VEIL OF TIME

VEIL OF TIME

CLAIRE R. McDOUGALL

GALLERY BOOKS

New York London Toronto Sydney New Delhi

G

Gallery Books
A Division of Simon & Schuster, Inc.
1230 Avenue of the Americas
New York, NY 10020

First Gallery Books trade paperback edition March 2014

GALLERY BOOKS and colophon are registered trademarks of Simon & Schuster, Inc.

For information about special discounts for bulk purchases, please contact Simon & Schuster Special Sales at 1-866-506-1949 or business@simonandschuster.com.

The Simon & Schuster Speakers Bureau can bring authors to your live event. For more information or to book an event contact the Simon & Schuster Speakers Bureau at 1-866-248-3049 or visit our website at www.simonspeakers.com.

Design by Aline C. Pace

Manufactured in the United States of America

10 9 8 7 6 5 4 3 2 1

ISBN 978-1-4516-9381-2
ISBN 978-1-4516-9382-9 (ebook)

ACKNOWLEDGMENTS

No matter that a writer is by nature a loner, a published book is a collaboration, and I am deeply grateful for the help and support I have received during the writing and publishing of this book. First of all, I must ask my husband and family's forgiveness for my broodiness while I was writing and my moodiness when I was not. A very big thank-you goes to my agent, Esmond Harmsworth, and my editor, Abby Zidle, both of whom screwed their courage to the sticking place in getting behind this book. The Aspen Writer's Foundation deserves sincere credit for backing this local writer and helping to put the word out. For those friends who gave of their time and creative energy I am grateful: Gail Holstein, Paul Jones, Naomi McDougall Jones,

Kent Reed, Ross Douglas, George Lilly, Barbara Bartocci, Deborah Lieberman.

Tapadh liebh, Allan Turner, who oversaw from Scotland my attempts at Gaelic, and *gratias maximas tibi ago* to Esmond Harmsworth, who brought his classical education to bear on my paltry Latin. Thank you to all who live at Dunadd, both past and present. But mostly I am indebted to the country of Scotland, for all of its history and its continuing quest to be free.

I

Long before my affliction was given a name, I was having dreams. Not passing dreams, but dreams in deep
sleep that weave themselves into the fabric of your mind
and won't let go. Even in bed beside Oliver Griggs, it
wasn't Griggs I was dreaming about, but Robert Burns
or Robert the Bruce or William Wallace. I was there,
not stretched out like a corpse beside my husband, but
in the bracken or in the shelter of a stone house with
thatch and a fire. I watched Burns with his head on his
desk after a night of brawling coming round slowly to lift
his pen; it was me in the trees, running from the English
with my hand in the hand of the Wallace.

So, I know how to get away. Don't think I don't. I
know, but I can't control it. An affliction buried in my

genes is the gate, and I have no way of choosing when I get to go through. Not very often, is the answer, not even as often as the seizures, because they don't always end in sleep.

I got away eventually from Professor Griggs. The dreams were too much for him.

"You always seem a bit removed," he said once, peering at me over his glasses like the teacher he is. "I'm not even sure if we inhabit the same world."

Oliver married me before he really knew what it meant to have to depend on phenobarbital to keep your day on a smooth path.

I tried to live in his world, tried the "normality" game as far as it would go. On the day of our wedding, I took twice the number of seizure pills, just to make sure I could glide through the "I do's," and so could Oliver. I suppose he was saving the "I don'ts" for later.

I married Griggs when he was someone else, before he hung up his jeans for a suit and his ideas for a curriculum. The years sort of flattened out between us, the endless days of child minding, the meetings and schedules at the university, the children who came and went, each in his or her different way.

Because she was there once, my daughter, my Ellie. She was there, and now I have no way of getting to her, whether through the fog or dreams; she is gone. My son, Graeme, took himself off to boarding school after Ellie died. I wasn't there anymore, and there was no point in his staying. So I left Glasgow, too, sold the house where we'd all lived under the illusion of being something stable and unchanging. But we weren't. The scene exploded or imploded, at least the center did not hold. After Ellie died, Oliver couldn't speak to me for weeks, couldn't actually look at me, open his mouth, and let out a sound. He blamed me, because that gene didn't stop with me. Ellie died during a seizure, and though everyone knows better, they can't help feeling I'm at fault, as though I had willed that horrid coil of DNA right into her.

Perhaps Graeme cried with his father, but he never did with me. He pulled up his fifteen-year-old self and said he had to go. We all had to go, so we didn't argue. His father had already left, perhaps not the house, but he wasn't there. So, with everyone already gone, Graeme moved to the east coast and I came with my suitcases to Dunadd.

What is this place called Dunadd? It is shades of green and all covered with bracken; it smells of moss and rain pouring for days on end. It is grey stone walls and cloud and bog and black slugs. It is sea and seagull cry, and the rough call of the pheasant. It is all these things and it is not that far from Glasgow, if you are a crow. If you are a bird, you fly high over a treeless mountain pass, over waterfalls and fingers of sea lochs that take a person in a car three hours to drive. Dunadd is a great rock rising out of a wide valley that runs from the hills that encircle it down to the sea at Crinan. It's not the place it once was, when Crinan was Scotland's main port, and wine and spices, jewelry and slaves were brought to Dunadd to be traded.

Mornings in my little cottage beneath Dunadd are so quiet now; the clouds are low and drizzling. Glasgow, where I lived another life with a husband and children, has no currency here. My children, who look at me from their picture frames when I awake, are not known here. Neither is Oliver Griggs of the University of Glasgow. Not even Margaret Griggs is known here, because I have unearthed the old Maggie Livingstone of childhood and pasted it over the Margaret I had become.

I wander around Dunadd in a sort of waking dream. There hasn't been much truck in humans here since the Dark Ages. In those days, when it was easier to travel by sea, there were no roads over the mountains and only foot trails around the lochs. These days there is the A83 from Glasgow all the way to this boggy land populated mostly now by ancient relics: standing stones, burial cairns, middens full of shells and bones.

When everything fell apart in Glasgow, I packaged up my life and drove here with boxes of books and postgraduate research on the witch burnings I had started once upon a time. Being an afflicted one myself, I suppose I felt some empathy with the witches, but I dropped all that when I married and for a while wasn't feeling like an outcast anymore.

But all things pass, and here I am with my cup of tea in the early morning, in the floral chair by the window looking out at the River Add that winds around the base of Dunadd. I bring my knees to my chest and pull my nightie down over my stockinged feet, watching the peaty red water swirl about the deep places. In the garden at the back of the cottage is a single standing stone to which one end of a washing line has been tied.

Only one other cottage lies alongside the trail up to the top of Dunadd. Except for the older man who lives there and me, the land here is empty of people. At night, there is nothing but the wind and the dark and the memory of the many islands that lie offshore. By first light, the tourists start driving in, to scramble up the path to the summit of this windy seat of the Celts, where the relics of the Pictish, then Celtic, then Viking fort lie in crumbles of tumble-down walls. Not even the archaeologists really know what was up there, because it was all too long ago, and not that long ago since the fort was handed over to the Scottish National Trust by the former feudal lord.

Archaeological digs come in from time to time and take Dunadd's treasures to the museum at the top end of the valley in the town of Kilmartin. What's left for the tourists is a Pictish boar carved in the rock, and a footprint where kings once placed their feet in the first coronation ceremonies of Scotland. The tourists smile at the camera with one boot in the stone imprint. They run their fingers along the outline of this early boar, barely visible now, that would eventually become the emblem of Scotland.

But in the evenings, when the sun swoons at the edge of the sea, there is only me on the edge of the windy hill. Up there, there is no sense of pace or life as life has evolved. On the edges of this glen, the Scandinavian firs that were once brought in for profit are slowly turning themselves back to ancient oak forests. Nothing but lorries carrying the last of the timber move fast here now.

You see, there is only one way out of my phenobarbital fog. I'm here at Dunadd for three months, October to January, to look at that thesis on witches again and to await my day of reckoning.

"For your type of epilepsy, Margaret, a lobectomy might be the best solution." My doctor calls me Margaret, because he comes from my Glasgow life.

I know all this. I know enough about my affliction to understand the dangers to my brain of repeated seizures. I know, because it killed my daughter. And where would Graeme be without a mother? He's in his last refuge, and I owe him this operation. It's the last thing I have left to give him. If it all comes out right, perhaps I'll move to a flat in Edinburgh and become a real mother again. If it doesn't, then these three months at Dunadd will be the end of Maggie, of Margaret, of me.

I came to this holiday cottage at Dunadd because I used to come here from Glasgow as a child. In those days my seizures were mild and undiagnosed. The nuns at my school used to put me out in the corridor if I had "an episode," as my mother used to call them. They told her I was just showing off. It took the doctors until I was in my teens to diagnose my epilepsy and then years more for them to bring the seizures under control—more or less.

The holiday cottage was different then, with a musty smell and small poky rooms. New owners knocked down walls, opened up the kitchen into the living room, and turned the windows into sliding glass doors. This is where I sit now with my crumpet and my cup of tea, hurling headlong towards the Day of Lobectomy. I came because I am scared of going forward, and time moves more slowly here. Sometimes at Dunadd time hardly seems to exist at all.

2

The man in the other cottage at Dunadd is Jim Galvin, a typical Highlander, a man of wry smile and few words, a man who had a wife, I understand—I don't know why he still doesn't. I've seen him at the museum in Kilmartin, a kind of relic himself. He nods to me and then looks away.

Whenever I'm on my way up Dunadd, when I creak through the stile by his garden, he looks up, one foot and his large hands on his spade, mulching in fertilizer by the smell of it. Behind him, roses and rhododendrons stand up tall in bushes or creep up the whitewash of his house. Outside my cottage door at Dunadd is an old trough with the remnants of summer pansies. Despite the cold, a hopeful purple pansy has pushed its face through the wilted leaves towards the sun.

I came to Dunadd just before Halloween and have been content to be nodded at and not spoken to, even by the little old lady behind the counter in Kilmartin's one tiny shop, which sells everything from cornflakes to Wellington boots. But Halloween by yourself feels a bit sad.

When I first arrived, I carved a turnip with a smile, lit him with a candle, and set him in my window. Still, after a week I would like to talk to someone apart from myself, and I think I should like to talk to Jim Galvin, the man on the hill. But I don't know how to get around the digging and gardening and the nods that are supposed to tell you what you need to know. I don't have skills for getting around people; if I had, I would have got around my husband.

I'm not looking for any man, let it be said, least of all some older Highland man who looks at me like I'm to be distrusted for coming from the city. I'm sure he already knows where I'm from. Information here travels on the small waves, like radio talk, and simply gets absorbed. There will have been tuts and sideways glances over me in the Kilmartin shop and even, I imagine, in the bigger town eight miles away. The annals of these people are always being added to. *In the year 2014 of the Common Era, a woman from the city of Glasgow took up residence at Dunadd. She arrived with books and papers and set a lit turnip in her window. To be continued . . .*

I don't even know how to think about a man anymore. Maybe I never did. Maybe that's why Oliver Griggs was able to take me unawares. But I am only thirty-eight, not that bad looking, I think. I inherited a helpful gene that has so far kept grey from my hair. The color of old rust, Oliver used to say in the days when such things didn't jar. Lately I've had to wear glasses for reading, but, if I wanted, I could still see well enough to add a little liner and shade to my eyes. My mother always said my eyes were my best asset, since my nose was a little broad to be pretty. Green eyes she said came from my great-aunt Ginny. She didn't say where the epilepsy came from.

I have stacked my books against the wall of my bedroom. Lonely little bedroom, for all that I want to be by myself. I am ill at ease among my own sheets these days. I suppose I could use a man. If he could just come and go; if I didn't have to look at him over the breakfast table and wonder what he was thinking. But it wouldn't be Jim Galvin on the hill. I hope he hasn't woken in the night and thought of me, the only female for miles.

Still, just for the sake of conversation I could make him a Halloween cake; take it over as a sort of neighborly offering, so it wouldn't seem silly to be stuck in such a remote spot with one other human and only a nod going between the two of us. I used to make Halloween cakes for my children, who would lick their little fingers sticky with black icing and orange trim.

Jim Galvin doesn't answer when I knock with one hand while balancing the cake on a plate in my other. The wind is brewing circles around me, making me think I should have tied my hair back into something more respectful for a neighborly visit. Along the way back home, when it starts to rain, a scrawny black kitten runs across the path in front of me. I stop and try to call it back, but since I can't put the cake down on the road, I have to leave the cat in the downpour.

In the bathroom mirror, I gather my damp hair on top of my head so that I look like a feather duster, but at least it gets it out of the way, and it doesn't look as if I'm going to be seeing anyone today. Except for the cat, which I see now sitting at my window, meowing so faintly against the rain that all I notice is her mouth opening. She comes running when I call for her at the door, and laps hungrily at the saucer of milk I set on the floor by the door. I don't know if it's a she, but if she belongs to no one I might keep her and name her Winnie, because it rhymes with skinny and with Great-Aunt Ginny.

She follows me into the kitchen, where I have set the uneaten cake. But cakes have a way of talking, and this one tells me it ought not to be left to go stale. I let the knife sink down into its swirls of chocolate and vanilla sponge and slither a thin slice onto a plate. I am so intent with my fork, separating the brown from the yellow cake, and I am in any case so unused to anything in my window that I jump when Jim Galvin appears. In a witch's hat.

I try to smile when I open the door to him.

"Sorry," he says when I slide the window back. He chuckles. "Didn't mean to frighten you."

As he steps in, Winnie runs out and then back in again. As Jim tugs his Wellies off, she uses his free leg as a rubbing board.

I point to the feather duster on my head. "I didn't mean to frighten you either."

I think that's a smile on his face. He says, "Right enough."

I point to the now incomplete cake, feeling guilty. Guilt comes naturally to me. "Would you like a slice?"

"With a cup of tea," he says, "that would be lovely."

I flitter over to my half kitchen and press the switch down on the electric kettle so that it lights up purple and the element begins to roar as though it had grander designs for itself.

He says, "I see you're taking in the farm animals."

"She's not yours, is she?" I ask.

He goes to set Winnie outside. "Not on your life."

"Oh, just leave her," I say. "It's awfully windy."

Jim smiles his wry smile, as though I must have a screw loose to think a cat can't survive when it needs to. I do have a screw loose, more than one, I imagine. It would be funny if that had been the diagnosis after all the years of tests: a screw loose. Oliver would no doubt concur.

Jim has obviously been brought up in an era when men had to be asked to sit in the presence of a female. I let him stand there uncomfortably for a moment, witch's hat in hand, until the kettle clicks off.

He looks down awkwardly at his woolly socks. "Where are you from?"

I pour the steaming water into a mug over a tea bag. "Milk?"

"Please."

"From Glasgow."

He takes the tea, still waiting to be asked to sit. "You're not far traveled, then."

I gesture towards the oversized blue couch. He may not sit in the floral seat by the window. That is mine. Winnie follows him and stretches along the length of his thigh as though perhaps he really did like cats.

"Far enough," I say, taking my own seat. "Have you lived in these parts all your life?"

"Apart from a stint in the merchant navy, aye," he says. "It does me fine."

I watch him take a sip of tea, trancelike in the way I get, studying people when I ought to be being polite. It's part of living in a fog; you have to look hard to see where you're going.

He says, "I saw you from the bathroom window. With the black cake."

I jump up, guilty again. "I am sorry, I forgot. Would you like a slice?"

This time, I slide a wedge of the colorful cake onto a plate and hand it over. Back in my armchair, I watch him dab the errant crumbs with the end of his finger before he starts in on the slice.

He tells me his father ran a pig farm to the south of Dunadd. He says he built his house at Dunadd himself when he was still fit enough for levering stones out of the ground and heaving them up for a wall.

He puts his hand flat against the base of his spine. "Fair jiggered the back, though. Now I'm not good for much but digging in the soil."

I say, "Your garden must be lovely in the spring."

I want to ask about his wife, but something tells me it can't be done. So I ask about his children. Two girls, he says, all grown up now with families of their own.

"How about you?"

I clear my throat. The conversation has turned and is heading my way. I can see he has noticed the wedding ring, something so far I haven't been able to let go of.

"Two."

Jim looks embarrassed. I'm sure he doesn't know why, but I don't have the kind of face that can rearrange emotions and pretend they're not there.

"I suppose you must be separated," he says. "Don't worry, I won't pry."

I try to order my face. "Divorced. As good as."

The question of the children hangs in the pause, so I resort to an expediency well honed by civilized humans: I change the subject.

"Do you know if any witches were burned at Dunadd?"

"Witches?" He shakes his head. "It was the church that burned witches. The fort was here before all that, during a time when your witches were women druids. '*Ban-druidhe*,' they call them in the old language, the Gaelic. It was about as high an office as you could get."

I hadn't even thought of the fact that Christianity was slow and sporadic in its spread across Scotland, that witches once upon a time ruled the roost.

Jim shakes his head. "No, there were no witches burned here that I'm aware of, though it wasn't that long ago the ministers used to build fires under the Standing Stones."

Jim is turning out to be more interesting than I thought. "Why on earth?"

"To crack them." Jim places a hand on his neck and pulls, as though rearranging his spine. "The stones come from thousands of years before any of this history we're talking about, way back in heathen times. The church saw it all as devil worship. Still does."

I point at Jim's witch's hat. "Don't they think that's devil worship, too?"

Jim laughs. "Aye, they probably do, but Halloween

is one of those church affairs that got stuck onto an old pagan festival. 'All Holy Evening' used to be the Celtic Samhain, the Day of the Dead, and let me tell you, it was not holy." He chuckles. "At least not in the Christian sense."

I am ashamed for having relegated this Highland man to an ignorance he clearly doesn't deserve.

"I've seen you up at the museum," I say. "Do you work there?"

"I help out two days a week. They don't pay me because I've nothing better to do with my time and because I make up my own mind about things."

He says he needs to be going, but I'm not sure I want him to. It looks as though he'll be a good resource of local history. And he's good company.

After Jim has left, I ring Graeme in Edinburgh. I wait with the phone against my ear, thinking of what to say. But it's always some other breathless schoolboy grabbing the phone off the wall as he runs by.

"Graeme Griggs?" I ask hopefully.

He shouts off down the hall, "Griggs! Your mum."

Whatever else they teach at boarding school, it is not telephone etiquette. I don't know who this boy is, but he obviously knows a mother when he hears one. I am still wondering how I manage to convey this when Graeme's voice takes a stab at me.

"Hi, Mum."

"Hello, love. What are you up to?"

"Racing off to class."

He's always racing off. Oliver went through that phase, too. Never any time to talk, not until he sat me down one evening and gave me the break-up speech: too much of this and too much of that, too much time, too much worry, too little freedom to be who he was. My too-muches didn't seem to enter into the equation. But just for the record: too much absence, too much blame, too much inability to cope in the end when Ellie went.

"Just wanted to say hello," I say, "see how you're doing."

"It's all right, Mum."

"Yes, I know. Are you eating all right?"

He laughs. Thank God for his laughter. "Of course I am."

I laugh, too, because it is all so formulaic, and I suppose that's why the other boy could tell who I was. The mother with her questions. He probably has one of those, too.

I say, "I just made a Halloween cake."

There's a pause as the weight moves back in.

"Got to go, Mum."

"I know."

"I'll ring you soon."

I don't answer. I know he will want to ring me, and I know that I will dread the call. I will want to ring him back, and he will be running down some corridor, needing to be somewhere else.

"Bye, then."

"Bye, Mum."

Off he goes, not quite laughing at something some other boy shouts at him as they flee.

I lie on the couch with my new cat purring by my head like a stick down a washboard. I smile, thinking of Jim Galvin in his ridiculous witch's hat. I smile, too, because it's all right between Graeme and me. The words just mix things up. He knows it's all right, and so do I. This is just a hiatus until things fall into a better pattern.

I close my eyes. Since I unloaded my boxes and suitcases in the living room of Dunadd cottage a week and a half ago, I have had only one seizure, and a mild one at that. But I feel heat in the soles of my feet, and I know one is coming on now.

Maybe it's the thrumming of the cat or some change in atmospheric pressure or perhaps I forgot to take one of those pills this morning, but the heat moves up my legs, and soon everything begins to dissolve back into the atoms out of which it came. The particles grow big and bigger, until I begin to squeeze between them, and then I am falling into whatever abyss there is once you remove the stuff that everything is made of. I never know anything else until I wake up with a head like a hangover. I can only guess at the dismal scene in between, all the hallmarks of epilepsy that make normal people step away.

After the attack comes sleep, and probably out of my conversation with Jim, I dream I am at Dunadd—not the present Dunadd, because in my dream there are high walls all up the side of the hill where nowadays the footpath meanders through heather and bracken. I am standing where Jim Galvin's house ought to be, looking down on the river, only this time there's a footbridge, and across the field aren't sheep but a village of houses, all thatched and smoking, not rectangular stone houses but round houses made of wattle and mud, houses that look for all the world like an African village.

I have had dreams before in the aftermath of seizures: I have argued points of theology with Mary Queen of Scots, who wasn't the blockhead history has made her out to be. I have strolled along the beaches of Saint Helena with Napoleon insisting to me that he was being poisoned. But nothing has struck quite so close to home as seeing Dunadd in this way, with goats tethered and children running barefoot, with great waves of drumming and singing, and at the back of it all, a low murmuring like a didgeridoo. I must have arrived during some kind of festival.

I wonder if Jim knew that a big boulder used to be on the site where his house now sits. I lean against it, trying to steady myself, to get my mind around the fact that Jim's house and that of any ancestor he could name are still more than a millennium away.

The sun is falling off the rim of Dunadd hill as I look up and notice two men approaching me. In the dusk, they look like a pencil sketch of medieval dress. They come towards me gingerly, as though they're not quite sure what they are seeing. I glance back at the stone to see if I can hide behind it, but the men are already calling to me.

They're speaking Gaelic. *"Co as a tha sibh?"*

It has been a very long time since I heard Gaelic, not since I last saw ancient Mrs. Gillies, who used to look after me as a child. I know enough to understand they are asking me where I come from, but I'm not even sure how to answer that question in English.

When the men turn me around and tug on the bottom of my sweatshirt, I begin to wish this dream would end.

I step out of their reach and start with my name. *"Is mise Maggie Livingstone."*

They shake their heads. No Livingstones at Dunadd in these days.

They repeat their question as to where I come from, but they are looking more suspicious now.

I fight to gather the Gaelic words I need. *"Tha mi a Glaschu."*

The mention of Glasgow makes them step towards

me. They aren't rough about it, just take me by the elbows and start walking me along the flat stones just above Jim's house that start the trail up the hill. One of the men is smaller than the other, so it is an uneven march to what turn out to be fine great oak gates set in the natural cleft of the rock and lit on either side by torches. I have climbed through here time and again but all it is usually is just a narrow gap.

It makes me laugh to see this grand entrance. I have often wondered how it must have looked. My captors glance at each other and tighten their grip. They shout in Gaelic with some urgency to whoever is behind the gate. I look up and see we are standing under a sort of portico; inset in the upper portion of the gate is a sliding hatch that opens now.

The man behind it is another picture from a book on ancient history, with his leather hood attached to a short cape that drops just below the shoulders. His mustache hangs over his top lip and catches on his teeth as he talks. He wants to know who I am and where they found me. I hear the words *ban-druidhe,* and I remember this is what Jim called the witches.

While negotiations go on over our admittance, I am able to step back and get a better look at the gates and at my captors, their knee-length tunics and hefty brown shawls tied at the shoulder with large buckles. The burning of torch wax floats heavily in the air, and the men are laughing now, almost as though they've forgotten I'm here. Part of me wants to run away, because I know who lives up on the hill of Dunadd. I know I am being taken to those in authority, and perhaps they won't have a favorable impression of me in my modern clothes. But even if I could run away, where would I run to?

When one side of the gate opens, we are let up onto the grassy flat part of the fort that is usually strewn with rubble but now is crowded with actual buildings. All of this I have seen in my imagination, and at the museum where they have tried to reconstruct it, but this is the real Dunadd, standing high and thick, lending the place the feel of an outdoor castle. Somehow I expect it all to look spanking new, but there is lichen on the walls, and I realize this place is ancient even to these ancients.

The singing and drumming from the village are fainter up here, and I can make out the crackling of a fire on the level above us. My captors pull me off the path to let pass a group of men and women bent under great loads of logs and sticks, presumably fuel for the fire. Another man, moving unsteadily with great stone flagons in either hand, steps in behind them. All the action is clearly above us, and I am getting so nervous about what that action might be that I stop walking and try to shake the men off. They watch me flailing and seem to be in some disagreement as to where I should go. For a moment, their fingers loosen their grip, and I would be free to run now, if it weren't for the guard at the gate. I begin to move in the direction of a spit that is giving off the smell of roasted meat, but the men seem to have reached agreement and pull me back.

The smaller man on my left points up the hill. "*Ban-druidhe.*"

I don't know if I am being taken to a Dark Age witch or whether, contrary to Jim's opinion, one is being burned up there. When I consider that the witch in question might be me, I start to struggle. This dream really ought to come to an end now.

But we keep moving up towards the top of Dunadd along a path that doesn't ascend this way in my day. We skirt a wall around the hill and then up higher and back along to a small half-sunk house near the summit thatched with heather and located exactly over a small lip of wall I sometimes sit on during my jaunts up here. The fire is so close now, I can feel the heat, but extras from some medieval film crowd around, obscuring the sight of it.

Because the small round house is partially built into the hill, the guard has to go down a few steps to get to the door. But instead of knocking, he calls out. Before long the door opens, and I am handed into the dark, where only an orange candle burning smokily on the wall sheds any light. The door shuts heavily behind me. Inside, the air is thick and pungent. I turn back to the door to make my escape, but something draws my eye:

a shadow moves, and I see an old woman leaning over a small fire.

I press my back against the rough wood of the door, gauging the distance between my hand and the torch to see if I could use it in defense, but the woman takes little notice of me. In the light of the fire, I see several brightly colored blankets draped about her shoulders, over which her grey hair falls in soft ringlets. She is busy with her fire, chanting in a language I don't recognize. My eyes wander from the pots of different sizes around the base of the wall to the drying leaves hanging from the rafters. If this is a witch, she wears no black hat; her nose is not warty and pointed, but she does have long fingernails, and her language is more guttural than Gaelic. She is tall and agile as she moves in a circle about her fire, from time to time throwing in flakes of something that fill the chamber with the smell of scented wood.

I move towards the only thing familiar to me, the little ledge jutting from the wall, and walk my head straight into the trailing leaves. For the first time, she looks at me, reaches out and touches my arm. She touches, then pats, curious about the fabric of my sweatshirt. Her fingers pull on the stretch of it, and then work down to my jeans; she stoops to run her hands over my sneakers. She stands up, turns my face to the light of the fire, then takes hold of my hands, turns them over and studies my nails, the gold ring on my finger. Her fingers are dirty and tattooed with Celtic designs. There are lines of tattoo about her cheeks and a circle of Celtic knots around her wrist.

"*Ban-druidhe?*" she asks. She turns her face to me, and I see that her expression is kindly.

I shake my head, smiling at the irony of her taking me for a witch.

She lays her hand on her chest. "*Is mise Sula. 'S mise ban-druidhe. Sula.*"

Sula. Her name lingers in my head, as does the smoke. Sula's smoky fingers on my cheeks make my eyes sting until I am forced to look away to the chinks of light around the door. I can still hear the fire on the hilltop crackling, the intermittent cheer from the crowd. I hear the word *Sula,* and I hear fire. I hear them loud, and then they fall off into the distance and become a whisper. I fight to stay with Sula the witch, but the blue couch has forced itself back in; the weight of the small black cat is upon my shoulder.

3

Fergus had been gone from Dunadd for months. After the long journey, his horse was tired, so he didn't want to push her. But he was nearly home; from here at the top of the Valley of Stones he could see the fire on Dunadd hill. The men he had ridden out with on his rounds collecting fealty from the lords of the kingdom had returned a week ahead of him. Fergus had sent them back to Dunadd with the cattle and the silver, while he rode south some short distance to stay awhile among the Britons and meet a young woman, a good alliance for the future, his brother the king had said.

The woman had been fine and gentle, bonny enough. There was no problem there. The problem was with Fergus, he knew it; he had heard it enough from his brother and his mother, the queen. What gain could there be, they said, in keeping his heart with the old wife, the dead wife? With Saraid.

But he had a daughter by this woman. It was no small thing to cast her off as though the heart could turn on its heels and leave. It had been two years since the plague, two years since the druidess Sula had cast her stones and seen the cloak of death around his princess. She had tried with her fire and her chants, but even druids must bow before the goddess. Fergus knew it then, and knew it now, but he still couldn't forgive either one of them, Saraid for rejoining her ancestors, Sula for failing to change the course.

Two years without a woman. Murdoch, the king, had ordered him to find one before he himself secured some company for his brother's bed. Sula said, *No, wait.* Murdoch said no more waiting. Sula said, *Wait,* something there in the way the stones fell from her hand to the ground, something in the pattern, she didn't quite know what.

Fergus ran his fingers between his black mare's ears, keeping before him the warrior stars, the cluster of seven twinklers to his right almost too faint to see tonight because of the moon. The dark had brought with it a keen sense of sound that made his horse's back twitch at every snap of branch or call of a late gull careening back to its rocky ledge.

The great fire burning high on Dunadd hill was for

Samhain, the Day of the Dead, and his horse did not care for the Valley of Stones on such a night. No more did he. His pony had thrown him here long ago when he was less than ten years in age and Murdoch had ridden up behind him with a stick draped with cobwebs and weed to scare him. On this Day of the Dead, Fergus kept to the hazels skirting the valley floor, measuring the distance between him and Dunadd in trees and shadows. Fergus leaned forward and soothed the mare with a shush—soothed himself, for she was not the only one to feel the small hairs rise on the skin.

To his left he passed the first of the ancient circles of standing stones that gave the valley its name, put here not by his own people but by the Picts who had ruled before. In the distance, the cry and chatter of voices at Dunadd held its breath. In a moment, the cheer would go up as the torch took its ritual path from the high fire down to light those in the villagers' houses for the start of winter. But for now in the dark, only the far-off song of the wolf could be heard, only small patters among the rusted leaves, perhaps the sound of the dead themselves, for this was the time in all of the year when the veil between the living and the dead grew thin enough to allow spirits through.

The horse's back twitched under Fergus's thigh. He sat up straight and pushed his hair back over his shoulders, trying to shrug off the voices of those ancient Picts who might demand the return of their land. Inside the neck of his tunic he found the godstone on the string of acorns that the druidess had given him before he departed. It had protected him on his long journey; he hoped it had enough strength left to keep him safe along this last uninhabited stretch.

The call of an owl muted the subtler sounds; wings fluttered suddenly to his left. A good portent, Sula would say. He had not meant to be away this long, too long since the day he left his daughter in the arms of her grandmother. Already, in his absence, the celebrations for her eighth year had come and gone. Two years since the plague had taken her mother, and now there was talk among the Britons of another round of the pestilence coming up from the Sassenachs in the south. If it spread this far north, he would take his daughter to the people who lived away from Dunadd, in the houses on the lochs, until the danger had passed. Illa was all he had left of Saraid, and he meant to hold on to her.

Fergus leaned forward into the smell of his horse, ran the coarse strands of her mane between his fingers. Horses were like the druids in a sense, hearing and seeing more than they should. Only a little while now and he would be home—not the home he had shared with Saraid, for he had closed that door two years ago after the body had been burned. He slept now on his mother's floor, just as the king himself sometimes did, though he had a wife and children and other women enough.

Like stone and like sand, these two brothers, their father had said. He had been dead since before either Murdoch or Fergus was old enough to take a wife. Ainbcellaig was his name, though the boys went by the name MacBrighde, since their royal line came down through their mother, Brighde. Murdoch was dark and brown-eyed like his father and the line of Scots that had sailed over from Erin two hundred years before he was born. But the mother had Pictish in her line and had passed blue eyes down to the second son, a point of scorn for the proud king, who wanted nothing to do with the Picts who made up half his kingdom.

"Pale-eyed Pict!" from Murdoch was enough to rouse his brother's anger and have them rolling in the dirt.

Still, Fergus had taken his wife from the Picts, and his daughter—rust in hair and light of eyes, long-legged like her mother—was more Pict than Scot, a stark contrast to the dark-eyed pale-skinned children Murdoch spawned. For the Scots came down from Scotta, a dark princess who had sailed across seas to Erin from a land far off to the east. It was she who had brought the sacred stone that those Scots had in turn brought from Erin to this land two hundred years ago. *Gaels*, the Picts called those sailors from Erin. *Strangers*.

Fergus's horse jolted to a stop just before a branch that hung low in the dark. The mare reared, and it was all Fergus could do to catch her reins and slip off her back. His foot came down hard on the soft moss, making him cry out louder than he should in this place on this night. He pulled his dirk from its halter under his arm.

Fergus waited and listened. "Sssh."

Even the dead from his own people shouldn't know his whereabouts tonight, in case they tried to haul him back with them. He had sunk his blade into the chest of a Northumbrian, cut the heart still quivering from a dying Sassenach, but he had no defense against the dead; nothing else could make his own heart quiver. While his fingers fumbled again for the godstone against his neck, the horse broke free and bolted.

All Fergus could do was run, not across the open fields, but weaving between the scrubby hazels, and now he didn't know if it was the trees or the dead ripping at his hair, blood from the scratches running down his cheek, down his shins, and him panting now, not from the running but from the tight grip on his throat, and surely the ghouls would suck this last drop of life from him. If only he could reach the houses, but his ankle shot pain up the length of his shin, and he was no match now for the spirits.

He called on Cailleach the goddess, who had sustained his people all these years, though she was turning in aspect now from the beautiful nymph of summer into her winter stage of the crone. She might be deaf now to his plea, but he kept up his petition, dragging his foot, asking for his life that he might return to his daughter.

His horse was gone clattering into the night, but the fire on the hill of Dunadd drew closer. He could see the torch leading off from the great fire on the hill and moving down towards the houses; if only he could keep going, he could run through the fire himself and purge this touch of death.

Coming at last to the village of many thatched huts at the river's edge, Fergus dragged himself forward into the faint smell of smoke and dung. Without offering any greeting, he ran through the maidens in their games of fortune hunting and kept up his pace until he was deep into the smell of blood sausage and boiling turnips. It was into the arms of Talorcan, brother of his wife, that he fell, a laughing Talorcan until the man saw that the look in the eyes of this horseless traveler was no cause for laughter.

"Fergus, I would rather take my chances with an army of Sassenach than walk alone in the Valley of Stones tonight."

Fergus bent over, touching the ground of the settlement with his fingers, needing to find himself safe here. The villagers came in a crowd about him, knowing who this was in his fine clothes, this brother of King Murdoch. Talorcan fought them back.

"My horse," said Fergus.

Talorcan patted his back. "She came trotting in a while ago. She is content now among the sheaves laid out for Samhain. Come, I will walk you across the bridge to the gates, unless you would stop and eat with us."

Fergus stood up, took in for the first time this tall brother of his wife, with the green eyes and the tattoo of the boar across his forehead. "I must go to Illa. How is she?"

Talorcan smiled. "She has grown tall in your absence."

He marked the place on his jerkin where the top of his niece's head came. Fergus smiled.

"Long in leg like her mother," said Talorcan. "Do you remember?"

Fergus nodded, though he wished Talorcan wouldn't torture him. "Yes, I remember."

Talorcan laughed. "She could take you to the floor even then."

Fergus did not speak. He wanted to get to the druidess and see if she could find the spirit of his long-legged wife tonight before the time passed.

"Where is Murdoch?"

A look of disdain crossed Talorcan's brow along the lines of the tattoo. "On the fort. His royal highness only enters the village when he has run out of women on high."

He wrapped an arm about this husband of his dead sister and led him through the houses along the lanes towards the rope bridge that crossed the river and separated the fort from the village. The common folk, some Pictish, some Scotti, parted to let them through. They liked this brother of King Murdoch, a softer type, good in battle, though fair defeated by the death of his lady. Many a woman would gladly have taken her place in his bed, but he was a strange one, this Fergus MacBrighde.

Before they reached the bridge, Talorcan nudged him. "A woman has been found. I have not seen her myself, but the guards who took her to the druidess say she wears gold and is dressed in strange clothing, unlike any they have ever seen on friend or enemy. She says she comes from Glasgow."

Fergus stopped walking. "Then why has she come so far?" He placed his hands on his knees and leaned over to grab his ankle. "Where was she found?"

"Just below where we stand now. She is not still young, but comely enough," said Talorcan. "They say she has the smell of the courts of the Romans."

Fergus said, "But the only Romans about these days are either slaves or monks. Is she a runaway slave?"

Talorcan laughed. "Perhaps, if you have a mind, you should see her for yourself."

Fergus shook his head. "Talorcan, she's just another woman, and I have had enough matches lately." A smile creased his cheeks. "This is not like you. You are the brother of my wife. You should know better."

"I know," said Talorcan. He patted Fergus's back. "But your druidess saw something for you in her stones, something strange. And this woman, so they say, is unlike any other."

4

Something in me it is that pulls me to fire. I tug my raincoat on and climb to the top of the fort in the wind today, stopping at the cleft in the rock where in my dream the gates stood. I remember them down to their heavy wooden smell and the knot in the wood above the sliding hatch. And I notice on my way up this time, and wonder why I have never noticed before, several holes in the rock where the gateposts must once have been lodged. There's a stain of rust leaking out from iron rods that must still exist somewhere deep in the rock. I gain the flat, grassy area where the houses stood in my dream, but now instead of buildings, I am standing among rubble, half submerged in grass, looking like nothing at all.

On the summit, I sit on the little ledge of stone left

from the original seat in the witch's hut. If I close my eyes, I can hear the snap of the fire, smell the drying herbs hanging from the rafters. Even now you can see why the ancient people picked Dunadd as a fort, for it looks straight across the Mhoine Mhor, a great stretch of peat moss leading down to the Atlantic. Off to the south, through the dips of the foothills, you can see mountains; to the north and east great forests rise and fall, and along the valley floor the River Add wraps itself around the fort before snaking through the Moss, as though it really would prefer not to get to the sea at all. The sun is setting behind the islands, casting the world in an orange wash. From below, only the raucous call of the pheasant interrupts the stillness.

When I get down from the hill, Jim Galvin is standing by his back door. He lifts his hand in greeting and looks away, the typical Highland gesture. But he is at the fence as I pass through the stile.

"I've seen you going up there every day," he says.

I didn't know I was being spied on. I pull up the collar of my raincoat against him. "Did there used to be a big stone where your house sits now?"

"Aye." He shakes his head. "It was moving that stone that did my back in. In the end, I had to dynamite it. But how do you know about it?"

I shrug. "I used to come here as a child."

I smile to have found an answer, both to his question

and mine. Of course, I must have remembered that stone from way back.

"You've a pretty enough smile," he says, "when you choose to use it."

This seems very forward for a Highland man, and I'm not sure how to respond. And anyway, I have other questions.

"What do you think that round wall at the top was part of?"

He sniffs, rubs his nose with the back of his finger. "It might well have been a dwelling for the chief druid, though the history books will not tell you anything of the kind."

I look into his face. A bit of a defensive face, I think, but raw enough that my gaze makes him turn away.

I say, "I was having a dream about a *ban-druidhe*, just this afternoon."

He looks back at me. "Is that a fact?" which is the Highland way of dismissing facts.

This time, I'm the one who looks away. When I look back, he's gesturing me through his gate. I don't want to give this man an ounce of encouragement, but I follow him through his back door into a kitchen that looks as though his wife had kept it well, but there has been little in the way of keeping ever since. Past the kitchen, a small living room seems crouched about a fire, its walls lined with bookshelves.

I stand in the middle of the room, fighting for something to say. "Quite the scholar you are, eh?"

Because of the books, I have to admit, I look at him
with new respect. I can't help it, because it's the way life
thinks of itself in the Western Hemisphere.

I want to ask him if he has read them all, but it would
sound insulting, and I have a way of offending people
just by the way I ask things. Oliver used to say I should
edit myself better, and this time I do.

"This is all very impressive," I say. "I'll have to come
up to the museum and pick your brains."

He stands by the fire rubbing his backside, I'm not
sure if as a gesture to me or just to warm flesh that in
this climate all too often needs warming.

"Any time is fine with me," he says.

I sit on the arm of a leather easy chair that must have
come from the era of the wife.

He steps aside from the fire, apparently having found
enough warmth. "So, you used to come to Dunadd as a
child?"

I ease myself down into the chair. "There was an
old lady downstairs from us who came from St. Kilda.
When the government evacuated them from the island
in the 1930s, they put them all over Argyll to work on
the land."

"They did that," said Jim. "Can you imagine, island
folk who'd never seen a tree put to work in the forestry?
They didn't have a word of English between them either."

There doesn't seem to be much Jim doesn't know, so I let him ramble.

"Of course, the old way of life on the island had disappeared long ago, but they still ate nothing but sea birds."

My mother paid the lady from St. Kilda, Mrs. Gillies, to mind me after school. I probably knew more about the life of St. Kilda than about Glasgow.

"Mrs. Gillies," I say, "was the last girl to be married on the island. She was proud of that."

"Och," says Jim. "It's quite a tale, right enough. And did you learn the Gaelic from this Mrs. Gillies?"

"I learned a type of Gaelic," I say.

"It was the old Gaelic. Those folks on St. Kilda were still living in the Dark Ages. When they were brought to Argyll, even the old folk had a job understanding them."

I stayed with Mrs. Gillies until half-past five during the school week and often all day Saturday, too. She stepped into the shoes of a granny, of which I had no natural ones. A few summers she brought me to Dunadd, to visit her brother, who lived nearby along the Crinan Canal. I probably picked up more Gaelic during those two weeks at the table of Hugh Gillies in his tiny kitchen than I ever had after school in Glasgow with his sister.

My parents weren't sure about their daughter learning Gaelic, which they thought of as backwards, but Mrs. Gillies was "a convenience," I once heard my mother say.

I look into the fire. "I don't suppose you have a Gaelic dictionary."

Jim shakes his head. "No, what Gaelic I know came from my mother, and that was a wee while ago. You got belted for speaking it in the school, so with an incentive like that, you were better to forget. But I'm being rude and not offering you tea."

If that was a question, he doesn't wait for the answer, but is off back to his kitchen, where I hear him moving about with a kettle and a match that lights a flame.

I am intrigued by these books, so I pull myself out of my chair and go to the nearest shelf, my eye immediately finding titles: *The Celtic Consciousness; The Druids; Life in Ancient Scotland*. There is clearly more to our Mr. Galvin than he lets on.

"Here, take this," he says, handing me a mug with a teaspoon in it. "My wife must be rolling in her grave. She'd never serve tea in anything but a proper cup and saucer."

I sit back down with the hot mug and wrap my hands about it. He drags a stool to the fire and perches himself on it. He slurps when he drinks, something I'm sure his wife would not have approved of. He must have been quite handsome in his day, a nice kind of father to have.

I watch him slurp for a while, until he knows I'm watching him.

"Who were they who lived up on the fort?" I ask.

He takes a deep breath through his teeth before he speaks. It's a Highland thing. "Well, the history books say it was the Picts until the Scotti sailed over from Ireland."

"Scotti? Who are they?"

"They're who we get *Scot*land from. The Scotti were Irish immigrants, though they called their land Erin in those days, not Ireland. The Irish thought, still do, that they were descended from this Egyptian princess called Scotta. Ireland, as you can see from the top of Dunadd on a clear day, is only eleven miles to the west, and there was probably always trade going on between the two coasts. If you ask me, it was always a mix of Pict and Scot hereabouts, sometimes more one, sometimes more the other. The Scots brought the Gaelic with them from Ireland, and by the time of William Wallace, it was the language of Scotland. It'll no doubt give out in the end, just as the Pictish language did."

"Have you ever heard the name Sula?" I ask Jim.

He says he hasn't and shows me instead a list of the kings that ruled from Dunadd, strange names mostly that mean nothing to me, names from the Dark Ages such as Ainbcellaig, Fiachne, and Eochaid.

On my way back to the cottage, rain is pelting against the side of my head. I stop to wade in a shallow puddle, watching the waves made by my boots wash up higher into the gravel, then fall back and disappear. Entire cultures come and go like this, empires rise and crash. The Picts moved off to the north and left nothing except a few strange words in the English of northeastern Scotland. They're just echoes, like the Standing Stones and like the druids.

Back at my pages the next day, I'm counting out witch executions, in huge numbers: for the year 1515, more than five hundred witches burned in Geneva; 1518, sixty-four burned in Val Camonica; seventeen hundred Scots burned at the stake between 1563 and 1603. I think about Sula in her hut at the top of Dunadd. She has no idea what would become of her kind in the future. There are no do-good clerics to drag her out of her hut yet, no edicts on the evil of women.

I set my glasses on the desk and go to the window to watch the river. The rain has stopped this morning, and a little way down the bank, I spot Jim Galvin with a fishing line running downstream as though it wanted to get away from him. Since he knows so much, I want him to tell me why the church did this to women. I want to know what he has to say for himself.

I shout my accusation at him across the river, earthy brown run that at least in my dream looked just like this a thousand or more years ago. Jim looks up and shrugs. After a length, he shouts, "Away round to the bridge and less of your shouting."

It's not easy going along the bank, semi-marsh as it is, piled with lumps of sedge that turn your foot sideways in your Wellie. As though in solidarity, Winnie the kitten follows behind.

The bridge is an old stone one with a fancy Roman arch for an underside, not that it came out of any great artistic vision, just out of the mud and practicality of the farmer who set it, stone against stone. It's a beautiful bridge, nevertheless, the mythical drawbridge in my mind that keeps me safe within the shadow of the fort, a recluse with my papers and my questions.

Jim looks up at me from his seat on the riverbank. "What is it you were saying? Quietly now, so you don't scare the fish, and take that bloody cat away or she'll be eating them."

I laugh. "It's nearly bloody winter. There won't be any catch, and even if there were, they'd have to be gae small fish for the cat to pose a menace. Is it minnows you're after?"

He looks back to his fishing. I look down at the dark river, harboring, so Jim hopes, some scaly vestige of life. A seagull lands and hunkers down against the wind. I sigh. Here in the presence of the river, even the burning of witches doesn't seem worth the noise.

I say, "I was saying nothing."

I sit down next to him and draw my knees up against my chest. Winnie rubs her back around my legs, as though I had just sat down for her pleasure.

He chuckles. "Sounded like an awful lot of nothing to me."

"I was just caught up in my work, research."

He looks at me, as though I've handed him a measure by which to gauge me. "Aye, they were saying in the village that you were up to something of the sort."

The noise comes back. "Something of what sort? What is that supposed to mean?"

He turns back to his line, which is bobbing all of a sudden. "No need to get your knickers in a twist."

Jim lands his fish, little shriveled thing that he ought to throw back, while I'm wondering about my dream. I can't put it away, because I want to know what the fire was about and who the privileged few were that made up the cheering crowd. I want to go into that village at the base of Dunadd on the sheep field and see the life there. Suddenly I'm finding myself wondering what effect it would have for me to miss a day's course of pills and perhaps find myself back in that dream. I don't know what year of the Dark Ages I was in, or if it even matters.

"Throw the damn fish back," I say, watching the poor thing writhe, its gills sucking hopelessly. I slide close enough to its tail to flick it with the toe of my boot. Using my foot, the fish bounces itself back into the water.

"Hoi," Jim shouts. "That was my dinner!"

I hadn't meant to throw the fish back, but I am suddenly giddy that it managed to do it for itself.

"Nothing to laugh at," he says. "Now it'll be beans on toast."

I say, "You wouldn't have found any meat on that thing anyway. I'll get your dinner for you to make up for it. I'm sure the fish will approve. It was probably some poor little fishy's mother."

"Bloody skinny mother, if you ask me," he says. "What'll you make me?"

I hadn't meant to promise him anything, not least of all more of my study time.

I sigh, "Sardines on toast?" I can't help but laugh.

"Oh aye, very funny. I'll be over at six."

"Fine." I walk off.

☯

He comes at five to six, and he's wearing a silly cravat tucked into the neck of his shirt. It might have worked when he was courting his wife back in the 1950s, but it doesn't work on me, and not because the "lady doth protest too much," just because I don't want his overtures, plain and simple. I'm thirty-eight, and not so desperate yet I need to ponder some old wrinkled bum.

He's brought me flowers from the local shop, a few white roses mixed in with fern. "It was the least I could do," he says, "after you threw back my fish."

I take them to the sink; the arrangement falls into a pleasing spray in a vase. "Not threw back exactly. Besides, you should leave the poor fish alone. You can buy a kipper at the shop."

He shakes his head. "Not the manly way."

I sigh. "I think we've had enough of men and their manly ways. Can't you just all lay off it?"

He takes a seat at the table and puts his elbows on it in the way I'm sure his mother told him not to. "You're not one of those ballbusters or whatever the hell it is the Americans call them, are you?"

He has defused the moment. I shake my head and smile. "No, not a ballbuster."

He nods towards my books and papers removed from the dinner table to a chair. "What's all that about, then?"

"That's the 'something of the sort' that local gossip has me working on. It's about witches, as a matter of fact."

"Oh, I see," he says, looking me over, as though I suddenly make sense to him. I wish I made sense to myself.

I set the vase on the table in front of him. "Did they ever have fires on the top of Dunadd?"

"Aye, they did. Even up into my day, every Halloween we would build a fire up there. We used to jump over it, and that's a piece of antiquity right there, though we didn't know it then."

I go back to the kitchen. "What was it for?"

He shrugs. "A purification rite from Ye Olde pagan times. They used to make their animals go over it, too, to ensure their safety through the coming winter. Most of the cattle, though, they'd have to slaughter, because there wasn't enough feed to keep both man and animal alive. It would be a lot of meat to salt, and innards, what have you, to preserve for winter, guts and sinew, they used the lot. Anything they couldn't preserve they'd stick in a sausage, including the blood, which is why we have black pudding to this day. And haggis."

I laugh. "Would you like to write my dissertation for me?"

"No," he says, clearly pleased, "I don't know that much at all, never did go to the university."

I retrieve the dinner from under the grill and set it down between us.

"Sardines on toast," he says. "I thought you were joking."

I shake my head. "I never joke. It's against my nature."

I don't know if he thinks I'm joking now, but I don't think I am.

He forks a fish into his mouth and follows it with a bite of toast. I remember now half a bottle of red wine in my fridge and offer it to him.

"Could you warm it up?" he says. "I'm not one for cold drinks, right enough."

I go into the kitchen, pour the unlikely red brew into a pan, and flick the gas on under it.

"Is that what you do over here," he says, "drink wine by yourself?"

I pour the sizzling red wine into two cups and return to the table with them.

I say, "I would call that prying. How does it taste?"

"Awful," he says. "Still, it takes the edge off awkward conversation."

I try my hot wine and wince. "Blah. I didn't think it was awkward."

"Not until I started prying."

"What do you want to know?" I ask. I take another sip of warm wine and try to gather strength.

He leans back in his chair, which creaks a little under the strain. "Well, here you are, divorced and without your children. I doubt the farmers around here are going to be of much interest to you, and you're a bit young to be giving up on life."

I'm glad at least that he's putting himself on the other side of the fence from my romantic interests. Maybe he's waiting for me to say I prefer older men. But there is too much to explain about my reasons for wanting to be lonely.

I sigh.

"Are your children with your husband?"

Here we go. I empty my cup of wine. It stings my throat. "No."

"If you don't want to tell me," he says, "that's fine."

"It's just that you will probably ask again."

He laughs, quite unaware of what is about to come out.

"Look," I say, "there's no secret about it. Oliver Griggs, my husband, teaches history at Glasgow University."

I sense that Jim is beginning to see, probably by the look or lack of look on my face, what he has got himself into.

He says, "Posh," in an effort to lighten the mood.

The wine is doing a better a job. "We have two children, as I said: Graeme, who is seventeen and at boarding school in Edinburgh. Ellie was eight years old two years ago when she died, so that's the story."

Jim leans back over the table. He doesn't say anything, and for that I'm grateful. I go back to my kitchen, rummage in the bread bin while I try to put myself back in order, and come up with a box of Jaffa Cakes. Jim stops me on the way back to the table with a hand to my arm.

"I'm sorry for your troubles," he says. "My mother used to say, *Cha do dhùin doras nach do dh'fhosgail doras.*"

I offer him a Jaffa cake. "My Gaelic's not good enough for that one."

He takes one. "No door ever closed, but another opened."

I sit across from him and try to size up this saying of his mother's, whether he thinks he is the door I'm looking for. "Well, if there's any other door, I've still to find it."

"So go on looking then."

I bite into my cake. I haven't been looking for doors. I haven't been looking for anything. There are times when there is no point in putting in the effort, when you just have to step aside and wait for the pain to ebb. This is what Dunadd means to me. It was for this reason I came.

I don't tell him about my operation in January, because then I would have to go into the epilepsy. It's not something I talk about. I take my pills and try to pretend I am not afflicted. My husband only rarely saw a seizure, my children never. It's not the kind of thing you want the staff at Glasgow University to know about, so you drink the cocktails and stay away from fluorescent light, like a vampire. And now it's just reflex to sit on it, and no point in baring my soul in any case, as I only have a few months before there will be no more dreams, because that part of my life is going to be fixed.

5

Talorcan banged on the gates of the fort with the heel of his hand. "Open up now. I have Fergus Mac-Brighde at my right."

Echoes of the name rippled back up the hill, and it wasn't long before a bolt shot back and the men walked through the gate. The torches had been lit up the craggy climb to the edge of the clearing where the royal houses stood, these and the granary, store, and bakehouses beyond. The smell of roasted deer meat from a spit outside the kitchen reminded Fergus that he had eaten little food since the oat bannocks and honey his host had sent with him for his journey. But for now, something more pressing than hunger insisted itself. He looked about for his daughter, Illa.

He heard her before he saw her. "Father!"

She came running with a shout into his arms. Fergus knelt to his daughter's level, although there was barely any need these days.

"You keep growing," he said. He ran his hand through the girl's rust hair and turned back to Talorcan. "She'll be as tall as that giant Finn M'Coul before she's done."

Looking down at his daughter's smile, Fergus wondered why he ever looked for his wife among the dead, for surely she was still here among the living. Illa's hair had grown long, gathered from the front and draped around to the nape of her neck. She looked up at her father with bright sky eyes, more his than her mother's.

She slipped her small cold hand into his and tugged him towards the house farthest up the hill below the summit. They could make out Fergus's mother, Brighde, standing by the curtain at the door, erect, stately, her headdress pooling around her shoulders.

She embraced her son. "Good to see you return safely." She patted his chest in the way she had done since he was a boy. "You must be hungry."

To Talorcan she gave a simple nod.

Illa waited patiently as her father set his bag down and went to warm himself by the fire at the far end of the house's one room. The girl couldn't help but hope that a journey of so many months might have won her a prize. But her grandmother ordered her out to the spit to bring meat for her father.

Fergus watched her go. "Where's Murdoch?"

"He's up by the fire," said Brighde. "But stay here a little and talk with me. Tell me, how was the Briton?"

Fergus laughed. "Fair, of course, or she would not have been thrust upon me. Bonny and generous, but too young to have anything of importance to say."

Brighde pulled her face tight. "You need a wife, not a war minister. Not a druid, not a bard—someone to give you children. Our line is only as good as its offspring."

Talorcan, who had been standing just inside the door, shifted his feet, making Brighde look up and sigh, for this Pictish man was a relative forced upon her. She had barely given Fergus's marriage her blessing and now even less so, for her son could look favorably upon no one else. She knew that Saraid had been as much counselor to her husband as any good advisor, but Fergus was asking too much, and he would have to succumb to the choice of his brother the king if he didn't act soon.

Illa came back, her thin arms laden with dishes and a cup of *fraoch*—for a dusty traveler, she said, making her father smile. Too much of her life the girl had spent with her grandmother and only an uncle for a father.

"Illa, bring me my bag!"

Talorcan came forward with the bag and handed it to the girl. She danced her steps over to her father, laid her hand on his thigh while he went through the deep pockets of his deerskin satchel, feigning frustration. But when he noticed his daughter's dismay, his hand closed around the small wooden box that had been given him by the Briton his mother now wanted to hear about. Illa took the box and kissed it.

"Wasn't she a good woman?" Brighde asked.

Fergus threw up his hands. Such questioning, always questions from the mother who had survived her husband but sometimes, he felt, should have gone instead.

"I was told she was both young and beautiful," said his mother.

Fergus laughed. "Beauty, what is that to me? A trinket in the moment for the man whose eyes do not see far. Youth I no longer have myself. Time has brought me forward with scars and knowledge. How could I entrust myself or my daughter to youth that knows nothing of these, that has not properly lived?"

He took the box from Illa's hands and showed her how to slide the secret door open. Illa gasped.

"Very clever," said Talorcan. "From the east, no doubt."

"I believe from the Far East. A bauble for trade."

Illa took the box and slid the top open for herself. She sat down in her father's lap and laughed as he poked her sides and nuzzled her face.

When she had struggled free and straightened the folds of her tunic, she said, "There's a stranger with Sula the *ban-druidhe*. She wears a short tunic and the leg bindings of a man."

Fergus looked to his mother. "Have you seen her?"

Brighde shook her head. "She was found wandering at the bottom of the fort, in strange clothing, probably one of the traveling people, though she wears gold on her finger and in her teeth. Murdoch had her taken to Sula." She gestured into the air with her hand. "I've heard nothing since."

His mother tried to smile at him, but her eyes showed no happiness. Fergus walked to her by the fire and fixed her wool wrap about her shoulders with the pin that had been his father's, a small golden shield studded with garnet.

"Then I will go to Sula myself and find out what she knows."

Illa jumped up. "May I come?"

Fergus motioned her to his side. "First, let me eat. Then we'll see what's to be made of a woman in the leg bindings of a man."

Illa laughed. Such a laugh, the same mouth and now the adult teeth same as Saraid. Brighde brought out from a heavy box a glass from the Gauls who brought the wine on ships and took away fine jewelry made by the Saxon Oeric at the forge, the same craftsman who had fashioned the brooch Brighde wore on her shawl. For the glasses she had traded two slaves brought in on raids from the south.

But Fergus had little taste for the Gaul's red wine. He gestured to Illa to pass the *fraoch*, ale made of heather, the common man's drink. He swallowed in great gulps, letting the bitter brew run down his gullet and warm his belly. The Britons had served sweet mead that did not sit well in his stomach. By the warmth of the fire, Fergus's eyes started to close, but he still had to climb the hill to greet his brother, Murdoch. More than that, he needed to seek out Sula and make use of this night of the dead.

Fergus wiped his mouth with the back of his hand as he emerged from the smoky house into the night made loud by drums and singing from the camp below, the black air redolent with the blood of animals and the cooking roots of the peasants. Illa was already running ahead, as though her father needed a guide. As they passed the house where Fergus had lived with his wife, he looked for her at the door. Tonight he saw only the door.

With his daughter running ahead, Fergus pulled Talorcan close. "I have heard it spoken of creatures half woman, half man. Perhaps this is what was found."

Talorcan looked puzzled. "Do you mean in stories sung by the bards?"

Fergus shook his head. "Not in stories, but real, a creature with all the parts of a woman and yet with the parts of a man, too."

Talorcan patted his back. "Too much *fraoch* drunk too quickly?"

Fergus nudged his brother-in-law in the ribs. "I am telling only what I heard."

They followed Illa up higher, to where the fire burned high and hot against the dark sky, almost starless tonight because of the bright face of the moon. Murdoch spotted them and came running in his wide stride, the belly of his tunic taut around a growing stomach. His hair dark and curly, his eyes set deep below his brow, he stood an inch or two below his brother.

"Come!" he shouted. "Come here." He grasped his brother by the hand, ignored Talorcan. "What of your travels? But come and make your jump. The fire is dying."

Fergus and Illa followed him, Talorcan dragging behind. Fergus had not yet shaken that touch of death by the stones, so he ran straight at the fire and launched a leap that only just carried him to the other side. He barely cleared the charred wood and slipped on a rolling log that brought him down and covered the back of his tunic with ash.

Fergus stood up, embarrassed, hearing Murdoch and the little girl laughing.

"It's a woman he needs," Murdoch said. "She would put the spring back in his jump."

Fergus dusted himself off. "Is there no end to this?"

Murdoch's face grew dimmer, too. "The Briton didn't suit his majesty?"

Fergus gave his brother a shove, so that he, too, was

now among the embers and covered in dust. Talorcan laughed. Illa stepped back; she knew the king well enough to expect the anger that often followed the tightened muscles of his jaw. But Murdoch got up and gathered himself.

He tapped Fergus on the shoulder with a broad hand. "Next time, my friend, you will pay for that."

Fergus waved him off and set off towards the hut of the druidess. Illa took Talorcan's hand; she knew to lag behind when her father had that look about him. Perhaps what he had to say to Sula was not for the ears of others.

Fergus stood at the door and called Sula's name. It was a few moments before she opened the door. If she was pleased to see him, little showed on her face, old grandmother of the people, actual grandmother to some of them. She barely nodded him in, and after the glare of the fire and the moon, it was hard for him to make out where the old woman had gone. He picked up an unfamiliar scent over the musty smell of Sula's incense. He had heard that Roman women bathed in essence of flowers, but this was not any flower he knew of, and then, when the stranger came into focus by the far wall of the cell, she was not like any woman he had ever seen either.

He started to move towards the shadow, but Sula held him back, feeling for the godstone about his neck, smiling when her fingers found it.

He caught her hand. "Thank you," he said. "Your blessings kept me safe, even in the Valley of Stones on Samhain. On foot."

She patted his arm. "You make yourself easy prey for the wandering dead on the night of Samhain, half dead you are."

"No," he said, "there is still life, just burning a little dim."

He wanted to tell her more about the night ride, about the owl and the voices he had heard. But his eye kept moving to the stranger coming in and out of focus by the far wall. Her hair was short for a woman's.

"What is this?" he asked. "Man or woman?"

He inched forward for a closer look. The woman did not seem young, and yet her face was smooth and appealing. Around her eyes she wore the dark lines he had seen in drawings of Scotta the Egyptian princess. Her defiant look held him, expecting him to look away. But he would not.

"Take off her leg wrappings," he said, "and we will see if she is man as well as woman. I have heard of such things."

The stranger fought off Sula's hands with words Fergus had not heard before. He picked up the word *no*. Like the Romans' *Non*. Perhaps a species of Roman, then. But a word he had heard coming from the Sassenachs, *fuck*—yes, he was sure she had said that.

But Sula was smaller than the woman, and though

she might be good with spells, she had no weight behind her. Fergus moved past the stranger's flailing hands, closed around her arm, and lifted the creature so that he could reach between her legs. The woman went still.

He let go of her and stepped away. Now that he knew she was a woman, he felt embarrassed for his lack of manners. This was more the art of his brother, and he did not like it. He took another step back, his fingers still warm from the touch of her.

Sula laughed. "A woman, then. But why do her breasts ride so high on her chest?"

The woman lost her calm again when Sula moved back towards her and tried to pull up her short tunic. In the light of the fire, Fergus could see her eyes darting from the druid's face to his own, and he touched Sula's arm, unable to see a woman frightened like a rabbit.

"Let the woman be," he said quietly.

The woman uttered a word. *Okay*. Fergus exchanged glances with Sula, knowing they should be careful. Perhaps this could be a spell. But when he stepped back, the woman smiled at him and lifted the tunic herself. Underneath, her breasts were caught in a sling pulled up towards her shoulders. Fergus noticed the outline of her nipple in the thin fabric. Sula leaned forward and pulled on one of the strings that seemed to stretch like sinew.

The woman said, "Bra."

In the tongue of Erin, *bra* meant forever.

Sula tapped Fergus's hand and laughed. "She wants you forever."

Fergus tried to laugh, but there was something about this stranger that had turned his mouth dry. "Where do you think she comes from? Is she Scot or Saxon? A slave or a free woman?"

The stranger pulled her tunic down and looked away. What kind of a tunic was this anyway that covered so little, that kept out so little cold? She must have come from the east, where it was always warm, so he had heard tell. Such a climate wouldn't suit the Scotti, who were hardy from birth, whose feet were toughened by a childhood without shoes, who slept wrapped only in their plaidies.

Her shoes, too, were like none other, with black strings that came up the front and tied near her ankle. The bottom was lined, not with leather as were his, but something else that sprung back from Sula's fingers when she knelt and touched them. They were fine shoes and fit well around her feet, not such as commoners would wear. Not even such as he might wear.

He stepped forward and laid his hand on the woman's shoulder, to show his shame for having treated her roughly. She was wrapped all over in this strange fabric that stretched under the tips of his fingers.

He smiled a little. *"Co as a tha sibh?"*

A smile flickered about her lips but fell back quickly. Her steady gaze did not shift from him, even when he forced himself to look into those eyes that were pale like his own and not free of pain. Her voice was quiet and her Gaelic halting as she told him that she came from Glasgow, which he knew as a small settlement along a burn to the south, popular with the Christians but of no strategic significance. He asked her if she came from the church, but she didn't seem to understand. It seemed unlikely that Gaelic was her native tongue.

He took a step around her, surprised that her short tunic did not even cover her buttocks. *"A bheil Gaidhlig agaibh?"*

She said, *"Tha, beagan."*

If she spoke only a little Gaelic, then perhaps her tongue was Saxon.

He asked, *"A bheil Sasunnaich agaibh?"*

She shrugged, then shook her head.

Fergus was confused. The woman didn't seem to know what language she spoke.

He tried another tack. *"De an t-ainm a th'oirbh?"*

He could tell she had understood, but she was slow in answering. *"Is mise Maggie."*

Fergus turned back to Sula. "Ma-khee? Have you heard this name before?"

Sula waved away his question. "No, but what of it, if she is a druidess from elsewhere?"

He turned back to the woman and repeated her

name. Ma-khee. He had never heard the name before, but he liked it.

Ma-khee placed her hand on his arm. *"De an t-ainm a th'oirbh fein?"*

"Fergus."

His name made Ma-khee smile, and he liked the way she muttered it under her breath as though it were a secret between them. He lifted her hand and turned a golden band on her fourth finger. This woman was surely no beggar. This close, he could smell the scent of flowers from her skin; he was about to put her hand to his nose when Sula took him by the sleeve and led him to the door. "Be off with you now. If this Ma-khee is a druidess, you'd better not tempt her with those eyes of yours."

When Fergus turned back, the woman had stepped out of the shadow of the wall and stood in her man wraps by the fire. Sula opened the door and pushed him out. Ma-khee. He said her name as he went looking for Illa, and he wondered in a small flickering of thought if this could be the woman Sula had seen for him in her stones.

Fergus found Talorcan and his daughter over the hill, throwing a goat's bladder from hand to foot.

"She is a woman," he announced. "That much we know."

"Catch!" shouted Illa.

But the bladder came at him too fast and bounced off his cheek.

Talorcan laughed. "It's a woman he needs."

Illa laughed, too—her uncle's imitation of the king was a good one.

Fergus kicked the bladder, shooting it at Talorcan's head, and then, when it came back to him, batted it gently to his daughter. He looked back at Sula's hut, trying to make sense of what he had seen. If the woman were a druidess, as Sula seemed to think, then she would not be released to him and could not be the one Sula had seen in her stones. Fergus stuck out his foot as the ball flew past him. Illa wanted his attention, and he knew he owed her this and more. His ankle hurt as he ran, and he wasn't disappointed when the ball eventually hit the corner of a rock and split.

"No fear," he shouted, "there will be plenty of bladders tonight."

The cull of livestock down below had brought the screams of goats, pigs, and cattle falling under the dirk. The store of winterfeed wouldn't be enough to keep these animals alive. Their meat would have to be salted in the next days and stored in the small stone cells that dotted the field between the dwellings.

As Fergus had done in the time of his wife, he went with Talorcan down to the village for the celebration of Samhain. He fancied haggis—fresh innards from the cull and good oats from the harvest—commoners' food, but a tasty change from the roasted meat they would be serving in the fort. Still his mind was on the woman, as they begged exit through the gates. There was something about the stranger that kept bringing his thoughts back to her image, half hidden in the dark, proud and yet bruised by life, it seemed.

They climbed down the crags and slabs to where the lights were all lit now in the villagers' huts, roof upon thatched roof as far as the eye could see in the dark, narrow lanes running in between; each doorway glowed with a carved turnip to keep the spirits passing. Fergus took Illa by the hand over the swing bridge and went to join the dancing about one of the smaller fires. The many drums sent their beat through the body; the horns sounded loud, but not so loud as the singing, singing in great swells as only the Picts knew how.

Talorcan ran under the hanging thatch of his own doorway to fetch the haggis; his people had taught the Scotti so many things, it was hard for Fergus to think of them as separate. And yet, if his sister had not married into Fergus's line, Talorcan might have thought differently. He might have joined in the talk about the new Pictish king Oengus in the north. Some men under the sign of the boar had already fled Dunadd to join that Pictish kingdom where, because of his own royal line, Talorcan would have office and standing.

The two men finished off a haggis between them, then threw the skin to the dogs. They interlocked arms and drank *fraoch* from the horns of the slaughtered cattle, Talorcan laughing so that the boar tattooed on his brow seemed to run of its own accord. Fergus danced past the pain in his ankle and fell asleep in the house of a Scotswoman with two daughters. But he kept Illa by his side so that the mother would not lead her daughters down beside him as he slept. It had happened to his brother before, a girl claiming his offspring after a night he couldn't remember.

As he closed his eyes and felt his breathing grow slow and heavy, Fergus struggled to remember the face of the woman in the strange clothing. He drew his knees to his stomach and thought about the outline of her nipple in the sling that held her breasts. He remembered her smell, and only then did it occur to him that he had forgotten to ask Sula about his wife, Saraid. The dead, like this night of the dead, were slipping away from him.

6

The prospect of missing that daily dose of anticonvulsant gets the better of me, and I do it almost without thinking, in the evening: a sin of omission, the nuns would say. There have been triggers before. Fluorescent light has been one, drumming, anything of a quick and intermittent nature. Rain taps at the window as I lie awake, but it is only enough to drive me into a short drowse before I awake in the dark and wander down the hall to the sliding glass door. The night is in its own drowse, the trees heavy with misty rain that manages to hang in the air somehow without ever falling. All the smells are hanging there, too, the comfrey and mint caught by the door in a world between sleeping and waking. I step out of the house, just enough not to break the spell; everything is unutterably still. I break off a leaf from a spike of mint and crush it in my fingers.

When I get back to bed, I feel myself drift, register the knee jerk, that precursor of sleep. I wake late and spend a perfectly normal morning at my desk gathering information about Joan of Arc, one of the first witches to be burned at the stake, and one the church in an about-turn later decided to canonize. The heady smell of mint is still on my fingers, and I get so dizzy inside those spectacles that later I have to lie down on the cobalt blue couch with the purring cat by my head.

With evening falling dismal into my kitchen window, I climb up Dunadd and watch the sun sink behind the islands. It is when I am sitting with my knees pulled up against my chest on the little lip of stone in Sula's hut that I begin to feel the telltale sensation of heat in the soles of my feet. It creeps up my legs, even while my back remains cold against the ruined wall of the witch's cell. This is no place to have a seizure, but I won't make it back to the house. My field of vision is already getting very very small.

Next thing I know I am lying on the ground with a bump on the side of my head. All I want to do now is sleep. The other next thing I know is that there is a man in the witch's cell, not much taller than I, and dressed in finer clothes than the men who brought me here. His tunic is more of a jacket with tapered arms, and though the candle casts a dim light, I can make out colored patterns down the front. His shoes are surprisingly well made, brown leather stained in colored diamonds and tied at the side of the ankle with a wooden toggle. A woven brown cloth is wrapped around each leg with a crisscross of string.

He could be Sula's son, though he bears little resemblance to her. At any rate, the two of them seem intent on finding out my sex. I can bat away Sula's hands, but I am so surprised by the man's hand suddenly around my crotch that I give up the fight. He seems to glean what he wanted to know, then stands back, almost embarrassed. I should be annoyed, but I can't help looking at him. He avoids my gaze by running his hands through his hair.

But Sula is more persistent, and this time her curiosity takes her under my sweatshirt. I'm slapping her away when the man steps forward and tells her to stop. I notice on the middle finger of his right hand he wears a gold ring with an insignia of some kind. Underneath the ring is a tattooed Celtic band. A Celtic knot tattooed around his wrist makes me want to take my fingertip and trace the endless loop.

I'm so grateful for his intervention, I offer to show them what's under my shirt, so all questions about my gender can be put aside. For some reason, I feel myself wanting this man to have no doubts about that.

He keeps glancing at me, and I keep digging into my brain for something to say in my rusty Gaelic. He wants to know where I come from. All I can tell him is that my last address was Glasgow, even though I don't know if Glasgow exists in his time. But I hear him say the city with a Gaelic inflection, *Glas-chu,* and I think he must have heard of it. I am able to give him my name when he asks, and again the Gaelic accent turns it into something else. Ma-khee. He steps closer to me than people do in modern times, but I feel no need to step aside. I take the liberty of touching him since he has touched me in places no stranger ever has. I can't help but ask his name.

Fergus. He says his name is Fergus, just like any old Fergus I know in the twenty-first century. When I say his name back to him, he smiles quickly and looks away. But there is nothing sheepish in the action. I curse myself when he lifts my hand and notices the wedding ring, but he seems undeterred and brings my hand closer to his face. Maybe it's only because I'm in a dream, but I begin to wonder what my hands would feel like in his hair.

But Sula has other designs for Fergus. She takes him by the sleeve and is leading him towards the door. I want to hang on to this man with the fleeting smile and the steady gaze. But the druidess, who has been watching the little play between us, pushes him out and shuts the door behind him.

She lifts my hands and smooths her thumbs over my palms, inspecting them, it seems. I would like to know what she finds there. She brings my palms to her nose and sniffs the air around me, honing in on my underarms, to which I applied a layer of deodorant this morning. While Sula carries out her inspection, I keep looking over at the door and wondering if Fergus is coming back.

The old woman takes a pinch of something from a glass bowl and throws it into the flames, creating that hot woody smell I remember from the first dream. She walks around the fire three times clockwise, then takes a dagger from beside the wall and draws in the dirt one vertical line and three parallel lines crossing through. I'm studying the lines, because I know they have to hold some meaning, but I'm not sure what. She reaches into her shawl for a handful of something that cracks in her hands; she shakes them and blows onto them. I see, when they fall lightly at my feet, that they are colored stones. They go here and there across the lines she drew, and it all seems to mean something to her. I see there are twelve stones. She looks at me and laughs. I smile in response, as though I know what she means, but for all I know I'm laughing at something evil that's to be done to me. I'm in a foreign land here, in this place I know so well.

She motions to me the universal sign language for *eat*. I nod *yes*, because oddly enough for a dream I do feel hungry all of a sudden, and I don't think Sula intends me any evil. She is a nice old witch, probably just like the nice old witches who were set fire to in the years to come, the ones the church decided they wouldn't suffer to live.

When she opens the door, I strain to see if Fergus is standing sentry. But he's not there among the stragglers still around the fire. We walk out into the breeze on the brow of the hill, and I have to stop. Sula stops with me, observing my surprise at what appears to be the sound of waves just below the cliff.

Sula must wonder why I am grinning at her, but what can I say? She may be a druid, but she would make no sense of my claim that one day the sea wouldn't come in to Dunadd at all. I follow her down the hill, past the place on the rock with the foot imprint and the Pictish boar, but neither one is there.

On what is in my day a grassy plateau around an abandoned well, we come upon a wooden shack. Only as we enter do I realize that it is set over the well, and that in this day the well is not dry but is in fact a spring that runs with a gurgle, giving off a dank smell of wet stone. On the wattle walls of the shack hang ribbons and little pieces of rag, and here and there a clay foot or hand. The druidess picks up a wooden bowl and, when she inclines my head towards the water, I see that I am to be given my second baptism, this time presumably into paganism. I take a moment of pleasure to think how this would sit with certain nuns of my childhood acquaintance, but freezing water running its icy grip down my neck takes me out of that thought. I shiver, and then shiver again. Sula laughs. She gestures for me to drink from the bowl. The thought of tapeworms crosses my mind, another of those dangers I have been taught lurk in the wild, but tapeworms come from sheep, and I am not at all sure that they have sheep in this age. Whatever this age is. The water is ice cold and tastes peaty, tangy.

A line of dead pigs and goats lies outside the door of the kitchen, as though waiting patiently to be granted their life back. Farther off, something is roasting on a spit. These people certainly make more of Halloween than we do. Everyone is crowding the druid, talking so fast I can't understand. I suppose it could be Pictish and not Gaelic at all. It depends who dominates the fort at this time.

A woman from a kitchen in a long tunic hands me a couple of grey bready articles that look more like something from the Middle East than a Scottish pan loaf. At the spit, a burly man with a beard cuts off a piece of meat from a small animal that I hope is not dog and hands it to me on the edge of his knife. Nice not to use his fingers, even in the Dark Ages. The druidess takes a piece of meat herself and ladles a piss-colored liquid with a lace of foam out from an earthenware jar set in the ground and into a wooden bowl. It is warm and yeasty, not an unpleasant drink. By the time I finish the bowl off, Sula is gone. I am left by myself on this heathen night of Samhain, crouched on the grass, glancing about for Fergus, feeling vulnerable and biting into the tough bread, which is made of some grain more mealy than I am used to. I put my head down and chew on the tender meat.

A dog barks suddenly down below the gates, the small bark of a lesser dog, but surprisingly clear over the cheering and the strange music and, of course, the drumming. A man comes from behind and fills my bowl with more of the hot, yeasty mixture. I see when he crouches beside me he has the tattoo of a boar right across his forehead. He steals glances at me as I sip and shiver in my modern clothes.

When I stand up, the man stays crouched. I try to walk, but the beery stuff has got into my step, making the men at the spit laugh. I see a smirk on the tattooed man's face, as I turn and take my feet up to look for Sula. Or Fergus. The man of the tattoo doesn't follow as I go back to the bare rock where the foot and the boar are still missing. There's nothing here but what God saw fit to decorate the hill with. It hardly seems like Dunadd without the only part of Dunadd that is going to be left for the tourists. As I wander up to the summit and the warmth of the fire, I keep glancing behind to make sure I am not being followed.

People are jumping over the flames up there, just as Jim said. A line of men opposite a line of women jumping from either end towards each other across the fire. I join the line of women, just so there's no question. Only now I see I have been spotted. A dark figure is coming towards me with the light of the fire behind him. He's a man dressed much like Fergus, but he wears a thin band of gold in his hair. I suppose that's why he acts like the king, gesturing and shouting, *"Siuthad! Siuthad!"*

I do hurry up, but down the hill towards Sula's hut where he is shoving me. He makes sure I am put inside and closes the door behind me.

It takes a minute to catch my breath and get used to the peat smoke and the warm smell of herbs again. It takes longer to brush off the violence of the king. The druidess is there, calm in her seat by the fire, and I have to sit down by the wall because I am shaking now, not from the cold so much as the fact that this is all a bit much, finding myself here with a king but no foot imprint, with a druid in her place at the top of everyone else, with a woman druid at all when I am spending my days with facts and figures about how the last of these people were simply wiped off the pages of history.

Sula rubs my arms and pulls out a blanket of roughly woven wool to wrap about my shoulders. She sits back down and watches me shiver. When I begin to feel a warmth in my feet, I suspect what I am doing is not shivering, though when it is over I am still sitting and this has been a mild attack, if that's what it was. That I could have a seizure in a dream induced by a seizure is a conundrum but not one I want to unravel now.

Sula is really interested in me now. She's running her hands around my outline, as if she can sense something. A seizure being an electrical storm, maybe she can. Once, before Oliver and I had kids, we climbed Ben Nevis in a storm, and I could generate bars of purple static between my hands. Oliver kept shouting over the wind for me to stop, that I would electrocute myself, but then, as I say, I have this attraction to fire. I set my bedroom closet on fire when I was a child by playing with matches and rolled-up pages of homework. The only thing in my life I failed to set on fire was Oliver.

Sula's cold hands wrap around my own and drop her twelve polished stones into the cup of my palm. She takes a dagger and repeats her pattern of lines in the dirt, then gestures for me to blow on the stones and throw them like a couple of dice. Feeling a fool, I do as she bids, casting the stones across the lines.

They fall in a kind of slanted line, which makes Sula mutter and obviously has some significance for her. She pats my shoulder and hurries out. With no guard on the door, I suppose I could scarper, but I have nowhere to go except wakefulness, and I'd rather stay to see if Fergus comes back. I crouch by the fire and prod the logs with a charred stick, still unsure if these people intend me any harm. If they killed me, I wonder, would I die in my sleep?

The door opens, and Sula hurries back in followed by a smallish man. She calls him Oeric and points at me. He comes over and looks at me for a long time, walking round me, touching my clothes but not manhandling me. Oeric is very, very dirty, in the way of a coal miner with smudges on his face but no tattoos. He goes back to Sula and shakes his head. She pushes him towards me again, this time apparently with an order to speak, because he starts in on something that does not sound like Gaelic, but now and then a little like Chaucer. If I had paid more attention to *The Canterbury Tales* for Higher English, I might have a clue what he is asking me.

I offer him something to see if anything strikes a chord, but I remember only one line from Chaucer and that only because it has its equivalent in modern English: *Every thing which schyneth as the gold, nis nat gold, as that I have heard it told.*

For a minute he chews around the word *gold,* then lifts my hand and points to my wedding ring.

"Yes," I say, "gold."

Communication has taken place. We have a word in common.

He turns back to Sula and says, *"Or. Gold."*

He places his filthy hand on my chest. *"Wiffman."*

"A'bhean," says Sula.

"Woman," I say.

Oeric shakes his head.

Sula places her hand on Oeric's chest. *"Fir."*

"*Mann,*" he says.

"Yes," I say, "Man."

I look into Oeric's square face with the cleft chin, but I understand not a word when he starts to talk in what must be Saxon. After all, hundreds of years separate modern English from Chaucer, and *The Canterbury Tales* was hard enough. I gesture with my hands that he is making no sense to me.

Oeric gives up and goes back to Sula, shaking his head. They must be concluding that I am not from South of the border, if the border during these times even exists. In their talk I pick up the words *Frank* and *Goth*.

"No," I say. "I'm Scottish!"

Sula leaves with the Saxon and doesn't come back as before. I lay myself out on the narrow ledge as much as I can with the blanket around me. It has been a long day, too much pissy liquid, and I have to close my eyes against the smoke. How I sleep in a dream that is already in sleep is another thing I don't ponder until later, but when I do awake alone in the cell, the candles are out, and the only faint light comes from outside. The door is unlocked, and things have quieted, so there is no one to notice me run onto the top of the hill, not even Fergus. The fire is down to embers and the sudden odd flare. Behind me, at the rim of the hills, the sun is forcing a band of light on the eastern sky.

I follow the sound of waves and stand over the cliff

edge, line my toes along the rim, and look down, as I have on so many occasions in waking. It has never made any sense to me that if Dunadd was such a central port, the boats had to stop miles away in Crinan Bay or follow the river upstream. And no wonder it made no sense, because here's the reason why: tonight the breeze that runs against the underside of my shirt, up my neck, and against my lips is salty. Down below me, in the time of Fergus, in my dream, the Atlantic Sea does not stop out in Crinan Bay as it does in my time. Tonight the waves are crashing right against the side of Dunadd fort.

7

There's no full moon and there is no sea as I pick my way down the trail to the car park at the base of Dunadd hill. I stop by the stile, incline my head towards the black ceiling of night, trying to pick out a constellation: the Plough, Orion, the Pleiades. Tiny pinpoints of light coming at me from distances too vast even to think about. But I've been on the fort for hours, and I need to sink into a hot bath. It's when I'm up to my ears in warm water that I think about Fergus. I see him crouched beside me with his dirty fingers in my water, with that quick smile of his and the glance away. If his hands were really here, I might pick them out of the water and kiss each one and then lay them against my heart for that part of me that is still living. And then I would let his hands go, to see if there is more than pain in his look. I would hope that there was longing and that the water would turn cold long before we unraveled ourselves and realized what we had done.

With only half the medication in me, I awake the next morning with a nice clarity. A morning cup of tea in my window, watching the river run, makes me hum something from my childhood or my children's, there's probably not much difference. I sigh with my head against the top of the chair as my thoughts begin to play with this Fergus character of my dream. I lift my hand to smell if there is any trace of him left. But logic rushes to inform me that dreams leave no trace on the skin.

I feel foolish for conjuring my medieval knight, but it has been a very long time since I longed for the touch of any man. Antiseizure medicine has in my adult life taken its toll on desire. As Oliver was wont to point out. But the choice was between a conscious wife and a randy one, and in the end, with all the demands of being a wife and mother, the sterile one took hold. But in my dream, with my hands on their way to Fergus's hair, sterile was the last thing I was feeling. For the first time since Ellie died, I caught a small intimation of hope just below the breastbone.

Jim Galvin appears in my window, taking with him my medieval scene. I'm sure I look at him a bit impatiently, because, as I say, I do not possess a face for social games, a disadvantage for the most part, but I suspect it's not something Jim cares about.

"I saw you coming down from the hill last night," he says. "What were you doing up there so late?"

I look at him to size up the possibility of his not thinking I am completely out of my mind if I tell him the truth, but decide I don't want to tempt fate. "Running around in my underwear?"

He laughs. "Oh, is that all?"

He stands around creating the kind of pause that makes anyone of British origin need to bring up the topic of tea. "Want a cuppa?"

He nods. "Would you warm up the milk, though? I like a really hot cup of tea."

I laugh. "That's a new one."

Winnie the cat arches her back next to the purple lit kettle, and then sidles over to be stroked.

"You'll never get rid of that one now," Jim says.

I want to tell him that I don't want to get rid of her, that I quite enjoy her company, actually, but I can see that I am not fitting in with the country way of looking at cats. I am after all a girl from Glasgow Toun, where cats live in tenement windows among the potted plants.

"She's all right," I say, "keeps me company."

Jim gives me a look as if to say he'd be better company, and no doubt he would, but I am quite sure, desire or no desire, I wouldn't welcome his hand about my crotch.

I hand him his tea in a white mug with ALBA on it in red lettering. "What do you think they used to drink on the fort when it wasn't wine?"

He balances the mug in his palm. "Tea?"

I throw him a sarcastic smile. "Very funny. Something else alcoholic."

When he looks over to the window, I see that he has a good profile. "Oh, you mean *fraoch,* the heather beer."

That would account for the earthy taste. I laugh. "I expected it to be whisky of some sort. Did that not come up with the Scottish hills?"

Jim shakes his head. "Whisky? No, that came up with the monasteries. They were the ones with the distilleries, you understand."

I watch him sip his tea, and then swill it around inside his cup, as though he were reading something in it.

I say, "I don't suppose you know if the sea ever came up to Dunadd?"

He looks at me for a moment. "Have you read that article, then?"

I shake my head.

He clears his throat. "One of the lords of the estate, a Colonel Malcolm proposed just such a thing, that the sea used to come up here. It was in *The Royal Geographical Journal,* I have it back at the house, now that I think of it. He thought that an earthquake some time in the eighth century tilted the land and sent the sea out to Crinan Bay."

Jim slips back into his slot. "It was way back at the turn of the century, though, and, by all accounts, the man was a bit of a nutter. Nobody took it seriously."

In my dream, the nutter wasn't so nutty. From what I saw, he was right on the money.

Jim says, "Why do you ask?"

I shrug. "An earthquake, though?"

"Oh, there were earthquakes, all right. At the time, earthquakes were recorded on the island of Islay and several in Ireland, one even causing a kind of tidal wave."

I can't find anything to say as we finish our tea. It's all too strange, this. After all, I was only in a dream. I suppose the case for the sea at Dunadd is fairly obvious and could have occurred to me anyway.

"Look," I say, "I have to go down to Glasgow. Would you look out for Winnie for me?"

He shakes his head. "Look out for a cat? If the entire human race were to vanish tomorrow, there'd still be cats scrounging off any cow in the field with a leaky teat. She'll be just fine couring down between the bales in the barn."

I've had enough of him now, and take his empty mug back. "I'll be gone for a week to sign the decree absolute on my divorce and visit my son at school in Edinburgh. There's some cat food in the cupboard under the sink. The door's unlocked."

After he's gone, I shake myself and do what I'm

supposed to do with the correct number of pills to get myself back on course for that drive to Glasgow. I don't want to see Oliver, but for this last time I have no choice. All he has to do is sign *I Do*, then I sign *I Do*, and then the marriage is finished in the way it was started.

The signature in any case seems perfunctory—it's not the way marriages really end. The end is something more like a slide from no determinate point that leaves you wondering if you ever loved, if you ever knew what love was. I don't know now if we ever loved, Oliver and I. Everything was aflutter for a while in the beginning, and the children brought a sort of bond. The rest seemed like a long process of finding out who each of us really was, and I suppose we didn't like what we found. In the end, losing Ellie was too much for either of us, and it all became just a bog, a numbness, a nothing.

As I step up to second gear just after that stone bridge, something makes me look back over my shoulder, maybe hoping for a glimpse of Fergus? But all I see is a straggle of tourists taking the hike up to the fort in single file, going up to the footprint where the kings were crowned, though not the king of Scotland in my dream. I think the Scotland of my dream is before Scottish kings, before Christians, or else Sula would not be giving counsel to men in fine clothes. The Sulas of that day could not have guessed what was waiting around that historical corner.

After an hour on the road, after stopping at the supermarket for crisps and Ribena and jelly babies, after a little contact with people at large, I begin to worry about myself. I have never played around with dosages before and certainly never tried to induce a seizure. By the time I hit the traffic along the cement walls and the garages outside Dunbarton, I am beginning to wonder if I should go back to Dunadd. Before I reach Glasgow, I pull off the motorway at a café and sip a latte by means of preparation for the ordeal ahead. May it be quick and easy. May Oliver not engage me in social niceties. May he not say I am looking well.

The Glasgow of my childhood was darker and grimier than it is today. The city council has been trying to pull it up to the standard of other European cities. They have dug the buildings out of their layers of industrial soot and uncovered some beautiful sandstone structures from centuries past that soar against the skyline. Once you get in from the horror of the council estates with their anonymous grey rows of houses, you find the Glasgow that was meant to be: museums and parks, rows of Edwardian houses on tree-lined streets. They have put up glass and modern architecture now, cleaned the river, and declared the city a center of art.

I park the car and sit for a while, because there is time, and because this is, after all, my city, the one that educated me and fascinated me all those years ago at Christmas with the lights around George Square and along the rows of shops. You caught the double-decker bus into the city center and sat upstairs at the front, feeling the lean of the bus around the corners, the crash of branches, and the giddiness that this was as close to a fairground as you'd get.

I wind the window down, because Glasgow has its own smell, a remnant of the days of coal dust, as though a fine black mist still sat in the air. I watch the Glasgow people, secure in their working-class look, in their dialect, safe in this city made rich from the days of slave trade. They are who they are, the Glaswegians, nothing more, and it makes me wonder why it was never enough for me, why I couldn't be another head-scarfed woman with my husband and my shopping bag, leaning in against the wet wind that comes off the Atlantic up the River Clyde, where old shipyards lie silent and rusted now, a vestige of former British glory.

Oliver and I meet in the hallway outside the solicitor's office and stand awkwardly, looking at the opaque glass of the door that bears the solicitor's name. He looks different without me, not the way he did when we first met, but middle-aged different, trying to hang on to something that has nothing to do with me. He looks a bit balder, more fussed over.

Oliver looks at his watch, one that I gave him for his birthday a few years ago. I look at it and see it in its box. I even see the saleswoman who sold it to me. He sees only the face and the time and the conversation to be made in between.

He says. "I think we're a bit early."

I notice how his hair has receded past a mole on his forehead that I didn't know he had.

He asks me how the thesis is going. I make it sound as though it's coming together much more than it is. I make it sound as though counting the deaths of witches is much easier than it is. I mention nothing about my trips to old Dunadd.

He says, "Glad to hear it."

He looks at his watch again. He asks me how life is at Dunadd, only he calls it Duntrune and I have to correct him.

He says, "Isn't it a bit lonely all the way out there?"

"No. Well, it could be, if it weren't for the cat. And for Jim Galvin."

He shifts his feet. "Who's he?"

"A local historian, quite an interesting man. Do you know the sea used to come up to Dunadd?"

He doesn't answer, because there's a pattern here we both recognize—me asking random questions, him seething over the waste of his time. I wonder why he doesn't mention the operation, since he was always driving me to get it done. But I suppose it has no purchase for him anymore. I'm in this by myself.

We do the deed in the solicitor's office, and afterwards we shake hands in a thoughtless act that ought to make me seethe. Why I have to wipe tears off my face with a half-dissolved tissue in my car later, I don't know.

It might be relief. But I do miss our house in Kelvingrove. I miss that it was safe for a while. We sold it and split the profit. It's what's keeping me going at Dunadd these days; though probably like a cat I would be fine "courying" down between the bales of hay in the barn. Fergus's people would have no argument with that.

One more stop before I leave Glasgow: Dr. Javed Shipshap, my neurologist. The name itself ought to make me laugh, but I have never been close to humor in the lift up to his floor of the medical building nor along the echoing corridor to his office.

He's jovial. Indian. Always seems glad to see me. "And how have you been, Margaret?"

I expect he sneaks a look at my chart for the right name seconds before I enter. I remind him that I am recently divorced, as evidenced by my visit to the solicitor this morning; that I am no longer Margaret Griggs but Maggie Livingstone; that I have moved away altogether.

He nods. "Just as well under the circumstances."

But what does he know? He probably had an arranged marriage. It makes me smile to think of him dancing in Indian dress under rainbow canopies. It makes him smile to see me smile.

"You're looking well, Margaret."

We run through the medicines, dosage, effects, all that. Everything a rerun of previous visits. He reminds me of the date of my operation. The third of January.

"You'll barely have time to get over your New Year's hangover," he says happily.

I tell him I've been having unusual dreams.

He looks curious. "Oh?"

"I mean, I always have had. But these seem more vivid somehow."

He nods. "Well, epilepsy is really the great unknown. Once the brain goes into overdrive, there's no telling what it might throw up."

This is new territory for us. "But what about things that the brain couldn't possibly know?"

His laugh is a bit condescending. "Ah well, we never know what our brains pick up on a subliminal level—something we heard but didn't quite register, things we've downright forgotten. A lot of clairvoyant claims by epileptics can be put down to this, I think."

All right, he's gone as far as he's going to go. I back off.

"Are you sure everything is all right?" he asks.

I sigh. No, everything isn't all right, but most of it is out of his expertise. "If living in a fog is all right."

He places a hand on my shoulder. I can see the very line in his textbook where this is suggested. He says, "Margaret, after the lobectomy, life will be so different for you."

I hate the word *lobectomy*. I wish he wouldn't say it.

He bites the inside of his cheek. "You know they have refined the surgery."

I have heard all this before. "There are no guarantees, though, are there?"

I shouldn't corner him. He's only a doctor. There are things he can say, and "no guarantees" isn't one of them. But I have read the literature. I know this operation works 85 percent of the time. It is brain surgery, after all, and things can go very wrong. I could end up with no speech, for one. But what is almost certain is that I'll lose my dreams.

He gathers up the leaflets and brochures as though I were about to take a holiday in Spain. "Here. Maybe these will help allay your fears."

I glance at them over lunch, somewhere off the motorway between Glasgow and Edinburgh. I have to admit, the thought of never having another "episode" is compelling. But brain surgery isn't. I don't like the idea of my brain being tweezered out of my skull by some specialist in brain removal.

"Don't be ridiculous," I hear Oliver say. "They only remove the diseased part, nothing that functions well now in any case."

Edinburgh is a different city from Glasgow. The capital city smells of hops and breweries, for one thing, a sort of sour Edinburgh smell. It housed Scottish royalty after they moved from Dunadd, and the industrialization that left its scars on other British cities left Edinburgh unscathed. Whatever accommodations were made for workers have been well hidden, and so Edinburgh held on to its sense of grandeur and never had to dig itself out later from anything.

Graeme's school is in the outskirts, among grassy playing fields and long leafy lanes of respectable stone houses. It looks more like a medieval castle itself, with a dome over its clock tower and little onion domes and turrets everywhere else. He comes running down a sweeping stone staircase, looking happy and waving to me in the school's car park. I watch him in the rearview mirror as I park, and I can hardly square this seventeen-year-old with the little boy who once fit so easily onto my lap. There's a photograph in one of the many albums of him at about three years of age, looking backwards over my shoulder at the camera, holding on like he knew that's where he belonged. Now he belongs here apparently. Holding him, slipping my hand onto his rough man's cheek, I wait to feel the familiarity. I wasn't good at balancing the love of the firstborn with the protection of the afflicted second. Perhaps it was an act of self-defense for Graeme to pull away into his own world, such a little world as it is, this life of the boarding school. It used to be an establishment designed for making men out of boys, but nowadays they are making men out of girls, too.

I'm obliged to hold conference with the headmaster, who in his high turreted study and flowing black robes so readily embraces the stereotype for masters of establishments such as these. In my convent school, flowing black habits held sway, thick black cloth that smelled of cupboards and things hidden away. The headmaster pats my shoulder as I'm leaving and tells me they are expecting great things of young Griggs. Such a sharp mind, such clear ambition. He will bring glory to his alma mater. I mutter that he is a clever boy, because Graeme is waiting for my comment, and I begrudge it only because of the masters in black urging him along their path.

Nobody urged me. The black habits wanted nothing but compliance. Chastity, humility, while in secret corners we sang the Beatles: "Oo you were a naughty girl, you let your knickers down." Naughty, hot things snickered at behind the door of the school bathrooms. Or you could become the Bride of Christ and take all that stuff and lock it just behind thought until it leaked and drenched your habit, swishing down the corridors of nice girls and brides of the church. *Forgive me, Father, for I have sinned.*

I shake the nice man's hand, but I refrain from thanking him. I take my son's arm and walk myself back outside, where lines of stuffed blazers make their way to the cafeteria.

I look at the rumbling navy sky. "You're doing well. I'm proud."

He sends me a side glance. "But you wish it was Ellie, don't you?"

I look at him and wonder what I've done. He has to look away because the truth of what he says is on my face: I would like to have swung into this car park and been greeted by my rusty-haired daughter at seventeen in her blazer and sensible shoes, watched her ponytail swing at her back as she walked. I would like to have shaken the hand of her headmistress and heard how bright she was and how far she would go.

I clear my throat. "If I do, it's only because it can't ever be again. You know that."

He nods. We are on eggshell ground. He says, "I'm doing it for her, too, you know."

I want to prostrate myself and sob into the concrete. He won't look at me, can't bear the catch in his voice, and tries to smile for the passing boys he is accountable to. Graeme never really cried when Ellie died.

I eat dinner with him in the school cafeteria. Such dreary food, nothing quite fresh but trying to be. It makes you wonder what you're paying all this money for. Graeme says it's better at the weekends. He says his dad came down last weekend. It's news to me.

Graeme has never seen me in the grip of a seizure, so for all good purposes I am a normal mum, except that after Ellie died, nothing was ever normal, though it tried hard to be. It was for him, no one else, that I moved through those days after she died, washing dishes, cleaning toilets, unable ever again to pick up the book I had been reading the day it all happened. Oliver was moving through his own layers of oblivion that were different from mine, in some different corner of the universe. But I had to stay on for Graeme.

"Let's go for an ice cream," I say. "There's something I want to show you."

Graeme shakes his head. "I'd miss study hall."

He's taking on the wider vowels of Scotland's upper classes, no Glaswegian scrubbers here. Not that we come from a family of scrubbers. My mother didn't scrub. She managed a cake shop on Argyle Street, and not any old cake shop either, but one that had been in business since Victoria. It required that she leave home every morning in a smart dress suit and a Sunday hat, and me in the care of Mrs. Gillies from St. Kilda in her Gaelic world of fish and bannocks. Her flat always smelled of fish.

I smooth a loose strand of hair back from my son's forehead over the little scar from the chicken pox he had when he was seven. "How about tomorrow?"

He agrees to take the period off before lunch, which will give us two hours. I hug him quickly and then drive away, feeling like a mother abandoning her newborn on the steps of an orphanage. He's seventeen and thinks he has a right to live by himself like this. Perhaps he does, but I can't see it in the waving figure that grows smaller in my rearview mirror, and then disappears altogether.

I am a woman alone in a hotel at the city center, nothing swanky, just the basics that a travel lodge will provide. A cup of tea with artificial milk in foil containers. I sit on the bed I did not make but hope the maid changed between the last occupant and myself. I suppose you would never know unless you came across a dried patch of something. For imagined reasons like this I sit on top of the bed, drinking my tea and watching a film on television that made me cry when I was Graeme's age but now just seems silly. The dying girl says, "Love means never having to say you're sorry." I almost blush for having thought this profound, but I suppose at the time it stood in contrast to the nuns telling me I should be sorry for everything, especially myself. I watch the film to its end, for old time's sake, but fall asleep without undressing and wake while it's still dark outside my window and the river of city traffic has reduced itself to an intermittent stream.

Five o'clock. The red numerals of the bedside clock declare the time and the fact that the television has been humming pictureless for the past few hours. And six hours of sleep will have to count as a good night, which it is for me in a hotel room, with or without clean sheets. The brewing electric kettle in its small hum says I am not alone. I take my tea to the window and look out on the gathering traffic, which I suppose is no less living than my river at Dunadd. And what does any of this have to do with an eighth-century Fergus conjured out of my need for something warm to wrap myself around? All these cars and the wars about oil and the age of reason, which slaps your hand for even thinking of times before it held sway. Fergus seems more real than this nothing flow of life from beds to clock-in to cocktails to beds.

Eating in restaurants by yourself is uncomfortable, no matter that it is a hotel restaurant and many others are feeling the same in their own circle of solitude— men with their newspapers, women with their phones, all trying to be someone by themselves, which is not easy, for we are social animals no matter how you look at it, no matter that some of us don't run so well with the pack.

You can't help but like a city that has only half a main shopping street, one that is dedicated to gardens and castles and maroon-colored double-decker buses. Edinburgh just seems to have its priorities right. I wander around a wintry Princes Street Gardens, then warm myself with a proper cup of tea in a saucer on the third floor of Jenners, the posh department store. A bookshop on the way back to my car cannot furnish the English-Gaelic dictionary I have been after, but it does have (on sale) a Gaelic phrase book.

As I sit in the school car park waiting for Graeme, I flip through the book, trying the unlikely pronunciations. Whatever Gaelic I learned at Mrs. Gillies's knee leaves me dumbfounded when I look at it written. Gaelic was an oral language until the nineteenth century, and it shows, because this mess of letters seems to bear no relation to the sounds it makes. On top of that, this is modern Gaelic, concerned with trains and shopping lists. There's relatively little for nature in its rudeness as life was lived on St. Kilda, and certainly nothing for Dunadd in the Dark Ages. Instead of asking for the wine list, please, I could use an idiom to explain how I am battered and bruised from my dealings with men, how that look of Fergus's makes me feel that he has bruises of his own. Rather than knowing how to ask the whereabouts of the nearest launderette, it would be useful to find the words for how available this man might be. Just in case I need to know.

I barely recognize *Is math ur faicinn,* which means "It is good to see you." I have to close my eyes and say it before it sounds like what Mrs. Gillies would say to me after the weekend.

Graeme knocks on the car window in his tie and blazer, pleated trousers, polished shoes. I would like to loosen that tie, let in a little air.

He gets into the car and says, "Did you not sleep?"

I laugh. "That bad, eh?"

He shrugs. "No, I just know you and hotels."

I smile that he still knows me and anything. "It was fine. I fell asleep during *Love Story.* How about you? How do you sleep with all those other boys snoring around you?"

He bats my knee. "Two other boys, and only one snores. I'm used to it. What's the book?"

I hold the little phrase book up to him.

He laughs. "Does no one speak English over there in Argyll?"

"Some of them don't," I say, and leave him to figure out what he can't figure out. At any rate, these Gaelic phrases are not going to help me out much with eighth-century Scots from Ireland. I start up the car and hand the book to my son. He lodges it between his thigh and the seat.

We head back into the center of Edinburgh and park at the Holyrood end of the Royal Mile. The street is narrow, cobbled and ancient, and still gives a feel of the crammed quarters people used to live in, with its tiny dank allies and its Tudor-like top-heavy buildings. Most of it these days is given over to tourism, and with Scotland's noble castle at the highest end, there is no helping that. The castle is built on a knobby hill, much like Dunadd, though this knob is bigger and the fort grander. It used to be called Dunedin, for good measure, but got turned around, as so many things did, under the influence of the English.

Our first stop is the new Parliament Square, and I point out where the old Tollbooth Prison used to sit, marked now by a heart-shaped mosaic in the cobbles next to the grand church of Edinburgh, St. Giles, which now sits on the site. The church has always been in the business of covering things up, a pun I make to Graeme as we set our toes on the heart.

"The Tollbooth," I tell him, "used to house the women who would later be burned for witchcraft up on the castle esplanade."

"How many witches?" he asks.

"In all of Scotland? How many do you think?"

He shrugs. "I don't know. Thirty? One hundred?"

I laugh. They haven't covered the topic at his posh boarding school. When I was at school, they weren't teaching Scottish history at all except for how it affected England. I learned about the War of the Roses and the houses of English royalty. I was taught about Cromwell, but I did not learn about William Wallace, Scottish freedom fighter, whose statue stands at the entrance to Scotland's royal castle, just beyond the spot where the witches were burned. History is such a selective bastard.

"In all of Scotland," I say, "upwards of four thousand, but that's a conservative estimate. If your case made it to the High Court of Judiciary in Edinburgh, you got a record, but most of these cases were tried in local courts, and next to nothing survives of those. In all of Europe over three hundred years, generous estimates run into the millions, conservative ones into the hundreds of thousands. Whatever, it was a shocking number."

I buy us each an ice cream on the way up to the castle esplanade, where the cobbled street becomes steeper and narrows even further. Graeme is quiet.

As I stand by the well that marks the burning spot, he goes off to find a bin to dispense with the ice cream.

The little brass sconce with its bright flowers seems like a hopeless gesture to the memory of what took place here, the mobbing crowd, the sanctimonious church officials. I stand by the wall like an extra brick, picturing Sula in one of those rude carts being brought to her death. How would she be feeling, knowing her innocence, perhaps longing for the end.

When Graeme comes back, he says, "But why did they kill the witches?"

I say, "The why is fairly simple: *Thou shalt not suffer a witch to live,* so the Good Book says. And they didn't."

"Yes, but why then?"

"It had a lot to do with the Reformation, going back to the letter of the law over Catholicism. There's that and then there's a deep-seated fear of women and sexuality— go back to the Garden of Eden for that. In fact, there was a handbook drawn up by two Dominican monks for trying witches called *The Hammer of Witches*, that went into great lengths about the evils of women. A lot of what they extracted out of so-called witches had to do with their supposed sexual conduct with Satan."

But we're onto tender ground here between mother and son. Graeme walks a few steps away from me as we pass beyond the esplanade, under the gaze of William Wallace and into the castle proper. The turret that holds Scotland's crown jewels is also home to the Stone of Destiny, a plain old sandstone block that came with the Gaels from Ireland and before that from the land of Jacob, a relic that goes back to Scotland's beginnings and is held dear, which is why the good English king Edward, known as the Hammer of the Scots, removed it to Westminster in London for its eight-hundred-year sojourn. It looks an odd thing among velvet and jewels, but this recently returned rough rectangle of stone, with its metal rings at either end, has come to mean more than the jewels.

It's a captivating story, Scottish history, now that we know it. In the Great Hall below, we watch a demonstration with swords by a couple of bearded men in Elizabethan dress, and so the chatter comes back and a few jokes about codpieces and men in tights.

On our way out of the castle, we merely glance at the burning spot; in the car words fail me. I can't dispel the image of that horse-drawn cart carrying the swaying, shackled witch, and often bands of witches, or druids, bumping over the cobbles, upwards towards the castle barricade, the clawing mobs after it. Sometimes the witches were garroted first; often they went live to the flame.

Maybe it's that that releases a tear when I have to say good-bye to Graeme. Perhaps it's the feeling of failure. He puts his arms around me like the man he isn't yet.

"I'll be all right," he says. "You know I will."

I shake my head. "No, I don't."

He hands me a hankie, like a man would. It's ironed and starched, in a way I would never have made it.

He says "Do you still think you might move to Edinburgh once you've had the operation?"

I hand him back his hankie. "I suppose I could if I got a job here."

"But even if you didn't," he says, "you could come here and use the university library."

I look into those grey eyes that used to be clearer, with fewer questions in them. "You'd like that, wouldn't you?"

He nods, tries to laugh, and makes me smile. "It's a bit lonely here all by myself."

I hold this little son of mine, desperate to make it all right for him. This is the first time since Ellie died that he has admitted any need.

He waves to me as I drive out of the parking lot, looking small and lost all of a sudden, so that it's all I can do to switch on the blinker and make the right-hand turn out onto the main road. I put on the radio and get an Edinburgh DJ. But the fast talk jars with the choking in my throat, and I have to turn it off.

Before I leave Edinburgh and head back to the west coast, I have one more stop. Oliver would say I want to wallow in the gloom, but I do feel the need to visit the university library's Scottish Studies section to locate some names and try to put faces to the bodies in the fire. Somehow I feel as if I owe it to them.

University libraries are stuffy places, not so much

because of the air but because of the faces people have, tortured student faces over the tomes they must devour or arrogant faces because of what has been achieved. I keep looking up at people as they pass my carrel, my finger on the lists of witches, the Bessies and the Isobels and the Joans, people with a network of family and friends, and enemies, too, apparently. It was often the nervous neighbors who would turn them in, churches that would try them, traveling courts that would sentence them. Pyres both recorded and unrecorded that would burn them. Whatever year it turns out I'm visiting in my dreams, it seems the church was making only squeaking noises in Scotland then, preparing in the wings for its great roar down the corridor of history.

As a child, I went to mass. I colored in the pictures of Jesus of Nazareth with his pierced hands turned towards the poor and helpless. For a time, I even wanted to die young so that I could sit on the lap of Jesus like the children in the coloring book. I suppose part of my interest in witches is just to understand how we went from Jesus meek and mild to this hell pocket in the history of the world.

It's hard to leave those women behind in Edinburgh, though history long since moved on. The last witch to be burned in Scotland was Janet Horne in 1727, a demented old biddy who didn't understand the pyre was meant for her and thought she was being taken for a picnic.

God, I want to throttle someone, as I wind this modern contraption over mountain passes to the coast upon which Dunadd sits. Surely I would have been a victim of the witch hunts; the nuns or the neighbors would have turned me in for my affliction. I wonder how many women were burned just for having epilepsy.

All the lights are out at Dunadd as I chug along the long lonely path, over the cobbled bridge to the small glow of the night-light in my cottage kitchen.

After I have banged the car door shut, the fields and the river seem very still. No sound, just the smell of soil and river. I lean back against the car, the hill fort towering over me asleep, like all good things at this hour. I wait for Winnie to make an appearance, but the only animals I can make out in the dark are the shadows of sheep in their field across the river where the village once stood.

But I am tired, and not only of driving. There's Ellie and the divorce; there's the son I have failed; there's the sheer brutality of the witch hunt. I look around for Winnie, but I expect she is still couried down among the bales, warm, back to her natural state.

The next morning, I'm still brooding on my Edinburgh trip, walking out into the farm's courtyard behind the cottage in my dressing gown, my hands around a hot mug. I call for the cat but hear nothing back. Then in among the bales, I see her curled black back, unmoving, something not quite right.

"There you are, Winnie."

I set my cup on the concrete floor, waiting for her to notice me, but the curled back does not unfurl. When I reach down and touch her, she is cold. I put my cheek next to her belly and feel her chest rising against my skin. But her eyes are dull and will not look at me.

I'm rushing for the car when Jim Galvin walks around the corner.

"The cat," I say, still running, "what's the matter with her?"

"Skitters," he shouts, as I open the car door and jump in.

I'm forced to let Jim climb in beside me, because I don't know where the vet is. I lift Winnie onto his lap, and he knows by my look that there will be no objection.

I have always been respectful of speed along the lanes out of Dunadd, as though keeping time with its ancient standing, but I am in third gear approaching the bridge this time and close to fifty miles an hour on the road out to the main road.

"If you knew she was sick, why didn't you take her in out of the cold?"

"Did you want shite all over the house?" he asks. "Don't worry. She'll be fine."

I turn hard into the traffic. "She doesn't look fine, does she?"

We drive in silence except for the directions I must accept. I am weak down to the foot that must depress the pedal and the hand that slots the gear stick into fourth. The vet is eight miles away. I glance at Winnie's half-slit eyes, and I'm not sure we'll make it. I slept all last night with her dying outside in the barn in the cold. I shudder with the familiar guilt of not being there.

"It's just a cat," Jim is saying.

Just a cat, but another life I was responsible for.

"Shut up."

We drive in silence except for "Turn here" and then "Pull up behind the green car."

I dash into the surgery in my dressing gown with my black bundle of fur and try to explain but cannot rightly answer the details. I wasn't there. I have known this before. I have known this before.

They make me wait in a chair with her on my lap, and then it's, "The vet will see you now."

They shake their heads, make me wait, shoot her full of fluid with a dash of electrolytes. I object to nothing, ask no questions. They give me antibiotics, probiotics. I do not object. I hang on to the possibility that it could all have some effect, and I drive home with Winnie eerily quiet in the backseat.

I fill the syringe and hold her tight to get the medicine down her throat. But she doesn't have much struggle.

I lay her back down, flat out on the table. She won't purr.

By the evening, she raises her head as I walk into the kitchen. Her eyes seem more awake. But she can't get up to take the water I offer. I use the syringe to get more fluid into her.

Jim Galvin taps at the window and mouths, "How is she?"

I shrug. He comes in, though I still have not forgiven him.

He starts to make tea, while I sit watching the feeble life of a stray cat that I need to survive suddenly more than my own life.

Someone has to be held accountable. "How could you leave her out in the cold? She nearly died."

"Aye, well." He drops a tea bag into each cup. "We all die."

I sigh. He's right. It seems we spend so much of living trying not to die. But then death happens anyway. Time is such a useless measure of anything. The most you can say is that we are born and that we die. What comes in between is a short pause. In the great expanse of the universe, the pause is nothing more than a few breaths. We try to make it mean something by adding it up in years, but it doesn't add up. We're here; we're gone. Something else takes our place.

I get up from the table and lean on the kitchen counter. Jim slides the cup of tea towards my hands, then leaves.

The next day, Winnie manages to pull herself up and

walk to her bowl of water. My heart jumps, and I'm smiling when Jim comes through the door.

He says, "I said she'd be fine."

"No thanks to you."

I pass him a bowl and a box of cornflakes. "You want your milk heated up for that, too?"

"If it's not too much trouble."

It is too much trouble. Life is too much trouble, but we can't help but shuffle it along. I crunch my cereal across the table from him.

He says, "Are you still in a bad mood?"

I sigh. "I'm not going to grace that with an answer."

Oliver couldn't stand my moods, either, but then, when I was having them, I couldn't stand him. They were often the precursor of a seizure, which gave him more reason to hate them. I wonder what Jim Galvin would do if I started one right here in front of him, and I am beginning to feel that heat in the soles of my feet, so it behooves me to get rid of him before I find out.

I take his bowl of cornflakes from him. "I have a terrible headache. Do you mind?"

He's saying he doesn't mind in the least and quite understands, but I am only seeing the part of him that speaks, the lips and teeth; all else has swum out into vague light, and he's only just out of the door before I feel my way to the bedroom and drop against the pillows.

8

Illa was gone when Fergus awoke from the Samhain celebration in the commoner's house, his head in the lap of the older daughter of the house. The thighs of a woman formed a soft-enough pillow, and he was still fatigued from the journey from the Britons, still a bit queasy from the *fraoch* he had swallowed in abundance. He closed his eyes again and feigned sleep, for there was no harm here in the lap of a girl, keeping warm in her woman smell beside the fire.

The mother of the house came through the door and set a pot of water over the fire, singing a song of supplication to the sun to rise each morning, and for Cailleach the goddess to stay close through the long winter nights. She sang in the strange minor tones of

Pictish, but this woman with her dark hair and sallow skin was no Pict.

The song brought with it thoughts of Saraid, and he remembered with a clutch in the region of his heart that he had not tried to contact her last night. His thoughts had become tangled and slipped from Saraid to the woman in men's clothes up on the hill with Sula. Perhaps it was happening, what his mother had said, the fading that came eventually after death.

He sat up and stretched, drawing to him the eyes of the peasant women. The mother handed him a bowl of brose, oats uncooked in milk, which he took but didn't know if he could stomach. He preferred the milk to be heated, but he nodded in thanks, belched a little, and felt better; after all, this was the food of his childhood. It gave him comfort, as it was designed to do, though what he required of his body this morning was getting back up on the fort to locate the whereabouts of the Roman slave, one of a few he had brought with Murdoch a few years ago from a battle with the Northumbrians. If some of the words he had heard the woman speak were from the Roman tongue, then the slave would be able to find out where she had come from and what her business at Dunadd was. She might well be a druidess sent by the colonies of druids that had been moved off the sacred isle of Iona.

First he went to make sure Illa was with his mother.

Fergus knew he should be more grateful to his mother, though he resented her meddling and had, at the time of his father's death, wished it were her instead. Still, she was the reason they were living high on Dunadd, the reason Murdoch was now king. She was as much of a mother as Illa had now, and that wasn't much.

He found Brighde, an unhappy bundle of shawls by her fire this morning, sipping her custard. Illa jumped to her feet when she saw her father come through the door.

"Go and find some meat for your father," Brighde said.

Illa's eyes met Fergus's in a moment of protest, but he nodded for her to leave.

Fergus went to the fire, stretching his hands out to the warmth. "Must you always send her off? We have slaves for that."

"Not on this morning after Samhain," Brighde said. "They are all like you, slumbering where they should find no slumber. Will you take another commoner for a wife?"

Fergus poked the fire. He sighed. "Sleep was all I was doing by a commoner. And Saraid was no commoner, as well you know."

He sat down and looked into his mother's face, still a handsome one in spite of the lines, her long grey hair swept up in coils about her head, her thick woven shawl in reds and yellows hiding the frailty of her shoulders.

"Where is the slave, the Roman who worked in the bakehouse?"

Brighde looked back at her son. "Still in the bakehouse, I suppose. Do you need a slave?"

Fergus met Illa at the door, took a piece of meat from her platter, and led her back outside.

He held the girl by her shoulders and kissed the top of her head. "Hurry. Go and tell the Roman in the bakehouse to come to me."

Illa ran off; the distance was short, and her legs were long. Fergus walked over to Murdoch, who was sipping *fraoch* by what was left of last night's spit. His large grey dogs were finishing off the carcass where it lay tossed off into the heather. Fergus knelt on one knee to get his hands closer to the embers.

"How was your night?" Murdoch asked. "I lost you."

Fergus didn't answer. He picked up a bone and pushed around in the ash with it. "The woman who was found. Have you seen her yet?"

Murdoch spat. "I chased her off."

Fergus saw Illa returning with the Roman and wanted to speak before they drew close. "Chased her off the fort?"

"Only from the fire. She might make a good trading piece."

Murdoch laughed at his brother's serious look. "Why didn't you take her to your bed instead of lying with the common women of the village?"

"I didn't lie with anyone in the village." Fergus got the words out before Illa and the slave arrived.

Murdoch's eyes left his brother and settled on his niece. "What's this? Do you have your own slave now, Illa?"

Fergus stood up and gestured Illa to follow. Murdoch and their mother were the same, always dragging their nails through his wounds.

Outside Sula's hut, Fergus asked the Roman his name. He came from one of the warm countries and spoke the Gaelic tongue with a strange inflection, like waves beating and retreating.

His voice was high, like a boy's just before he comes to manhood. "Marcus Paullus."

Fergus pushed his hair back and stood strong before the druidess's door though he didn't feel so strong inside. "Sula!"

They could hear her moving about, before the door opened into the dark space with the small fire at its center. As his eyes adjusted, Fergus could make out the stranger in the recesses. He stayed back by the door and kept Illa with him. He wasn't yet sure about this woman, and strangers had been known to bring in disease.

The druidess seemed only vaguely to register their presence.

Fergus left Illa by the door and pushed the slave forward. "I brought Marcus Paullus to see if the stranger can speak to him."

Sula looked up. "I had her cast the stones, and I see again that she doesn't come from our world."

Fergus took a step forward so that he could see the woman better. He caught her eyes on him, but she looked away when his gaze fell on her.

"But she is not brown-skinned like the ones from far off," Fergus said. "She looks more like a Pict, like some of the women in the village."

Sula interrupted him. "More like Saraid, you mean?"

He shook his head. He didn't want to give himself away before he had even had time to measure his own feelings. "Like her people."

Sula patted his arm. "She is strange and came to us at Samhain. I can only think she comes from the place of the dead."

Fergus could feel his heart speed as it had the night before in the Valley of Stones. How careless of him to grab her like a woman. How quick he had been to relish the warmth in his fingers. He feared what he might have brought upon himself.

They turned to the stranger now because she was uttering a few words. She was looking at him and saying it was nice to see him again in his own tongue. *Is math ur faicinn.* It didn't sound exactly like it should, but it made Fergus smile.

He stepped closer. "Don't be afraid."

Fergus nudged Marcus forward. "Speak to her. Find out where she comes from."

Marcus seemed to have a bad foot. He kept his weight off it and pulled on the hem of his tunic like a child who must answer for his misdeeds. *"Ubi domus tua?"*

The woman's eyes looked to Fergus and then back at the slave. He liked that she seemed to trust him.

"Don't worry," said Fergus. "He's a eunuch."

A smile came to her face. Fergus took a step backwards, because it took him off guard how she put her hands into her hair and shook her head. Her face was struggling, and she shook her head in a comical manner. She did have a look of Saraid, it couldn't be denied.

She put her hand on her chest. *"Caledonia."*

Marcus was excited. *"Tu es romana?"*

She said, *"Non sum romana."*

Marcus asked, *"Tu venisti per mare?"*

The woman shook her head.

Marcus looked back at him. "She says she's not Roman, and she did not come by sea."

Fergus stepped forward again. *"De tha sibh as iarraidh?"*

Fergus liked that she blushed when he asked her what she wanted at Dunadd.

It made Sula laugh. "It looks as though she wants you, Fergus."

The Roman slave laughed, too, making Fergus turn on him and send him out of the hut.

He drew Sula to one side. "Tell me what this all

means. This woman, is she the one you have seen for me in the stones? Look at her. I do not believe that she comes from Samhain. She has nothing of the aura of the dead."

He went back to her and touched his fingers to the warm flesh at the center of her palm. "Look, there is heat coming from her."

He was surprised when she wrapped her fingers around his hand. *Tha mi a Glaschu. Tha mi a Dunadd. Is mise Maggie Livingstone.*"

She seemed so badly to want him to understand her that he wrapped his other hand around hers. But when he asked her how she came to be at Dunadd, she looked away. When she laid her hand upon his shoulder and spoke in a language he didn't understand, he turned back to Sula.

But Sula only shrugged. "Spells perhaps from her native land?"

Fergus let go of the woman's hands and stepped towards the door. He put his arm around Illa's shoulders and led her out. If this woman was a druidess, he had better watch out, and yet something about her made him lean back against the door once it was latched behind them.

Illa looked up at him. "Did you find out where the stranger comes from?"

Fergus took his daughter's hand and led her a good distance from the hut. She looked back at him with eyes that were her mother's. Fergus went to speak, but the words were slow to come out. "I don't know where she comes from. But Sula says she didn't understand Oeric's Saxon, and the Roman wasn't able to speak to her in his tongue."

Illa squeezed his hand. "Will she live with Sula now?"

Fergus crouched beside his daughter. He was confused by the odd weight of his thoughts. "Do you remember your mother, Illa?"

The girl looked perplexed, and why shouldn't she, since he had seldom talked to her of her mother. Brighde never did. "Her face is less clear to me," she said. "But I remember sitting on her lap in our house, how she played games with my fingers. Talorcan says she had a fine voice."

"Talorcan?"

The girl shrugged. "He comes to the wall sometimes, where no one can see. I can climb over, though I know I shouldn't."

Fergus noticed her eyes fill and rubbed her arm. "Talorcan is a good man, whom your mother loved. You should see him when you can. But don't let your grandmother or Murdoch find you climbing over the walls or there will be a beating for you." He prodded her side and made her squeal. "And me."

Illa nodded. She needed this secret world with her father as much as she needed anything. "Will you teach me the game of blue beads on the board?"

Fergus looked over his shoulder at Sula's hut. He would go back later, try to find out more about the woman. Sula was stubborn when she made up her mind, and Fergus feared she would persist with her belief that the stranger did not come from their world. He almost wished he felt the same, for he couldn't rid himself of her. This might be the woman the druidess foresaw, and yet she had come out of nowhere and was stranger to him than any person he had seen from other lands, even the black-skinned ones. He didn't know how to approach this woman. All he knew was that he wanted her to be from the land of the living. As he watched his daughter run down the hill ahead of him, Fergus hoped that this woman Ma-khee would stay at Dunadd and have no more thoughts for the place she had come from.

9

The first thing I see is light breaking into the hut through small chinks and Sula in the doorway in what seems like half a dozen blankets. As she steps to the side, I recognize the figure behind her as Fergus, and my pulse speeds up to jogging rate. My eyes are not yet adjusted to the glare of daylight, but I can make out a small girl behind him across the doorway. I can't see her well, but from her height she must be about Ellie's age. Ellie's last age.

Fergus nudges a smaller, older man forward, and tells me he is Marcus, the Roman. He tells me in the next breath that the Roman is a eunuch, which makes me smile. But I am more interested in Fergus standing there in his leather jerkin belted at the waist, his tunic coming to midthigh and the leggings crisscrossed with string. It seems he has made some effort with his hair, tying back strands from the front with lengths of cloth. The short hair around his forehead and neck is curly.

Fergus sees me looking and shifts his feet. I wonder what this man of the Dark Ages makes of me in my androgynous clothing, springing from nowhere, speaking a language that doesn't exist yet. I tell him I'm from here, but then there are things I cannot say in his native Gaelic. When he touches my hand, my fingers automatically wrap around his so that I am standing holding hands with this man I hardly know, but planning already to take this feeling away with me. *Fergus, I don't know how I got here, and I don't even know who I really am, except that I am thirty-eight years old and am as nervous as a teenager before you.*

He goes to pull away, but I grab his hand. Now I'm acting like a teenager.

"It's okay," I say.

But that offering of English makes him draw back as though I were casting evil spells. With only O Level Latin, I can't do much better with the Roman. Suddenly everyone is nodding and talking too fast in their Gaelic for me to follow. Fergus retreats to the door, making me wish I had never said a thing. He's gone, and all I have is the space in front of me where he was standing. Sula takes a blanket from her shoulder and wraps it about mine. I am shaking, and I don't know why.

I ask her in Gaelic what his full name is.

She says, "Fergus MacBrighde." And then she tells me an entire history of the man, which I catch only some of.

I say, "Is he the king?"

Sula shakes her head. "No, he is not the king himself. He is King Murdoch's brother."

Prince Fergus, then. Sula is watching me, studying my face, which is bad news for me, because I might as well have I LIKE FERGUS tauttooed across my forehead. She goes to the door and calls the eunuch back in. He takes a seat by the fire and undoes the one lace on his much-worn leather shoe. There's a cut on the inside of his foot, and Sula kneels down to attend to it. She points to one of the pots on the floor and asks me to hand it to her, only I can't really follow the direction of her finger in this semi-darkness.

I get up and make a stab at one.

"*Chan e,*" says Sula. *No.*

I keep going through the pots, sniffing. Cloves. Dill. Coriander. Saffron, surprisingly. Something very foul smelling, like sweaty feet. Bark. Chamomile. Mint.

When I lift the lid of a pot containing evil-smelling dried leaves, Sula says, "*Tha!*"

She pulls out a pinch of leaves, grinds them in her palm, and spits to make a paste, which she daubs along the jagged line of Marcus's cut. She blows on it and sings a verse. The Roman is most pleased and keeps saying, "*Math, math.*"

He even turns to me and says, *"Tapadh leibh."* Thank you.

I'm not sure why he would be thanking me. But he is a nice little eunuch.

Sula sends Marcus off and squats by her fire staring at me. I wonder if she has anything in her pots for my affliction. Perhaps in this day it wouldn't be counted so much an affliction as a blessing. I desperately want to ask what year this is, but if we haven't come into Christianity yet, there will be no way of gauging my time against theirs. Not from here anyway.

Marcus comes back with a pitcher wrapped in a cloth and bread with something that tastes like cottage cheese slathered over the top. The pitcher contains warm *fraoch*. Warm anything is welcome, so I down a few cupfuls from the same cup used by the other two. But it's all a bit much for the middle of the day, and I doze off.

When I come to, Sula is gone and Marcus is watching me, almost like a man who isn't a eunuch. When I sit up, he offers me more food, but I know I'm not going to shake the drowsiness unless I can get some fresh air.

I go to the door with Marcus close behind. He trails me across the top of the hill and stands in front of me as I get close to the cliff edge. The wind rushing up off the sea billows my shirt into a balloon that I try to hold down and then let go, spreading my arms like a supplication to the sea. Only now do I notice Fergus sitting farther down the hill. He must have been here all along, and he's not alone, for his arm is about the shoulders of a young girl.

Suddenly a commotion of bells has us all looking back, and the girl breaks free from Fergus and runs over the crest of the hill in her tunic that falls to her ankles, her reddish hair bouncing on her back. Without thinking I start to run after her. I've seen this girl before, but not for a long time, and I desperately don't want to lose her.

I hear my voice come out as though it belonged to someone else, less a call, less a name, than a wheeze. "Ellie!"

But I am making the slave panic. He spreads his arms as though herding a runaway cow. I stop because I am beginning to choke on nothing but my own breath. The little girl doesn't hear me anyway and runs down the hill out of sight.

I turn to Marcus. *"Puella quisnam est?"* Who's the girl?

Marcus holds my arm to keep me from following her. *"Puella filia Fergi est."* The girl is Fergus's daughter.

As Marcus leads me back to the hut, I catch a last glimpse of Fergus on his ledge below the cliff. Just for a moment, he turns his head and takes me in, all in my distress, confused, my face wet with tears.

Sula is back in the hut when we return. She bids me squat by the fire, where she takes my arms and runs her hands along the insides of my wrists. After Ellie died,

I used to find her sometimes in fleeting dreams, those dreams that taunt you and leave you on the other side of sleep with lead in your chest.

I turn to Marcus. *"Puella nomen?"* What is her name?

Sula pats my wrists, then sets them back by my sides. "Illa."

"How old is she?"

I almost don't want to hear. I think I know the answer.

Sula says, "She was born eight years ago."

I should ask about her mother, but just for this moment I want to be the only mother in this dream.

When Marcus brings us meat and more bannocks, I begin to wish potatoes had already made it to Scotland, because dry meat and bread needs an awful lot of *fraoch* to help it slip down, and this warm ale of yesteryear is stronger than what it would become. I fall asleep, and when I wake, Sula is snoring by the embers and Marcus is making of himself a useful draft block by the door.

I pull my shawl about my shoulders and lift the stick to poke a flame to life, but the fire has been left too long. I've noticed a lattice of peat blocks stacked around the outer wall of the hut, and have to step over Marcus to reach the door. Outside, the wind has died down and a rosy glow is creeping up over the horizon, so I am able to find the peat and start making a smaller stack to carry inside. I start to hurry, because I have the sense that someone is watching me, and I don't want to be chased back into the hut by King Murdoch again.

But it's not the king. It's his brother. Fergus is suddenly crouched beside me, gently nudging me aside and lifting bricks of peat into his arms.

"It's still night," I whisper. "Why are you here?"

I don't mean to question his appearance. All kinds of things have been appearing lately.

He says, "I was waiting for you."

I stand there, not knowing what to say in English or in Gaelic.

He takes the peat to the door and drops it. "I want to show you something."

He looks awkward, as though I could wound him by declining. But this is a dream, and in the way of dreams I hold out my hand. He lifts my palm and runs his hand over it, a gesture that might have its meaning in this day, but I'm not quite sure what to make of it. All I know is that I'm not going to let go of his hand this time, even as he leads me down the hill, past the cookhouse that is beginning to stir, to the wall, where a small gap in the masonry allows us to pass through. On the other side, we crouch down, listening for any sign of life.

"Don't come here by yourself," he says.

A goat bleats down in the village, followed by an answer from another of its kind. But the people are still waiting for first light, and the village is dark as we drop down into the lane that leads from the fort to the bridge.

Out of nowhere, a heavily tattooed man is in our path on a small bay horse. In what light there is, I can see the horse's breath as the man dismounts and hands the reins to Fergus.

Suddenly Fergus's hands are under one of my feet, and I am being lifted onto the horse as the man who brought it here drops back into the darkness. Fergus jumps up behind me and kicks the horse into a trot. He doesn't lead it to the bridge, but away to the hills on the south side of Dunadd. I haven't ridden a horse since I went through that phase as an adolescent, but Fergus's body lodged behind mine manages to keep me in place.

Once we are out of sight of the fort, Fergus slows the animal to a walk. I can feel his rough cheek against my ear.

"Where are we going?" I ask.

He breathes the words against my cheek. "A sacred place."

I only know the word for *sacred* because Mrs. Gillies used to use that word to describe Dunadd. Maybe that's what drew me back here.

Fergus doesn't talk; at least he utters no words. There is plenty of talk between the front of his body and the back of mine, and I don't mind in the least that half an hour passes before Fergus pulls the horse to a stop. When he jumps down and holds my waist for me to dismount, I hardly care anymore what it is he has brought me here to see.

He reaches for my hand and leads me to several large slabs of rock. There is more light now, but it is still hard to make out what he crouches down to trace with his finger in this sacred place. He takes my finger and sets it in the groove of what I trace out to be a circle, and then within that circle another, and another. With my other hand I trace other circles within circles; all over the rock this pattern of rings repeats itself.

I look into his face. "What is it?"

He places his hand in the small of my back and I feel his fingers trace a vertebra or two, as though I were another of the patterns in the rock. "Sula used to bring us here when we were children. These marks were left by the ancients, the stoneworkers. Do you know who they were?"

Right now, with Fergus's hand on me, I am not particularly interested in who they were, but I get the feeling his question has more to do with where I come from.

I take his other hand and hold it against my solar plexus. "*Chan e.*" No.

He says, "Sula says they are raindrops on water set in stone. She says life on earth and life in the stars is like this, one circle within another, crossing others." He looks away, then says a word I don't recognize: "*Eadar-thoinnte.*"

When I look to him for an explanation, he laces his fingers with mine. "*Eadar-thoinnte* means 'many strands woven together.'"

He lays his mouth against mine, not a kiss, just a question of some kind. "Tell me who you are, Ma-khee."

I could tell him something that is not true, but it would jar against this moment.

I take my lips from the warmth of his, and say, "I don't know who I am."

He looks back at the rings in the rock and slowly takes his hands from me.

"Who are you?" I ask, drawing his eyes back to me. "I know you are Fergus, but I don't know who you really are."

He flashes his fleeting smile. "I'm just the king's brother," he said. "The king's sad brother."

A weight comes over him and stays that way as we ride home. Yet, moving to the rhythm of the horse, his chest against my back, the questions and answers seem moot. We know who we are and why each one hopes there is no end to this journey. There is nothing I can tell him of what I am that will make any sense to him.

But when we reach the fort and he helps me dismount, he says, "Ma-khee." In his eyes the question remains.

I hold on to him and let that be my answer. Before he leaves me at the gap in the wall, he touches his lips to my cheek. I watch him run down through the rusty bracken before turning in the direction of the cookhouse, which is bustling now with servants running to and fro from other buildings, smoke sidling from the chimneys. Those bells that had caused Fergus's daughter to run off yesterday morning are being rung, though I can't see where. They chime in my head as I climb back up to Sula's hut at the summit. They vibrate loudly, then fall off, and just before I slip out of the dream altogether, I see the girl Illa running between the adults below, glancing up at me, and then moving away.

10

The girl comes and the girl goes. As I turn over on my pillows, my eye falls not on Illa but on the bright square in the wall that is my bedroom window. From the fold-out frame by my bed, Graeme and Ellie look back at me. This picture of Ellie hugging Mickey Mouse in Florida has no reference for me anymore. I can't find her face in any of the photos, just sometimes there in a flash of memory, like her little self in a high chair sucking melted chocolate from her fingers, or waiting by the back door in her first school uniform, her little baby neck in an oversized collar and tie. And a world away on the hill, I could have sworn it was Ellie; the pain under my breastbone suggests it is so.

I curl around myself, bringing back the movement of

Fergus behind me on the horse, the damp warmth of his lips on my face. He smells like the wall and the bracken. His scent is not separate from his surroundings, in the way that I, in this distant land, here but not really here, smell not of myself but of something manufactured. He asked me who I am, but there are many me's—like looking into a broken mirror, I am scattered all over. And yet, there is something scattered about him, too. He is the king's brother, son of Brighde; he is the father of his daughter, and perhaps, who knows, the husband of his wife. I know so little of what makes up Fergus Mac-Brighde. But I understand that sadness he speaks of. I feel it in his eyes.

We never brought Ellie to Dunadd—only to that refuge of cold Scots, the beaches of Spain, and once to Disney World. I close my eyes and will myself back into sleep, perchance to dream. But nothing is coming to Dunadd in the twenty-first century except a dimming light behind the spray of dead grasses in the window. The birds are not yet quiet, but settling.

In the kitchen I crack open a tin of beans and slot slices of bread into the toaster, everyday actions that edge Fergus and Illa out. The heat from the burner warms my face. The kitchen is in full view of the glass doors, so there would be no hiding from Jim Galvin even if I wanted to, which I'm not sure I do. Alone in my kitchen, watching my beans begin to bubble, I suddenly feel quite lonely.

Soon enough, Jim opens the door. "Came to see how your headache was doing," he says. "And the cat."

My hand goes over my mouth. "Where is she?"

"Running after a mouse, the last I saw. Do you know you have been asleep for eight hours? I almost called for an ambulance."

I smile and relax my defenses. He takes a step into the house, followed now by Winnie, the very skinny black cat. "I came an hour or so ago, but you were out for the count, so I gave her a saucer of milk. Later, she wanted to go out, so I let her."

I don't like the thought of this man wandering around my cottage with me asleep in the bedroom. My door wasn't even closed.

I pick Winnie up and snuggle her against my face. "I took a strong painkiller, that's all."

Jim nods and steps back towards the door. "Well, I was just checking."

"Thank you." I gesture towards my paltry meal. "If you haven't already eaten? It isn't much."

He looks glad that I want to share my beans and toast with him. I make him his tea with warmed milk. We don't say much, as though our main business is eating. After the beans, I find a few chocolate biscuits in the bread bin and arrange them on a plate.

He unfurls the wrapping from one. "How was the trip anyway?"

For a moment, I think he means my dream. I have to

tap my fingers on the table to refocus myself. Glasgow. Edinburgh. The well on Castle Hill.

"Fine. Divorce finalized. Son educated and on his way. Myself appalled by what I turned up at Edinburgh University. Did you know the last woman to be tried under the Witchcraft Act was in 1944?"

"Aye," he says. "Crying shame, that. Old Winston Churchill got involved. It's him that had the law abolished, you know."

I am studying his face, as I often do with people until I realize what I'm doing. "Is there anything you don't know?"

He chuckles. "Oh, aye. Apparently I don't know much about women."

I'm not sure I like where this is going, but I ask anyway. "Why do you think that?"

He gets up and goes to the window, and now I know I definitely shouldn't have asked. "Well, take you, for instance. You seem to like that cat better than me, and I'm the only man for miles around."

I sigh. "Come and sit down."

He comes back, but shuffles his chair back a little before he looks at me. For every part of me that could want him, a much larger part steps away. It's not that he is unattractive, not that he couldn't be a nice refuge, but I've just had enough of slotting into someone else's idea of me.

So I change the subject and watch his face drop. "When were you in the merchant navy?"

He goes for a laugh. "I'm sixty-two, if that's what you want to know." He takes a breath, as people do when they are heading into muddy water. "I had a wife, you know, before this one, before Janet. I was already in the merchant navy when we met, and it paid well, so I kept going. We had two daughters. But I was away much of the time naturally. When I came home on my last leave, she'd shacked up with someone in Liverpool, hadn't even bothered to tell me, just vanished with the wee ones. I had to find everything out from her sister." He laughs, not happily. "Here I was turning up at the door of my flat in Glasgow, expecting a welcome, and my key didn't fit in the lock. I'm about to break the door down when this fellow comes to the door, says he's the new tenant and I'd better scarper or he's going to call the police on me."

I watch him ramble on, as my mind drifts away to Fergus. "What did you do?"

"Punched him in the face."

"Did he call the police?"

Jim shrugged. "I didn't stay to find out."

I sigh. "How long until you met Janet?"

He lets out a breath, seemingly relieved to be on a happier note. "A couple of years. But it was out of the merchant navy for me. I wasn't going to risk that again.

We came up here, lived in a council house for a good many years, until I built this one here at Dunadd."

I want to ask what happened to Janet, but I still hardly know the man.

He says, "How about you?"

I say, "Oh, you know. The marriage didn't survive after Ellie died. It was just too much. Some things are."

He's not the first person I've told, but I feel my voice run off a little shaky, perhaps because I just saw Ellie again not more than half an hour ago. Men of Galvin's ilk weren't schooled in what to do with shaky women, so we both wait a second until the emotion passes.

He shifts in his seat. "What about Graeme?"

I like this note better; it takes me out of my freeze. "Graeme's after a place at St. Andrew's University. More tea?"

He hands me his cup. The little activity lasts long enough to change the tone.

"It wasn't a headache," I say.

He looks interested.

"Why I slept all those hours wasn't because of a headache."

I have to force out the next words, which never come easy, not even to Dr. Shipshap. "I have epilepsy. Complex partial seizure disorder, to be precise."

He looks at me as though I had just told him the bull in the field has only one testicle. "Is that a fact?"

I shrug. "As close as we'll get."

He looks at me sideways, as though not completely sure he should be asking. "You shouldn't be driving, then, should you?"

"Luckily, I have very distinct auras before each seizure, so I always have a warning."

"Which is why you kicked me out earlier before I'd finished my cornflakes."

"Correct."

I gather the plates and go to the sink with them. "Anyway," I say, "after a seizure I normally sleep deeply for a few hours, which is how you found me when you came uninvited into my house."

He brings me the glasses. "I was worried about you, and now I see I had good reason."

"Not good reason." I turn the tap on, hoping to drown out the conversation. "It's just a sleep like any other. Only deeper."

He picks up a tea towel and waits for the first wet plate. "Is that why you're always on about your dreams?"

The man is fast to catch on. I nod.

"I've been wondering, right enough, how you could have known about the sea coming up to Dunadd. As far as I know, no one but the nutter who lived on the estate a hundred years ago ever proposed such a thing."

I'm not saying anything, just handing him dripping

knives and forks and letting him draw his own conclusions. Maybe he could make sense of it for me.

He looks perplexed. "Anything else from these dreams of yours?"

"Well—" I stop and wonder if I should. "There's a Fergus."

"MacErc? The annals say he was the first to come over from Ireland."

I shake my head. "MacBrighde. He's the brother of the king."

"The list of Dunadd kings doesn't mention brothers. I suppose Fergus was a common enough name."

"And a witch named Sula."

He shakes his head. "You've got me there."

"She lives at the summit in what is now just that part of the round wall. It's a cell with a heather thatch and herbs hanging from wooden rafters. They think maybe I'm a Saxon or a Roman."

He's scratching his stubble. "Do they now?"

"In my dream."

"Aye."

I don't know whether Jim thinks I'm entirely insane; he isn't giving much away.

I stand up. "Anyway. All nonsense."

"Och," he says, "would there be anything left if we took away all the nonsense?"

I empty the washing-up bowl and drape the dishcloth over it. Winnie paces behind the taps, purring.

"And this Fergus bloke," Jim says, sitting back down at the table, "is he a handsome brute?"

I try to look calm and completely with it. "It's my dream. How could he not be?"

He laughs. "Could you find a good-looking grannie for me in that dream?"

To make him feel better, I place my hand on his shoulder, and before I know it his hand is on top of mine. I take mine back and go to the kitchen. It's not long before he gets up to leave.

But there's one more question. "I don't suppose there's a rock around here with rings on it?"

He shrugs. "Out at Achnabreck, aye. The cup-and-ring marks, you mean?"

I take a deep breath. If this is a dream, it's turning out to be awfully accurate.

He laughs. "Now, even I have no theories about what they are all about."

I have to bite my tongue, hold back Sula's explanation of the stars and the way the earth turns. I watch Jim as he walks home, skirting the puddles in his sensible brogues, berating myself for telling him anything. He'll no doubt be telling the postman, who comes in his own time three days a week, *Yon woman from Glasgow's as loony as you please.* You couldn't blame him for thinking it.

I keep insisting to myself that it's all just a dream, but I'm finding it harder to believe that. I certainly wish it were more. I like Dunadd in the Dark Ages. I like that Sula lives above everyone, and ministers to them with her herbs and her stones. I like that the king's brother listens to her. I like the king's brother, period. I like his lovely hand on the place the priests have so much trouble with, his fingers in the palm of my hand, his mouth resting softly against my lips. I like the way his hair curls where it meets his shoulders, and the way his nose is just slightly off-kilter. I smile when I think of the look of amusement on his face when he told me Marcus was a eunuch, and I am very glad Fergus MacBrighde is not one. I don't know that for a fact, but something in my pulse registers it. Something in the way my fingers fidget with the latch on the window tells me this is so.

II

Fergus came back up to the fort through the gates this time and climbed up to the house of Brighde, his mother, to the house where he had been a young boy with his brother and father. He found her by her fire with Murdoch, her firstborn, her ally in a way Fergus had never been. Murdoch had a wife and five children but often slept in his childhood house. Fergus was more like his father, Ainbcellaig, who had not himself been king, just the consort of his royal wife. The gold band would never sit on Fergus's head either; Murdoch was much better suited for king anyway, for the ceremonies and the honor. Murdoch had always known his station and lorded it over his brother.

For a moment, they didn't register him, but kept

talking and drinking wine from the glasses their mother loved so well, the ones the Franks had traded.

Murdoch noticed him first. "Here he is, the night rider."

Brighde beckoned him to the fire. "Come and warm yourself. Where have you been?"

Fergus accepted a glass of the blood-red liquor from his mother's hand. "I did not know your spies were out, Murdoch. Since when could a man not go where he pleases?"

Murdoch dashed the remains of his drink into the fire and stood up. "Since when did a brother of mine sneak around in the darkness like a criminal?"

Fergus pressed the heel of his hand against his temple. He always tried not to go along with Murdoch's games, but it was hard not to feel the anger in his stomach. "I only went to the ring stones. Perhaps it would do you good to go there, too, and remember what Sula taught us."

"We don't live in that age anymore," said Murdoch, "when rain patterns in stones could hold any sway."

Fergus said, "No, we live in the new age of suspicion and division."

Brighde laid her hand on Fergus's shoulder, anxious to steer the conversation clear of argument, but Murdoch had to get in one more comment.

"We know who you took there."

Fergus stood up and handed his glass back to Brighde.

She caught his hand. "Stay a little. There are things to discuss."

Fergus sat back down but turned his shoulder away from his brother.

Brighde said, "I have decided to keep you at home for a while, send some others out for the next collection."

"Or have them come here," said Murdoch. "It shouldn't be our job out risking our necks for a collection. I have heard it told in other kingdoms, how the lords come and bring with them a bag of soil from their land. They empty their bags out in the presence of the king, set their foot upon their own soil, and then swear their allegiance. We could have the stone mason carve a foot into the rock itself to mark the spot. Fergus should be at my side, not running his horse all over Dál Riada collecting fealty."

Fergus shrugged. He had no argument with this. And he was glad for the change of topic.

But Murdoch couldn't let it rest. "If you won't take a woman from outside Dunadd, I know of one for you here from the clan of Scotti."

Fergus stood and walked towards the door. "I have heard enough of your plans for me, Murdoch. Don't you understand these things can't be found in the schemes of others? Especially yours."

Murdoch caught his tongue between his teeth, a sign that Fergus knew of old was the rumbling before the storm.

Brighde laid her hand on her elder son's knee. "Murdoch."

She turned to Fergus. "The marriage is no matter."

"And besides," said Murdoch, "I already bedded the strange new woman myself and soundly until she rejoiced with joy unspeakable."

Fergus made a lunge at his brother.

Brighde pulled them apart. "Stand back from each other. Have you lost all dignity, the king and his brother fighting like boys? Murdoch, you were bedded here last night. Say so."

Murdoch would not say so.

"Besides," said Brighde, "the chief reason your brother wants you to remain at Dunadd is in case of trouble with the Picts."

Fergus let his brother go. "From the north and east?"

Murdoch rearranged his plaidie and pulled the brooch back up to his shoulder. "From the Picts of the Boar among us."

Fergus spat his words. "Is there any sign of trouble?"

Murdoch stood astride the hearth as though he were about to issue an edict. "The Christians say this new King Oengus is gathering a large band to the north, and some of our own men are leaving to join them."

"Which men?"

"Cousins of Talorcan and your former wife."

Fergus sighed. "The way you treat Talorcan, it is a surprise that he himself has not already gone."

"Talorcan has to learn his place," Brighde said. "There has been no Pictish rule at Dunadd for over two hundred years. We would like to keep it that way."

Fergus shook his head. "There will be no trouble, as long as we stay civil with the Picts. They want peace as much as we do. They have no intention of rising up and taking Murdoch's crown."

Murdoch said, "Talorcan has been seen by the lookouts stalking around the castle walls. Such behavior suggests only one intention."

Fergus laughed. "To see Illa, you fool. He comes to see the girl."

Brighde said, "It is not forbidden for him to see his niece."

"No," said Fergus, "but neither is he welcome."

"You should not bring him up here," said Murdoch.

"Why not?"

"Because you can see the mischief in his eyes."

"You see only what you seek, Murdoch," said Fergus. "If you want to find trouble, look to your Christian friends with their infernal bells, spreading trouble, passing laws over our heads about what we can and shouldn't do."

"A bell is not a sword," Murdoch said. "We need not fear their words."

Fergus held his brother with his gaze. "We have reason to fear. These Christians are filling up the lands with their ways. Only four years ago they fought a battle fifty thousand strong against the Moors in the land of the Franks. Now I hear that they chased the druids out of the land of the Sassenachs to an island and murdered them to a man. To a woman. They allow no women. See what they have done to Iona, the Isle of the Druids. There is your enemy, my brother, if an enemy is what you're after."

Fergus turned to go, but Murdoch got between him and the door. "Do not turn your back to your mother."

Fergus turned round. "I'm sorry, Mother. I promised Illa I would teach her to play one of the board games."

Brighde nodded her assent to his leaving. Fergus did not look back at Murdoch. There was love there, of course, but since childhood he had always felt put upon by his elder brother. His tale of bedding the stranger was typical Murdoch taunting, but it cut Fergus more than it should have, he realized, as he went out and found Illa. Still he was glad of the news that he didn't have to leave Dunadd anymore. It would be good for him to spend more time with his daughter. And he wanted to find out if this woman was the one Sula had seen in her stones.

As soon as the door closed behind Fergus, Murdoch turned to his mother. "I'll arrange a meeting with the woman I have chosen for Fergus. If he were married to one of his own people, his allegiances would soon change."

Brighde sighed. Since he was a boy she had found little luck in persuading Fergus onto a different path. "Who is she, this woman?"

"She is the widow of my friend Erc, who died in the battle with the Northumbrians. Her name is Colla, and she has a daughter just about the age of Illa. Erc used to say there was no woman with a faster tongue than Colla."

Brighde laughed. "Then she might suit your brother. But we must work quickly, that he doesn't become entangled with this strange woman in the meantime."

While Fergus showed Illa the board game, his thoughts kept wandering off to Ma-khee. When he had taken her to the ring stones, he felt her ease under his touch, and he had thoughts of seeing how willing she was. But the stones had always had a strange effect on him, and this time was no exception. His finger moving in the circles within circles brought a sense of his insignificance in the great workings of Cailleach the goddess. Despite what he said to Murdoch, Fergus felt that things were changing around him, and part of him didn't like change. A mood of emptiness had fallen over him, and so he had been quiet on the ride back to Dunadd. He hoped the woman had understood.

When Fergus looked up, his daughter was waiting for the answer to a question he hadn't heard her ask.

"So," he said, "the eleven blue beads must capture this single white one."

He waited to see if he had given the right answer. Illa smiled, but then she always wanted to please him.

"It's been a long time since I played," he said. "It was your mother who really liked games."

Illa said, "Especially the new one with the figures on squares carved like kings and queens."

Fergus nodded. He had traded furs for that game with the fair people from the land across the North Sea. But trading was all he ever hoped to do with those people. Something about the berserk warrior pieces in that game disturbed him, one biting the top of his shield. He would not want to meet such men in battle.

After the game, Illa went to fish at the mouth of the river with some of the village children her age. It was on just such trips as a boy that Fergus had grown accustomed to the Picts and their ways. When he got older, he found Saraid, still a girl then, but he liked the way she could gather mud balls and sling them farther than any boy. He liked the small boar tattooed on her shoulder. She quieted down as she got older, but there was still fight in her, as he discovered when they lay together beyond the field of oats. Murdoch had done the same with other Pictish girls, but when it came time for him to marry, his mother made sure it was to a Scot of some standing.

Fergus climbed to the top of Dunadd. The view had always cleared his head; the salt air and the acid smell of the marsh soothed him. He had the sense of this slipping from him, with all the talk of the new Pictish king and the way the Christians were changing the world about them. He sat down facing the sea and let the wind stroke the hair back from his face. He glanced over at Sula's hut. Fergus knew that Murdoch did not necessarily stay in his marriage bed, and that was his prerogative as king. But Fergus wanted this Ma-khee for himself, and he had no interest in a woman sanctioned by Murdoch, especially not one Murdoch had already brought to joy unspeakable.

When Illa tired of fishing, she knew she would find her father at the top of the hill. She brought a wrap from her grandmother's house and placed it about his shoulders.

"What's this?" laughed Fergus. "Do you think your father has not enough strength to bear the wind against his chest?"

Illa looked ashamed. "Grandmother sent it for you."

Fergus shook his head. "Then I have become weak in her eyes, too. Here." He twirled the woolen blanket off his shoulders and around his daughter's.

But Illa shrugged it off. "I said my prayers to Cailleach at Samhain. She will protect me."

"Yes, she will."

"Look," said Illa, pointing, "the stranger and Marcus."

Fergus glanced quickly. His heart was running ahead of him like a scared animal. But when Illa made a move to go to them, Fergus held her down so they would not be seen.

"Why do you not want her to see us?" Illa asked.

But Fergus had no answer and didn't have to give one. He waited until Illa had run off before calling his name outside Sula's door. Marcus let him in, and then went back to arranging blocks of peat on the fire. Fergus closed the door behind him and leaned back against the wood for a moment. A torch on the wall cast its light on the woman crouched by the druid's pots of healing herbs. He picked the torch off the wall and took it close to her. She looked into his face hard, studying first one eye then the other. She placed her hand over the beat of her heart so that he saw what fine white fingers she had, unused to work.

She said, "How are you?"

Fergus wanted to touch her, but he didn't know if she would be willing after he had withdrawn from her at the ring stones. Just like her, he didn't know who he was. His life for so long had been one of in betweens— neither wholly a Gael nor a Pict; royal but not king; a father and husband but with no wife, and not really wanting one until now.

He handed the torch to Marcus. "Go to the queen and bring the woman some clothes."

After the slave left, Fergus stood apart from the woman, by the wall, awkward to be alone with her. She seemed wary of him, chewing on her lip as he had never seen a woman of any standing do. She seemed nervous, like a slave who had been beaten.

He came close again and touched her hand, just to let her know that she could trust him. Her skin was soft like a child's, and he noticed again the band of gold on her finger. This woman was no slave. She smiled, and he liked that smile so much he touched her other hand. His fingers itched to move around her waist. But she seemed wary, looking away and running her hands through her hair. Instinctively, he caught her hand on its way back down. She searched his face, but he couldn't tell what she wanted of him. Did she have a family, and did she want to go back home? He didn't ask, because he feared the answer.

Still he kept hold of her hand, and after a moment, since she seemed willing, he laid each of her fingertips against his mouth.

When Sula came in and saw what he was doing, she pulled him away by the sleeve to the door.

"If she is a druid in her own place, you should leave her be. She needs her power, and you should not be stealing her off at night like your brother does the wenches in the village."

Fergus lowered his voice. "You have to tell me if she is the woman you have been saving me for?"

Fergus saw the wrinkles gather above Sula's eyes. He wasn't used to seeing her perplexed. "I don't know. She confuses me."

Marcus came back into the hut with a bundle of clothing, and handed a tunic to the Ma-khee woman. Fergus watched as she pulled it over her head and down over her breasts. She did not seem to know what to do with the leg wraps.

"Never mind," said Sula. "But she needs a brooch to hold her wrap closed."

"I will fetch one," said Fergus.

Just as Sula went to latch the door behind him, Fergus touched her arm. He had a question that must be answered. "My brother," he said quietly. "Has he visited the woman Ma-khee?"

Sula patted his arm. "You must go. The tinkling bells tell me the Christians are back again from Iona. You must speak for us, Fergus. I will take the woman with me—there is trouble with a certain family below in the village. If she is indeed a wise woman, I can use her hands. Go now, and know your brother did not come."

Fergus closed the door of the hut lightly behind him. He brought his fingers to his nose and breathed in Ma-khee's smell of flowers.

12

I keep time now by how many days since my last seizure. The operation looms like a wall in my way back to Fergus. Just dreams, I tell myself. Just an electrical storm playing havoc. I park my glasses on my nose and run my fingers down the list of women held guilty of witchcraft, half expecting to find Sula's name there:

The year 1662. Isobel Gowdie, a young housewife, *"confest guiltie of the horrid cryme of witchcraft."*

The record shows Isobel confessed her pact with the devil, that he had placed his mark on her shoulder, sucked blood from the wound, and rebaptized her with it. This trial gave rise to a whole new wave of persecutions.

I set my pen down and pick up my copy of the *Mal-*

leus Maleficarum. In its time, this witch-hunt guide was second in sales only to the Bible. "All witchcraft," it says, "comes from carnal lust, which is in women insatiable."

Carnal lust. This would be funny, I think, if you could find anything funny in a book of hate. This is woman perhaps as we can't imagine her anymore. It's not the fainting woman of courtly love, or Victorian woman with her sexless sex, not even the sex kitten of modern day. It's not me either, except for vague memories from before the medicines started to kick in. And me now, perhaps, when I think of crouching in the dark with the hand of a Dark Age prince against my spine.

Back to the book: it says that witches also have the power to steal men's penises. I know Freud would have a heyday with that one. No wonder they needed torture for confessions. It's true someone stole Marcus's, but it wasn't a witch. I smile to think that I would have made a poor witch, because I wouldn't steal Fergus's even if I could. That part of his anatomy should stay exactly where it is.

I go to the window, where the sight of the river should make me calm but is not having much luck today. It says in the book that if a woman doth protest too much, she is automatically a witch. How different things would have been if women had stayed in power and the priests had been kept in check. I can't help but wonder how women changed as an entire sex in the aftermath of such a holocaust. Wrap up that "carnal lust," my girl, tie it secure, force it down, and bury it deep. And pay no attention at all to that man in his black cassock behind the curtain and what he's doing to the little girls and boys of the parish. It shall never be spoken. Woman, cover thy shame! Honor thy father, God. Honor thy priest.

The Sabbath day dawns, and all I want to do is to go looking for the cup-and-ring stones Fergus took me to. Jim says I'll have to wait until he's done at the museum, and so, for some perverse reason, I fill my time with the enemy in a pew at the local Church of Scotland. It is Protestant, not what I'm used to: no incense, no Hail Marys. No Mary at all. I suppose at least the Catholic church got that much right: it kept the goddess. But then they made up for it double by putting men in charge. Eunuchs, or would-be eunuchs.

I sit in the last pew by the door, just to make sure everybody knows I'm just an observer looking for evidence, hoping to find some John Knox snarling at the mouth, leaning over his lectern and condemning "carnal lust." But this minister isn't Knox and looks as if he never heard of carnal anything.

The pews are hard, the backs set at the wrong angle. The wood is so old, its brown is almost black. Broken stained-glass windows have over time been replaced by ordinary glass, lending a view of trees and a hillside that perhaps the old windows were designed to obscure. The remaining stained glass allows a filtered kind of light through its gory biblical scenes. But nothing in the church is as old as the air. Once the walls were put up and the door closed, I think the first air was afraid to leave.

I look around at the congregation, a cross section of the older population of the area. Jim Galvin would look at home here. I half expect to see him, but instead I see purple-rinse perms and older farmers scrubbed out of their shite and muddy Wellies, half dozing from the early-morning rise to milk cows and muck byres. They stand to sing hymns familiar from childhood, and sit to doze during a sermon given in the speak of a litany long since dead. There's nothing here, I decide, but a remnant, nothing that could be tried and found guilty anymore.

The sermon is about redemption. It is about getting our dues on the other side, but the minister appeals to no "woe betides." In this church, sin is about letting the side down. It's the private shame we feel for not doing the good we ought. No burning witches here. No burning souls at all. Just guilt. In that the Protestant and Catholic faiths did not diverge.

When we stand to sing the hymns, I do not sing. I don't think anyone notices. *Amazing grace, how sweet the sound, / That saved a wretch like me. / I once was lost but now am found, / Was blind, but now I see.* The red hymnbook, bound in mock leather, has a musty smell that adds to the dim light and dank air and makes for somnolence. After the benediction, the church turns me out on the other side, sapped of fire.

I drive from the church to pick up Jim, and find him in the map room talking to a group of Americans about sacred springs.

"The way the pagans saw it," he says, "the earth supported the people instead of the other way around, and a spring was where the spirit of the earth ran out."

He shows them the light-up map of standing stones in the area. It looks like a flat green room full of Christmas lights. "These all follow the path of lay lines, another place where the spirit of the earth was supposed to leak."

Jim lets the switch go, and the map falls back into greys and dark greens. The Americans move on. We go out through the door into the museum shop, where you can buy silver replicas of the finely wrought jewelry from Dunadd, the brooches that once held shawls about the shoulders of a rough-hewn people.

All along the Kilmartin Valley road to Achnabreck, we pass stone circles.

Jim says, "They used to call this Gleann nan Clachan, you know, the Valley of Stones."

I shake my head. I didn't know. "How far do the circles date back?"

Jim points to our right. "Temple Wood there goes back about five thousand years, twice as long as the pyramids of Egypt."

"Then all of this," I say, "was already ancient in the time of Fergus MacBrighde."

Jim nods. "Compared to these stones, Fergus Mac-Brighde happened only yesterday."

Not yesterday enough, I think.

The cup-and-ring marks at Achnabreck have, like Dunadd itself, been taken over by the Scottish National Trust, and there are fences all around the slabs of rocks where I crouched only recently with the prince of Dunadd.

Jim shakes his head as I climb over and squat with my fingers in the circle grooves.

"They put the fences up for a reason," he says.

But I can tell he doesn't mean it. Without Fergus stroking away all sense, I can focus better on the markings now. The slab almost looks like what happens to a pond in the rain.

"I don't suppose rain was sacred to the pagans," I say.

Jim shrugs. "What do you think? This magical stuff that falls from the sky and makes your crops grow."

I climb back over the fence. "Everything's so mystical, isn't it, until you know the science of it."

"Och," says Jim, "science, my arse. Everyone assumes these people were just ape-men making random marks in the stone. They were just like us, worried about the same things, asking the same bloody questions."

I want to go now. This place is bringing Fergus too close without getting me any nearer to him.

Later, I head up to the fort with Winnie in tow. I

wave to Jim in his window as I pass his house and squeak through the stile gate.

The top of the hill is just what I need, windy enough to take your head off. I wish someone would pry open my head, make enough room to squeeze out all the facts and nonsense I've been filling it up with. They should hold church services on hilltops and see how much is left when they are finished.

I sit among the rubble, while the wind rearranges my hair and nips at my face, while the declining sun on Crinan Bay sits back and licks the quicksilver sea. Looking out past the white hotel at Crinan, past the castle out at Duntrune, I could be back in Fergus's time. The islands are secrets, dark and mounding out of the water, but forever keeping themselves from you.

I smile, for the relief of finding a Sunday up here— Day of the Sun, after all.

I don't feel like going back to the pages. I don't like that my thesis has turned into a feminist manifesto, though I don't know now what else I thought it could be. I'm not in the business of being a feminist, at least not a ball-busting one. A sheep bleats from the field below, setting off a chorus of sheepy panic.

On my way back down, I pass a group of German tourists coming to set the inevitable foot in the stone imprint. Future king of England Prince Charles of the Battenbergs once did this, so it says on the board down below. It is a wonder the entire hill didn't cleave in twain and erupt with lava flow. Whatever this hill is, it belongs to the history of Scotland, no matter that its present-day inhabitants are a mix of Scots and Picts; in Fergus's day, those Viking ravagers hadn't yet done their dance of rage and brought their fair hair with them.

Before bed, I stand at my sink and roll my pills around in my palm, studying them as though they held an answer. I set them on the counter when the phone rings.

"Mum, it's Graeme."

"Who?" I tease him, because I think it's odd that he thinks I wouldn't know which son of mine it is, given that I have only one. Only one child, when it comes down to it.

He laughs just loud enough for me to pick it up across the miles of country between us.

He says he should be in bed. I wait for an explanation as to why he is not.

"I've been thinking," he says, "that I might take the bus up to see you one weekend, if I could get away early on a Friday."

I can see that little-boy smile spread over his face, even as he holds the phone against his man's cheek. "I won't mind, if you don't mind."

"I don't mind," he says.

I say, "I would like to show you Dunadd. It's very ancient, very interesting, everything that went on here."

"What did go on there?"

My mind flies to Dunadd in Fergus's time: the village of thatched roofs, the smoke, the tattoos, heather ale, and the way the necklace of acorns lies just inside the neck of Fergus's shirt.

I say, "Oh, battles, takeovers, trade and slaves, kings of antiquity, all the usual stuff."

He laughs. Even the sound of his laughter makes me feel better, as if I have a place here in the present.

He says he has to go to bed. I concur.

He smiles. You can't hear a smile, but it has a resonance.

After he hangs up, I go back to the sink, pick up my pills, and toss them onto my tongue. A gulp of water and they are gone. Better to stay on an even keel. That's what I've always tried for, what everyone around me has always been hoping for.

13

Even without missing any medication, I succumb to a seizure a few days later, on the blue couch with the curled cat once again doing drum duty by my head. Now, if I were being objective about these dreams, I would be forced to ask why it is I go back into them at the place I last left off, like lifting a bookmark out of the pages of a book.

In the semi-darkness of the hut, I crouch by Sula's fire, remembering now that I forgot to ask Jim for that list of Dál Riada kings. I know the Romans left in 410, and so I could work out the time of King Murdoch from then. I wonder how the years were kept before the birth of Christ. Perhaps they didn't worry about years, and perhaps it doesn't matter anyway what time I'm in.

I am in Once Upon a Time, not of the fairy kind but of the druid, and perhaps here I might even discover who I really am, underneath it all, a woman filled with "insatiable lust." Marcus looks over as I laugh. Because the way your mother told it, the way the nuns at school leered down their noses, this was the prerogative of the male population, something you were taught to guard yourself against.

I glance at the door, wishing for Fergus. But Sula has other designs for this day. She covers my outfit with a brown woolen wrap in herringbone weave that hangs heavy and would go twice around me. She pushes my hair back and covers my head with a triangle of cloth that she crosses over my throat and ties at the back of my neck like in pictures of Mrs. Gillies when she lived on St. Kilda. When Sula thinks I'm ready, she gathers a leather pouch and leads Marcus and me down the hill. We can hear the clink of bells as we descend past the buildings on the lower level, and a noticeable change comes over Sula as she ushers me quickly by. The men at the gates bow to her, then let us through.

The village below takes me by surprise again, just because it is so sprawling and jostling. Each of the round, mud-colored houses has a thatched roof and its own square of yard bound in by wattle fence, along a maze of narrow lanes. Above it all between the highest roof and the cold sky sidles a layer of smoke.

Sula nudges me on, but there is no stile down at the

base of the fort, no Jim Galvin's whitewashed house, no bridge made of stone, just a swing bridge of wooden slats held to either bank by rough rope. To my left, standing by itself, as though on sacred ground before the river, is the standing stone that in my day will hold a clothesline, only now it is but one of a complete circle.

I can't help but clap my hands and run to find the one I know. Marcus darts nervously after me while Sula stands by, watching. And I can't keep my thoughts in, so all they must hear is a nonsense stream of words that will one day be modern English. I am so happy that my one stone is now among friends that I have to run my hands over them. From across the river come the happy sounds of goats bleating, the cries of children running and playing.

We rejoin Sula and move off to the swing bridge, which sways as we cross. The fibers of the rope cut into my palm as I steady myself. I stop on the other side, as barefoot children run by us, some leading goats. Groups of men sit in the doorway to their yards; women pass, weighed down by burdens of peat and kindling. The ever-present smoke stings my eyes, but I can hardly bring myself to blink. I notice the clothing of the people down here is much less colorful than that worn by the inhabitants of the hill, just a few drab rusts and greens; nothing fitted, heads and shoulders covered over by yards of woven shawl.

Sula is watching me as I turn back to get a sense of

the fort from down here: its high stone walls wrap around the hill, its smoke lifted by the breeze, so different from what it will be when it becomes part of the Scottish tourist trade. She takes my arm and leads me along the tight worn lanes of the village. The people stop what they are doing, touch me, and ask Sula who I am. Sometimes she answers; sometimes she doesn't. All I can do is follow in our little troupe, with Marcus at the rear.

The hut we are going to is at the far end of the village, close to what will one day become the Oban road, Motorway A83. This is no road there now, just the flat of the valley rising up into the familiar rise of camel-hump hills.

Our eyes have to adjust to the interior of the house we enter, a round room with someone on a mat on the far side. It smells a bit rank in here. A child of about four or five sits on the dirt floor by the fire, wrapped in a bundle of blankets. Its smudged face is bound by long and curly hair. Whatever sex it is I can't tell. A man I assume is the father follows us in and bows to Sula. When I go with them to the bed, I see our patient is a woman in labor. I look back at Marcus to see if he has left by his own discretion, but he is as interested as I am, and no one seems to bother about a eunuch being there.

The labor is different from the image of labor I grew up with. The woman does not appear to be in distress. No frantic breathing, just eyes focused on the floor in front of her. I don't even know if she's aware we're here.

The man is speaking to Sula, but not in Gaelic, so I don't understand. He is shaking his head, seeming to indicate the cross of the sun over the sky, perhaps saying his wife has been in labor too long. Sula strokes the woman's forehead, and then lays her hand down at the base of her belly, where a couple of intertwined snakes are tattooed just above her pubic hair.

Sula turns back and indicates that I should hand her the leather bag she has brought. She pulls out a small pouch of dried leaves and asks for a cup, into which goes a handful of dusty green leaves and a splash of water from a pitcher. She stirs them, and then lifts the woman's head for a drink.

But I am not going to be let off that easily. Sula takes my hand and places it on the woman's protruding stomach right over the tattoo. Because I have felt this on myself, I know that such a full belly should feel solid at the bottom and less packed at the top. This woman's feels the opposite.

"Breech," I say, but they think I mean Brighde, mother of Fergus. They shake their heads and look at one another.

Now I see that Sula has designs for this breech baby. In my day doctors deliver these by Cesarean section, and it's funny to think that this operation exists even now, if this was the way Caesar was born. Still, the odds wouldn't be good for the mother, and Sula obviously has other plans.

The woman's body seems less tense now, and I wonder if it is because of the leafy brew. Sula wants my hands in this operation, and she guides me the way I should push, around to the outside on one side, while she tries to manipulate the baby going down from the top the other way. I keep my eyes on the woman's face, because I am very uneasy about pushing so hard. Sula catches my hands, presses them to my chest, and then puts them back on the woman's stomach. Perhaps she is telling me to feel my way by instinct, and I try, but women of my era were not trained this way. In the nunnery, instinct was the enemy. Inside myself, I will the baby to move. I picture my hands as instruments of healing instead of just paddles.

I look up at Sula. Her eyes are closed. She removes her hands and blows into them, then starts back in the circular motion, almost not touching, as though she could insinuate the movement by hovering slightly above the skin. My hands are still touching. But the baby is beginning to give. I have to see Sula's movement and mine as one. Where I leave off and start back to the bottom, she takes over and smooths her hands over the top of the mound.

Every so often the baby gives a kick, for which I am grateful—at least I know it is still alive. Once we get it to center point, the baby does the rest itself. Soon we have a solid mass at the bottom. Sula quickly grabs a band from her bag and ties it around the woman just above where the baby's bottom must now be.

She takes herbs from a different pouch and gives them to the woman in another drink, then sits back and waits. I do the same. The man seems happier now. Just like a contented modern man, he whistles as he sets a pot on a tripod over the fire. The child moves in closer to throw on sticks. I walk over to see the stew, I suppose it is, with lumps of meat and other objects, some of which I can identify, like turnip, but others I'm not sure about. No carrots, I notice, no potatoes. Strange to think how food made its way across Europe in drips and drabbles. Potatoes, that British staple, wouldn't make it here from the Andes for hundreds of years.

Sula has the woman up and walking about, then squatting with her elbows on a stool. Sula gestures me over. It is my job, she shows me, to smooth my hand down the base of the woman's spine, while Sula eats from a bowl by the fire. She and Marcus and the husband are talking about me; that's a feeling you just know, whether you speak the language or not.

The woman is pushing softly, and then I'm not quick enough to catch the baby that falls hard onto the dirt floor. The woman picks her baby up, puts it to her breast, and remains in a squat until the placenta slips out. A dog should come in and eat the afterbirth at this point, but there actually seem to be very few dogs down here. Instead, the child scoops it up and adds it to the stew.

I want to make all the modern noises of objection,

but I sit back on my haunches and keep my peace. I just won't be having any of the stew myself. The baby is a boy, though no one seems to be paying any attention to that. There is a joke about the size of his testicles, and that must be one of those things, like the shape of the hill on the other side of the road, that time does not change.

The wife lies down in the bed with the baby at her breast. Her older child lies beside them. I worry that the baby has not cried yet, though he is making some powerful sucking noises. Maybe if you're not being born into original sin, birth is nothing to cry about.

Suddenly through the door a man enters. He is tall with reddish brown hair, and I recognize him as the man with the tattoo of the boar who followed me around the fort on the first night. As he steps closer, I see the tattoo stretches right across his forehead and down on either side of his temples. The tail and the snout run off a little into his hairline. His eyes glance over me, but the person he is looking for is Sula. Like everyone else, he approaches her with respect, though he is unable to hide his eagerness for her to step aside and speak to him. Sula is reticent to leave. She checks back with the woman and her baby, and then brings the man over to me.

She pats his shoulder. "Talorcan," she says. I can't keep my eyes off his tattoo. He bows slightly in my direction, keeps his eyes on mine as he begins to talk. I don't pick up everything he says, but I do hear the name Fergus and next to it the mention of a wife, and I do register the drop of lead into the pit of my belly. He keeps talking, but I'm not hearing anything else. After a while, his nod to Sula seems to indicate he has more urgent business.

He talks to Sula by the door with fewer smiles than he had for me, and eventually, she leaves with him. I stand by the door and watch them walk through the gate of the yard, and then I can see only heads and shoulders moving along the top of the wattle fence along the path that leads away to the farthest houses. Their conversation is quick, secret. She seems to be so much the center of things down here: midwife, teacher, counsel. I wonder if that is why the church objected to the witches: it didn't want little old women at the center of things. I remember now from the list in the Edinburgh library how many of my witches were midwives.

I feel selfish to be preoccupied by the news of Fergus's wife, when life has just taken place and I have had a role in it. From the way he acted towards me, I couldn't have gathered that there was a wife. But this is not my age, and why wouldn't I think other principles hold? Fergus might have ten wives. But I am gloomy now, abandoned by Sula, shuffling around the strangers' house, taking in the vat of *fraoch*, the rudimentary loom set against the wall by the door. I know nothing about weaving, but I can admire the quality of the tweed that is being woven. The yarn of the warp hangs down the back of the loom, weighted with round stones into which holes have been bored.

There are no trees in this village, just yards backed onto other yards, peaks of heather-thatched roofs. The yards are of hard-packed dirt, kept clear by the twig broom that leans against the wall of the house by the door. Racks of drying peat are set up against the lower part of the fence, and there is a small stone hut with a wooden door to the side of the house. I notice similar stone structures in all the yards, though they are too small to be dwellings. My curiosity leads me to push the door a little with the toe of my shoe, but it's too dark in there to see. It doesn't smell so fresh, so I pull the door closed.

The orange glow of sun in the far distance is disappearing behind the islands, just as it does in my day. The air is very still, interrupted only now and then by bird cry. The child follows me back into the house, where mother and baby are asleep. I play a game with the child of pick-up sticks made with small pieces of kindling. The child is quiet like its baby brother, unspeaking but contented on the floor by the fire.

I sit cross-legged by the fire and ease the child onto my lap, nuzzling my nose into its unwashed hair. I'm not sure the last time I smelled a small child this close, but I have a powerful compulsion to kiss that head. I wonder when Sula is coming back for me, and I wonder what Fergus wants from me if he already has a wife.

When the child wanders off, I go over to the woman

and place my hand on her forehead to make sure there's no fever. She is asleep and doesn't see me watching her. She is like me, with two children. I hope she can stay that way. I hope that fate won't wrench one of them from her when she is away one evening. The woman opens her eyes and smiles. Her baby's head is black, not a patch of red gossamer as Ellie's was when they handed her to me in the hospital. She closes her eyes again but resists when I try to take the baby. I know how she feels. Keep holding on to him, I want to say, and perhaps you'll never have to let go.

Marcus seems to think it's time to leave when the sky turns black, not as much light, now that the moon is on its wane. We weave through the houses where the doors are shut against the cold, and over the river on the bridge whose give seems a little more alarming in the dark. My foot keels a little, torqueing my ankle, but I don't have time to register the pain before I notice Talorcan waiting on the other side.

Marcus hangs back and lets Talorcan take me by the arm up towards the gates. He talks quickly as though he thinks I can understand everything, when all I want to ask him is about Fergus's wife. He is telling me something about the Picts, how they used to rule Dunadd, how his ancestors were on this land long before the Gaels. I'm not sure of this man, what his hand in the small of my back means. It is with some relief the guards bar him from entering the fort and Marcus is put back in the role of lead. I hear the slam of the gates closing as I follow Marcus up to the flat esplanade where the houses sit. I wonder about this Talorcan, what he wants from me.

Before we have gone much farther, Marcus reaches back and slows me down; in front of us, a figure is taking shape out of the dark.

Marcus's voice is quiet as he says, "King Murdoch."

I already feel apprehensive before we get up to the king, so I hang back a little. He is shorter and stockier than his brother. His hair is curlier and somehow there is less intelligence in his gait.

He doesn't speak to me, barely looks in my direction. His orders are directed at the slave. Marcus bows and leads me to a house from which I can hear the music of a harp. There is light and warm air seeping out from under the door. I hope Fergus isn't in there because I don't know how to be with him now. After Murdoch has left, Marcus announces us. *Marcus Paullus agus Makhee.* When the door opens, he leads me inside. Unlike the house we have just come from, this one is rectangular, with a fire and a rude clay chimney at the far end. Superior torches in silver clasps on the upright beams illuminate the tapestries that cover the stone walls and the carpets strewn over wooden floors. The underside of the turf roof is lined with wooden slats, and the furniture is fine, the chairs and table carved with animals in Celtic design. A man seated on a stool by the door with a lap-size harp is singing in a falsetto, a little raucous to the ear.

Fergus rises as I approach the fire, and my heart stops. He wants to meet my gaze, but my gaze wants to be anywhere else. There are other people in the room, but I am not looking at them either. Marcus pushes me gently in the direction of an older woman seated between two monks. I suppose they're monks because of their coarse brown cassocks, which apparently aren't going to change over the next millennium. One of them holds in his hand a pole with an ornate copper bell at the end tied by a leather thong. Welded onto the face of the bell is a crucifix. The woman gets up with regal bearing and circles me in a way that would be rude in my day, but I'm not caring. I have Fergus in my peripheral vision; he has turned away from me.

Marcus tells the woman my name is Maggie. The woman's heavily embroidered robe swishes over my feet as she stops in front of me. There's a look of Fergus about her, in the eyes, in the shape of the brow.

I imagine this is the queen mother, with her gold and garnet brooch and the ornate chain about her neck. Her bony wrists and fingers are bedecked with other finely crafted gold pieces. Her braided hair is wrapped around a band of gold and sits off her shoulders.

At any rate, she seems unimpressed by me and goes back to her chair. I see Fergus motion Marcus forward, and the slave shows the queen all the aspects of my clothing that were of interest to him and Sula earlier, including the bra. I'm particularly interested to see what the monks make of that. I catch Fergus smiling to himself when they make a show of looking off to the wall. I wish I could smile back at him, but I have already taken too much for granted.

Marcus shows the queen my fingernails, which I suppose betray a life of ease. But the monks want her attention, and have more luck, redirecting her towards a leather-bound book.

All of a sudden, the door opens, and Murdoch comes in leading a handsome woman he introduces as Colla. The harpist ceases his song. The woman's long hair is very dark and ringed with a coronet braid. She is not young, but younger than me. Fergus seems annoyed when Murdoch sets the woman next to him. Perhaps this is the wife Talorcan mentioned. She certainly seems to have her eye on him, certainly shuffles her bum as close to his as possible. I begin to think Talorcan might be my best ally—he knows what these royals are up to.

Fergus indicates to Marcus that I should be led out. Before I turn, he shoots me a look that concedes he is not happy. I tell my face not to show what I am feeling. I think I have already let down too much of my guard to Prince Fergus. He can have his dark-eyed woman. I don't know why I thought Dark Age men would have higher standards, but I have to admit he put on a good show.

After the well-lit room, the outside is very dark, so much so that I almost fall over Fergus's daughter. Like any child, she has been hovering about the doorway listening to adults through the cracks. I can't see her well, but just finding her makes me fight for breath. I wait a moment for my eyes to adjust, to make out the features of this girl who looks so much like my Ellie. Her hair is longer, of course, the front strands twisted and pulled back to a piece of twine at the nape of her neck. She must think my staring at her has to do with her misbehaving.

"Hello," I say quietly.

I place my hand on her head and say her name. Illa, not Ellie, but still the word strangles in my throat. She turns her head slightly towards me and then back to the crack in the door she is peering through. I take a step and touch her back. When she looks, I smile. She doesn't flinch this time but looks back with a smile I have seen a million times before. But Marcus is tugging me upward towards Sula's hut. I wave to the girl and hope this is a universal signal. She nods, not understanding, I think. I nod, too, anything to bridge the gap between her in her time and space and the thing that is me, here and now, confused. Marcus is confused, too, not understanding the tears, as we walk around the final fortress of wall and up onto the hill.

Sula asks me what's wrong when we walk into the musky air of her hut. Her eyes are wandering all over me, but it is my heart that is in pain, and I'm not sure she has anything for that in her pots. She kneels by my twisted ankle and bids me sit. She holds her hands skyward, then rubs them together so quickly I expect to see sparks. But they feel warm and afford some relief when she wraps them around my ankle, pressing in at certain points on my foot. It feels good to be back in the care of Sula, like it used to feel sitting on the lap of Mrs. Gillies when I was a child.

I begin to wonder if Colla was any more persuasive with Fergus once I left. I wonder if he is now touching the tips of her fingers to his lips. Still, I am quite hungry, having declined that stew earlier. Sula seems to know and sends Marcus off for food. When he is gone, she starts telling me about the monks. She does a very good impersonation, walking tight with hands folded, ringing her imaginary bell with a sour look. She throws her arms up in a dismissive gesture. But Marcus is back with food, finer than I have seen yet; perhaps the monks are being treated to dinner. What seems to be a kind of custard fills one bowl, and it tastes very good, a sort of sweet scrambled eggs, with a flat cake sweetened with honey. He brings whisky in a small earthen jug, which I don't normally like, but I sip it and it sears my insides enough for me not to notice the cold so much, not to pay as much attention to the thought of Fergus.

Once the meal is over, Sula wraps herself in her

cloak and lies down by the fire. Now I am glad for the extra material in mine. It doesn't make the floor any softer, but it provides a couple of layers of heat. The room is hazy from the smoke and dim, lit only by a stone lamp. I bunch up one end of my cloak for a pillow and let my eyes close. Sleep comes, but dreams do not.

Some time later, I am awakened by the plague of many a tenant in Glasgow on a Saturday night—drunken singing outside the door. They're not singing they belong to Glasgow, for I'm not even sure if Glasgow properly exists yet, but whatever it is they are singing about, it seems to be funny to them. The racket doesn't appear to awaken Sula or Marcus. But I creep to the door and, still wrapped like a mummy, peek out. The stars are bright against the waning moon, and I can just make out two figures lolling upon each other, one of which I realize quickly is Fergus. I close the door again.

But Fergus has seen me. In a moment, he is banging on the door. *"Ma-khee, mo chridhe."*

Mo chridhe. Mrs. Gillies used to call me that when she was in a good mood. It means "my heart." And my heart has picked up on it, because it is beating faster than it should.

He bangs on the door again. "Ma-khee."

But Maggie takes her shawl and lies back down by the fire. Prince Fergus should go back to his wife. He isn't in any state to know what he is saying. And he should stay away from me with his lack of eunuch-ness and his *mo chridhe*. I don't want to think about this now. I want only sleep. And will get things straightened out in the morning, if the morning in this Dunadd ever dawns.

14

Fergus woke up shivering by the midden on the far side of the fort. He emptied his stomach onto the grass, and then stood up, wiping his mouth with the back of his sleeve. He hadn't often had whisky, but the monks from Iona had brought bottles from their distillery, and he had decided to drink himself to the point that he could no longer hear their speeches and the tinkle of their bells.

Brighde had served them custard and cake as though they were royalty, not eunuchs from an island where sacred women once lived. The thought of women brought back the image of himself banging at Sula's door. He bent over double, fearing there might be more to lose, but only retched, and then groaned for having played the fool in front of the woman Ma-khee.

Fergus heard a voice off to his left and found the king, his brother, low down among the bracken, rubbing his face.

Fergus offered his hand. "The monks will be the death of us," he said.

Murdoch stood up, shivering. "At least we will die happy."

Fergus laughed, nudged his brother. Murdoch laughed, too, making himself stagger and almost fall. They were boys again, hiding from their mother, free for just a few more moments.

"Colla is a good woman," said Murdoch. "What did I tell you?"

Fergus shook his head. "Not for me, my friend."

Murdoch wagged his finger at his brother. "That is not what I saw last night."

Fergus rubbed his eyes. Things might be worse than he feared. "What did you see?"

In truth, Fergus couldn't remember much of the evening of drinking. He had a vague recollection of holding the woman on his knee, but he also recalled it was more of a taunting for the monks than for the woman.

"I saw a good match," said Murdoch. "I saw my little brother with a wife of his own kind. I saw a woman who would give him counsel and love him well, whose daughter would be a friend to Illa."

Fergus began to walk away, past the druid's hut and down towards their childhood house.

"I hope you will not reject Colla," Murdoch called. "I have already told her of your interest."

Fergus turned back. "Then you told her wrong."

They found their mother and the two monks just as they had left them, their heads inclined over a book. The language of Erin had never been written in books. The druids counseled that the life in the language would dwindle if it were reduced to scrawls on a page. Everything there was to tell could be passed on by voices. It took many years for the druids to learn the history by rote. Sula knew much of the tradition, too: she was the one who knew the exact number of summers from this to that, from when MacErc and his brothers left Erin, the summers measured back to Finn M'Coul and all the heroes from the other country. But Sula's main use to the people of Dunadd was in her predictions, her charms, and her healing ways. There were other druids living within the fort who kept the history better, who knew the patterns of the stars and their meaning; a few boys who were learning the trade.

Brighde looked up. "I am glad you came back. There is more to what the Christians have to say than comes out of a bottle."

Fergus laughed. "The spirits of the bottle speak the most clearly."

Murdoch sat down on a stone by the fire. "What is in the book?"

Brighde said, "It is a story of a savior, not here but far to the east where winter never comes."

"To be saved from winter," said Murdoch, glancing at his brother, "would please the people well."

The monk with white hair spoke. "From a winter of the soul, brother."

Brighde said, "This savior performed wonders of divination and brought men back from the dead."

Fergus drew closer. Could this savior from the east bring his own father back? Could Saraid come back even now? He asked, "Where is this savior?"

The young monk barely had a beard yet. "The Romans killed him."

Murdoch shook his head. "The Roman armies killed many with their chariots and armor."

"But if he is on the other side himself," said Fergus, "how can he bring back the dead?"

"He sits at the right hand of God," said the older monk.

"Which god?" asked Murdoch. "The horned god?"

"No," said the monk, laughing, "the horned god is no god. There is only one God. It says so in this scripture."

Fergus was confused. The mightiest power was Cailleach, the triune goddess, who kept them through the dark days, who nourished the earth with sun and rain in the spring, and who put seeds in the belly of woman.

"He is the god of Moses and Abraham. His name is Yahweh," said the young monk.

"A man?" Fergus laughed. "How could the only god be a man? How could a man give birth to the world by himself?"

"A father," said Brighde. "A spirit father."

Fergus was in need of a father. Still, he didn't like the monks and their strange ways.

He took a step towards them. "Why is woman now banished from Iona?"

The younger of the two monks looked embarrassed.

The older one spoke. "Columcille, who brought the gospel of Jesus Christ to this land, decreed it."

Murdoch said, "Columcille? Didn't he come from the land of my ancestors across the channel in Erin? He took no such habits from Erin. He must have taken this from Rome."

"Woman," said the older monk, bowing slightly to the royal woman in his company, "it says in the book it was woman's fault that suffering came into the world. She listened to a snake and defied God; she tried to have more knowledge than she should have."

"How can a woman have too much knowledge?" Fergus asked. "What good would a woman be without knowledge?"

The old man spoke. "Woman tempts man from his

spiritual path. This is why we have neither women nor any female beast on Iona."

Fergus began to pace. "This is madness." He stopped and raised his arms to his mother. "How can you listen to this—you, the chief woman of this band of Scotti?"

Brighde coughed to interrupt and directed herself towards the monks. "It is true that the island of Iona bears the bones of the royal line from Fergus MacErc on. My mother and her mother are buried there. If you will admit no women, then how should I be buried with my line? I would want nothing less."

The monk seemed to feel he was losing ground. "As a royal woman, of course, you would be admitted to the island and permitted to lie with your ancestors."

"As a royal dead woman." Fergus turned to the young monk. "What kind of a man shuns the female kind? You are yet young; do you not wake in the morning with the need for a woman?"

The young monk tried to form words, but no voice came with them. The older monk stepped in. "There is no carnal lust where there is love of Christ our Savior."

Brighde coughed quietly. "The Christians have brought other news. The Picts in the north have been moving south. They say their new king Oengus is a ruthless man."

Murdoch furrowed his brow. "So I tell my brother, who would sooner marry a Pict than fight one."

Fergus felt his arm move to strike.

Brighde stepped in. "The Christians say we must reject the gods and the ways of the Picts, allow them no purchase, or we will be overrun once the forces from the north join with their brothers here under the sign of the boar."

Fergus's breath was coming fast. "If we make enemies of our Pictish brothers and sisters now, we will drive them to ally with their cousins in the north. There has never been conflict between us. Their gods and customs have served us well enough. We understand each other."

Brighde glanced at Murdoch. "Take the Christians," she said. "I will talk to Fergus alone for a while."

"Come," said Murdoch, helping them from their seats. "Our Saxon metalworker makes all manner of gold ornaments. Perhaps there might be something for your cape."

The monks followed Murdoch out, leaving their book in the hands of Brighde.

"Pay no heed to that," said Fergus. "So many words on a page telling us how we must live. They care only for selling their wares, nothing more."

"Still," said his mother, "there is much in here to be admired. Peace instead of war, love instead of hate."

"If they love so much," said Fergus, "then why do they hate women? Do you think your kind brought suffering into the world?"

Brighde shook her head and laid down the book.

"Still, we would do well to learn this writing from the Christians."

"No," said Fergus, "you know my father believed the druids on this matter. The Romans wrote everything on this paper, and look, where are the Romans now? The words of the heart beat louder than this."

"But Fergus, if we could have it written down that we, the Scotti, own Dunadd, then perhaps there would be no need for battle."

Fergus shook his head. "Even if we believe what the written word says, the Picts would trample such words into the dirt."

He sat down on the rectangular stone by the fire. "I have heard of these Christians and their written word among the Britons. They take the power from the *ban-druidhe*. They do not allow the lines anymore to come down through the women, but only through the men. They spit on the spirits that have sustained our race through winters and wars. It can come to no good end, these eunuchs with their hatreds. It is no wonder they make whisky to dull their pain."

Brighde rolled her eyes. "Last night, my son, you were happy to dull your own pain with the Christians' drink."

She walked to him and laid one arm around his shoulders. "I know it is difficult for you to see the Picts with anything but the kindness you showed your wife. But you have failed to come back to life. Saraid is dead, my son. The ways of the past are changing. The Picts of the north have become hostile, and unless we see the threat, we are in danger ourselves."

"But what of Illa?" asked Fergus. "Look at my daughter. She is a Pict."

"Which is why I have tried to keep her from Talorcan."

"You cannot turn back what is already so, Mother. Talorcan is my brother. He would not turn against me. Talorcan's mother was also of a royal line. The people listen to him."

Brighde went back to the fire. "I hope you are right."

"I know I am right." Fergus had heard enough. He went to leave but stopped in the doorway, his back to his mother. "Will you invite Sula and the stranger to your fire? The woman is not a commoner—she wears gold upon her finger, and her manner is fine."

"Sula is always welcome at my hearth. But the stranger, what is she, another *ban-druidhe*? We already have our own."

Fergus turned back to Brighde. "For my sake, will you invite them both this evening?"

Brighde sighed. "My son, was it not enough that you took a Pict for your bride, gave me a Pict for a granddaughter? Now you want to take a druidess who speaks no language anyone knows?"

Fergus smiled. "I will tell their slave to bring them."

"Go," said Brighde. "Would that you were a eunuch

like the monks with their hands folded. Would that I sent you to Iona, that you do not embarrass me with any more ill matches."

Fergus closed the door behind him, laughing. As with his brother, the moments of love he felt with his mother were few.

Fergus caught Marcus on his way to the bakehouse. "What does the woman Ma-khee say? Did she see me last night with my brother?"

Marcus shrugged. "She was at the door."

Fergus cursed.

"She is not a common woman," Marcus said.

A look of pain came over Fergus. "I know."

"She covers her lips when she belches."

Fergus became impatient. "Yes, I know this, Marcus."

"She has fine manners," he said. "And yet she helped Sula with a difficult birth today. When she saw your daughter, she called to her as though she knew her. If she is a druidess, then perhaps a powerful one."

Fergus sighed. A druid this powerful would not be released to him as a wife, even if she did still have respect for him.

He said, "Tell Sula to bring the woman to eat with my mother tonight."

"I think she does not like our food," Marcus said. "That's what I see."

Fergus touched the slave's sleeve. "What would you eat in Rome?"

Fergus saw how the slave smiled, how glad he was to remember. Perhaps even he didn't like the food of the Scotti. Perhaps the food of the Scotti was not tasty.

Marcus said, "Olives." He narrowed his eyes. "Fruit such as you have never tasted: grapes, melons, plums. Yogurt and sauces; white bread made with wheat from Alexandria and dipped in olive oil."

"Marcus, this does not help. White bread? Olive oil? What is that? And there are no fruits here except apple and pear."

"Apple and pear, then, in slices, mixed with honey and served with roasted hazelnuts and cream from the top of the milk."

"But what about meat? No one can live on fruit and cream."

Marcus slipped back into his dream. "Mutton, ham, bacon. Peacock. And sauces." His tongue sidled slowly along the inside of his lip. "Yes, sauces."

"I have tasted this ham," said Fergus, "but I doubt the kitchens have such a thing, unless there is some salted boar left from the hunt this summer. I will speak to the cooks."

Marcus followed Fergus to the bakehouses.

"What of drink?" Fergus asked.

"Wine," Marcus said. "Wine mixed with honey and spices."

But the look on Marcus's face told Fergus he was not thinking anymore of food. "What is the matter?"

"The woman, Ma-khee. I think she has a child. I think she has been taken from it."

Fergus grabbed the slave's shoulder. "Did she say as much?"

Marcus shook his head. "Her tears tell me as much."

Fergus walked over to the kitchens, wondering what this could mean. He needed a mother for Illa. Still, perhaps not a child but a husband was the cause of Ma-khee's tears. He gave his dinner order in the warm-smelling air of the kitchen, but the cooks had only goat's meat from the slaughter on Samhain. They did not know about Marcus's sauces, but they could prepare the pears and apples as he requested. Their stock of honey was full after a good summer's harvest.

Fergus turned back to his mother's house. He knew his mother had kept the robes his father, Ainbcellaig, had worn, but he wondered if he might borrow them for this evening without rousing too much suspicion. He could borrow from his brother, Murdoch, for he had more clothes than anyone needed, but any such request would only inspire taunting.

This woman was older than Fergus, he knew, but not too old for childbearing. He liked her look, not so much the contours of her face or the shape of her nose or mouth, but that look in her eyes was his own look, the hope that sorrow would not in the end win over. A little more time, and Illa would walk into her own woman years; it was time for her to have a mother again. With her knowledge of herbs and healing, Ma-khee would make a good one.

Ma-khee. Strange name. Not like Saraid, whose name came from the history of the land. His wife still had her hold on him, but the thought of her didn't catch in his stomach as it had once done. Murdoch wasn't always right, but anyone could tell his bed had grown cold with no woman there to warm him. Not any woman, not one of the matches his mother or brother had made for him. But perhaps the woman Ma-khee was the one Sula had foretold, the woman for whom he had been holding himself back.

15

The moment I surface, my line of vision is filled with the arm of the blue couch. I close my eyes and ask some unknown god, any god, even the Christian one, to send me back into the dream. But even as I make my petition, I feel myself floating like a disembodied someone farther away from the night on the hill where I am still sleeping. In spite of Colla, I have to smile at the thought of Fergus playing the drunken troubadour.

Winnie the cat is perched on the back of the couch, ready to jump down on me, now that I am conscious and of some use to her. She's after food. I push my feet off the end of the couch and notice a slight pain in my ankle. I am halfway through chopping up cat food in a saucer before I realize the cause of the injury wasn't here and now, but there and then.

After a quick change, I leave my papers and head over to Jim's house, because the question of which king when is burning in my thoughts, more burning right now than the burning of the witches. On the way over, I try to remember if I had had a sore ankle before I went into the dream the last time.

"You were passed out," Jim says when he opens the door, "so I left you to sleep it off."

I smile. "Too much stress, I suppose. What's that smell?"

Jim taps the oven. "Scones. I thought you might be hungry."

He sits me down in his living room by the fire and goes off to rescue his scones. I settle back into the chair, watching the bricks of peat glow, thinking how strange that after twelve hundred years we're still taking our fuel from the same banks of peat left by antiquity. After a while, I get up and try to look for the list of kings myself. Instead, my eyes keep falling on books about cancer, so I know now what took his wife.

When he comes back in, I pretend I'm looking at the view from his window.

I take my mug from him. He sets a hot buttered scone in my palm.

I tell myself not to, but I find myself asking anyway, "Doesn't *mo chridhe* mean 'my heart' in Gaelic?"

Jim sits himself in what must be *his* chair by the fire. "It does, literally. More 'my love,' I suppose."

I should know better, but there's no hiding the grin that takes over my face.

He says, "Anyone I know?"

I take a bite of that scone and let the lovely buttery crumbs dissolve in my mouth. "Could I see that list of kings again? I need to find a King Murdoch."

Jim sets his cup on the hearth, but only has to pull himself up a little to reach for a piece of paper from the shelf by the side of his chair. It is a handwritten list.

"King Murdoch, eh?"

I take another bite of scone and have to use my hand to catch the crumbs. "I'm thinking around the middle of the eighth century."

I can tell Jim knows I'm after something in my dreams by the way he tilts his head and peers at me. "Close to the earthquake, you mean?"

He sets a pair of half-rimmed glasses on his nose and runs his finger down the page. "According to the Irish annals, one King Murdoch mac Ainbcellaig ruled Dál Riada from 733 to 736."

My heart begins to thump. "What happened after 736?"

Jim shakes his head. "There are no recorded kings again until after 750." He picks his cup up. "You know, not only was there an earthquake in 736, but that's the year the Picts overran Dunadd. That's probably what happened to your Murdoch." He sips his tea. "What's the matter?"

If the Picts overran Dunadd, did they kill Murdoch and his house? What will become of Illa? What about Fergus, *mo chridhe*?

I try my best to look calm. "Jim, there's a King Murdoch in that dream I've been having. There are monks with handbells. There's a sea that comes right up to the base of the fort and cup-and-ring marks in the rock. How the hell do you think I got all that right? I've never even heard of the Irish annals."

Jim takes his time answering. "I don't know about handbells."

I want to grab him and shake him. "Neither do I. But it's such an odd detail, isn't it? And that heather beer— did you know they warmed it up in earthen jugs over embers set in little pits?"

Jim shrugged. "No bloody wonder. They didn't have central heating, you know." He chuckles. "Yes, I suppose you do know."

"And that field out there, you can't even see for thatched roofs with stones hanging off ropes to keep the thatch on. Every house has a yard, and there are odd little stone structures belonging to each house."

"Cleits," he says. "Little storage houses for peat, dried meat, and provisions. It's how they got through the winter. A kind of ice house, if you like."

I can't tell from the look on his face whether he's

mocking me or not. "It's all right," I say. "I know all this sounds completely bloody loony. It sounds loony to me, too. I'm just having dreams, aren't I?"

Jim is beginning to look uncomfortable. He takes his glasses off and twirls them by one of the stems. "God, lass, I don't know."

We finish our tea without speaking. Maybe he is just waiting for me to go.

I stand up. "But what if time isn't what we think it is, one damn thing after another? What if what we know isn't just a series of pictures, but more like a hologram? If the whole thing is contained within each piece, then traveling through time isn't so much a question of traveling anywhere so much as looking deeper into the image."

"You've lost me," says Jim. "I don't see how it could all be happening at once if one thing causes another. Look, in this list of kings, your King Murdoch comes directly after King Eochaid."

I throw up my hands. "I know."

Jim senses I am anxious to leave and stands up too. "I have to go up to Oban tomorrow, if you'd like to come."

He tells me he has a car in his garage, but it must be a small car because I thought his garage was a shed. I shouldn't go anywhere because I have to keep working on the witches, but I am about to explode.

"All right," I say. "I could do with the distraction."

I have been to Oban only a few times and not at all

on this visit. Jim is pleased. For one day, I just want to be normal, though that would be a new feeling for me. I can just see Oliver giving me his deadpan look. I can just see the psychiatrist he sends me to telling me that the subconscious often produces a colorful reality to compensate for the prospects of a dull one.

The next morning early, Jim backs his ancient car out of the garage onto the gravel drive. He has had the heater going, but car heaters in the 1970s weren't what they would become. I can see my breath as I wait for him to turn the car around, stamping my feet on the gravel to generate some modicum of warmth in my toes. At least the sky has decided to show itself from behind cloud.

The road to the tourist town of Oban dips and curves around lochs with sailing boats surrounded by forest and through scenes that would be at home on any calendar. And always the sea stretches out around the islands and beyond to the edge of the horizon.

Oban comes into view, a stately town with the houses built up on a grade from the harbor to the top of the hill where sits an old folly like a small coliseum. The Castle of Dunollie sits on a hill at the far end of the town, one of the first but now just a collection of ruined walls overrun with moss and ivy.

Swans float in the harbor among dismal seaweed like fairy boats; seagulls preen themselves on the harbor wall and on the backs of benches; large ferries pull silently in and out of the long pier, destined for Mull and the many Hebridean islands farther north. We walk along the front and go in for lunch at one of the older bakeries for a piping hot cup of tea, chips with tomato ketchup, and thick slices of bread.

I hum to myself, sitting here with Jim, making my chips and bread into a butty, doing the normal stuff.

Jim says, "I bet they didn't have those in the eighth century."

After a while, he says, "Maybe it's not good for you, spending so much time by yourself."

I have to laugh. I suppose to the onlooker I am showing all the signs of derangement. "It seems to suit you fine."

He shakes his head. "It doesn't suit me fine at all, which is why I was after you finding me a grannie in that dream of yours." He forks a few chips into his mouth. "There's not much you can recommend about living alone, eh?"

"No," I say, "but at least you can have your epileptic fits in peace. Not counting nosy neighbors, of course."

"Och," he says, "you're lucky you have a neighbor, one with an imagination, I might add. You're lucky I haven't summoned the wee men in white coats."

"What if you could go back in time?" I ask him. "Where would you go?"

"Aye, well. That's a question all right," he says. He tilts his head for a better slant on the problem. "It wouldn't be to that last king of Scotland, James the sixth—he disappeared off down to the English court and nothing was seen of him again. A right disgrace he was to his mother, Mary Queen of Scots. It was him, you know, who put a light under the fire of the Great Scottish Witch Hunt, so to speak." He took a deep breath and let it out slowly. "I think it would be to the time of the Bruce, right after the Battle of Bannockburn—what a glory it must have been to know his army had sent the English packing and Scotland was free at last after all the struggle. I think I would give away most of my life just to know how that felt."

I am in my staring trance. Sometimes you just happen on the thing in a person that stirs the quick. It's a nice thing to see, the quick, and I have to stare. But it makes Jim look away.

I nudge his arm. "The eighth century isn't that bad either."

He laughs. "Take away the strapping Fergus, and all you have is plague, wars, a serious lack of heat."

"You have the witches. Dunadd has Sula, the druidess. I bet in the sixteenth century, the witches were still just doing what witches had done since the beginning of civilization, practicing their herbs, midwifery, a bit of fortune-telling; only now the church was running scared."

After lunch we walk farther along the front to the cathedral, which is made of the pink granite the islands are famous for.

On the way back to the car park, my ankle is bothering me.

"Probably turned it on one of your jaunts up the hill."

"Probably," I say. But I don't believe it.

For all this being normal, I would swap this tourist town in a second for the chance to be standing by the door of Sula's hut watching Fergus stagger about with Murdoch.

Jim and I don't say much on the first part of our journey home. It's getting dark, and the yellow headlights on the single-track road keep our attention forward.

"I'm sorry about your wife," I say, somewhere between one small town with a GO SLOW sign by a tiny stone school and the next.

Jim looks over at me, then back at the road. "Aye, well. Life has a way of throwing things at you. I'm sorry about your daughter. That must have been very hard."

I don't know whether he can see me crying in the dark. I try to take silent breaths, but they want to turn into something more. He says nothing. The branches that arch over the road from their tall hedgerows seem leafless and grim.

I know he is waiting for something more, and for some reason in the dark I want to tell him. "She died during a seizure. She was with a babysitter, one of Oliver's students, while we went to a god-awful faculty party. I think the thought of her fighting for breath while I sipped on a glass of sherry was the hardest thing of all. I was barely there at all for the funeral, just going through the motions, trying to fend off the pitying looks. Oliver couldn't speak to me for weeks after. I couldn't speak to myself."

Jim reaches across the gear stick and places his hand on my knee. "It wasn't your fault, any more than it was my fault that Janet got cancer." He clears his throat, takes his hand back. "She got thinner and thinner. She was in so much pain I wanted to put the pillow across her face and be done with it."

His pain is so palpable, it almost eclipses mine. We sit in the silence of it for the rest of the journey.

Dunadd is already in view before I say, "By the way, why did you have to go to Oban?"

He turns and winks. "I didn't."

He flicks the noisy indicator on, and we swing in right to the road that has no special name except the Road to Dunadd. Ahead of us, the hill looms in the darkness, just a presence in the dark, nothing clear about it at all tonight. Nobody there, not even the tourists.

He wants to drive me round to the cottage, but I tell him I can walk the short distance and better to get the car back under cover before it expires altogether.

I hear his back door close, and it is my main intention to get back to my house and let the cat in, but Winnie appears out of nowhere, and I see no reason now not to climb up the hill.

She follows me in the dark as though this had been

the plan all along, running out from behind boulders as though she were being pursued, and maybe she is. It feels like I am. You can hardly distinguish the eighth-century fort from the present one at night, even despite the absence of gates. I run my fingers into the holes left by the iron rods, while Winnie balances on the ledge above my head, her tail twitching, a proper black Halloween cat.

The brow of the hill is cold and windy. The one remaining segment of Sula's wall does nothing to block the elements. Out beyond the fort, the sea, which the tide has taken out even farther than usual, harbors everything it ever knew and kept secret. None of the peaks and valleys between hills has changed since Fergus and his people. But they are not telling either. Real history, the part that is not written down, is mum. No matter if time is a long thread running into a vanishing horizon or a mass of simultaneously moving circles, nothing is being said tonight or any night.

I slip and slide back down the hill on my bad ankle, back onto the path I was supposed to take in the first place. I nip across the garden, which is a shorter way to my sliding glass door than the road. But I stop at the lone standing stone. No one knows about Standing Stones. Even history draws a zip across its speculation here.

Winnie arches around my ankles. I run my fingers over the top edge of the stone made smooth with lichen and wish it would speak. But at any rate I can thank it for remaining firm, for withstanding wind, rain and fire, and for sitting in a twenty-first century garden, still knowing something.

It is late when I return to the cottage, but I switch on the table lamp at my desk, push my glasses on, and sit with my pages, trying to form chapter headings. I'm not sure what I can do for the poor witches, the many Sulas who were dragged from their homes, tortured, and burned. I suppose I could nail my ninety-four theses to the door of the Cannongate Church in Edinburgh and demand an apology. But I can't undo the division of the world into God and Satan that pitted the Good against the Evildoers in the first place.

And then there's Fergus. What's to become of him? Should I warn him that the Picts will overrun Dunadd? I'm not sure where in the three years of Murdoch's reign we are; how much time I have left. Or is it even going to matter, if the Vikings are set to destroy Dunadd anyway? I don't know if all this will be poised to happen when I go back next time. If there is a next time.

16

It comes sooner than I thought. No more than a moment after I come to in Sula's hut, I'm up and shaking
Marcus awake. He stares into my face blankly. But I
need to know what year of Murdoch's reign we're in,
no matter that Marcus's eyes are closing on me.

I shake him again. *"Murdoch Rex. Quo anno?"*

I am surprised I can even come close to conveying
my idea, even more surprised that Marcus catches on.
He's a clever little eunuch.

He fixes his eyes on me. "Annus secundus."

The relief makes me sigh. Marcus is watching me
carefully, confused, while I work out that this must be
the year 735. Of course, 736 starts in not more than a

month, and that's the year Jim said the Picts take over, the year of the earthquake.

I prod Marcus's arm again. This time he seems a little impatient for someone who is supposed to be a slave.

I clear my throat before I speak, because I'm not sure I should be saying this. *"Pictii Dunadd vincent."*

I'm sure it's hopelessly wrong, but something seems to dawn on him.

He gets to his knees, dipenses with his blanket and with Latin. "When?"

"After the new year."

Marcus bumps into Sula on his way out. When she asks him where he is going, he tells her it's for food. But I'm still trying to read the change on his face that this news about the Picts overrunning Dunadd has brought. I'm sure now I should have kept quiet.

Sula takes me by the hand and leads me to her rows of earthen pots. She seems to have a lesson in herbology for me this morning. When Marcus comes back in with the food, he sets a wooden board of flat bread, a dish of sour cottage cheese, and a jug of milk on the floor. The milk, I judge from the smell, is not from cows. It tastes like the smell of manure.

I take a bite of bread dripping with cheese, then turn back to Sula. But Fergus is on the other side of the door announcing his presence. I swallow hard. When Marcus opens the door, Fergus walks in, looking uncomfortable, glancing first at me and then at Sula. Perhaps he's embarrassed by his musical performance outside the hut last night, but he keeps his gaze from me and simply hands Marcus a bundle of clothes. He is turning to leave when Sula tugs my arm to draw my attention back to her lesson.

I try to take in what she is saying about herbs and the circle she traces at the center of her palm, but I have the sense of Fergus hovering by the door.

She nudges me, points into a pot, and tells me a name in Gaelic. "For fever." Marcus tries to help by giving me the Latin, *salix alba*. But I keep on glancing over at Fergus, and he keeps on not leaving.

Sula takes my hand and crushes a dried mint leaf into it.

Marcus tries to illustrate this one by holding his buttocks open and making noises. Sula gives up, sits down, and laughs. Marcus's antics even have Fergus laughing. I smile despite my brooding, even though I feel sad watching his unconscious laugh with his head back and the grooves rising into his cheeks. Why couldn't this lovely specimen have been wifeless?

Fergus steps forward and takes the bundle of clothes he brought from the stool where Marcus laid it, and this time he hands it to me himself. When I nod, as a way of saying thank you, he starts to fumble in a leather pouch with yellow and red design, not quite a tartan but getting there, then brings out a brooch and indicates it's for tying my robe about my shoulders. I turn the piece of jewelry over in my hand, such finely worked strands of gold in filigree about a polished green stone.

"Thank you." I smile. *"Tapadh leibh."*

"Tapadh leibh," Fergus says. A smile spreads over his face, pulling his lips back from surprisingly white teeth. I suppose until sugar makes inroads, teeth will stay the color God designed them.

"Your singing was nice last night," I say.

I stare at him boldly. He just looks embarrassed. I want to push his embarrassment by telling him he called me his love, but what would be the point if he isn't free to do anything about it? I should resist, but I let him lift my hand and run his thumb over my fingers.

I look at him and think *mo chridhe* but try not to let it show. Fergus brings my hand up to his cheek, then kisses it before he goes to the door. I watch while the closing door takes him from me, but hold the feel of his fingers in the palm of my hand.

After he leaves, I move back to Sula, but she has apparently given up with the lesson and is poking around in the fire with a stick. I unfurl the bundle Fergus brought into a beautifully woven robe, almost like a tapestry and almost as heavy. The colors are deep and rich with tiny strands of gold. I want to pull it on, but Sula indicates not to. This must be for another occasion. There is a pointed hat of purple silk that clashes, to my modern taste, with the robe, but I can see I'll be wearing it nonetheless. A small bundle of hair ties fall from the inside of the hat. Marcus picks them off the floor and braids them into my hair.

Sula seems to need to sleep. She wraps her shawl about her and stretches out by the fire. Marcus disappears, and I am left to poke the fire. Anything will do to keep my thoughts from Fergus. I wonder why I am taking the moral high ground—whether he has one wife or ten, he is showing me how much he likes me. This isn't 2014, after all, but 735, and the rules are probably different here. Still, it's hard to shake the laws of the abbey, even though I might not get to stay here long. I only hope that where I am going in my fancy dress has something to do with Fergus.

Marcus comes in with an armload of rude wool and what I know to be a drop spindle—I have seen them in museums, and this method of making yarn was very slow to be displaced in Scotland. Drop spindling sheep's wool would be hard enough, I imagine, the spindle being little more than a twirling weight, but whatever wool Marcus hands me not only does not smell that fresh, but isn't given to holding together. I laugh at my failed attempts to get the spindle spinning uniformly, let alone to draw out a line of yarn. The look on Marcus's face is one of contempt.

Sula sleeps the sleep of the dead and does not wake until the sun is beginning to set and the dismal light in the hut has become even more dismal. While Marcus lights the torches on the wall, Sula reaches for the bundle of fancy clothes and hands it to me.

She says, "Put these on now."

I don't know where we're going, but all of a sudden the excitement in the hut is palpable. Marcus leaves, not to provide me with any privacy, I suspect, but on some other errand. He comes back with a saffron belt tied around his tunic, his hair smoothed back off his face with oil.

When I pull on my new robe, I realize that it, too, has a belt. I tie it tight, like a trouser belt, but Sula loosens it to sit low on my pelvis. The hat stands up a little at its point, and all I need now is a chiffon scarf hanging from the peak. I don't know when mirrors were invented, but I'd like one now. I'd like to see how Maggie Livingstone transforms into her Dark Age counterpart.

As Marcus ties the brooch to the shawl that hangs heavily over one shoulder, I begin to wonder why this period came to be known as the Dark Ages. It doesn't seem to be dark to anyone living in it. As Jim says, the lack of heat can be a problem, but it doesn't seem to bother anyone else. The village children run barefoot, no matter that it is almost winter. Mrs. Gillies's flat in Glasgow was always cold. She said no one had central heating on St. Kilda, and no one ever took ill with a cold. I suppose our age may someday be designated the Soft Age.

Marcus grabs a torch on our way out of the hut and

shines it on my path so that I don't trip on the long robe over my feet. I have to lift it in little puckers, in a way I haven't done since I was playing princess as a child. As we make our descent off the top of the fort, there is a clattering of metal on stone. Every so often a ping is added to the percussion.

"What is it?" I ask Marcus.

He points to his foot and then to the ground. Foot on the ground. This is Dunadd. Yes, I know exactly what is being carved into the rock. Not the Boar yet, but the foot imprint. But I don't know why this is happening now unless there is a new king to be crowned.

We are being taken back to the house of the queen, and now I understand my colorful clothing. I like the custom of announcing one's presence by calling from the outside. The unplaned wood of these doors certainly wouldn't do your knuckles any favors. Sula calls her name and mine, but doesn't mention the servant. In fact, when we go inside, Marcus remains outside.

It's much brighter inside this house, and the once beautiful queen sits on a wooden chair by the fire. A thin golden band encircles her grey hair, but my attention is quickly drawn to Fergus, who stands by her chair, and to Illa, who's sitting on a stone at the hearth. So far, no wife. I try not to meet Fergus's gaze, but he looks even more appealing in a purple jacket tailored to the waist and leg wraps that appear to be made of tweed. My impulse is to curtsy before a queen, but Sula merely approaches her. Fergus moves another wooden chair from the wall towards the fire for the druidess; I am left standing, until he taps Illa's shoulder and gestures for her to give up her seat. I notice she is wearing shoes tonight and a scarf in her hair. She lifts her long pale green dress at the front as she jumps up from her stool, a sandstone block with curious handles at either end that seems oddly familiar to me.

A wiry man with red hair comes in and sits by the door, stroking his small lap harp, humming something of a harmony to its melody. Another musician comes in and joins him with a reedy-looking instrument that sounds like the chanter from a set of bagpipes. My fingers automatically play with the ring handles on my stool.

A servant who is not Marcus, and, I suspect, neither Roman nor eunuch, comes into the room holding a jug from which he dispenses an amber-colored liquid into glasses on the carved table. I take a sip, glad that it is not a spirit, tasting something close to mulled wine. When Illa is offered a small glass, I almost object. She is only a girl, after all.

The queen takes a sip and eyes her glass accusingly. Fergus says something about *Romanus*, so maybe the recipe is left over from the empire. Fergus seems disinterested in the drink, more occupied with looking at me in the clothes he brought. He keeps finding excuses for moving closer to me, and I can't say I mind. I suppress the urge to brush my shoulder against his thigh or lean in and rest my head against him.

The queen doesn't seem pleased with me. It suddenly occurs to me that these clothes I'm in might come from Fergus's wife, and perhaps she is a particular favorite of the queen.

"Why is her hair so short?" she asks without looking at me. "Did her husband die?"

I feel Fergus waiting for the answer. Illa comes over and gently gathers the ends of my hair in her hands as though they must hurt. My hair must seem short compared to the other women at Dunadd in 735. More like the length of her dad's.

"Where is your husband?" the queen asks.

If it weren't for the fact that Fergus's face is quite well represented in hers, I don't think I would like this woman.

She says, "Are you married?"

Fergus is looking at the floor and doesn't see me shake my head.

"No," I say, loud enough for him to hear. But I don't know if divorce has any status in this time, so I follow it with, "My husband died."

The queen pats me on the shoulder. The haughtiness goes out of her eyes. "How old are you?"

Fergus looks at the ground again. I tell them I'm thirty-five, which isn't exactly honest, but it's close.

The queen speaks more gently now. "Where is your country?"

My country? I've tried Caledonia, but it doesn't seem to work.

I say, "Alba."

They just look at me.

So I say, "Dunadd," in the way people in 2014 say Dunadd. They correct the pronunciation. "Doonadd."

They nod their heads and seem well pleased.

I say, "Before that, Glasgow."

Again a moment's pause and then the proper pronunciation. "Glaschu?"

Only Fergus seems to know this one. "Glaschu," he says, and then he tells them of a small dwelling by a stream to the south. I have to smile that Glasgow was ever this insignificant. He says it's popular with monks.

"Is she a Christian?" the queen asks.

"No," I am quick to say.

Now the queen knows a little more, she seems better disposed towards me. I am pleased because Illa seems less wary, too. From the corner of my eye, I can see the disbelief on Sula's face. The queen gives me her hand and offers me her seat. It's not until I turn and glance back at the stone I have been sitting on that I see what has been nagging at me ever since I first sat down.

For there on the floor, being sat upon like any other seat in the world, and much less worn around the edges, but undeniably, in the heat and flicker of the fire, is Scotland's famous Stone of Destiny.

Sula seems to understand my shock. She comes over and holds my arm because I am almost shaking. Nothing has brought this strange reality I am living home to me like seeing this icon of Scotland being used as a seat by the fire. I want to tell them what's going to become of this stone, never to let it out of their sight, because England's King Edward has his eye on it. But Edward, the Hammer of the Scots, is still five hundred years from the start of his hammering.

The musicians have stopped playing. The queen is speaking to her son in low tones that I can't make out. Illa seems quite amused by the spectacle that I am, and have always been. It's only by looking at her that I manage to calm down.

I really want to sit back down on that stone, but Illa has perched herself on it again. When I smile at her, she smiles back, though I can tell she doesn't know why she is smiling. The queen is studying me. Fergus orders the musicians to continue.

Fergus brings out a nicely crafted board game with blue glass pieces and one white one, which seems to be a favorite of his daughter's and has her up and jumping around. This girl is less interior than Ellie, more excitable. Fergus gestures for me to watch them play, but it seems a good deal more complicated than I can pick up without a proper explanation. As far as I can gather, the goal of each player seems to be to capture the white bead, and the rules seem somewhat similar to backgammon. I suspect Fergus will want me to play next, but there's no hope. So I study him instead: the quick smile of regret that comes when his daughter gets the better of him and laughs; the hair that falls forward over his cheeks as he studies his next move; the square hands that run through his hair when he is frustrated; the golden ring over the tattoo on his middle finger.

I am glad for the arrival of the food brought in by Marcus and the other slave. Marcus has a broad smile on his face, not something I have grown to expect from him. They lay the food out on the table in wooden dishes, except for what have to be bannocks in a pile by themselves, small bready rounds that will survive to become another symbol of Scotland. I note the fruit salad with relish, though the only two fruits in it seem to be apple and pear. I suppose grapes without air travel would be a bit much to ask.

Illa leaves her game and pulls out pieces of fruit from the bowl with her fingers in a way I would never have let Ellie do; I follow suit. Fergus reaches for a strip of meat from a different dish. I take one, too, but can't quite place the taste through the saltiness, something like pork, only gamier. The queen does not appear to be eating. She exchanges her glass of mulled wine for something else poured for her by Marcus from a stone bottle.

I signal for Ellie to watch me as I kneel down, take up seven of the blue beads, and then cast them down in front of me. I used to be good at jacks as a girl and used to play with my children when they were little. I throw the white bead up and scramble for a blue bead before the first bead drops. She comes close and kneels by me, drops the weight of herself against me. I throw my white bead up again and this time catch two blue beads before it drops.

Illa likes this game. Her smile is like Fergus's, and I would like to kiss that face. Both of them. She puts her hand out for the beads, and that hand is not what you would call clean, but I would still put my lips on it. Fergus says something that makes her withdraw the grubby paw, and everyone, I realize, is waiting for my next move. The game of jacks gets considerably harder after two and especially with glass beads instead of spiky modern jacks. I try, but drop one of the blue beads before I catch the white one.

Fergus swivels down onto the floor by his daughter, catching my eye and taking the beads from my hand with fingers that leave a sting at every point they touch my skin. He starts with one and makes it up to four before he hands the beads over to Illa. The girl doesn't have much luck after one, so I try to show her how to throw the white bead straight up so that it's easy to catch again. My eye follows Fergus as he moves away. Illa keeps going. I can hear Fergus and Sula in low conversation with the queen, and the word *Boar* keeps coming up. The queen holds a book up to him that has *Vita Colum Cille* and *Adomnan* on the front. Fergus refuses to take it. I am sure I have seen that title somewhere before.

Marcus refills our glasses, including Illa's, and soon she has to abandon my game because she is too giddy. After a while, after the talk has died down, she falls asleep on the hard floor. I want to take my cloak off and lay it under her, but I suspect this is part of the toughness training. I wonder if Fergus sleeps on a hard floor, too. I wonder how it would feel to have the weight of him against me.

When Sula gets up to leave, I stand, too. But Fergus wraps his hand around my arm and bids me sit back down. He himself goes out with the others, leaving me in an uncomfortable silence with the sleeping girl and the silent grandmother. Now that her father is gone, I take off my hat and slip it under Illa's head. I am just wondering if I am supposed to sleep here tonight when Fergus comes back in with a small bundle. These people like their bundles.

He unravels the cloth and brings out a fine bone comb in the shape of a hand attached to a wrist handle. He holds it so carefully that I know it has meaning for him, and I am scared to touch it.

When he places it in my hand, I think I catch the glint of a red hair caught in a crack of the bone. Maybe the hair of a different wife than Colla. I hand the comb back, managing a smile. But then with his mother looking on, he starts running it through my hair. I try to remember the last time I washed my hair. He combs it gently, stopping when it catches. Every stroke of the comb, he follows with a stroke of his hand.

I don't even want to know what the queen is thinking, so I keep my eyes straight into the fire, just above the Stone of Destiny, and wonder how it became my destiny to mingle here. All I came to Dunadd for was to get away, and here I am under the hand of a medieval lord, whose touch, I might say, is very kind to me.

When the queen falls asleep in her chair, he wraps me about with his own shawl and leads me out into the cold night. We stand by the house with a question between us.

He says, *"Tiugainn comhla rium."* The question is in his face as his hand gestures up the hill. *Come with me.*

I look at his outstretched hand, but I cannot take it. I know where this question is leading. I can read it in his eyes. But moral high ground or no, I can't make love to another woman's husband. I shake my head. He drops my hand.

I can feel him watching, but he doesn't follow as I make my way back through the dark to Sula's hut, holding up my dress to navigate the ascent but feeling nothing like a princess this time. I sit by the embers of Sula's fire, my knees under the fancy robe pressed against my chest, wishing I could leave this era with its complications of history and love.

I try to sleep, to induce my return to the blue couch and my view of the river and the open fields, but I am having no luck ordering things the way I want them tonight. Later, when Sula and Marcus get back, they quickly take up their spots by the fire, and everything descends again into stillness.

Sometime later I am aware of coming to. It takes a moment for my eyes to adjust, but even then there is no light to speak of under the door or through the wattle walls. Someone is calling so softly, at first I can't make it out, but then, by the way he says "Ma-khee," I know it is Fergus.

I have to step over Marcus to reach the door. I stand there, biting my nails, listening to Fergus moving around on the other side. It is so quiet I can hear his breathing. I try to breathe slowly so he can't hear mine.

Maybe he puts his hand on the door, because it moves slightly towards me.

"Ma-khee."

My hand goes to the latch but stops short. I know what answering this call is going to mean and that I shouldn't put myself in its way when I am not going to go through with it. I am drawing on all the reason my age has given me, but my brain seems disconnected from the rest of me, and my fingers push the cold iron latch out of its catch.

He has his arms on either side of the door, unexpectant, it seems, of my response. When he sees me, he steps back. For more than a few moments, we stand opposite each other, me still on the inside, him part of the night outside and just as threatening.

And then he clears his throat softly and speaks. "Tiugainn comhla rium." Come with me.

He looks at me with his cheeky smile as though he's asking to be kissed, if kissing has even been invented.

"I can't," I say, stepping back over the threshold.

Fergus is not listening to my words. Why should he? They don't even convince me. He pulls me against him, and I feel his hands spread out over my waist and fold me into him. His shoulder belt presses into my chest bone where it slots between my breasts. My hands go around his back and rest on the belt as it crosses his shoulder blades. I can feel his breath against the top of my ear, and all I have to do is tilt my face back slightly and his mouth falls against mine, infinitely warm in the cold night air.

His hand slips down around mine, and I feel him tug. "*Tiugainn comhla rium.*"

I shake my head. "I can't."

He breaks away and stands a little way off. He is breathing hard.

He says, "Because your heart is still with your husband?"

"No," I say. "Because yours is with your wife."

He comes to me and holds me by the shoulders. "You are right. It has been for too long. I didn't think I could love another woman, but I want you, Ma-khee."

He holds me again like I was his last refuge.

I push him back. "You need to go to her."

When he pulls back, I see his face is confused.

I give him another push. "Go to your wife, Fergus."

With all my heart I don't mean it. But I should. And I don't know why he is smiling all of a sudden, but I see those blessed even teeth flash in the dark.

It's a reflex to get defensive. "Colla. Go to Colla."

He finds this even more amusing. "Colla's not my wife, only a woman Murdoch wishes were my wife."

Now I'm the one to be confused. "Well, who is your wife?"

He smiles a quick, unconvincing smile. "She is dead, like your husband. She was Talorcan's sister."

I am breathless and reeling all at once. I want to sing "Hallelujah," but it doesn't look as though he would take that very kindly. I am not simple enough to think a dead spouse is less of an obstacle than one in the land of the living. Still, it does clear the way. It does make me take his hand and kiss the palm, his not-altogether-clean palm.

He waits in case I have more words for him, and I do, but I can't even begin to formulate them. I want to tell him to go easy on me, that it has been so long since

I have been loved and now I am all fingers and thumbs with it.

He takes my hand and tugs. *"Tiugainn comhla rium."*

I walk with him, tied to him, my side moving against his, through the starless dark away from Sula's hut, down the hill past the spot where the mason has abandoned his tools for the night, down to the buildings on the grassy level. The cookhouse is also dark and silent as we go by and stop outside a small rectangular building. He hesitates before he lifts the latch, and I begin to wonder if this is the place he lived with Illa and his wife when she was alive.

The door swings open into only one room, which, judging by the greenery now decorating the floor, hasn't been used in some time. The measured way Fergus steps around the room, the way his eyes dart from the floor to the ledge where a bed must once have been, and where there is still a stack of blankets, I know where I am, and I'm not too comfortable with it.

I wait for him by the door, but he comes back for me and leads me in, shutting the light out so that all I can do is feel him in the dark and hear his breath in my ear, as he lifts my tunic and runs his hands over the skin of my back.

He drops to his knees and wraps his arms around my buttocks, pulling me against his face, his mouth right at the place his hand took hold of on our first encounter.

The man wants the woman, and there is no doubt in the dampness of the place where these things get registered that the woman wants the man, too.

He knows more than I about the unraveling of lady's clothing. The brooch and the sash come off easily and drop into his hands. The robe unsuspended drops about my ankles. He holds me at arm's length and peers into the dark when my knickers stretch out under his touch then snap back like an extra layer of skin. The bra proves more difficult, but then it is difficult for modern man, too. I don't linger long over the humor of the situation but, pushing his hands aside, wriggle free from both items of underwear and draw him again down to his knees beside me. If this is a dream, then please let it play on, please may this gasp as his cold palms come against my nipples be real. If there is a god, and especially if she is a woman, may I sink into the hold of his arms and never recover.

Without letting me go, Fergus reaches for a blanket from a pile that sits on the floor and lays it on the ground and me on top of it.

There is no moving in slowly; this is what he brought me here for, and this is why I came. I fumble to untie him, but I don't know where the knots are, how he is to be unleashed. Fergus knows. He unloosens his belt, and the string and leg wraps drop away as though everything had been designed to do just this, and maybe it was. I reach up and lay my hands on his chest, feel the pounding of his heart. For just a moment he hesitates before moving towards me. The knife that he wears under his arm still sits against his skin in its halter. I grab it and hold it against his back as he inches down onto me, cupping my shoulders against the hardness of the floor. His knees step between mine, and there is no thinking now. The gates have been opened and he sails in, pausing only to wait for the wall in me to give. I want to hold on, hold back, don't let it slide so soon. If we could only stop breathing, stay still, and keep ourselves here for a moment longer. But it's too late. I am falling. Everything is giving way and I am over the edge, grabbing onto him because on the other side of this there is only a fall.

I can hear him saying, "Ma-khee." He brings his mouth against my ear. "Ma-khee."

Ma-khee. The scene begins to fade. I fight to stay on, running my hands over his back, stepping my breathing in time with his.

But a voice rattles in from another world. "Maggie." Under a different veil of time, someone is trying to waken me.

I close my eyes, breathing hard. "No."

Fergus kisses the hair by my ears where the tears fall. "Stay with me, *mo chridhe*."

He slides off me, covering me over with the end of the shawl. There's a faint line of light under the door now, and pots and pans are being set down in the cookhouse. I have to keep touching him to reassure myself that this all happened, at least this once. The tears are in case it never comes again.

I can tell by Fergus's rhythmic breathing, the slow rising of his chest against my side, that he has fallen asleep. I smile, because no matter what the age, some things never change. Right at this moment, I wish they never would again. But they are going to change. Only eight weeks until an operation that is precisely designed to ensure that they will.

I nudge Fergus a little to see if I can rouse him. I lift his hand, but it drops from my fingers. *Fergus, mo chridhe.*

My hand slips down onto the rise of his flank. "Fergus."

I wait to see if he stirs. Not a muscle moves. I smooth the line of his eyebrows.

"Fergus."

I clear my throat. I don't know if I should say this, what it might mean to history. But if I never come back, I have to warn him before I go.

"Fergus, the Picts are going to overrun the fort soon. And an earthquake is going to tip the land and send the sea too far away for decent commerce. You don't even know about the Vikings yet, but they are going to come down on you like hell itself, only you don't have hell yet. You will, when the Christians take over. Eventually,

Kenneth MacAlpin, half Pict himself, will be crowned first king of Scotland here at Dunadd, but not until 843."

I stroke the back of his head and down to where his hair stops just over his shoulders. "You want to know who I am, but if I were to tell you, you wouldn't believe me; before I was Ma-khee, I used to be Margaret, with a husband who is not dead but might as well be. I had a daughter once, too, just like Illa."

I lay my forehead against his chest, and let my tears roll onto his skin.

"I come from Scotland in the twenty-first century, where there are no more witches except at Halloween, and even then they are not proper witches, but just cartoons. We don't depend on the druidess anymore but on stuff, on cars and houses and Rolex watches."

I stop speaking when Fergus moves slightly under my hand and groans. I wait until he is still again, watch the morning force itself under the door and me further from him. I can feel it slipping.

"Maggie," says Jim, *"are you all right?"*

I wrap my arms about Fergus's back and press myself against him, every inch of me that can find an inch of him.

"Fergus," I whisper, though he wouldn't understand what I am saying in a language that doesn't even exist yet. "Fergus, you're going to find electricity and gas and bombs and turn into such a queer people, whose men turn against their women and burn the strong ones alive.

Eventually, there'll be a car park at the base of Dunadd, and people from all over will climb up here to put their foot in an imprint in the stone that isn't even here yet. Nobody then will believe the sea ever came up this far, except some English nutter who lives on the great estate that will make its millions on the backs of slaves in far-away sugar plantations and will possess all this land as far as you can see."

I stroke the back of his thighs. Perhaps, if Dr. Shipshap is right, he might absorb some of what I'm saying into his subconscious, except that hasn't been invented yet either. Before I leave I have something else to say. "Fergus, people are going to go out from this nation and take over entire continents, a bit like the Vikings are set to do, killing off the natives like there is no tomorrow, and perhaps there is no tomorrow. Everything gets very crazed, except on a much larger scale than you can imagine. What I have to tell you, *mo chridhe*, is that, as far as the moon is from this place, I come from your tomorrow."

I slip the wedding ring off my finger. It doesn't come off easily, wedged as it is in a little groove of me. I get to my knees and bind the ring onto his belt with a tie from my hair. I lie back down and press myself against him. I suppose he will find the ring in the morning when he is without me, and it will tell him whatever it is he wants it to.

17

After the woman had left, Fergus went to lie near his daughter by the dwindling fire in the warmth of his mother's house. But too many thoughts weighed against sleep tonight. Illa's head still rested on the hat the woman had worn. He liked that the woman was kind in that way, and it made him smile to remember how she had felt in her strange wrap about her backside, about her breasts. He rolled over, and his eyes fell on the stone by the fire. How odd, Ma-khee's reaction to that. Of course, this was no ordinary stone, but came from far to the east. Perhaps it was because Ma-khee also came from the east that she recognized what type of a stone it was.

Her ways were strange. Her language was nothing he recognized, even though he had traveled as far as

Gaul. It sounded more like Saxon than anything, but had a lilt to it. He had feigned sleep as she talked, felt her hand on his backside, her fingertips on his eyebrows. He smiled when he remembered she had called him *mo chridhe.*

Illa moved suddenly in her sleep and touched Fergus's hand. She could not know that on this night her father had moved on from her mother. He had waited until Illa was sleeping to bring out the thing her mother had loved, the comb that came in a bag of loot from an attack on the Northumbrians. It had felt odd to hold it in his hand and run it through another woman's hair. Still, he had liked the way his hand slipped so easily across her hair down onto her shoulders. His fingers lingering there had sensed no resistance.

Fergus wondered about Ma-khee's husband, what manner of man this could have been to leave a woman with such a weight about her. Marcus thought there had been a child. So she was like him, this Ma-khee. He hoped that she could forget her old husband. He lay on his back with his hands behind his head, running over the scene in the other house. It had been so long since he had brought himself this close to a woman, but how sweet the cry of the woman in his embrace as it mingled with his own. He had forgotten, had for too long buried himself in a cave with no light and no sound. Ma-khee had brought him back to the edge of his darkness and shown him the sky. The thought of it made his heart a little fearful for all that can be lost in love.

It was the mason who woke Fergus in the morning with his clattering at the rock on the hillside just above his mother's house. The fire had gone to embers and offered little heat. Fergus got up and threw a triangle of peat onto the fire before he walked out to the mason Murdoch had hired to fashion the shape of a foot in the rock. For once, his brother's ideas concurred with his own. Fergus wanted to stay at Duandd now, not just for Illa but for Ma-khee. But he worried that Murdoch's antagonism towards the Picts might incite them to revolt after all.

Fergus found Illa in the bakehouse, where the cooks often gave her dough to roll. Leaning against the door-jamb, he ate a dish of oats boiled in milk and looked out on a morning that was damp and quiet under thick clouds. He would gladly have stayed by the ovens, but he had to go down to the village and find Talorcan.

As Fergus followed the path down to the gates, the clouds began to release icy drops, and they did not have far to fall. It was his custom to exchange a few words with the guards, but his thoughts were heavy this morning as he juggled this new woman with his duty as a royal son of the house of Dunadd. He hurried through the gate and down across the bridge which swung under his step and reminded him of the injury to his ankle on the night of Samhain.

Morning in the village smelled of baking bannocks and the yeasty sour smell of warming *fraoch*. Talorcan lived on the far side by the hill in a house surrounded by a tall fence. His wife had borne no children, and so he had sons and daughters with other women. Today he was alone by his door.

Talorcan caught his brother-in-law by the arm. "Fergus. Come and eat."

Fergus walked into the house and squatted beside his friend at the fire, not willing the time forward for his telling about the new woman. Talorcan had loved his sister Saraid and would not take the news easily.

He spread a bannock with cheese and handed it to Fergus, then set a cup of *fraoch* on top of a few embers in a hole in the ground.

Fergus ate in silence. After a moment, he lifted the warming brew to his lips. It would make the speech easier.

"There have been rumors," Fergus said.

Talorcan nodded. "I have heard the rumors. I heard you have taken the foreign woman for yourself."

Fergus sighed. "Do not think it is easy for me to let Saraid go."

"It is time, though," said Talorcan. "The dead don't fit into one of your boxes to be kept. They have their lives, no longer with us except for the times when the veil lifts. But that is not up to us."

Fergus nodded.

Talorcan slapped his back. "If you had not, I would have taken her for myself."

Fergus drank from his steer horn cup. He knew it meant nothing for Talorcan to boast about women. Still, it made Fergus anxious to change the topic.

He said, "But these are not the rumors I came to talk about. My brother and my mother are worried about news from the north and east about the new king Oengus. They worry that you Picts of the Boar will rise up and join this king to take Dunadd from us."

Talorcan picked up a stick and idly drew a boar in the dirt. "I have heard rumors, too," he said, "that the druidess has visions of this image on the rock inside your fort."

Fergus shook his head. "How do these rumors come to you?"

Talorcan offered him another bannock. "Remember, the people who serve you and prepare your meat do not come from your stock."

Fergus looked into Talorcan's face, traced the handsome outline of the boar on his forehead. Talorcan looked away.

"Then is it true? Should we fear those from whom we have taken our wives, whose goddess we have worshipped? Must they come in the night and murder us?"

Talorcan looked into the eyes of this Scot he had

known since childhood. He laughed. "Not as long as my brother draws breath. Not as long as my sister's girl sleeps sound."

Fergus finished his drink. He gave Talorcan his hand. "Thank you. I can trust you. But what of the others?"

Talorcan walked him to the opening in the wattle fence. "We have lived peacefully with your people these two hundred years. You took my sister as your wife. No Scot will fall by my hand. Those who want to fight must do so under the sign of the beast of King Oengus in the north. Still, you should tell your people to listen to the druidess."

Fergus felt uneasy as he walked back through the village. There were many mixed bloods living here, but also plenty of the tall red-haired Picts. If the Picts to the north chose to march south, who knew what others they would pick up on their travel? If the Scots were going to stand against such a force, all the men of the islands and in the larger Dál Riada kingdom would have to be brought in. Perhaps even from as far as Erin. But the word would have to go out soon. Such an army could not be brought together quickly.

He shook off these thoughts as he climbed back up to the fort and was admitted through the gates. His thinking should be of lighter things. After all, he had found a woman he liked well and was eager to see. He hoped the thought of him pleased her as much as the anticipation of seeing her this morning made him run the last stretch up the hill to the houses.

But she wasn't in Sula's hut nor at the bakehouse. A moment of panic suggested she had escaped and gone back to where she had come from. But he found her with his daughter and Sula, watching the mason carve the foot in the rock. He stood close to her, hoping she still wanted him.

She turned to him. "What is the foot for?"

He found a softness in her eyes that made him smile and want to touch her. His fingers went around her hand. Her squeeze tightened his grip. He could feel Sula watching them, but it made no difference now whether Ma-khee was a druidess or not. Too much had passed for Sula to take the woman back.

He said, "The foot will be the place for the payment of fealty by lords from the outlying lands. It means I don't have to travel to collect it."

He took a step in until his chest was touching her back. But she was distracted now by the mason asking Sula to step into the imprint that he might take its size from her foot. It seemed to bring the woman Ma-khee much joy, talking quickly in her own language and clapping her hands.

Fergus took the woman by her hand. "Come," he said in the soft way a man has of speaking to a woman he is not yet sure of.

He led her back to his house, where they had lain the night before. As they walked Ma-khee pulled her shawl to her face against the rain; it pleased Fergus when she slipped in the mud and his hand had to wrap about her waist to save her from falling. He took Illa this time, too, for it was time for her to go back into the house where she had been brought into life. These past two years they had not liked to go in there at all, and it felt strange to him to kneel by the old fire pit with another woman's eyes on him.

As he had taught her, Illa brought sticks and built them into a pyramid, while Fergus took a leather pouch from his belt and laid out his steel instrument with the two finger holes, a round piece of stone, and a dried piece of fungus. He set the fungus to the side of the fire on a pile of old charred wood, and then began striking the steel shoe with the stone until it produced a spark or two, which he caught in the fungus and blew on as it began to smolder. It wasn't long until the sticks began to crackle, and the fire rose up out of Illa's pyramid. He caught the woman's eye as he gathered his kit back into his pouch and sat back with his hands on his haunches, watching the fire rise.

The woman seemed happy with Illa on her lap, braiding her hair, singing some strange-sounding song with her lips close to the girl's ear. Fergus stood over her, ran his fingers down her arm; she looked up and smiled. He tried to busy himself moving things about, but his eyes kept finding her, wishing for it to be dark in here again. By the look on his daughter's face, it would not be hard for her to accept this Ma-khee as a new mother.

When the house had gained some heat, he left them to find Sula, for there were things to discuss. Outside the house, he stopped for a moment while he gathered himself and took a little more leave of his dead wife. It was simply a new feeling of release, and it lightened his steps as he scaled the hill and came to Sula's door.

He called out his name and stood back, the woman's gold band in the cup of his hand.

But Sula was not by herself. In the dim light of her hut, Fergus saw her leaning over Marcus's foot. He was anxious to talk to her, but he kept yawning from his lack of sleep the night before, and he had no choice but to sit down on the floor and wait. The smell of the poultice Sula was applying overwhelmed Fergus and made his eyes heavy. The next thing he knew, she was bending over him, shaking his shoulder.

"Wake up," she said. "What is it?"

Fergus opened his eyes. He stood up and moved aside to let Marcus leave. Sula beckoned Fergus to sit on the shelf that jutted from the wall, where Ma-khee had been sitting the first time he saw her.

"This woman Ma-khee," he said. The very words made him smile.

Sula nodded. "It is time."

243

"Will you cast your stones again, see if this Ma-khee is the one you saw before?"

Sula shook her head. "I am afraid to cast my stones these days. What I see no one understands. Not even I understand."

Fergus edged forward on his seat.

"What do you see? The boar in the hillside?"

Sula walked to Fergus, this man she had known since he was a scrawny boy; she took his head in her hands. "Yes. The Boar in the rock by your footprint. I see a time when these are all that will be left at Dunadd, just the bracken and the carvings in the rock."

Fergus looked into her face. "When?"

"I cannot tell. But I see black ribbons running down the land. I see carts without horses moving very fast. I do not think this time will be soon. But you must leave."

Fergus ran his hands through his hair. "How could I leave? Murdoch will never give up on Dunadd and neither will my mother. We will stay and fight."

"Some things you cannot fight," said Sula. "You can kill every Pict from the north to the east to the south, but their carving comes to the rock, whether you slaughter us all or not. Fergus, your people will not last here for long."

She lifted his hand and patted. "I am telling you these things because you have ears that listen. Murdoch is deaf these days to signs given by an old woman. Speak to your mother; speak to your woman."

Fergus warmed to the touch of the old woman's hands, as though he were still a child. He caught her hands and brought them together within his own, such fleshless fingers now. "What of the woman?"

The druidess shook her head. "I have no sense of her. I ask my stones and they say this woman has traveled far, but she says she comes from here, and I do not take her for a liar. I can only think she has traveled from the land of past bones. And yet, you are right, she has all the marks of the living." Sula looked hard into his face and smiled. "Why this woman now? Your mother, your brother, have found other brides, younger, more beautiful than this one. Is this the young Fergus who must always say no?"

Sula took her hands away and squatted by her fire, looking into the flames as though she could find an end to her questions there.

Fergus crouched beside her. "Who can say why? It is not a question for argument." He turned Ma-khee's ring over in his palm, and it touched him that she would not have given this up lightly. "Even if she is not the woman in your stones, I would want her to be. You can argue until dark about the right arrow for the job, but in the end the arrow that will make its mark feels right in the hand."

Sula uncupped Fergus's hand and picked out the ring. She looked into his eyes, then set it back across those lines of his palm that she knew so well, that told so much.

When she stood up, Fergus saw for the first time that she was old now; her legs could not hold her for long in one place. He watched her run her hand over her face and look back at him.

"These things I see I do not fully understand," she said. "The shaking of the fort—I do not know whether this is a game of pictures or a quake such as fell once on Erin, but you must take this woman of yours and your daughter. You must leave Dunadd, because the time is coming when it will not be safe for you here. I see it more frequently now."

Fergus stood and laid his hand on her shoulder. His breathing was fast and shallow. "You know I cannot go."

Sula stood up. "Leave Dunadd, Fergus, while there is still time."

Fergus went out from Sula with his thoughts like daggers. He ran to the house of his brother's wife. She had not seen Murdoch for a night and a day. He ran to the house of Colla. She said Murdoch had left with a company by horse at sunrise.

Fergus found his mother seated by the fire, the book of Colum Cille's life in her lap.

Fergus knelt before her. He could do no other. "I just came from Sula. You must listen, Mother."

"I have listened," Brighde said. "It is you who has not paid her any heed. Even today your brother is riding to the farthest reaches of Dál Riada to round up men. We cannot defeat the Picts by ourselves. Murdoch will march north with an army and face this King Oengus before he ever gets within sight of Dunadd." She laid her hand on the top of Fergus's head. "Will you join them? Murdoch has a strong arm, but you have the trust of the people."

Fergus shook his head. "Sula says they can't be beaten. They might kill King Oengus and they might defeat his forces, but she has seen the boar carved into our hill."

"She's just an old woman," said Brighde. "The monks say she should be carried beyond the fort and burned."

Fergus grabbed his mother's knees. "You have to listen to her, Mother. She says the Picts will reign over Dunadd, and that in short order."

Brighde withdrew her hand. "Will you run away from me and leave Dunadd, this land of our mothers that we came from Erin to conquer, that we have fought to keep?"

Fergus looked up to see his mother's face. "Of course I will not run from my duty towards you. I will never leave Dunadd. How could I?"

Fergus ran down the fort, through the gates, across the bridge that swung under his feet, across the beaten earth of the village back to Talorcan.

Once in Talorcan's house, Fergus bent over to catch his breath.

"What is it, Fergus? Speak to me."

"Murdoch," he said, "he has ridden out to gather the men of Dál Riada to ride north against King Oengus."

Talorcan let out a sigh. "I have just heard they left before light. How many men can he gather?"

Fergus stood up. Talorcan fetched him water in a wooden dish. "There is a list. Each settlement I collect fealty from has so many boats. The druids know the details. The island of Jura has twenty seven-benchers, the isle of Islay, ten more than that. The hills down to the Strath of Clyde will yield more. Perhaps two thousand men in all."

"Oengus's army is greater than this and is familiar with the territory to the north," said Talorcan. "Remember that fifty years ago the Picts defeated the Northumbrians, who were a strong force. Murdoch doesn't stand a chance against the Pictish army." Talorcan turned to Fergus. "What will you do?"

"No, my brother," said Fergus. "What will you do?"

Talorcan's wife came into the hut with one of his daughters, the unusual one, who also bore the mark of the boar on her forehead. She saw the faces of the men and said, "What is the matter?"

Talorcan drew his wife to his side. "You must take Fergus and his family away. They will not be safe here."

"I could take them east across the land to my mother at Loch Glashan," said the wife.

Fergus shook his head. "I cannot leave Dunadd."

The wife said, "The loch is well hidden. The people there still live in their houses on the loch. You will be safe out in the crannog."

Fergus said, "No. My mother will never leave. I will stay at Dunadd."

Talorcan grabbed his arm. "Then you will die, my friend. Surely you must heed the warnings of your own druidess."

Fergus took his arm back. "Sula has been wrong before."

Fergus left. He didn't know which way to go. It was not in him to run away and hide. Yet he could no longer feel himself on the same side as Talorcan. He thought of the woman's golden ring beside his dirk in the sheath he wore under his arm, but now the question of taking her for a wife seemed small next to the possibility of having to leave Dunadd for good. He felt foolish for even thinking of her when everything was dissolving about him.

When it grew dark, he went back to the house to find her, so strange to walk to his old house anticipating another woman. He laid his fingers on the latch, but he could not go in to her. He could find no peace in his thoughts after what Sula had told him. Now that he finally had a woman for himself and a mother for Illa, the ground had been pulled from beneath his feet. How could he lie with the woman now that he couldn't put a hand on any of his feelings?

He strode quickly away to find the slave Marcus and set him to guard his house, though he didn't know what he was guarding against. He ran to the top of Dunadd and sat in the heather above the sea. A strange light spread out from behind the islands into the dark dome of sky. Day or night, he needed this view from the fort like a child needs a mother's lap. His family had always lived here, and he could not conceive of living elsewhere. How could they command the area, continue trade with other lands, without the lookout of the fort, its proximity to the sea? He would defend Dunadd to the last, even though he knew it could mean he would die.

18

I hammer on Jim's door, my eye on the bare finger where my wedding ring used to be. I bang my knuckles hard against the wood. When he opens up, I walk in without comment.

"You were asleep on the couch for hours," he says. "I tried to wake you."

I walk to the oven, then back to him. "Will you make me a cup of tea?"

He nods. "What's the matter with you?" He peers into my face. "You don't look well."

He turns away to fill the kettle.

Before I speak, I have to catch my breath. "Was the Stone of Destiny ever at Dunadd?"

He goes to his kitchen door and lets Winnie in. "So

they say. But it ended up in Scone in Perthshire, where the seat of the king was moved, away from the marauding Vikings. There, away in and sit by the fire now, and I'll bring you your tea."

I can't help myself; I grab Jim by the arms. "I couldn't just have dreamed that."

He looks a bit worried. "Aye, but it's not an unknown fact."

"It is to me." I am almost singing it. "At least it was unknown to me until I sat on the bloody thing up there in the queen's house!"

Jim is sort of squinting at me, as though if he waits I might come into better focus. "Go and sit down. I'll get the tea ready."

He pours enough boiling water into the teapot to make the tea bags float at the top, and then he carries the tray into the living room and sets it down on the table by the fire. I start to speak again, but he shushes me so that he can pour the tea and offer me a biscuit from a rose-patterned plate. The astringent scent of tea competes with the acrid smoke from the fire.

He takes his cup to his chair. "Now," he says, "what is it you're blethering about?"

I set my cup by my feet and the biscuit beside it. "It's not blether, Jim; you have to grant me that."

He takes a noisy sip. "Do I now?"

"You do, and here's why: I asked Marcus the slave

how long Murdoch had been in power. He said two years. That makes it 735, right? They are carving the foot into the rock even now, and, guess what, it's a woman's foot and has nothing to do with crowning kings."

He sets his cup in its saucer. He's interested now. "What does it have to do with then?"

"The lesser lords paying fealty, putting their foot in it, so to speak."

Jim chuckles. "Swearing allegiance to the king in it."

I sigh. At last he is on my side. "Did you already know that?"

He shakes his head. "No, but they took the custom over to Perth with them. There's a mound called Boot Hill there, where they did the same thing."

I am breathless. "So do you believe me now?"

He shakes his head, as though it could save him from making such a wild leap. "Did you really see the Stone of Destiny?"

I have to laugh. "I got invited for dinner by the queen, and I was sitting on this stone by the fire until I realized that it was the Stone of Destiny, for God's sake, just sitting there by the fire."

Jim takes a deep breath. "Have you told any of this to your Fergus brute?"

I shake my head. "What am I supposed to say, that I am come from his future and know how all this plays out?"

Jim takes a sip of tea. "Suppose not. But he'd better get himself out of there. You'd better get yourself out of there, too."

I sit back in my chair. Jim's right, and I had better get back there to warn Fergus and Illa that they have to leave. I don't care if history needs them dead. I want them with me in the land of the living.

Jim says, "Your cat's drinking your tea."

I pick Winnie up, stroking her back until she purrs.

"Not to mention, there were monks there," I say, "which is another fact I didn't know. They're trying to get the queen on their side, leaving her Bibles, and another book called *Vita Colum* something by Adam somebody, something else I've never seen."

Jim jumps up and goes rummaging on his shelf. "Saint Columba's biography. *Vita Colum Cille* by Adomnán."

He hands me a copy of this selfsame book, only this one is bound in glossy paper, not cloth and hide like the one I saw. I take the book and hold it against my chest. "Sula doesn't like the monks."

Jim chuckles a little. "I'm sure she doesn't. I'm quite sure the monks don't like her, either."

I get up and look out the window. "In 735 that one standing stone out there belongs to a complete circle."

"Well," he says, placing his cup and saucer on the hearth, "it's a lot to swallow."

When I turn back, he smiles. I don't know whether

he believes me or not. I don't know whether I believe myself. It is a lot to swallow, and every bleeding psychiatrist who ever built on Freud is laughing his head off. But then, these were men dedicated to the march of reason. There is nothing reasonable here. I am strictly in nonreason territory.

"Fergus has a young daughter called Illa," I say.

Jim looks away. "Well, he'd better get her off Dunadd, too. It's not just the Picts you have to worry about. Don't forget the earthquake. You may not have much time."

I kneel by his chair and take his hand. "Thank you, Jim."

He taps my fingers, and at this moment I can tell he will believe anything I want him to believe. We finish our tea and stack the cups in their rattling saucers, stare at the uneaten biscuits.

I take myself home, still jumping around inside, walking meekly along the path that I recently walked with Sula. I stop by the circle of Standing Stones, at least by the one the Presbyterians left. More than a millennium separates the me who is here from the me with Fergus, and it shows on this stone with its grooves and the top that is no longer square. I lay my cheek against its lichened surface, as if it might talk to me and tell me all that it has seen and what the outcome is to be.

When it gets dark, I lie down and sleep heavily for a while. Somewhere in the night, I find myself awake, caught between my life with Fergus and this other life hurtling me along its corridor to a hospital bed. It is merciless in facing me with a choice I cannot make. From the doorway of the cottage, the field seems lit by a strange light. The outlines of hares move among the sleeping sheep, their feet in a sort of haze rising from the grass. Who's to say that this is where I belong, that this is any more real than my life in the heyday of the fort?

For the next few days I scribble on my notepads and take walks, but always in the background is the urgency to get back to Fergus. I worry that the events of ancient Dunadd are scurrying along without me, though I have no evidence that they do. I want to know what happens next in the story of Fergus and Maggie. But most of all, I need to get him out of Dunadd. I stand by the sink with my bottle of pills and know I can't keep taking them. I need to get back now.

But nothing happens. Only the rain. Each morning when I get up, the rain persists under low grey cloud. I go back to my thesis and read over my descriptions of the witches who were tried, how they were made to admit all manner of foolery about ice-cold devil penises and having their blood sucked and flying through the night on brooms. It strikes me then, with my reading glasses pushed onto the top of my head, my back hard against the chair, that maybe witches flying through the night is what I have been doing. What Sula is doing when she throws her stones onto the floor is flying through the night on her broomstick.

I don't see Jim for a couple of days, so I leave my pages and get into my car to find him at the museum. As I drive past his house, I pass a couple of rain-hardy travelers in sou'westers and knee-length raincoats, struggling against the wind. They wave at me as though I might rescue them from their decision, but I am only rescuing myself today.

I find him with a group of schoolchildren in the interactive displays. He throws a handful of grain into the top hole of the quern and shows them how to use the stick to turn one stone against the other to make flour.

When he's done, Jim takes me to the hanging gardens of the museum coffee shop for scones. Through the large window by our table, we can look out on a full circle of standing stones, and in the distance more. The rain runs rivulets down the glass and patters off the roof. But it is a well-lit and exotic place, this little eatery, at odds with the damp dark places it represents.

I look around at the other patrons, tourists or more permanent imports. The locals don't drink coffee and don't walk around museums even when full of artifacts fashioned by their ancestors. They still live in the dark and damp, and it's what they know, not that much different from the people in the village at the base of Dunadd. They have bigger houses, and some may have central heating, but they are still driven like the rain.

They are elemental, as people always were, until they became dispensable.

"You're quiet," Jim says. "Not like you."

I shake my head. "Actually, very like me. You're just used to seeing the excitable, far-fetched me." I laugh. "You don't know what to make of me, do you?"

He shrugs. After a while he says, "Now, I don't know much about physics. As I say, I never did go to the university. But I was reading in the dentist's office the other day that yon fellow Einstein had a few things to say on the subject of time." He taps his finger on the back of my hand. "It seems to me he was saying time is relative, just like you were telling me. So maybe you're not just crackers."

"I wish," I say, "that I could introduce you to Fergus's mother. She's the queen and quite good looking."

He tuts. "She'll not be looking for someone of my station."

I tap the back of his hand with my finger. "She would be lucky to have you. Any woman, say, over the age of fifty-five, would."

He tries not to look embarrassed. "Are you going to pay for these scones or what?"

I laugh, though I don't feel it. "Jim, if I did warn Fergus about what's to come, would it upset the outcome of history?"

He shrugs. "It might. We might end up coming

from *Pict*land instead of *Scot*land. Perhaps we would be speaking Pictish now instead of English."

"Then maybe he should stay."

"No. He should leave. What if he gets himself slaughtered?"

I can't imagine the thought of getting rid of Fergus is too displeasing to Jim, but he's being kind. I pay the waitress, counting out change without thinking about it.

I am not happy to wake the next morning and find myself in a white house, which is what Mrs. Gillies used to call any house with windows. I wake to find myself in the pitch-dark, but not the kind of dark out of which Fergus emerges. I wonder why I was ever taking pills in the first place if I can't induce a seizure when I need one.

I spend my time at the computer, surfing through theories about time and its workings. I find out that traveling through time is not actually ruled out by Einstein's theory of relativity. I learn that a group of scientists, who worried about having their very serious discipline being transformed into science fiction, got together to prove that time travel is not possible. They have been trying, but they still haven't been able to prove this.

I rub my eyes under my glasses, push my desk away from the computer, and take a walk to the top of Dunadd, looking up at the configuration of stars in their slow sweep of the sky. It strikes me that the constellation

Orion with his belt and tunic actually looks like Fergus in his cloak and belt.

But what if this is the end of traveling for me? What if this is as far as the story goes?

Off and on and without enthusiasm I push my cart around what passes for a supermarket in these parts: narrow aisles of enormous bottles of pop, whisky, and endless sliced bread. The checkout girls chatter to one another in an almost undecipherable accent but talk to me at a speed reserved for the mentally challenged. I come from Glasgow, after all. *Glaschu.*

I sit on my blue couch after a dinner of rarebit, with Winnie asleep on my lap, turning my bottle of pills over in my hand. *Do not exceed the stated dose.* No fear of that.

Jim knocks on the window and rescues me from my dilemma. I don't know why he has come. He doesn't say when he lets himself in.

"I'd offer you a cup of tea," I say, "but I can't move on account of the cat."

He sees to the kettle himself, but he is quiet.

He sits beside me with his tea, a little too close with the side of his thigh. I don't know what to make of him tonight. Winnie arches her back and stretches.

He picks the yellow bottle of pills from the table. "What are these?"

"They regulate seizures. I haven't been taking them, but it's still two weeks since my last one."

"Maggie," he says, "maybe you're not going to go back." He picks up my left hand. "I see you're not wearing your wedding ring anymore."

I take my hand back. If he only knew where my wedding ring really was.

"Look," he says, "I know I'm a bit older than yourself."

"Are you angling?" I ask.

He says, "A wee bit. But we get along like a house on fire, don't we? The way I see it: we're two lonely people who need not be lonely."

I take his cup. "I already have someone."

He leaves, and I feel lonelier than I have ever felt in my life. I am lying on my couch with Winnie on my chest when I first notice the heat in the soles of my feet. The world narrows down, first to the patterns on the wallpaper and then to the particles of wood that went into making it. The particles swirl, then spread apart until I am looking down into the atomic, subatomic world, and everything is getting heavy, and at last, at long last I am falling through.

19

My movement in time doesn't match up exactly this time, and I find myself back with Illa beside the fire on the floor of Fergus's house, waiting for him to return.

That was two weeks ago, and I am dying for his shape to fill the doorway, to get close to his smell of moss again, the drape of his hair between my fingers, the texture of the woven cloth on his arms. I want to place my cheek against his again and breathe against his ear, feel his chest expanding against mine.

Illa brings to me a little wooden bowl with a carved top. Inside is a handful of what look like old sixpences, but which on closer examination turn out to be Roman coins. I tip them into my palm, heady with the realization that not all that long ago, these pieces were being exchanged at the Roman marketplace. Perhaps Illa has stolen into her old home at times to play with this shiny booty. I tip them back into their little bowl, smiling at the pleasure Illa has found in sharing her secret with me.

I touch her arm and bid her come close. She nestles against my side, and perhaps being back in her old place permits her something I'm sure she wouldn't do in front of her father: a few tears make dirty paths down her cheeks. She doesn't resist when I pull her against me and the tears turn to sobs. Perhaps no one else has held her since her mother died. I play with her fingers like I used to play with Ellie's, tracing the spaces between hers. She laughs when I tickle the palm.

I study Illa's face, trying to extract from it Fergus's features to get at the mother. But there is not much of Fergus here, not even the hallmark nose. I am looking straight at my competition. She slips her head into my lap. From time to time I reach out and prop up the pyramid with more kindling. Almost automatically I start to sing the bedtime song that Ellie liked: *Golden slumbers kiss your eyes, / Smiles await you when you rise. / Sleep, pretty darling, do not cry, / And I will sing a lullaby.* We had it on a Beatles record, too, and Ellie preferred the jazzed-up version, but not when she was going to sleep. Illa's eyes close. She is after all just a baby. I have no idea how long I stay by the fire with the weight of my daughter's head against my thighs. It feels like all I ever wanted.

I notice the spot on the floor where Fergus and I slept the night before and, as I have so often over the last two weeks, replay that scene. The blanket he laid under me is tossed against the wall. I set Illa's head on the dirt for a moment while I reach for it, and fashion a makeshift pillow for her head with another from the pile of blankets that must have come from the wife.

I begin to wonder if Fergus aims to return to me tonight.

When I open the door, Marcus stumbles in. He has obviously been set guard, and thankfully so, because I am able to ask him for *aqua*, and when I do a little play illustrating the need to wash, he goes off in the direction of the spring and comes back in a while carrying water in a pitcher with designs of black horizontal and vertical lines.

I leave him again at the door, take a sip of the water, then get out of Illa's line of vision and strip off my undergarments, made up as they are now of stretchy knickers, string, and ancient leg wraps. The water is icy, but I am able to do a decent job, first with a splash to the face, and then, in the absence of a sponge, with a cupped hand to my nether regions. I dry off with the dusty corner of one of the blankets and feel ready, should Fergus ever come back.

Illa sleeps on, so I take the extra blankets outside,

past the sleeping guard, and shake them out. One on the bottom is a tapestry of a man and a woman, but not this woman. I think I had better keep that one out of sight. Back inside, a little way off from Illa, I set it on the floor as a pad and stretch out under the others. They smell of mold and years of sitting by themselves in an abandoned stone house.

Fergus doesn't come and doesn't come. I can't sleep because of wondering about Fergus and because I fear I am hoping for too much here. The fire burns to embers, and I begin to doze. When I come to, Fergus is standing over me, only I see as he moves into the light of the fire that it is not Fergus but Talorcan. I feel his body come close and kneel beside me; in the shimmer of light sent up by the flames I follow the pattern of the boar across his forehead. His fingers close around my arm.

I sit up and say his name. He says Ma-khee, and then he is earnest in what he has to tell me. "You have to come with me, Ma-khee. I will take you and Illa to Glashan where you will be safe."

I don't like his hand on my arm. I say, "I'm waiting for Fergus."

He shakes his head. "You will wait a long time."

I shake his hand off and scramble to my feet. "Why? Has something happened to him?"

"No," he says, "but he won't leave Dunadd, and the Picts won't spare him." He tries to take my hand. "Come with me and you will be safe." He slices his throat. "Let Fergus die here."

"*Cha tig,*" I say. I will not come.

He says again, "Come."

"*Cha tig.*"

He kisses my hand before he leaves, then steps across the sleeping Marcus, just as he must have done to get into the house in the first place. I go to the door and deliver a kick to the slave's backside.

I bring him inside the door and make him sit.

I say, "Stay," in a voice that gives him no choice. "I'm going to find Sula."

The path to the druidess's hut is hard to negotiate in the dark, and slippery from the rain. I choose to ignore the protocol for calling at her door and slip right inside. I duck under the first row of drying leaves, expecting to find her asleep, but finding her instead sitting on a stool by her fire, as though she had been waiting.

She gestures me over; I've been gone for two weeks, so I'm glad to take her hands in mine.

I kneel beside her. "I have something to tell you."

I have gone over a line or two in my head on the way up, but all those escape me when she fixes me with her gaze. I wish that I could lapse into English and that she would understand, but I have to struggle through with the Gaelic I know.

"Sula, I told you I was from Glasgow, which is true.

As a child I lived in Glasgow. As a wife and mother I lived there, too. I also said I came from Dunadd, and that is true, too, but I don't come from the Dunadd you know."

Sula nods. "You come from the ancestors."

It would be so much easier to explain if I did come from the ancestors. I shake my head. "I come from tomorrow."

Sula looks confused. "Tomorrow when the sun rises?"

"No," I say. "Tomorrow and tomorrow and tomorrow, from many generations into the future."

I don't know the Gaelic for "generations," so I say "families." But Sula is nodding, and she must have understood.

She opens my hand and smooths her whole hand over my palm. "My teacher told that there was only one time. This is why we see the dead on Samhain."

I touch her arm. "Sula, I know what is to happen at Dunadd. The Picts are going to take it back, and there will be an earthquake so big it will send the sea out to Crinan Bay."

Sula is nodding. "And the boar in the hillside?"

"That will come, too."

She grips my hand as though I'm a life raft. "These things have already come to pass in your time?"

I nod. "You have to tell Fergus. We have to take Illa and leave the fort soon."

Sula squats by the fire, running her hands over the flames. "I told Murdoch and then Fergus what I have seen in my stones, but Murdoch went off this morning to gather an army, and Fergus sees only his duty." She shakes her head. "Their father Ainbcellaig taught them well."

I go to the door, but I don't know where I'm going, so I come back again. "I have to get to Fergus, but he won't understand about this one time of your teacher, will he?"

Sula stands and fixes my gaze. "Only the druids have understood this." She steps closer. "In your time, are you a *ban-druidhe*?"

I shake my head. I am no druid, not like this witch of Dunadd before me, with her magic stones and her very unchristian notions. I go back to the door. "Do you know where I can find Fergus?"

She comes and opens the door before me and points into the cold night. "As a boy when he was troubled, he could always be found on the ledge below the cliff."

I turn and hug her, this little woman with her long grey ringlets and her tattooed fingers. I have the sense that our paths are about to diverge. There would be no point in telling her what's to become of her kind when the priests take over.

I hear her close the door behind me, as I walk out onto the crest of the hill under the stars. Everything seems so peaceful now, belying what must take place here on this fort in the coming years, the bloodshed, the crosses that will be brought in, the ruins that everything will fall into until people of my age are stumbling among them trying to find some inkling of what they were for.

I see him, but he doesn't see me, his face turned towards the faint line of light on the horizon. I drop beside him and take hold of his cold hand. He doesn't so much as turn his head.

I squeeze his hand. "Sula has told me that she sees you must leave."

He doesn't want to hold my hand now and wrestles it free. Like anyone who must face what they cannot, he pretends it isn't there.

"Fergus, you know I don't come from the dead, but I do come from a place very far from here, a place where the druids have become sick and women must see in their dreams what once only the druids saw. I need to tell you that I have seen the shaking of the fort, and that carving of the boar in the rock that Sula sees."

Fergus is silent. He wipes his face with both hands and breathes hard to gather himself, but he still won't look at me.

I get up to go. "If you won't leave, then at least let me take Illa."

He turns to look at me but says nothing. Somehow, without thinking it through, I have come to this decision. All I know is, this is the choice I didn't get to make with Ellie.

I climb back onto the hill and make the descent to the house where Illa lies. I guard my heart with feelings of anger at Fergus, with plans to find Talorcan in the morning.

When I open the door into the house, I find Illa where I left her, but Marcus is stretched out on the blankets where I was lying. It makes no difference; I don't anticipate sleeping.

When the door opens finally, my heart jumps; my breath is suddenly in a race. But the man in the doorway seems hesitant. It is Fergus, a heavy Fergus, one who would rather crouch by the fire instead of by me.

He turns to look at me. I notice him fingering my wedding ring tied to his belt. For the first time in too long, he smiles.

I move to him and touch his shoulder.

He says, "Is the sea going to go away soon?"

I nod. "I have seen it."

He stands and takes hold of my shoulders. "Gather what is here. Talorcan is below the fort waiting for us."

20

Fergus led Ma-khee and Illa over the gap in the fort wall. He had to leave without being seen by the guards at the gate in case his mother had warned them that he might flee. It was rough going in the semi-dark where there was no path through the bracken, especially carrying bundles. But Talorcan was there at the bottom as they had arranged, waiting with his cart and horses, in a short, fringed cape whose hood covered the tattoo on his forehead.

Fergus had spent half the night with Sula, trying to persuade her to leave with them, but she would not change her course. She was a Pict, after all, and too old for travel, she said. As Fergus threw their bundles onto the cart, he still felt a pang for stealing away like a coward, the very thing his father had schooled him not to be. Ainbcellaig had taught Fergus to fight, to use his fists and eventually his dirk. Murdoch had inherited their father's jeweled knife, taken from the Sassenachs long ago, but the dirk that Ainbcellaig had carried with him through the days Fergus carried now under his arm at the level of the heart. Still, their father knew better than Murdoch to listen to the druids. Fergus had turned it over a hundred times, but nothing could be done if Brighde had chosen to follow the monks.

Marcus came running down the hill after them. Fergus had bargained the slave's freedom for his help in getting to Glashan. The Picts over there had lived in loch dwellings since even before the arrival of Fergus's people from Erin. Talorcan had agreed to take him, because his wife came from these people, and he would be glad to get her out of Dunadd ahead of any fighting.

Talorcan helped his wife into the cart along with Iona, the strange daughter. Young as she was, this daughter was already thought of as a *ban-druidhe*. Fergus had thought to bring her along even if Talorcan had not—without Sula, they were going to need someone to speak on their behalf to the spirits.

Once Ma-khee and Illa were in, Fergus and Talorcan closed up the back and latched it. The sun was spreading a thin light over the eastern sky, the direction their road would take them. Fergus looked back up at this place of his childhood, the fort that still held his mother and the druidess. He stretched out his arms and leaned in against the rock. He had eaten nothing since the evening before, but he felt as though his stomach might try to empty itself.

Talorcan called to him. "Come. We must be out of sight before we lose the cover of dark."

But Fergus couldn't move. Talorcan came to him and placed his hand on his shoulder. "Hold on to what Sula says. Murdoch can alter the direction of the river for a while, but eventually the river runs to the sea. Not all the armies of the world can change that."

Fergus knew what Talorcan said was true. He glanced at Ma-khee and Illa huddled together in the cart and found again the resolve to leave. Still, this woman could never know what it cost him to ride away from Dunadd in the early morning, looking back at the outline of the hill against the lightening sky, not knowing if he would ever return.

The ride over to Glashan was going to take the better part of the day. Fergus had visited the loch before, but not since his marriage. He had told Illa about the wooden crannogs sitting out on the water and the people who still lived in them. Much of the leather that was used at Dunadd came from Glashan, for Glashan's tanners were well known. These days they even had a forge, and Oeric had traveled there a few times to teach the smith his craft.

Fergus caught his last sight of Dunadd as Talorcan fought to keep the horses on the trail through low hanging hazels. A moment later, in the shadow of the trees, the great rock was lost to him. He caught Ma-khee's eye, but not even she could understand the dagger in his chest. He sat heavily against the side of the cart, watching shadows play games over the other faces, expressionless faces, resolved, but unwilling, swaying like dolls with the movement of the cart.

Iona, the flaxen-haired daughter of Talorcan, stared at him with her pale eyes, unblinking. He heard Ma-khee ask Illa who she was.

Marcus answered in Latin. *"Aegyptius."*

"Ceard," said Illa. "Her name is Iona."

Iona didn't register the discussion going on about her but kept her eyes on Fergus. He knew the ways of druids often seemed strange to a common man, but it made him uncomfortable enough to leave his seat opposite her and sit with his daughter and Ma-khee.

"Is she Talorcan's daughter?" Ma-khee asked quietly.

Fergus shrugged. "So he tells me, but the woman Rhada is not her mother. She comes from the traveling people, the *Ceard.*"

The sun was beginning to penetrate through the forest and warm the travelers. Talorcan pulled his hood down. Marcus handed out bannocks from a cloth.

Ma-khee said, "How long can we hide at Glashan?"

"We will be safe for a while," Fergus said. "It will take Murdoch upwards of a month to assemble anything of an army, and then with the march north, another few weeks unless they meet Oengus's army already on their route south. The time of the darkest day will already have passed before there is any news."

At midday, Talorcan stopped the horses by a waterfall that splashed down beneath the path over stones and through the roots of oaks before emptying into a pool where beavers had built their home and the air was thick with garlic. It was a relief to their backsides to stop and walk under the spreading trees, and Marcus was ready with a dish of curd and more bannocks. Iona didn't stop to eat but climbed down to the pool, ignoring the beaver slapping his tail. She knelt on a slab by the waterfall and scooped water over her head.

After a while, Fergus and Ma-khee sat down against a mossy trunk, watching Illa pull garlic bulbs out of the wet ground into the apron of her dress. Fergus was hungry now and chewed on his bread round.

Ma-khee put her hand on his knee. "If Murdoch's army is defeated, will we have to keep moving?"

Fergus nodded. "But we won't have anyone to lead us. Talorcan will go no farther, and Marcus will be free and able to choose his own way, which, if he is wise, will not be with us, I fear."

He tossed his bannock and stood up. "Perhaps I

should leave you with Illa at Glashan. You are neither Scot nor Pict, and Illa looks enough like you she could pose as your daughter. It is I who needs to keep moving."

His words brought tears to the woman Ma-khee; he knelt beside her, stroking her hand.

She said, "Why do I always have to choose?"

Fergus didn't understand. He watched Ma-khee take Illa's hand and wander down to the pond. When they pulled their shoes off and dipped their feet in the water, he could see how pale Ma-khee's skin was, as though she had been locked in a cell all the years of her life. He asked himself if her other life would eventually come between them.

The women of Dunadd had never been protected in this way and in the past had ridden out to battle with the men. His own wife had done the same, until the monks came in trying to change their ways. Even far back in Erin, this had been the way. Wasn't it Scotta, mother of all Scotti, whose sons became the high kings of Erin, who fought and died in the Battle of Slieve Mish?

The children of Dunadd were taught early to be strong against the wind and cold. Their mothers bathed their feet in cold water even when snow lay on the ground. Many had been the night when Fergus had slept in the open with his brother or with the army before a battle, with nothing but the cloak and the hard ground. His father had taught him how to dip the blanket into the river, for the dampness brought its own strange warmth.

Fergus watched Ma-khee's foot recoil from the touch of the water. Quickly she slid her soft foot back into her boot. His heart grew heavy with the thought that she would never fit into a life that was not always easy, where the sun did not bring as much warmth as to other lands, where it was necessary to hold close to the earth and know her secrets.

Back on the road, the sun had climbed high, although Ma-khee kept tight within her blankets. Every so often, a deer bolted out of their path; birds scattered into the treetops. After the early start, Illa fell asleep against the woman's leg. It took until the sun was on its descent for the forest to thin and Loch Glashan to appear as a glint of silver in the distance. Over each new rise, the glint expanded until they could see the near end of the loch with its strange structures of straw and stick built out on the water, the long wooden walkway out across the water and the massive roof with stone weights hanging on ropes from the peak to hold the thatch down.

Illa jumped to her knees. "The crannogs!"

Ma-khee stood up in the cart to get a better look, and made the others laugh when she tumbled back into Fergus's lap.

Although this was not a large body of water, the far end of Loch Glashan disappeared out of view. Other crannogs populated this and the other side of the loch, but the one to which they were headed seemed to be the largest. Even before Talorcan brought the cart to a stop, Rhada's parents came running to greet them. From the shore, fishermen left their boats; from the small fields that ringed the loch, women and children came running. By the time they stepped down from the cart, there was a throng encircling the visitors. Ma-khee kept Illa within reach and tried to keep them close to Fergus, but he was still the prince from Dunadd, and the crowd carried him forward, separating him from them until he was led by the aged parents out of sight across the water to the round squat building sitting out on the loch.

Ma-khee made her way with Illa back to Talorcan, who was unhitching the horses.

Talorcan tied the horses, then took Illa's hand.

"Will you not come?" he asked Ma-khee. "There will be food in the crannog."

"I will," she said, but waited so that Talorcan knew that for now she must be alone. It wasn't late in the day, but the clouds were low and the hills beyond the water on the other side of the loch seemed to belong to the sky instead of the earth. The air was still except for the orange-beaked birds that flitted over the water with their shrill cry. Ma-khee walked by the shore among the abandoned curraghs. She picked up a stone and skipped it across the water.

Fergus found her there as it was getting dark. He was lighter now that he was here, now that he had enjoyed the food and the company. He stood close to her to see if she would move away. He didn't know why she had stayed by herself on the shore, whether or not she still wanted him. Standing by the edge of the loch, this strange place that echoed like the dead on the night of Samhain, he felt lonely. When she brushed her arm against his, he caught her hand and brought it to his mouth.

"Come and meet the parents of Rhada," he said. "They have been asking about you."

Ma-khee sighed. "What did you tell them?"

He squeezed her waist. "I told them you were a strange woman from the Far East."

Ma-khee smiled. "I am not from the Far East."

"I know." He squeezed her waist again. "You are from Glaschu, and yet there are many mistakes in your Gaelic."

She spread her hands over his cheeks and laid her lips on his, touching the edge of his teeth with her tongue. "How many mistakes?"

He kissed her back. "No mistakes."

Her laughter spread out across the water. "Why don't we sleep out here?"

Fergus smiled. "There are too many dangers for sleeping in the open this far from the sea. Do you have no wild beasts in that country you come from?"

She shook her head. "In Glasgow? No."

He tugged her hand. "We must go into the crannog now so that we will be given a place to sleep together."

He led her through the gate and along the walkway where the water grew deep beneath their feet. They passed Talorcan on his way back to the cart. He did not seem to share the others' feeling of relief at having arrived at the loch after their long journey. He would not look at Ma-khee and only grunted in Fergus's direction. Fergus glanced after him as he passed; he had never seen Talorcan like this.

As they came under the roof of the crannog, the woman looked all around in the dusky light—she must never have been in such a dwelling as this before with its reedy smell of thatch. Illa brought some of the speckled fish to Ma-khee, and Fergus brought her brose. She offered him part of her fish, but Fergus wasn't fond of the muddy taste that came with these fish from freshwater. At Dunadd they ate fish from time to time, but only from the sea and more often shellfish and eels, which could be trapped by the shore with a willow trap.

He kept Ma-khee close so that the others would know she was with him and so she would know he wanted her under the covers with him when the chatter died down. He longed for her now, as the night set in; her fingers along his thigh made it hard to concentrate on the singing that started up and for which these people were well known.

She wanted to walk by the loch, while others were leaving or lying down around the fire or in couples out of sight in a corner. Fergus marked their spot by the door from the entry room by laying down his shoulder belt and his father's dirk.

By the water's edge, he stood back and looked at Ma-khee's face upturned, as the moon lifted over the hills on the far side of the loch. Only the small sound of waves broke the stillness. She stooped and splashed her face with water, perhaps for some ritual among her own people. And then she clung to him as though he were a rock, as though she were afraid she might be washed away at any moment. Her fingers found the golden ring he had tied back onto his belt. He didn't know what that ring signified, but it had meant much to her, and so he kept it close and fingered it from time to time.

He took her hand, and they walked back along the path to the house, where Marcus had set their blankets by the door. They stepped over Talorcan, lying not far off. From all over the crannog came the sounds of sleeping, and the occasional bleat from one of the goats that had been brought in for the night. Only the mother of Rhada still stirred around the fire, saying her prayers for the evening blessing of the house. Fergus stopped to hear the words in Pictish he knew so well from childhood:

Deep peace I breathe into you
Deep peace, a soft white dove to you
Deep peace a quiet rain to you
Deep peace an ebbing wave to you.

In the silence that followed, Fergus called on Cailleach to watch over them, to stand under his world and
hold it up with her strong arms. With Cailleach's blessing, he lay down beside the woman, turned her gently,
and looked into her face, far into the eyes that searched
his face. He pulled the blanket over their heads so that
they lay facing each other in the dark, breathing in the
same air. He waited until her mouth came to his, until
her hands reached down around his buttocks and pulled
him in against her.

Under the cover he unwrapped her from her tunic,
slowly brought his own over his head. It was easy to let
her words *mo chridhe* turn him from his heavy thoughts
and simply fall into her as he had on occasion fallen into
the sea. She caught the hair at the nape of his neck and
kissed each of his eyelids, traced the line of his nose with
her fingertips. She did not look away from him, even
though Talorcan's eyes were open. She was eager for him,
moving with him, biting his shoulder so she would not be
heard.

Fergus slept with his arm about the woman, for it
was not easy to stay warm in these houses made of willow and mud. Only a good stone house half buried in the
earth could keep out the wind. He kept Ma-khee close,
because he had noticed how the old man of the crannog
had looked at her.

When Fergus awoke late on his belly, the woman was
gone. But he heard her in the next room talking by the

fire with the old woman. He strained to catch a glimpse, and what he saw made him smile: the old woman's hand was over Ma-khee's, teaching her how to turn the quern and grind the flour for bannocks. It was child's work, but the days of privilege at Dunadd were behind them. Ma-khee was going to have to learn these things that she must not have learned as a child of privilege in her parents' home. Fergus could hear Illa playing along the shore with the other children. She was going to have to learn, too.

Fergus folded his arms behind his head and lay back, staring at the apex of the roof with its abandoned nests. His thoughts quickly shifted to his brother rallying his troops, and to his mother at her fireside on Dunadd hill. He knew he could never leave Glashan until he knew she was safe.

He got up and squatted by his woman at the fire, noting the red grooves the stick had made in the palm of her hand. He wanted to pick it up and kiss the sore, but he didn't want to embarrass her in front of the matri-arch. He took a pot of bubbling oats from its stone shelf by the fire and looked about for milk. Some things from childhood didn't change, and this first meal of the day had always been Fergus's favorite.

Ma-khee looked up at him and smiled.

The old woman said, "The goat is tied to the gate if you've a mind for milk with your porridge."

Fergus hesitated. He had been used to milk coming

in a pitcher. He took Ma-khee by the hand and led her to the goat, hoping she would offer to help.

He waited, but Ma-khee was more intent on stroking the rough fur between the beast's strange staring eyes.

Fergus cleared his throat. "I've heard it said that milk flows more freely into a woman's hand. The hand of a man is too rough."

The woman smiled her disbelief. "This goat is a woman, and I'm sure she appreciates the hand of a man better."

Fergus smiled. She had confused the word for goat with the word for danger.

Ma-khee gave him a shove. "You don't know how to milk the goat."

He handed her the pot of oats and gestured for her to hold it low beneath the animal's rear legs, while he reached for a teat. His fingers around the dangling appendage felt more like grabbing a fellow man than grabbing a woman, and his instinct was to let go, but Ma-khee was watching, and there was much face to be lost here.

Fergus squeezed without producing a single drop.

"I know how to," he said, "but it has been some time."

Ma-khee laughed. "I think you don't know how."

"I do." He grabbed the teat again and squeezed harder. A single drop fell into the oats and was lost.

Fergus stood up. "Like all women she needs to be warmed up."

He stroked the goat's back. He tickled behind her ears, tapped gently the fur between her eyes, then tried again. There were two drops this time, but they quickly ran into the oats.

Fergus stood up. "It's clear this goat has already been emptied."

Ma-khee set the pot on the ground and took a teat in her hand. She squeezed and pulled, producing a jet into the oats that swirled around the edge of the pot and stayed there. Fergus was so excited he gave a shout that brought Illa running.

"What has happened?" Illa asked.

He placed his hand on her hair. "Nothing."

"Come," she said. "The grandfather is teaching me how to mend nets."

Illa tugged so hard, Fergus had no choice but to take the pot of oats and follow. He glanced back at Ma-khee, who was laughing as she walked over the walkway back into the crannog. The old man called to Fergus as they approached the shore. He was painting pitch onto the bottom of the curragh he used for fishing and for visiting the other crannogs on the loch. The smell of the hot tar made Fergus turn his face away. Illa went on with the net she was sewing with a bone awl.

The old man lowered his voice so that Illa couldn't hear. "There are young women here at Loch Glashan," he said, "who are in need of a man to provide children such as your Illa. We lost too many men in the fight with the Northumbrians, and now there are not enough to go round. I ask in the name of Cailleach, let me know which one you would like to go to first, and my wife will arrange it."

Fergus looked at his feet and then back at the old man. He knew this duty to Cailleach could be asked of a man, and his brother Murdoch would be glad to help in this way, but he feared his love for the woman Ma-khee would make him unable, like the goat he had just tried to milk.

"I will look," he said in a way that didn't convince the old man.

"What is this woman you have brought with you from Dunadd?" the old man asked. "Marcus says she is not your wife. Is she a slave? Could I take her if she likes men grayer in the face?"

Fergus shook his head. "You can't take her, old man. She will be my wife."

Now it had been said. Only he wasn't sure yet that the woman agreed with it. And then suddenly he saw her coming from the woods with Marcus, carrying willow wands, perhaps for a screen for their sleeping area in the crannog. The old woman came out of the crannog and called to Marcus to stand the willow in water or it would be no good for bending.

When Fergus went back into the house, Ma-khee was kneeling by the old woman, who was showing her how to make wattle with old willow wands that had already been soaked. But Ma-khee's hands were not tough enough for such work. She kept putting her fingers in her mouth, bringing storm clouds over the woman's face, making Marcus laugh, though, because of his low rank, he should be keeping those thoughts to himself.

Fergus pushed Marcus forward. "You're not free yet, and my lady needs help."

Ma-khee looked at him and smiled. Fergus longed for the warmth she was in the night, though her limbs were soft and hairless such as he had only ever seen on a child. It was no wonder she was always cold. Perhaps Iona might know of an herb to make hair grow on her body as it did on other women.

The women had settled Iona out in one of the field huts so she could be alone, and the wattle Ma-khee and Marcus were making was for her hut. Talorcan had nailed honeysuckle over the doorway to mark the place as sacred. Fergus intended to visit the girl and have her cast her stones.

As the days passed on to the time of the winter solstice, snow began to fall on Loch Glashan, as it rarely did in the sea air of Dunadd. Ma-khee stayed inside by the fire and worked the quern. She did not often go out with the other women. Fergus began to wonder if she was with child, the way she guarded herself.

He laid his hand on her belly and asked, *"Torrach?"* She shook her head. *"Chan e."*

But if she wasn't pregnant, then why had she not sat in the hut with Iona for her time of the month? He had noticed no blood in the time they had been at Glashan. He would like to have a son to teach in the way his father had taught him. Perhaps Sula had given Ma-khee herbs to close her womb as she had once done for Saraid. But Ma-khee was not young; perhaps it was already too late.

It pleased Fergus to get up in the morning and see his daughter running free along the shore with other children, or casting off with the old man on his fishing trips. Illa had found a small black cat and taken it for her own. Cats were kept by the grain houses in the village at Dunadd and about the bakehouse on the fort itself. But they were not black like this one. It paced along the shore while the girl was out on the water.

Fergus rowed along the shore in the old man's curragh to the tanner and brought back a satchel for the woman, who seemed well pleased by it. He bought a jerkin for himself, which kept in the heat of his body now with the days so cold, the snow on the ground coming and going like the thin ice on the edge of the loch. Soon it would be the shortest day, and they would need Iona to be one with Cailleach in the celebrations.

It was then the messenger came from Dunadd, a servant, not a slave, but a friend of Marcus, though he spoke no Latin. He spoke in Gaelic, and Fergus heard his words by the edge of the peaty water that had become his haunt. All was not well at the fort. Word had come of Murdoch's exploits in the north, his men running wild among the Pictish people, even before they had yet met with Oengus's army.

Brighde had holed herself up at the top of the fort with the monks and sent Sula down to live with her people. She had stationed guards all about, and no Pict was permitted to come or go. No traders were allowed in, and grain and salted meat were being rationed. With Talorcan gone, there was much scheming now among the Picts of the boar.

Fergus sent the messenger off to the crannog to eat. He sat on the shore, looking out across the water dotted with the thatch of crannog roofs like this one. Men were out in their curraghs fishing and sometimes sleeping. All was peaceful here; and yet, if they had to, would these people not sign their allegiance to King Oengus? How long before Radha's family could no longer keep them or risk their own throats? Fergus wanted to return to Dunadd and take his mother off the fort, by force if need be, but he knew she would call on her guards before she let him do that. And he would be able to persuade Sula even less, now that she was down among her own people.

Ma-khee sat down beside him and wrapped her arms about his knees. He took her hand between his and kissed the knuckles, rougher knuckles these days, as a woman's should be.

He spoke slowly so she might understand. "I don't know how long we will be safe here. It has begun, everything Sula foretold. It rips at my heart to keep pushing us farther from Dunadd, but I see no other course."

The woman seemed to understood. She picked up the black cat and laid it in her lap.

"I would have you with me," he said, "if you will abandon the place from which you came and seek a new life with Illa and me."

He set her hands in her lap, patted them, and patted the cat. She seemed to want to speak but couldn't find the words. He noticed a tear drop off the end of her nose.

"I no longer have a husband or daughter," she said. "But I do have a son."

She held on to his knees so that he could not get up. But she need not have feared, because he was pleased by the news. "Then I will take him for my own. Where is he?"

"He is at a school," she said.

"In the east?"

She nodded. "Yes, in the east."

He wrapped his arm about her shoulders to steady her. He worried suddenly that she might choose the son over him. "When we have fought and won or lost Dunadd, then I will take a few men and travel to bring your son to you. I make this promise to you, Ma-khee."

She didn't seem as pleased as she should have. She sighed. Fergus laid his lips against hers and felt her teeth with the tip of his tongue. He had seen pieces of gold in her mouth, surely a sign of high standing.

"I think in your land you are a queen," he said. "You have run from that royal house and fear you might yet be captured. For this reason you say nothing about this place you come from." He placed an imaginary crown on her head. "This is what I think."

She laughed and shook her head.

"Perhaps we should go there," he said, "take over that kingdom and live there in the east with your son."

She said nothing. They watched the black cat run around them with its back arched. Ma-khee reached for it and placed it against her cheek. She said the word *Winnie,* but he did not know this word, or if the woman's tears were happy or sad. She was strange to him, strange in the way things affected her, like the stone that Fergus MacErc had brought from Erin, the stone of Scotta. And then Fergus remembered the stone itself. How foolish not to have brought it, though the cart might not have borne such a weight. Now it would be left to the Picts, and they might not treat it so kindly, especially being a thing from Erin.

The woman left, and yet he couldn't keep his thoughts from her, couldn't help reaching for her in the nights that followed, tracing the contours of her spine even while she cried. He didn't understand what her tears were about, but he hoped she loved him and would shed tears over him, if things did not turn out in the end as he planned.

21

When I come round from sleep this time, Jim is holding my hand.

He says, "You've been out for an entire day, you know."

He says I've been crying in my sleep.

I sit up. "Where's Winnie?"

He laughs. "You're not going to believe this, but I found her coming down from the fort."

I sigh. This is all too much—first me, then the cat. I guess the witch hunters had this much right, that the black cats were in cahoots. I know from my research that the witch hunters tortured and strung up black cats just as they did the women, but no historical records hold their names dear.

Jim gets up. "Let me make you some porridge. I'll pour some milk on for extra strength."

After he's gone off to the kitchen, I lie back down. My tears run into my ears, picturing Fergus and that goat he was pretending to know how to milk. I succeeded only because I'd seen it on television once. Squeeze and pull, that's what they said, and no one was more surprised than me when it worked. No one, except Fergus. He made me jump the way he called out, and then every face was turned to him as though he had been bitten. I conjure over and over that quick embarrassed smile while I listen to Jim bubble up the oats and come back along the hall to the bedroom with my serving in a willow-patterned bowl.

He sits on the bed and hands it to me. "I heated the milk."

"You're a jewel," I say, and then smirk as though I might not have meant it.

He throws my pills between my knees. "I thought you might need those."

When I pick them up and turn them over in my hand, they rattle in their plastic container, little yellow pills with a very loud voice. Every time I open the top they shout out their question: Which life is it going to be, Maggie— this one with Graeme, with the thesis and a PhD, maybe a teaching job and a move to a house in Edinburgh, where life can begin again? Or do you want your life with Fergus on the run from the Picts, with Illa?

If I don't make my choice before this year is ended, I'll find myself on the operating table and then the choice will be made for me.

Jim looks at my desk strewn with papers and stacks of books. He notices the piles of paper on the floor. "How's the work going?"

I shrug. "I have the material. I just need to organize it. Problem is, it's hard to be impartial when you know a witch personally. Two witches now. Another one has appeared, only this one is young."

I look at the disbelief on Jim's face and say, "We don't have to talk about this if you don't want to."

I rifle in my bedside drawer and find a bag of jelly babies. Jim picks out a green one and bites the head off. "Don't hold back on my account."

"This new witch is really young. Her name is Iona, oddly enough."

"Not odd at all," he says. "The old Gaelic name for the island of Iona was *Eilean nan Draoidhean,* the Isle of the Druids."

I bite the head off a red jelly baby. "You're joking."

My mind runs back to the look on Sula's face when she heard the bells of the Christians. How else would she feel towards the Christians who had usurped her sacred isle?

"Marcus said that Iona was *Aegyptius.*"

"Gypsies," he says. "That's where we got the word. Today they're just Tinkers."

"She is like a ghost," I say. "Pale, otherworldly in a way that Sula wasn't."

Jim reaches for another jelly baby, a yellow one this time. He doesn't bother dismembering the thing, just throws the whole baby into his mouth.

He says, "*Wasn't?* What happened, did she die?"

I shake my head. "No, we've left Dunadd and moved to a place called Glashan. Have you ever heard of it?"

"Aye," he says, "it's not that far from here. Of course, they built a hydroelectric dam up there in the 1960s."

I smile, because this Loch Glashan is another thing I shouldn't have known about. "We're living in a crannog—a word, by the way, I didn't know until Illa told me."

He looks away, embarrassed, but I can see him smiling. Sooner or later the facts, I hope, are going to overwhelm him.

"If you like, I'll drive you over there," he says. "But the road is a bit iffy these days."

I am excited to go and start moving towards my coat. "My car would be better, then."

He laughs. "No, I'm not going in a car with you. It's not safe."

I stop by the door, put my hand on my hip, and tut. "Fine."

He pauses. "But there's no crannogs left there now, you know."

Of course there aren't, but it catches in my throat

nevertheless. Houses of sticks and mud weren't going to last to tell their stories like the buildings at Dunadd. I have lived with these people, and suddenly I have to see them as wisps of air, barely that, not even a mention in a history book.

It takes me a week to work up the courage to go, a week of nights alone in my springy modern bed. A whole seven days without one glimpse of Fergus. Winnie has become restless and wants to be out at night. Graeme calls and wants to know what I've been up to. Fergus is what I have been up to, but I can't tell him that. If I did, he would hear in my voice how much I want to get back there.

I sit in the car with Jim, waiting for him to turn on the ignition. My fingers are drumming on the dashboard.

He says, "We don't have to go out to Loch Glashan, you know."

I clear my throat. "No, I want to."

A week away from Christmas and the roads are a dull, grey brown and bowed down under sogging vegetation. Jim and I seem to be the only ones about, driving past houses smoking from their chimneys, Christmas trees lit in the windows. The skeleton trees manage only a few spindly fingers over the road.

"What do you do for Christmas?" I ask Jim.

He takes his eyes off the road only long enough to glance at me. He shrugs. "Remember, I do still have two daughters. I get asked down to England, to whichever one is not entertaining their mother." He's quiet for a minute. "I wouldn't want to see her, not now, not after all these years."

"Is she still with the bloke she ran away with?"

He laughs. "God, no. But she is married, which is more than I can say for myself."

I don't push it any further. Maybe he will go south for Christmas, and maybe I will be ringing in the bells with only Winnie for company. Graeme is to spend Christmas with his dad in Glasgow, where there'll be festive lights to ogle over, and Oliver's parents will provide Christmas hats, Yule log, brandy-lit plum pudding. We spent a dismal Christmas there last year with the vestiges of a marriage still hanging on like a broken tree ornament.

Along the rough forestry road to Glashan, Jim's low-hanging car dips with a splash into potholes. We are driving up through rows and rows of Scandinavian conifers, such a different look from the oak forests that covered the hills the last time I was here. Sight of the loch comes and goes until we pull over by the new dam. The slam of the car doors echoes off the water. It is not until I am standing by the imposing concrete wall that I realize it has been erected directly across the bay where our crannog once stood. Gone is the smell of smoke and dung; all the tilled fields have grown back in now. There's no shore here for a young girl to run along, no curraghs to cast from; just a wall of water and below it a great drop.

Across the loch, the outline of hills has not changed, nor has the peaty color of the water, but the place feels very empty. An oystercatcher flits across the water, casting its shrill intermittent call back at us.

I say, "There used to be wolves, you know. I can hear them at night."

We walk along the edge of the loch to a mound of stones just breaking the surface of the water. "They excavated it," says Jim, "and found a lot of leather and spatulas, a midden of course."

I think of the satchel Fergus brought for me from the tanner along the loch, finely crafted, light tan, with a running thread of darker leather through the flap, like something you'd find at a craft fair these days. I could walk around with that satchel at any Highland Games and no one would be any the wiser.

And then, of course, there would be traces of a midden, the ever-present midden. It's all I can do to stop myself objecting to them chucking stuff over the side of the crannog, but I am bringing my sense of a planet sinking under a burgeoning population to these people and their counterparts all over Europe barely making a mark. The forests back then haven't been cleared, the seas polluted; no holes in the ozone. Everything is ticking along as it should and will do for almost another thousand years.

It has started to rain, but we pull up our hoods and walk down to the gravelly shore where the tideless water is repeating itself in pointless waves. Some old man's curragh must have once sat upturned here with its hide skin catching a glare off the sun. I picture Fergus pulling up the curragh to this pile of stones in the water, which in my imagination is back to being its old crannog self. It hits me with a pang, as though that life back then were my real life and this projection into the future the phantasmagoria.

Jim fishes in his trouser pocket and hands me a hankie.

On the way back home, the wipers are having trouble keeping up with the downpour.

Jim asks, "Are you sure you'd never heard of Loch Glashan before?"

I shake my head.

"I wish," he says, "there were some way of testing it all, but I suppose there's not."

When we get back to Dunadd, he wants to drive me round to my cottage.

"No need," I say. "I won't melt."

I'm too distracted, too much still at Glashan to make small talk over tea and biscuits. I haven't been taking my pills, but so far it's been to no effect. I keep waking up in a room that does not smell smoky, keep pushing my spectacles onto the bridge of my nose and carrying on with my notes.

Winnie meets me on the way back to my cottage, jumping over puddles ahead of me. Here I am, a witch with my defamation of the church and my own black cat. I round the final wall of the farm and notice something bedraggled sitting on my doorstep. Winnie runs off to investigate, but I need not look any further to know my own child.

"What are you doing?" I call to him.

He smiles with rain running off his chin. "Having a shower, apparently."

I let him and his duffel bag in, strip off his duffel coat, and hang it over the bath. I bring him a towel and kiss his cheeks as I rub his hair dry.

"I thought you were going to Grandma and Grand-dad's for Christmas."

I stop rubbing to hear his answer.

He says, "But you were all alone."

I hold him to me, feel his breathing against my chest. "I was all alone. Thank you."

Looking like he has just come from a bath, his face shining and his hair standing straight up from his fore-head, he seems like my little Graeme again. I don't have a fire to sit him down beside, so I pull a tartan blanket off my bed and wrap it around him on the sofa, put a hot water bottle between his feet.

"Where's your ring?" he says.

Fergus has it. I look at my bare finger, still indented where the wedding band used to sit.

He looks at me with his father's grey eyes. "You and Dad aren't going to get back together again, are you?"

I shake my head and stroke his cheek for the little boy that he still is.

As I make him hot chocolate, he calls to me in the kitchen. "No Christmas tree either."

"Oh well," I say, "Our Little Lord Jesus was probably born in midsummer. You don't hold a census in bleak midwinter. Perhaps we could get a palm tree. It was the church that plunked him down in winter."

I hear him laugh. "Why did they?"

"To quash the winter solstice celebration. Why are you smiling?"

"Nothing," he says, tugging the blanket up around his shoulders. "It's just that you're getting awfully militant in your old age."

I run my hands through my hair. I suppose he's right.

He says, "It must be the witches that have done it to you."

I nod. "Must be."

I want to tell him that I've known a few witches in my time, but he wouldn't understand about "my time." I let it drop, bring him his hot chocolate, and sit with him, share his blanket. We watch his choice of television programs until we both fall asleep.

Graeme is at the table eating cornflakes the next morning when Jim makes an appearance at the window. He says he's come to say good-bye before he leaves on his trip down south for Christmas.

I wave him in, proud that the young man at his

breakfast is mine, that I can barely separate who he is from what I am myself.

"My son," I say, laying my hand on his head. "Graeme, this is my neighbor, Jim, local historian, big know-it-all."

Jim laughs. "Oh, thank you very much."

Graeme looks suspicious.

"Do you have a Christmas tree, Jim?" I ask.

It's a good excuse to send Graeme off to Jim's house and see what he makes of this newfound friend of mine.

"He fancies you, Mum," Graeme says when he comes back with a well-battered box under his arm. "Plastic tree," he says. "I suppose it will have to do."

Jim follows him in with another battered box of baubles. Graeme looks away when I kiss Jim's cheek goodbye. If my son only knew what I have been up to in the eighth century with the brother of the king of Dunadd.

"Mum?" Graeme says, as we watch Jim's car cross the bridge from our window. "Once you've had the operation, you won't be coming back to Dunadd, will you?"

He has to say "Mum?" again, because I hear it on the periphery of my awareness, while I try to get myself around the notion of not coming back to Dunadd.

He touches my shoulder. "Remember you said you might move to Edinburgh?"

I nod. "I did say that, didn't I?"

His face suddenly looks old and heavy. He says, "I suppose you've probably changed your mind."

He goes and sticks the star on the top of the tree.

"I haven't," I say. "Of course I haven't."

He hangs up another bauble. And then another, but his actions are mechanical, and he is taking no pleasure from this. I feel guilty for the disruption to the life of what should have been a normal boyhood. I am paralyzed by the window and don't know how to get to him. He kneels by the Christmas tree, but not in worship of our Lord Jesus.

When I see his shoulders begin to shake, I go to him, crouch down beside him, but I don't touch him.

"It's such an awful tree," he says, and tries to laugh.

But then he is in my arms, sobbing, and it is so unexpected, I feel as if I am being driven backwards off a cliff. I guess I retreated to my corner after Ellie died, just like he did. I abandon any hope of finding something to say, a question to ask that might stop this avalanche. He curls up against me, big boy that he is, in a retreat to the unblemished fetus. And he stays there, we stay there beside the bare Christmas tree with its star until he can look up and I can kiss his forehead and there is a sense of getting back home again.

That night, after we have said good night, I sneak to the door and quietly don my Wellies. With my hood pulled tight around my face, I walk along the path to Jim's house, then through the stile and up over the stone slabs towards the top of Dunadd. It's one of those oddly balmy winter's eves. The wind is set to push me right over, but it's a kind, nonbiting wind, and I can set my weight against it and walk, after a fashion.

Before I reach the top, I pass the place where the mason traced around Sula's foot.

I wonder what they would say at the museum if I announced that the foot at Dunadd belonged to a woman druid. We're too far gone along the man track even to allow the possibility. In the dark, I stoop and run my finger around the outline of the boar.

At the top, I find shelter in what is left of Sula's hut and picture her tattooed fingers working her herbs and remedies, her long grey curls bouncing off the small of her back. Herbs drying from the rafters, the smell of mold and dirt and stinky roots. I picture Fergus's outline in the doorway and feel his hands about my waist, lifting me against him.

At the edge of the cliff, I drop down to Fergus's little ledge. Instead of the moon, there's a muted light over the islands. I relax into my own solitude. For the couple of miles between the sea and me there is only the flat stretch of the Great Moss, *Moine Mhor*, boggy and sinking in its peat bath. All the birds are quiet on the Great Moss now; everything is still. No wolves or bears or beavers here anymore, only the faint bleat of a far-off sheep. The lights of an airplane blink high in the indigo sky, unaware of this solitude here on the hill in the grass.

I have no choice but to walk forward off this cliff in

the dark, this cliff of unknowing. The modern world has its answers: it knows how my brain functions and why it fails. It has noted the lesion on my right temporal lobe, and the answer is as easy as the way airplanes fly. It lays its silken path before me and bids me come. *Tiugainn comhla rium.*

But it has no answer for one value against another. In the scale of my hands I hold Graeme on one side and Fergus on the other. Ellie sits right between. How can I choose? It's not a function of the brain; it's not the way man comes to the table and divides his counters into piles. It's not a table at all, but a night sky and an ocean spread before you, and not the countable minutes of the clock, but a tunnel that starts and ends in this moment. You can't walk through any of those things, only hover.

I leave Fergus on his ledge looking out to the islands, his hair blowing back in the wind. I leave him there for now, but can I leave him forever? Graeme wants me to try, to let them tease out the parts of my brain that don't work for them. I will be saved from the best and the worst of myself. This, I decide in the dark of Dunadd, is what I must do. But not yet. I have to go back once more. Please, just one more time, let me go back to Fergus.

22

I find myself in the woods with Iona this last time picking hazels and acorns from the leafless trees and looking for something she calls *druidh lus*. I look around for Fergus but see only Marcus sauntering nearby with a dagger tied to the end of a long stick. As we push into an area of dense thicket, something large moves quickly away from our feet. Marcus lifts the goat's horn that has been hanging from his hip and calls back in the direction of the loch. Iona pays it no heed. She tugs on my sleeve and shows me how to pull a withered plant for its roots, which she snips off with her fingernails and drops into a jute pouch tied around her waist.

My day brightens when Fergus, the old man, and several others come running past us, some with spears, some with daggers like Marcus's, all with their tunics bouncing off their backsides. Iona doesn't look up, just keeps picking and dropping things into her bag. It's been so long since I saw Fergus, I have to hold my hand by my side to stop it from catching the hem of his tunic and pulling him back to me. I strain to catch a last glimpse of him, but Iona is calling; she has found her sacred plant growing halfway up an oak tree.

"Druidh lus," she says, pointing, with as much animation as I have yet seen come over her.

"Mistletoe," I say.

But Iona is not interested in learning English names. Her pale blue eyes pass over mine only fleetingly. I am glad that the tradition of mistletoe and Yule will carry forward all those years into my time. God only knows, and only if she is a pagan goddess, how far back it goes the other way.

Iona pries the plant off its oak host with a stick and lays it carefully on top of the greenery and white berries in her lap of nuts. Somehow I think the mistletoe of these people has more significance than a means to a kiss.

There's a clattering through the bushes, and then we jump back as a wild boar tears past us with the men in pursuit, all of them laughing for the distraction or just for the anticipation of hog meat tonight. I am half excited myself. The tradition of roast turkey at Christmas must come later.

All the way back to her hut, Iona holds on to my sleeve. When she closes the door, we are in almost complete darkness, except for small chinks in the mudded wattle where the light slips through. It takes a minute before I see her moving about near the floor. She takes a knife from her belt and starts carving off small pieces from a root.

She holds one out to me. *"Seo."*

I don't understand what I am being administered or why, but I take it despite my mother's warnings. The root is damp and slippery in my hand, bitter to the tongue.

The men are still out when I get back to the loch. I am still trying to break the fibrous root into pieces I can swallow. Before I go into the crannog, I spit it out on the ground and cover it with soil.

I find Illa sitting with the old woman at the back of the crannog, gutting small fish from a barrel. It is Illa's job to toss the entrails over the fence into the loch. When I lay my hand on her back, she turns to me. I wish Graeme could see that look in her eyes. I wish he could look in through this window and see that Ellie was not just one moment in time, but a kaleidoscope of moments. I go back through the crannog to let the cat in at the gate, straining past the lap of loch waves to the noises of the now distant hunt. Illa comes running with a handful of fish guts, which Winnie wastes no time clearing up.

The old woman takes my offering of hazelnuts and shows me how to set them around the fire to roast. I see now the holly strung around the wattle, another tradition that will not be lost. I wish Graeme could be here on this eve of winter solstice, for this is a better Christmas than at my house.

When it begins to grow dark, I worry for the safety of the hunters. I wonder about Iona, who rarely joins us in the crannog; I wonder whom she plans to trap beneath her mistletoe. With Fergus gone so long, I hope it is not him.

Eventually, the men come back with much noise and excitement, telling the tale of the hunt with large gestures and much cheering. They gut the boar on the beach, bringing in the dogs for their evening meal, and then string the beast from the rafters with a bucket beneath its noisy dripping. The old woman chants, walking clockwise about it, saying prayers of thanks for a successful hunt. Outside, a steady snow is dropping into the loch.

I am glad to slide in next to Fergus when we all lie down on this Christmas Eve without the Christ. The church Christ wouldn't approve of what we are about to do, though I imagine that radical Israelite knew where he came from and didn't care. Oh Lord, I am trying not to care either. Fergus taps my nose to draw me back from my distraction. Our noses touch and then our lips. I run my finger along the ridge of his eyebrows and kiss each eyelid. When he reaches under my wraps, the earth falls away. A bit like time travel, I suppose.

In the morning when I awake, Fergus is still sleeping. I slip out from under his arm, wrap my shawl tightly about me, and go out to find Winnie along the shore. The hills across the water are quietly snowed under on this Christmas morning, and I feel fresh, too, like the loch with the first touch of dawn. The snow is beginning to clear, but I see no cat, just groups of men tending a fire in a crater they must have dug before I awakened. Illa and some other children are running along the path gathering kindling. None of them are wearing shoes on their poor red feet.

Back at the fire in the crannog, the old lady is saying her morning prayers, stirring the embers to life. Most everyone else is awake, pointing and laughing at the slumbering brother of a king. They glance at me, and I am proud to be the source of his exhaustion. I smile to let them see I know what they're on about, making them laugh more.

This Christmas Day is abuzz, everything is, just like it would be around a Christmas tree with children and stockings and a turkey in the oven. Radha is letting the hog down from its hook. The beast weighs so much she must set her whole weight against it to stop it from slipping. I offer to help, but she waves me away, then lets it drop to the floor. What she wants me to do is carry the thing out to the fire. I suppose it needs a hoist of some kind onto my shoulders, but unlike modern pigs, this beast is massively prickly. I don't think I have much time to decide how to go about this before the others will start to wonder what's wrong with me.

Dragging gets me nowhere fast; the hog feels stuck to the floor. The women are looking at me in disbelief. I look away when Fergus appears, but he comes over and lifts the forelegs, gesturing with his head for me to get on the other end, so we can sling it along to the gate and then out along the walkway to the pit, where its fiery end awaits. Fergus's eyes glance off mine a few times. I don't want him to know how my shoulders ache from the effort. Talorcan joins us to help the hog down into the embers, and then the children form a circle to pile earth on top.

All morning, we're making custard and bannocks, gathering more roots from the fields where the soil is hard and unwilling to yield its crop. The plants are too withered in the cold to tell what type of roots we are gathering. All I know is, they are not carrots.

The smell of slow-roasting pig escapes from its earth oven in little gasps of steam as people begin flocking in from roundabouts, some on foot, most in curraghs from other parts of the loch. The last to arrive are the musicians, who, in their colorful matching hats, seem to be something of a troupe.

Iona spends the day working alongside us. When Radha deems we will need more bread, I am set to grinding the grits of some kind of wheat, greyer than the one I know, together with oats and tiny balls of millet and the odd acorn. The stone quern I turned at the museum was not that different from this one; the smooth wooden handle feels warm in my palm. But it is not long before it is wearing a groove in my skin, and then blisters form that I have to let pop as I carry on. The quern yields little flour for the effort.

The bannock dough is heavy and unleavened, mixed with a drop of sour milk. We sit around the fire patting balls of it out flat between our palms while the large bannock stone, *clach bannach,* heats over the embers. The old woman works her hands over it, offering words of thanks, then spits onto it to test its heat. She arranges batches of the rounds across the stone, and they give off a hot floury and nutty smell. It is my job to flip them over once they have browned on the underside. This is not so very different from watching Mrs. Gillies roll out and cook girdle scones on the top of her range.

The morning mist on the water clears and burns off the overcast sky. Children are running about their tasks in the sun, not a hot sun but enough to melt the snow and become a source of warmth a child could lift its freezing toes against. I go out to suggest it to Illa, but her feet are covered in ash from the pit, and she is using the fish bucket to catch what must be some kind of bloated animal innard. I stand by the gate and smile at these children, far rougher than their descendants will be, but children will always be willing to chase a ball around.

Somewhere between one child kicking the ball and another catching it, there's a rumble. I look off to the far hills for black clouds, but the sky is quite clear. Then a louder rumble tilts the world for just a few seconds, and I have to stagger to keep my balance. I notice Illa fall against the edge of her empty bucket. But she gets up and keeps trying to capture the ball in it. Surely this can't be the famous earthquake. No one else pays it much attention.

I almost forget about it, as dusk brings a stillness to the farthest reaches of the loch. I want to check to see that the pig is not burning, but I suppose I am the newcomer here, and the men seem to have the bake in hand. I sit with the other women wrapping holly about orange candles that we hang on the wattle walls, making this night feel like any Christmas from my childhood.

When it is dark and everyone is gathered, the singing begins, sort of out of nowhere. There is no conductor tapping his stand to draw everyone in on the same note, same beat, but somehow they manage it. We are gathered in a circle that fills the room under the high thatched roof, and the voices fill the quiet that had settled on the loch, move into the space between every person, loud singing, like the Welsh will be famous for. I hum along to its strange melody, sure that no one can hear me. It's a song of many verses, no doubt chronicling some saga of the past. There is something magical in the strange guttural sounds of Pictish.

Without warning, suddenly the singing stops. The circle parts, and Iona walks in ceremoniously, dressed in a bright red woven robe, trailing ivy and wearing in her hair the mistletoe we gathered. As the circle closes behind her, she throws spices and wood shavings into the flames. They crackle and have a short life of their own, sputtering and fire flying before they expire in the dark. As the fragrant smoke drifts out from around the edge of the fire, the people waft it towards their heads.

When they lift their hands to the east, Iona begins her chant. And then the direction changes—all hands and bodies turn to face the west. To each direction she has a prayer and then up towards the roof of the crannog the people bend back, offering their hands. The smoke smells sweet, and I feel a little dizzy as I strain my head back and notice deserted birds' nests at the apex of the thatch.

Lastly they all crouch and splay their hands flat on the floor, their eyes closed as though they were at a prayer meeting. Iona is chanting, staring straight ahead. She's talking to the fire, spreading her arms out wide. I pick out the words as she repeats them: *Brigid Queen of Fire, behold your child this night as I honor thee and thy realm. I stand humble before thee, asking for thy blessing and favor through the remaining dark months. Lift now the veil between the worlds that I may come to you.*

Afterwards we stand out in the courtyard of the

crannog bounded by wattle fencing, and look up at the moon that is not full but crescent-shaped and weaves in and out of grey clouds as though in a dance. Iona is still moving trancelike, up and down on her toes, saying her prayers to this sliver moon. She spins until she drops, her veils blurring behind her, then lies shaking on the ground.

As though the show is over, everyone turns and leaves Iona to herself. The musicians strike up inside where the old man is pulling the cooked boar apart. Only I hold back, hovering over Iona, trying not to give in to the reflex to help her to her feet. Nobody else seems to feel the need to.

I go in eventually, because Illa tugs at my sleeve. We squat by the fire, waiting for the meat to make its way around the chain of hands. Not exactly sanitary, I think, but when I look down at my own hands, I see they are no cleaner than anyone else's. I pass the meat that is put in my hands until the people at the end of the circle take and eat of this flesh and this blood shed for us.

I take a strip of meat and tuck it inside a bannock. Illa finds this funny, but follows suit, perhaps her first-ever sandwich. The bread has a nutty flavor and complements the meat, which is not tough and must have been a young member of its family. The boiled root we gathered earlier stands off to the side of the fire in an earthenware pot. I try one with my sandwich and find it oddly pungent, something like parsnip. Great stone jars of something that I would wager is heather ale are brought out, into which cups are dipped. One eventually reaches me, a stronger ale than before, but I take the communion drink, and then take some more. Everyone is coming under the influence of the *fraoch*, drinking more, and the singing is loud and drives any thought out of my head. I drink until the clear flame of the candles blurs, and I am not entirely sure anymore where or in what era I belong. For now I am where I should be.

When Iona wanders in, she sits by the fire, and the people take turns touching her head. I line up and place my hand on her flaxen hair under the wreath of ivy and mistletoe. I don't know what she is supposed to be giving off, but whatever it is, I could use it. I sit back down and lapse into a kind of drowse.

Then suddenly out of nowhere, a man in a stag headdress bursts into the circle, startling his audience and rousing everyone to their knees. It takes me a moment to see through the smoke and din that the stag is Fergus. A fit of giggles wants to take me over, as he paws the ground with his shoe and dances in towards Iona and back. I see to my astonishment that his steps resemble those of what will become known as the Highland Fling. In and out, then back in towards her. I get the feeling that this dance is more sexual in nature than the Highland Fling, and my impulse to laugh flees.

There's no singing now, just a lot of jeering and calling. Iona seems fairly oblivious—her head back, her eyes shut. Every time Fergus dances towards her, the women shout, trying to grab him, sliding their fingers up around his crotch and backside while the men whistle and jeer. I have to fight myself not to run out or jump up and keep the other women off him. I shrink back against the wall, looking for Illa, but she is occupied with the other children and doesn't appear moved by the sight of her father dancing around the women in what is clearly a heightened state of excitement.

One more approach, then Fergus is on his hands and knees swooping over Iona, and I can tell from his face what is going on in the folds of his leg wraps. Down and up without ever touching her. I find my feet and I start to move towards the door. But then he stops moving and is standing tall, adjusting his antler headgear and dancing within the circle with the women still reaching for him. He dances once around the outside of the circle, and then dashes out through the open door to much calling and whistling.

I go for more ale and don't find myself until the morning. The first thing I register is that Fergus is not beside me. My mind flies back to all I witnessed the night before, and it makes no more sense now than it did then. Iona is Fergus's niece, for God's sake, though she certainly wasn't acting like a niece last night. Perhaps it was all only a passion play, but I feel oddly betrayed by it.

At any rate, no one saw fit to stay sober enough last

night to tend the fire, so it is a pitiful specimen, being poked and rearranged by Illa to no great effect.

I get up and nudge her aside. "Illa, will you bring bigger sticks?"

She goes off as Fergus comes towards me wrapped in a blanket stitched over a deer pelt. The gaiety of last night has evidently worn off him, because his face is serious as he moves about, gathering things, several daggers, I see, that he slips into a fold of cloth.

"*Cait am bheil thu dol?*" I ask him. Where are you going?

He says, "Dunadd."

"*Carson?*" Why?

Talorcan comes in dressed very much like Fergus. He sees the question in my eyes and moves out of range for answering. When they leave together, I follow after them, but Fergus walks back to me and holds me by the upper arms. "I'm going to Dunadd to get the queen. You must stay here with Illa. I have asked Iona to teach you what she knows about healing arts."

In spite of last night, I take his head in my hands and kiss that crooked nose. "Will you come back?"

But he's all business this morning and doesn't answer. He and Talorcan start saddling the horses. But I can't leave.

He takes me by the arm and leads me towards the water. "You have to be strong, Ma-khee. You must learn to be like Iona."

I shake his hand off my arm. "I can tell you like Iona."

He watches me walk away, before he goes back to Talorcan packing the horses with bundles of food and daggers.

He nods farewell to me as I stand far off by the crannog door. I watch them ride away, all knotted up in my throat because I don't know if this might mean the last of Fergus for me. I find Winnie and curl with her at the fire. I hate to know so little of what is going on. I don't understand these people and what they do, what that fondling ceremony last night could have meant.

Illa comes back in with a hefty load of sticks. I want to pull her close beside my cat and me, but I content myself with watching her move: the way she squats and decides which stick to put where, the intent look on her face. She seems unperturbed by her father's sudden absence.

But what if Fergus has no plans for coming back? What if he was only ever here for a while to settle us out of danger, and now he's returning to whatever it was he couldn't risk our being around? It suddenly occurs to me that with winter solstice behind us, the new year might already have begun, and that as far as the ancient calendar goes, we are already in 736. If the Picts are about to take over Dunadd, Fergus could be in real danger. I know his people are not going to come out of this conflict well.

But history is moot on the point of Fergus, son of Brighde. No one knows what happens to Murdoch and his war, except that this year, still a week off on the Gregorian calendar, marks his last.

I sit on the covers Fergus and I have slept under, smudging tears on my already dirty face, unwilling to get moving this morning. But the old woman needs my help dragging water in for boiling breakfast oats. She shows me how to drop the leather bucket over the side of the crannog wall where the fence has been cut shorter for such things. The rope attached to the bucket is coarse and rips at my hands, and a bucket of water is no small weight to pull up on a rope; by the time I get it on board, half the water has splashed out. I want to cry again, for Fergus being gone and for my being no use here. The women laugh, not to be rude, but I must be a strange thing to those who carry large bundles of everything and think nothing of it. Even the old woman carries more weight than herself in firewood. I would laugh, too, except that I've never been that good at laughing at myself. Especially not today, because of that spot on the path from which Fergus just disappeared, perhaps forever.

Close to dusk, when I am still hoping for the sound of hooves on the hard ground, Illa comes in and sinks down by the fire. I notice straightaway her flushed face and bring a blanket for her to lie on. She doesn't want to move. Her hands feel hot.

I come close to her ear. "What's the matter?"

She lifts the edge of her tunic to show me a gash on her thigh that has become swollen and infected. I remember now her fall against the bucket. I'd even forgotten about the rumble that caused it. The old woman comes over and shakes her head.

She pats my back. "Take her to Iona."

As I begin to rush off to fetch the witch, the old woman takes my arm and gestures for me to carry the girl there myself. All a panic, because I have enough medical knowledge to know the danger here but not enough for a remedy, I thrust my arms under her and lift. She is solid, no small weight, but the urgency makes me move fast along to the gate, where one of the other children lets me through. I move heavily through the trees to the hut where Iona lives.

I'm surprised when Marcus opens the door to my call. It is smoky and dim inside, but I can make out Iona by the far wall and allow myself a fleeting moment of jealousy. But I lose it fast enough and set Illa on the floor by the fire.

I lift her tunic to expose the gash. "Iona, you have to help her."

Iona gives the wound a passing glance. She comes over and blows into it, chanting her prayers. She has not been here long enough to have collected Sula's array of jars, but on pieces of leather by the wall there are small piles of what look like pressed flowers, roots of various sizes, and finely chopped bark. She reaches for a flattened piece of yarrow and crumples it into a hollowed-out stone, which serves as mortar to the pestle she grinds into the hollow, adding what look like dried hops. She pours water from a stone jar into a cup and sets the whole concoction by the fire to warm, then goes about making a poultice.

She reaches for a root, which she grinds in the mortar until there is a small amount of juice to pour into her palm. To make the paste, she spits as Sula did and mixes with her forefinger until she has something she can spread across the swollen cut. I lift Illa's hand and put my lips to the dirty skin. I wasn't there to save the first Ellie, but I promise myself I will keep this child from harm.

Illa's forehead still radiates heat, and I think the infection must be bad to have caused this level of fever. Before long, the cup of flowers and bark begins to simmer and I draw it against Illa's lips. Though she pulls back against the acrid taste, I bring her lips again to the cup. I am the mother here.

She lies down and curls up, so that I can have no thought of moving her again. But neither am I going to leave her. I did that once before.

Iona goes out with Marcus, and they stay away much too long, because I am in a panic alone with the sick girl. My thoughts wander back to the ceremony last night, but I can't think of that now. The book of childhood ailments on my shelf at home in Glasgow tells me that the infection can get into the bone or turn to gangrene and then to septicemia. Iona comes back in with a ring of some kind of woven plant, chanting while she sets it all about Illa. But my confidence in Iona is not such at this moment that I can believe in garlands of herbs or mere words.

I turn to Marcus. "Ride out and fetch Fergus!"

Marcus looks nonplussed. Only now do I remember Fergus's words for me to stay strong, almost as though he knew something was going to demand it. Marcus stays put, so I sit by the wall and close my eyes. Illa sleeps, but I don't. I just sit with my eyes open, listening to Iona's murmurings, hanging somewhere people go in the middle of endurance, a floating island of semi-detachment.

In fact, I float all the way out of the eighth century back to my pillowcase and the photographs of my children on my bedside table. The window is dark, hit intermittently by the splash of a large raindrop. I close my eyes and try to push myself back. This is the second daughter I wasn't there for. Perhaps now there will be no time to get back and find out if she survives?

23

Fergus loved the woman, though she sometimes seemed weak as though she had an illness. It nagged at him that she had stood back from the circle last night at the solstice ceremony, ill at ease with his role as the horned god. She should have been proud, but perhaps she did not understand that he was not himself in the ritual, and the hands of the women on him were only the hands of Cailleach the goddess? Surely every people had such ceremonies at the midpoint of winter.

When he was getting ready to leave that morning, he was pleased to see her, but he did not want to touch her in case she should hold him back. He had to get to Dunadd. Even before the messenger came, his mother had been in his thoughts. But now that he knew she was trapped in the fort, he knew he had no choice but to return.

He had consulted Iona, who was too young to be re-lied upon entirely, but she had cast her stones and they had seemed to say he should go. He had asked that in his absence she take Ma-khee into the woods to teach her of the plants that grew there. If Fergus's people from Erin were no longer going to rule, then they were going to have to learn these ways.

Still, he longed for her, as he moved about the cran-nog in the early morning, folding dirks into a cloth wrap and glancing at her as she slept. He didn't know what he was going to find at Dunadd, but in case of trouble, a man had no better friend than his dirk.

He didn't like to leave Ma-khee, so he turned his horse away quickly and followed after Talorcan through the trees until the smell of the cooked pig and the smoke of the fire was lost to the air. It was good to put it behind him; there was work to be done.

Talorcan rode up behind him and slapped his back. "The woman Ma-khee has you slumped over like an old man. I saw she was not pleased by your dance last night."

Fergus's smile escaped him when he thought of how she had shaken his hand from her arm.

"When it is time for the spring festival," Talorcan said, "how will she feel then?"

Fergus knew Talorcan was right. During winter, Cail-leach took on the aspect of the crone, and so the stag god could only pretend copulation with her. But at Beltane, when Cailleach appeared in all her youth, there would not just be prayers of thanks, but ritual copulation with the druidess. That was why Iona had to be kept away from men from day to day; she was being saved for the Beltane ceremony. The success of the summer cull and harvest would depend upon it. Being her father, Talorcan would not be able to play the role of the stag god, and so it would probably fall on Fergus to do the rites. Murdoch always played the stag at Dunadd, and for this Fergus was glad, for though he loved Sula, she was not young and pleasing in that way. Still, it was the way of things, nothing to hide from. The druidess would lie back in her ivy and her mistletoe, and the people would chant as they circled the goddess and the stag god celebrating new life to come.

Wives accepted this, but Fergus could tell Ma-khee would not. For at least this reason, it would be better for them to be gone from Loch Glashan before Beltane.

"Why does this woman disturb you?" Talorcan asked. "And why is she not bursting out at the front already?"

Fergus wondered the same thing. He had asked Iona to give her herbs for childbearing. But like any man, he could only wait for the goddess to smile on him. Even during last night's celebration, as he watched Ma-khee across the fire from him, he wanted to take her out under the stars, even when it was time for Iona to come in wearing the druid's weed and speak to the queen of fire.

On a night such as the Day of the Dead, such a

prayer would be dangerous, but the dead were in their winter sleep now; even his wife Saraid no longer slipped into his thoughts. When he wanted a woman these days his thoughts turned to Ma-khee.

"If they cut me down at Dunadd," Fergus said to Talorcan, "you must take care of Ma-khee."

Talorcan nodded.

"They will not cut you down," Fergus said, "because you share the same blood. But they will not spare me."

Talorcan laughed uneasily. "Nor me, brother, for joining with you."

"But is it not your right to be king of Picts, because your mother was of the royal line?"

"There are others who would claim that right, others who have not played traitor."

Fergus sighed. "Then I should not have brought you. I should have chosen another man."

"You could have chosen Marcus, the Roman." Talorcan began to laugh.

Fergus couldn't help but smile, too. "When a man's *clachan* are cut from him, the fire runs out through the hole."

"Yes, he is best left among the bards and musicians. But there are others. Gavin the Hairy."

Fergus shook his head. "Much hair, little brain. A soldier would do better with a bear than a man with no cunning."

Already, one day after the shortest day, the light

would stretch further, though not by much. Fergus's plan was to hobble the horses, then steal into the village quietly and hide until dark if things seemed hostile. But on this slow walk through the oak forest, there was only his time with Talorcan, the trees and the sun reaching playful hands onto their shoulders.

"I will not return to Glashan with you," Talorcan said, almost in a whisper, as they drew close to Dunadd.

Fergus pulled his horse to a stop and turned to see what he could read in his brother-in-law's eyes.

Talorcan looked away. "Iona told me. She saw only one horse and rider coming back along this trail."

Fergus counted Talorcan a friend and brother; he could not bear to lose him. "Perhaps it will be you, not me, on that horse."

Talorcan shook his head. "I am going to stay."

Fergus kicked his horse forward. He didn't know how to take what Talorcan had said. Was it merely a way of changing allegiance?

"But what about Radha?" Fergus called back.

"It will be best for Radha to stay with her parents. Iona will need her. She will be safe once you have taken your daughter and left Glashan."

"Taken my daughter and my woman," said Fergus.

Talorcan shook his head. "You have seen the way she is. You will put yourselves in danger with her along."

Fergus knew what Talorcan said was true, but if he made it back to Glashan, he would not leave again without Ma-khee. They would have to stay there until she had gained some strength, learned their ways better. But he kept quiet. He felt suspicious now, as though Talorcan might be up to something.

They came out of the forest just north of Dunadd at the first group of standing stones in the Valley of Stones. This far, no lookout would see them, and here they tied the horses and left them to graze. The hazel groves that edged the forest provided good cover as they weaved along with the fort in sight, such a pleasing vista for Fergus, and for a moment he had to stop to rid himself of the longing for the days when his father was alive.

Talorcan placed his hand on Fergus's shoulder. "Do you see anything?"

Fergus shook his head. "Only ghosts."

Talorcan overtook him. "Let the dead sleep. Today we have work to do in the land of the living."

They moved along the route Fergus had followed after his last journey, when he had returned on the Day of the Dead. Soon they came to the place where his horse had bolted. The village was well in sight now, and nothing looked different: still the children running, still the bleating of goats and the smoke trailing up from the thatched roofs. The fort itself looked the same, from here just a run of tall stone walls on the hillside.

Fergus kept his voice quiet. "Do you think it will be safe to slip into your house?"

Talorcan shook his head. "The women who bore my children will almost certainly have gone to live there."

"But you can trust them."

"I can't be sure. Some of these women have husbands now." Talorcan started moving. "Come."

When Fergus hesitated, Talorcan reached for his sleeve and tugged. "We'll go to one of the elderly. Alban, the man who taught me archery."

Fergus followed. Talorcan's father, and Saraid's, too, had died young, and other men had had to step in to do the work of a father. Fergus's own father had shown him how to shoot an arrow straight to its target, and for that he was grateful. But Talorcan could hit a target blindfold. His teacher, Alban, had been a good one.

The hut was small and closer to the tilling field than Talorcan's own house. They kept low, hoping no one would see, but there was no escaping the children who ran up to them. Many of them knew Talorcan; a few, Fergus knew by the look, recognized him as father. But they did not follow into the hut of Alban, and Fergus soon saw why. The old man sat by himself in the dark, and his eyes, when a cast of light from the door lit him, were opaque and dead. He sat in easy reach of his fire, a bundle of sticks close to his right hand.

Alban recognized Talorcan by the hand; it alarmed Fergus that the old man knew to turn his voice to a whisper.

The old man spoke in Pictish. "Who's that with you?"

Talorcan let the old man's hand drop back into his lap. "Fergus, son of Brighde."

"You should take him away from here," the old man said. "His brother's army has been smashed at Brechin."

Fergus stepped forward and asked his question in Pictish. "Is Murdoch alive or dead?"

The old man shook his head. "I have heard no reports, only that there were many dead. The rest fled."

It was the worst news Fergus could have hoped for. He quieted himself with the thought that Murdoch might have escaped, that even this King Oengus would be loath to put another king to death. Almost in concert with these thoughts, the ground rumbled beneath them, sending the old man's blind eyes searching. Talorcan covered the distance between himself and Alban and grabbed his teacher's hand.

Fergus glanced at Talorcan after the short quake had passed. "What is it?"

"It has happened before," said Alban, "in the time of my grandfather. It is a warning from Cailleach of changes to come."

Fergus made towards the door. "I must go to my mother."

The old man let go of Talorcan's hand and stretched his arm out to stop Fergus. "After the news came about your brother and his army, the druids of your people escaped with your mother and the Great Stone towards the eastern sea, bound for Scone. Your people no longer rule Dunadd. A council of Picts of the Clan of the Boar now sits in the fort until King Oengus reaches us from the north."

"Where is Sula?" Fergus asked. His heart had stepped up and was banging in his chest. He knew very little of Scone, except as a druid center and place of learning. He knew Glashan would not be safe for long, and it occurred to him now that this was going to be the way for him, his woman, and daughter to follow.

"Sula is where she belongs, with the Picts. Most of your people fled, but those who remain are held across the river by the base of the fort. They are fenced in and guarded. You will join them if you do not leave."

Fergus sat cross-legged on the floor and prodded the fire. He could not flee and leave his people captive here at Dunadd to await the arrival of the brutal King Oengus. He knew without any doubt that he was going to have to free them. But even if he did, how was he going to lead a march back to Glashan? Most at the loch were Pictish and might not accept the dark-haired ones from Dunadd, even for a short time until they moved on to Scone.

Fergus caught Talorcan's eye and gestured him to the door where they could speak in private.

"Did Iona say only one horse would return to Glashan, but with many behind it on foot?"

Talorcan smiled. "I forgot to mention that."

Fergus sighed and tried a smile for all the impossibility of what lay ahead. If he could kill the guards during the night, he might be able to lead his people out of sight under the cliffs of Dunadd, and then circle around the back. But the tide wouldn't retreat until morning, and by then it might be too late.

Talorcan took Fergus's arm. "I cannot go with you through this."

Fergus sighed. Everything was getting harder. Even his brother Talorcan was deserting him.

"Perhaps I should have brought Hairy Gavin, after all," said Fergus. Talorcan did not smile. "How long a march is it to Scone?"

Talorcan shrugged. "A week or more. But there are many crannogs along the chain of lochs that take you there. Some of the lochs were settled in years gone by by your own people. You will have shelter and food. It is a good plan for you to move to Scone. I have heard the soil is rich there."

Fergus tried to gauge the time of day by the amount of light that sneaked in through the walls of the old man's house. Talorcan lit a torch and hung it from the wall. He glanced at Fergus, who was saying nothing, just fingering the hilt of his dirk and wishing there were another way.

As soon as there was enough dark for cover, Fergus left the old man's house and went to find Sula. Her house was a new one, close to the river, the heather thatch still green in places. He stole in without announcing himself and found the old woman asleep on a mat of woven reeds by a small fire. As he crouched over her, she seemed to him much frailer and older than he remembered.

She stirred and sat up, keeping herself well wrapped in her blanket, for it was damp by the river. "Fergus, I saw you would return."

She got up and reached for a jar, from which she took a piece of bark to chew. Fergus could tell from her small movements that her bones ached. The chew would be of willow to ease the pain.

He crouched beside her to keep the talking low. "I need to know. Is Murdoch alive?"

She patted the back of his hand, as she had done when he was a child. "He lives."

Fergus let out such a sigh, he had to catch himself from falling back. "Will you cast your stones and see what is to become of us?"

She blew into the fire and set dry sticks on the flame. She called to the queen of fire to help her see through the veil, while she walked around the flames three times. It was a well-worn ritual for Fergus. He handed her his dirk to mark her lines in the dirt, and when she reached inside her wrap for the stones, he sat on the ground, the better to see how they might fall. One straight line and three crossing it; the stones fell over the lines like a flock of flying geese.

She looked at him. "You must move fast," she said. "You must go forward with your plan."

Fergus sheathed his dirk down into the warmth under his arm. "Did my mother come to you before she left?"

Sula nodded. "She came and the stones said the same as these. She left with my brother druids. She will be safe."

Fergus took hold of the old woman's bony hands. "Sula, can you help me? I would prefer to release my people without the blood of friends on my hands."

Sula searched among her jars and brought out a bottle that had not been made at Dunadd. She smiled. "From the Christians."

The smith had long ago fashioned Sula a bowl of bronze, hammered thin with a handle attached. She dropped into it a concoction of flowers and leaves, added water, then let it simmer. She let it cool while Fergus told her of his plan to follow his mother east to Scone.

"The last crannog along the long loch belongs to my sister druid. Her name is Birog. It is not a good time of year to make such a journey, but she will give you shelter before you turn across the land to the smaller loch that leads east. When I was young, I made the journey to Scone to learn from the old druidess who held court there. She has long since joined the dead, but she told of a time to come when Scone would be as Dunadd is to your people today, a place of kings, and in time a place of desolation."

Fergus picked up a stick and poked the fire. "Why must desolation always follow?"

Sula laughed a little. "My son, there is only fire and

those things consumed by fire. All comes down to ashes; it is the way of things."

"But not of the goddess. The eternal goddess who sustains us will never turn to ashes."

Sula placed her hand on Fergus's back. "Even the goddess, Fergus. Gods and goddesses rise; gods and goddesses fall. Nothing escapes the fire. The task is to burn bright while you can. Fergus, I always knew the goddess had chosen you for this."

Fergus didn't like the weight of Sula's words. He didn't like the task before him, and he didn't like that his efforts would eventually come to nothing but words in the mouth of a bard.

"How is your woman?" Sula asked.

Fergus looked straight into the old woman's eyes. "Sula, I do not understand her ways."

Sula shook her head. "It doesn't matter. She is a mystery. You must honor her."

She wrapped the edge of her shawl about the pan's handle and tipped the herbs into the bottle of whisky.

She smiled as she handed him the bottle. "The guards will be children in your hands."

"But who will take it to them? They surely will not accept it from me."

Sula nodded. "But from the hands of an old woman, something to warm them in the night?"

Fergus took the old hands and wrapped them about the bottle. "Thank you."

When he brought her head near to his breath, he could smell the scent of her herbs and spice, the way she had smelled when he was a boy and she had run her fingers through his hair.

He left into the dark, his step heavy because this feeling was becoming too familiar, always leaving things behind. With Dunadd, he would leave Saraid once and for all. This was her land, after all, the place where her ancestors were buried. He was angry that Murdoch had muddied the waters that could have remained smooth if he had only taken Sula's word and moved his people out of Dunadd quietly. Now Fergus had the task of stealing them away, and it was not going to be easy.

He sneaked around to the bridge and crossed, staying low behind the top rail, and then, because this was the place of his childhood, he took his childhood path around the outer wall of the fort to the low space where he and Murdoch had squeezed in and out of the fort as children, the same place Illa had found as a meeting place for herself and Talorcan. Fergus could not squeeze through now, but he could see through to the place where the guard inside turned his back for a moment, just long enough for Fergus to vault on his hands over the top of the wall and land softly.

Inside the fort with his hood over his head, he was just another Pict moving about the place, walking past his old house and then the house of his father and mother, past the well and the forge. Only the light from the bakehouse shone across the flat part of the hill. Fergus moved quickly away from the familiar smell of bread and pushed into the bracken, where a little way up the hill he found the place where the mason had recently carved around Sula's foot. He lay flat against the rock and saw now, almost with relief, the predicted boar chiseled so finely on the sloping edge of the rock. The Picts had wasted no time in placing their mark there, although they would have to live with the foot, as there was no easy way of erasing what had been put into stone. If the people from Erin should ever regain control of Dunadd, they would have to live with the boar, a handsome female boar at any rate.

Up on the top of the hill, there was no one to disturb him as he stood at the cliff edge and smelled the salt air rushing in against his body, paying no heed to the thin wrap of woven cloth that was a human being's only defense against the elements. At best, it would be a long time until he cast his gaze again across this water to the western isles. He did not know if the sea to the east had the same look or smell.

He knew every stone on this hill, each place where heather gave way to bracken. This was home as much as any place could live inside a man or woman. For a moment he felt it would almost be better to be penned in with his own people down at the base of the fort than to have to remove himself from everything he knew. But his father had not trained him in the way of being a slave. If the future for his people lay in Scone, he must follow the path his mother had already set.

He scaled the wall again unseen and pushed down through the rusted bracken to the small pond against the side of the hill where the spring collected. It was here the fence had been constructed high against the side of the hill, and here where he heard his people talking quietly among themselves. He followed the fence around to the gate where three guards stood.

He would have to wait until Sula came with her offerings, and this was not the place to do it. He shrank back against the side of the hill, into a scallop of rock where he had hidden once, waiting to ambush his brother. As he waited, his thoughts danced back and forth around Ma-khee. The night before he had awoken more than usual, glad to feel her breathing beside him, glad to wrap his hand around her breast and drop back into sleep.

Fergus tried to bring his thoughts back into a straight line like Sula's stones. As the moon started to cross the sky, his mood fell. He began to worry that Sula had drifted back asleep, or even that Talorcan might have warned the guards. For the first time he saw that he was alone at Dunadd, without friends, and that just as he had come into life here, this night might see him slip out of it.

24

Winnie hasn't been back for days. Her empty dish on my kitchen counter is too depressing, so I put it out beside the wilted pansies. With the days inching towards the light, small clusters of snowdrops dangle their bobbleheads over the riverbank; in the lengthening evenings, hares race about the field looking like small dogs, sensing, I suppose, that the fight for mates might be close at hand.

Only a week to go now before my operation, and I put in a call to Dr. Shipshap to ask if there is any way of rescheduling it for February.

He says, "You have nothing to fear, Margaret."

"No," I say, "there's something I have to get done."

"I talked to your son," he said. "I quote verbatim: 'Don't let my mum wriggle out of it this time.'"

Poor Graeme doesn't understand what is at stake here. My speech, my sight, my personality, my memory are all up for grabs in this operation. But more than that, so are my dreams.

There is silence on the other end of the phone.

I hang up. On doctor's orders, I haven't been taking my pills for a week now. They need all those chemicals out of me before they can start their probing. I keep waiting to slip back into Fergus's world, but my feet plod heavily on the road, in the puddles, with no sign of going anywhere but here.

Ironically, without the medication, I have only minor seizures, plenty of them, but nothing that would rock the ground, nothing that would get me back to the eighth century.

I enjoy the lack of fog. In the clarity that God gave me, I scramble to put together the outline of my thesis. I spend a week at my desk: papers, books, words, time ticking slowly on the clock in the kitchen. I try to keep Fergus and Illa away from my thoughts. After all, they might have only ever been functions of scarred brain tissue. The weight inside my chest says they are more than that.

"The Burning of Witches, and the Loss of the Sacred Feminine." The thesis has a title now. The outline comes together quickly, and I see my way forward, now that I may not have any way forward.

Dr. Shipshap rings me back and assures me he is a very experienced surgeon and has never had anything go wrong. But that is what I am afraid of. Once I wake up in the antiseptic hospital room with my head in a turban of bandages, will normality just be deathly dull?

"Och," says Jim. "Everyone else has to put up with it."

I am leaning my backside against the edge of his kitchen counter. Inside my Wellies, I shift my feet at the ordinariness of this smell of gas from his cooker, these bread crumbs on his table, the drip of the tap, this feeling of everything going on as it should.

"Do you want to go up the fort?" I ask.

He reaches for his boots. "It's raining, though."

Just by way of emphasis the wind takes a bucket of water and dashes it against the window.

I sit down at his table.

He sets his boots back down. "It'd be a bugger up there in this."

I know he's right. I stretch my arm along his table and lay my head on it.

"Are you all right?" he asks.

I pick up a large acorn from a bowl of them on his table. "Fergus has acorns on a string around his neck and a funny little stone with a hole in it."

He sighs. "You don't have to go ahead with this operation. Nobody's forcing you."

I have to laugh, there with my head on my arm on the table, a sort of sideways laugh. "I know. It's just that the timing isn't great. Fergus left for Dunadd, and I think the earthquake's coming. Illa has an infected leg, and I really want to be there to help her, not here in your kitchen with the bloody rain going like the hammers on the window."

Tears fall sideways, just like the laugh. Jim rests his hand on my shoulder. "You'd get used to not going back there, if everything straightened out."

I sit up. "Would I?"

I don't believe so, but here I am choosing to stay in the present for good. I will have Graeme, and he will have me, which is why I am going through with this. I won't have Ellie. Instead of Fergus, there will just be a gaping sad hole.

"I still want to go up Dunadd," I say.

Jim goes to the window and pretends he can see through. "If you keep walking out with me, people will be talking."

I look at the back of him: his short grey hair, his broad shoulders, the dark green corduroy trousers that run into no particular shape across his backside.

"They'll be saying you're an old goat, running around with younger women and your wife not four years in the grave."

I see his breath rise heftily and drop inside his knitted jumper. "Aye, they like their scandal, people do."

I stand up. "I'm going up the fort anyway. Are you coming?"

He doesn't turn. "No."

I slip out of his kitchen door stealthily like a thief, plant my feet on the wet gravel, pull my hood down, and head up the hill. Even the tourists have decided to stay in their cars, fogging up their windscreens as they wait for this lot to clear up. They don't know about rain here, how it's out to get you and keep you off the land. It will win, but not today, not against me.

The metal stile is cold and wet as I push the bar back and step around in the mud. My Wellies slip on the stone, and I have to grab handfuls of heather to pull myself up. The heather has learned better than most to grow slowly and gnarl itself into the bedrock. Higher up on the plateau where the houses were, my feet squelch in the grass, trip on the jutting rubble. The well is not dry today but flowing as it did when I was christened here once by a druidess.

The final ascent is blinding, and the view from the top of Dunadd is a sheet of driving rain. I have to imagine the hills and the islands, because today they have been swallowed by the demon sea. Dunadd doesn't want me here today; it wants all that history of people wiped clean. But I sit on Fergus's ledge and defy it. The small voice of defiance is all I have left.

Back at my desk, I order my data into time periods: the rise and final ebb of the witch hunt in Scotland. Only, I want it to be seen against the arm of the patriarchal god, the deus ex machina of the church. That is my thesis, the one I will write when my brain has been fixed and I see with the clear light of day.

I pack the papers and the books into boxes, the ones I first walked through the door with. The cottage will revert to its spring holiday status, and there will be others at this window with their tea in the morning, people who think Dunadd was just a place for crowning kings, who have never heard of Fergus MacBrighde and his daughter Illa, but who might open the window to a small black cat one day if she ever comes back.

Jim knocks at my window later, holding a bunch of early daffodils from his garden.

"You'll need someone to drive you down to Glasgow," he says.

I make him jump when I stretch out my arms and wrap them around him. He doesn't hug back, but we stand there in some kind of understanding for a moment.

"If all goes to hell," I say, "and I lose my marbles, I will come and live with you. You can feed me soup through a straw and wipe my bum when I need it."

I hope, once they maneuver my poor lobe out, they won't take my sense of humor with it, because I haven't had it for long and I rather like it.

Jim is blushing when I pull out of the embrace. I punch his arm.

He punches my arm back. "All right," he says. "It's a deal."

I turn him round and push him towards the door. "Get out of here."

Dr. Shipshap is back on the telephone, asking me if he told me he's going to wake me up halfway through the operation to make sure he doesn't cut out anything that governs major function. Standard procedure, he says, though it is not exactly a comforting thought. What is comforting is the thought of being wrapped up in a blanket with Fergus MacBrighde, of holding in my arms the daughter I never wanted to lose in the first place.

On the day of departure for Glasgow, the sun decides to make an appearance. The sky is clear and vivid blue over Dunadd. Jim appears with more daffodils.

"For your mother," he says.

I wrap them in plastic in my empty kitchen and set them on the backseat of my car on top of sheets and pictures of my children. They smell like a hill fort in the rain.

He waits outside for me to make a last check, make sure I haven't left anything, at least not anything I can put my hand around. On the blue couch, on the table by the bed, in the small cracks around the windowsill I have left everything, and it takes longer than it should to decide I can walk away from it and turn the key in the lock for the last time.

"Don't you have any luggage?" I ask, as Jim slides down into the driver's seat.

"Do you mean clean underwear, that sort of thing?"

"That would be a start," I say.

He shakes his head. "I only changed them last week."

He winks and makes me smile in spite of the engine moving me away from my view out of the window, away from the barn and the remnants of animals that once lived there, away from the stile at the base of the fort, over the bridge, a little dip in the bottom of the stomach. I cannot bring myself to catch a last glimpse of Dunadd fort, great elephant back of a mound in the sea.

Tiugainn comhla rium. Come along with me, it says over my shoulder. *I will keep you here.* How could it not? It's not a place, after all, but a state of dream.

25

Fergus stumbled against the rock, hitting himself hard. He stood up, rubbing his hip, but when the ground began to shake again he fell back. Stones slammed and cracked as they bounced off the hill above his head, first one or two and then a great torrent, louder than thunder. It would have been a vain effort to throw himself forward and try to crawl out of their reach. There would be no time now to wait for Sula. He must get his people out and away before the entire fort fell to its knees.

As he crouched in his hollow, he saw the end of the bridge come loose and the whole swinging structure drop heavily into the river. Beyond, many of the houses that had stood in the fields stood no longer. The men guarding his people, some of whose faces he recognized, were crouched close to the ground like him, but no one was worrying about allegiances now. No one even thought to call out while the ground kept shaking, the boulders kept falling, and Fergus had to keep in sight Iona's vision of the trek back to Glashan. He inched out, covering his head and steeling himself against the rubble falling against his back.

There was a pause in which he managed to run free of the stones, but then another great shaking brought his chest hard against the ground. Great clouds of dust and rumbling rose as though the fields themselves were rolling away. When things grew still again, Fergus turned onto his back, wincing where the stones had cut through his jerkin.

"Fergus MacBrighde," he cried out. "I am here."

It took a moment when he stood up to get his balance, but then he made for the wattle prison that was all a tatter now; the people were pushed against the side of the hill, separated, men together, women by themselves; the two monks who had befriended his mother were crouched by the men, clutching wooden crosses and muttering in Latin from their leather-bound books.

"Gather yourselves quickly," Fergus said. "We must leave."

No one was going to argue. The women called for

their children and stood by their men. The monks closed their books and came towards Fergus, but he would not let them near.

He started walking in the direction of the sea, the monks close at his back, and then the women with their children, the men coming up behind. But Fergus stopped suddenly as they came out from under the cliffs and saw for the first time the tide run out as far as they could see, as though the islands had decided to keep the sea for themselves. In the distance, they could make out Talorcan, his back to them, standing far out on the new stretch of sand.

The older monk turned and waved his book against the line of people behind him. "It is the judgment of God against your wicked ways."

Fergus caught his arm. "Take your curraghs and sail back to Iona."

The monks looked to the men for support.

The older one spoke. "Will you follow this heathen or shall our Holy Father smite you again? Must he send lightning bolts to turn you from your evil goddess?"

Fergus ran at their backs and shoved them hard against the sand. Their coarse brown robes slopped in the water, their sandaled feet floundered in the muddy sand.

"Swim!" he said. "May your God make you float!"

He ran at them again until they crawled backwards

like crabs against the ridges of sand, dropping their books, flailing out towards the water's edge with cries that matched the cries of the children that could be heard now coming from the village.

Fergus picked their sopping books out of the sand and hurled them after them.

"The One God sees all," shouted the younger monk, stabbing the air with the blade of his hand. "You shall be punished."

Fergus turned his back on them and gestured for the others to follow. When he got to Talorcan, Fergus laid his hand on his shoulder.

"What use will Dunadd be without the sea?" asked Talorcan quietly.

Fergus gripped his arm. "Come with us."

"No," he said. "You can take yourself to Scone, but I belong here. Sula says Dunadd will belong to us, and I believe her." He took Fergus aside by the arm. "You will leave Iona at Glashan. I shall fetch her when the time is right. At Scone you will find your own druids among your own people."

Fergus nodded. Ma-khee would be glad for this.

Talorcan took a step back. His words faltered as his voice rose. "May the goddess glide gently in your steps, may she clothe you in righteousness and make life abundant."

He waved, and they watched him walk back towards

the village that was no village any longer. Fergus wiped his face with the back of his sleeve and waved at Talorcan's back. He knew these Picts who had endured from the time of the standing stones would persist. Sula had said so, and now, with their boar carved in the rock of Dunadd, it was sure they would come to rule this land again. Fergus and his people must flee.

No one followed them, but not until the land curved up into the hills of Dunamuck did Fergus stop the procession with his hand in the air. A child shouted to see Fergus's horse running across the valley towards them. Talorcan must have ridden out to free her, and now Iona's vision would be true: Fergus at the front on his horse, two hundred women and children and men behind.

It was dark now. Fergus kept looking back to Dunadd in case anyone should be following. But there was no need, he knew, unless some vengeful Picts had relished the thought of making the people from Erin slaves. He could see the smoke from a fire out in the field where the villagers lived. With no homes to protect them, a central fire would be the best way of staying warm and warding off animals.

After Fergus had tethered his horse, he came back to the procession. There was no point in stumbling in the dark, he told them, they would stop here now for the night, build a fire like the one over at Dunadd. He tied his horse, and then set about clearing a space for the fire. Women and children went about gathering wood, while the men dug out a shallow pit with whatever tools of branches and flat stones came to hand.

An older woman with a crooked back and grey hair bent over her flint, feeding in dry moss from her pouch, striking the smooth stone that finally gave a spark and set the moss smoldering. But the wood was damp, and it took much cutting with Fergus's dirk, the only weapon they had, to get tinder enough for a flame and then a fire that didn't care how wet the wood. The fire smoked a great deal, and the people could not come in close. There was no food, nor would there be until they arrived the next day at Glashan.

Fergus stood among the huddle of his people. They were quiet, accepting what they already knew. Fergus looked at them, a concentration of dark heads and smaller bodies than the Picts. He had never seen them set apart like this, but he knew he belonged to them and that he would have to lead them.

He said. "Tomorrow we will reach Loch Glashan, but we will not be safe there for long. King Oengus's army is moving south to Dunadd. After we have rested, we will move to Scone by the eastern sea. Our people have already settled there, and we will be welcome."

An old man spoke up. "But we are traveling without the protection of the druidess."

"I spoke to Sula before we left," said Fergus. "She

and the girl Iona both saw our path away from here. We can do no other than go forward." He crouched down by the fire. "Sleep now. You will need your strength."

Fergus saw little sleep. The wolves had gone deeper into the trees, but he could still hear them. If the troupe had been carrying food, there would be bears to worry about. The women slept with their children under their blankets; men lay close to their families. There was no one for Fergus to lie near, no eyes that beckoned him, so he tended the fire and wondered about Sula. As he began to doze, he held tight in his chest the hope that Ma-khee and Illa were safe. He hoped they had not been in the crannog it dropped into the water. He hoped that Ma-khee had not run away.

When he awoke, the dew had frozen on Fergus's face. He could see the smoke still rising from the field below Dunadd but no one in the valley between. The sky was still dark; the wolves had left off their night hunt and were silent in their dens. He roused the others for what would be a four-hour walk with the children and the few old ones. Their bones were cold and slow to move as they followed on the path that may have been beaten down at some time but now was overgrown with withered weed and bracken. They noticed the sun rise behind clouds in the east and steered their course to the left of it, keeping in sight Fergus, who led his horse and let the children ride in turns.

They would have to wait at Glashan for better

weather before they tried the trek east to Scone. Fergus hoped the land and the loch would support this many more people. He hoped the Picts there would not grow hostile to them when they learned of their people's victory at Dunadd. But all that was hope for now, nothing to be counted on. He felt for the godstone about his neck and smiled when he saw a hawk circling above. Cailleach the goddess was watching over them.

26

In my childhood room in Glasgow, it is only street dark through the velvet curtains; the house is very still. I don't want to be here on the eve of my surgery. Sitting on the edge of the bed, I hear Graeme shift in his sleep next door in what used to be my brother's room. It has been more than a week since I left Fergus, ages since I didn't know if Illa would be all right. I've been lying awake wondering about the books on general pediatrics my mother has kept downstairs in a glass cabinet since my brother and I were children.

It's quiet in the house as I set my bare feet on the stairs, and make for the front room. The cabinet door squeaks; under my weight the floorboards speak, too. In the semi-dark, my fingers run along the spines of dictionaries and encyclopedias and finally find *Diseases of Childhood*. I sit down with it at the polished table that hardly ever saw any use and, by streetlight, flip through gruesome pictures of complications from infected wounds: blackened flesh and stumps of legs where proper limbs once ran down into knee-length socks. Antibiotics, of course, are needed. A tetanus inoculation—at the very least, stitches to close the wound against further infection. None of these modern antidotes is available to Illa. I hope against hope that Iona knows what she is doing. I wish I could just move them all like chess pieces: Illa would move forward; Fergus would come in like a knight.

Graeme flicks the light on. "What are you doing? It's two o'clock in the morning."

He hovers by the door as though I am about to take flight.

"I couldn't sleep."

He shrugs. "Me, neither. What's the book?"

I close it and set it on the table, as though it had unwillingly flown into my hand. "Nothing, really."

"Are you frightened?" he asks, standing there in his pajamas.

I shrug, and then I nod, because I am frightened. Terrified. Scared of the operation not working, scared of it working, scared of losing my mind, scared of finding it. Scared most of all of losing my time out of time forever.

He comes over and takes my hand. "I don't think it will hurt, will it?"

"No." I kiss his cold knuckles. "But I don't like the idea of being woken up in the middle of the operation to take an IQ test."

He smiles. I replace the book and walk my boy back up to bed. He even allows me to tuck him in and kiss him, as though he were the patient, and thank God he's not. I climb into bed, back on course now, sucking in my breath and going forward for the sake of this son.

I lie down, thinking about Iona, how pale and other-worldly she seems, almost as though she doesn't exist. The only way I wish she didn't exist is under Fergus. I can't erase that picture from my mind. Everything she is—seer, healer, goddess in a fertility ceremony—and everything she knows about the earth are the things for which women will die all over Europe in another eight hundred years.

The walls of my childhood room close in on me. The small noises of the sleeping house flood over my thoughts, and then the tick of the grandfather clock in the hall gives itself to the sound of a woodpecker in the trees where I am walking with Iona. In spite of everything, I am so glad to see her, and I hold on to the sleeve of her robe as we walk. With the sun painting the floor of the forest in shades of light, she leads me to a spring bounded by flat stones, making a little platform on which she stands. She makes sweeping motions with her arms, saying her prayer to the element of water as she did to the fire on Christmas Eve.

She gestures for me to come to her.

"Kneel down," she says, forcing my head lower than my knees. I remember now this was the first action Sula performed, and I shiver in the same way, as the freezing water sinks into my hair and runs down my neck. She must not be satisfied with the way it takes the first time, because she pushes my head down again below the level of the highest stone and pours water from her cupped hand. *May the waters from the hills bring health and peace. May the spring waters bring calm to you, and may the rains always be tranquillity to you.* I have never been so baptized in all my life.

I stand up, shaking the water from my head, wiping my eyes with the back of my sleeve, shuddering as tiny rivulets run down my back to my waist. Iona doesn't seem to like the look of me or the way I behave. As we walk silently and separately now back towards the loch, the earth rumbles, just once, but enough to make me stagger.

Iona catches my arm and takes me quickly back to the hut. There is urgency in her step and something about her that still sets me ill at ease. I wait outside the door before going in, then find her crouched by a sleeping Illa. The roof is creaking on its supports. I close the door and rush to the sick girl, not wanting to touch in case I wake her. Iona starts circling the fire, throwing into the flames little pieces of bark and leaf that send up a pungent smoke.

Iona says, "Take your coverings off."

I hesitate, because of all that nunnery training and because I was sitting on my bed in Glasgow about five minutes ago. I pull the tunic over my head and undo the strings that hold on my leg bindings, but that leaves the underwear I came with.

"Those, too," she says.

She sets the tip of a braid of grass against the edge of the fire and starts to waft the smoke it makes over her face and the top of her head. I wave the sweet smoke over my own head, making my eyes weep. Tears are running off my chin and onto my breasts, as I undo the bra and let it fall, then step out of the stretchy knickers. Iona picks up both and tosses them into the flame, adding the smell of burning rubber to the mix. And here I am naked, glancing at the sick child, trying to resist the urge to crouch and cover myself with my hands.

My eyes accommodate to the smoke. Iona is intent on covering every inch of me with it, including the parts appreciated by Fergus. She has me kneel, and then she chants as she places her hands on the top of my head. I think a priest once did that, perhaps during my first communion, but I am quite sure I was not naked at the time. I am quite sure it didn't evoke the reaction that Iona's hands do. I begin to shake. It is cold, I am without clothes, but I know that is not the reason for my shaking. I wait for the burning sensation in my soles, for consciousness to work its way through the atoms until it falls away altogether. But none of that happens. I go on shaking and calling out until there's nothing left to come out. When I am finally quiet on my knees in a heap, I look across at Illa, who is still sleeping; when I look up at Iona, she is smiling.

Up again. Now we must dance around her fire, a trudge clockwise. I try to give in to it as much as I can, for Illa's sake, but I can't help thinking how damning this would be in the eyes of the clerics to come—naked women dancing around the fire. No wonder they thought the witches were in league with the devil.

Iona is chanting herself into a frenzy and must sit down. I am tired and sit down, too, my backside in the loose dirt, my cold and filthy toes up to the flames. She stares into the fire until her eyes close and she is lost to her spectator.

My thoughts are racing. Iona sits on, unmoving. Eventually, I close my eyes, trying to settle my mind, watching thoughts spin about me with no plan to leave. What seems like hours go by before I lapse into a sort of nonthinking, aware of my thoughts but only in passing.

This space reminds me of the timelessness that comes in the aftermath of a seizure. Illa's eyes are still closed. I hope she is just sleeping.

I was sleeping, but now I am awake, watching the morning light penetrate the curtains in my room of dolls and horses. Downstairs in the kitchen, Jim has won my mother over by baking scones for breakfast. The daffodils from his garden sit on the linen tablecloth in a ceramic vase too ornate for wilderness flowers. Everyone is looking to see how a person might look before brain surgery. All I know is I am hungry because no food or drink is permitted for patients.

"I'll save you a scone." Jim smiles.

I wink at Graeme. "Save me two."

Everyone is forced into a jolliment this morning. Peering over the chasm, what else can anyone do? On the way out of the door, I even receive a phone call from my ex-husband wishing me all the best. Oliver Griggs, the name that once held so much weight, now floats out of my hands and up the chimney. Oliver has heard through intradepartmental gossip that I handed in my thesis outline on the way through Glasgow. "Interesting title," he says. There's a pause before he asks, "Who brought you down?"

I am on the point of brain surgery, and perhaps I should not be so petty, but I tell Oliver that I came down with Jim Galvin, my neighbor, and I do not punctuate the pregnant pause with any disclaimers about his age or the lack of anything that would qualify as a proper relationship. I let the pause take Oliver Griggs wherever he wants to go, and then I say thank you and hang up.

My mother points to her watch and ushers me out of the door.

When I get into the car beside Jim, he smiles. "To Oz?"

I am glad for this man this morning and almost want to take back the words I didn't say to Oliver about him.

"To Oz."

Graeme laughs in the seat behind me, and I grip onto that laughter because otherwise I might sink. We wave to my parents in their car and set off in a convoy, trying not to lose each other in traffic on the way to the hospital, trying not to glance behind as we swing through the hospital doors and check me in, leaving the light and the day and the city and perhaps life itself outside. For the most part the hospital has few surprises: the squeaky floors, the polished chrome, the female nurses, male doctors—all conform happily this morning. And at a juncture such as this, conformity seems like no small commodity. It is something. Something to hold on to.

Everyone who came through the doors with me suddenly looks lost, as though we had just been marooned on an island. My parents' bodies tend back towards the exit. Jim steps back so as not to crowd. Graeme holds on to me and I hold on back, like two drowning rodents. Our faces are wet, and now he is the boy, not the man, just a little bundle of him in his mother's arms.

The nurse steps in stage left. "Please come this way."

I ease Graeme off me and hand him to Jim, who has never hugged a boy in his life and doesn't know what to do with a sobbing seventeen-year old. I step after the nurse, setting one foot in front of the other as though I had just learned to walk, leaving the loved ones at the swinging doors, trying to get a last look. In the small room of hard edges, I submit to the undressing and the immodesty of a hospital gown. I allow myself to be snagged and tagged, my statistics written down, and my growling stomach to be laughed at. I submit because I am outnumbered. I am in a cathedral with a priesthood in blue scrubs that will cut me open until the devil flies out.

Hours move slowly around the face of the clocks on every wall it seems. I am laid out like Christ, a crucifix of a woman, so they can thread their tubes and needles in, so they can pump in that first release of relaxant. I am vaguely aware of the shaving that drops my lovely locks to the floor, of the Magic Marker that maps the path of their incision.

"Margaret?"

I close my eyes. I will not speak to the devil.

"Margaret?"

"Maggie?"

"Yes?"

"Ma-khee? Mithair?"

I open my eyes to find Illa sitting up and looking at me. She called me "Mother." I scramble to my knees and bring her face into focus; it is no longer hot. Under her tunic, the infected slash has receded under the poultice.

"Margaret, can you hear me?"

No, I cannot hear you. I can hear only the creak of the thatched roof in the wind. I can hear only the small waves lap against the shore. I can hear my daughter's breathing and the crackle of the fire. But I cannot hear you anymore.

I put the cup holding Iona's medicine into Illa's hands, but it falls suddenly and rolls towards the fire as though on a track. The rafters supporting the thatch begin to groan. Iona comes through the door, moving quickly, gathering her piles of herbs and roots. The small waves at the shore turn into a great sloshing. The ground on which we sit begins to heave, not shake as it had done before, but as though a great rift were splitting the earth.

Iona is shouting at us, urging us towards the door. Marcus flies in, grabs Illa under the armpits, and drags her free of the building. I follow though I am naked, and get out just in time to feel the roof collapse behind me with a gust of dirt and air

We're on the ground, because there is no mechanism of the inner ear that can adjust balance this quickly. The walls of Iona's hut fall in, sending another layer of dust over our backs; a louder crash from the water means the crannog has come off its stilts. Winnie runs across my field of vision, but I have no sense of where she came from or where she's going.

The shaking is interminable. A few rotten apples roll and bounce on the ground like Ping-Pong balls, but, like the swirling contents of a tornado, nothing is real or reachable. If there were a moment of distraction I might amuse myself with the thought that that old fuddy-duddy Colonel Malcolm had been right after all: the shaking of Dál Riada came just the same.

27

When the sun had cleared the clouds and gained its highest place, Fergus held his hand up to stop his people by the waterfall where the beavers lived. The children ran off to gather bulbs of garlic and chew a few pieces before they traveled the second half of their journey. Sorrel and watercress lay along their path, but it had been made bitter by the cold. As the afternoon wore on, the children straggled behind, but the singing of the women added strength to their steps. Many of the songs were in the Pictish language, and it seemed strange now to be separating themselves from what had become part of their own heritage in the long years since the first people from Erin had arrived.

Fergus began to recognize the slant of the hills as

they approached Glashan. Not much farther and they could see smoke rising above the trees.

"Look!" he shouted to the children. "Not long now."

He brought his people slowly into the bay, but he could do nothing to stop the children running ahead along the shore, mingling with the people who were gathered around a large fire. It wasn't long before Fergus assessed the damage caused by the quake: the thatched roofs now floating in the loch, men fighting over the small huts that still stood in the fields. Women were weaving wattle as fast as they could soak and bend the hazel and willow into new fences.

Out of the crowd, the woman who had come to be known as Fergus's ran to him, her face dirty and shining. Fergus tried not to smile. She threw herself against him while he struggled to keep the horse calm. Despite their weariness, the people in the line behind him laughed a little.

It was good to see her, too, but he would show her that later. For now he had the business of settling his people among this lake population. He noticed Illa leaning against a tree and nodded to her.

Radha came out of the wood with her father. Her scratched and bruised face fell when she saw that Talorcan was not among the travelers.

"Murdoch's army has been smashed. Dunadd has been taken," said Fergus. "Talorcan will come when he can."

Radha's father stepped forward. "Why have you brought these people here? You can see we no longer have homes ourselves. We do not want the force of Oengus's army on us for harboring his enemy."

Fergus had thought out his strategy along the way. "We will not deplete your winter food supplies. We will stay only long enough to help you rebuild."

Days or weeks. It was a lot to ask. The old man walked the length of the line to see what he would be inheriting by taking these people in. The young men would be of some use to the women at the loch with no husbands. He liked the look of some of the Scotti women, a few with cockiness in the way they stood. He would take them and explain to the people of the loch later. He pointed to his curragh and the net that lay drying on the shore.

A handful of men and women stepped forward and pulled the boat into the water. There was no time to waste; the children were hungry.

Radha's father took Fergus by the elbow. "Your woman said the druidess at Dunadd knew of this shaking before it came."

"Yes. She didn't know when."

"What of Dunadd? Does it still stand?"

Fergus laughed. "Dunadd will always stand, no matter who rules."

The old man dropped his voice. "There are those here who say we should go there, take what is ours."

Fergus ran his hands through his hair. "Since the earth shook, the sea has left Dunadd. It will be a sorry trade that cannot moor its boats to the western side, but must steer up the river against the flow. Picts or no Picts, Dunadd will not last as the center of anything unless the sea comes back."

The old man nodded, perplexed. "Iona sees something new. I am telling you this because you brought her here, although she is one of ours, not yours." The old man stopped to see how Fergus would react. "She says great boats with many oarsmen will come down from the far north and fight bloody battles. They are many and tall, with hair like strands of gold. This is what she sees since the earth shook."

Fergus waved for Illa to come over and join him. He noticed the child's limp without thinking; his mind was still on the large boats with the yellow-haired people.

"My mother went east to Scone," he said. "It is a walk of about ten days. If you want, you should bring your family and follow, too."

The old man shook his head. "With your help we will rebuild our crannogs. The oarsmen from the north will not find us here. We are well hidden. When the time comes, you shall go to your mother, but you must leave Iona here."

Fergus nodded. He looked at Illa's pale face properly for the first time. "What is the matter?"

"My leg," said Illa. "It was bad, but my new mother took care of me, and now it is getting better."

Fergus lifted his daughter's tunic high enough to see the gash under the dried poultice. "Your new mother did well."

He stood up, looking for Ma-khee now. But his mind drifted to the long trek ahead: so many people and no healer, no link to the spirit world. In what little time they had at Glashan, Ma-khee would have to learn the ways from Iona. He looked out on the loch to the men and women in the curragh who were bringing in fish. Even though they were tired from the journey, the children on the shore were running and shouting. Some of the men came out of the forest dragging a deer that had died under a falling tree.

It would be a celebration, though Fergus was wary of celebrating yet. Two hundred more people to feed from this land and this water. There would be no grain except for where the crannog people along the way deigned to give some. If the crannogs on the way to Scone had fallen, their people would be reticent to help at all.

At Loch Glashan, the crannogs sank up to their walls in water. Tomorrow they would start the process of lifting them back onto their islands of rock and tree trunks. Tomorrow the loch people would be glad of the help. For now, some of them stood by the water's edge, scowling. Fergus knew that he had no dominion here, that these people would soon hear about the victories of their new king in the north and would not suffer Fergus and his people long.

He set off to find Ma-khee. He had waited for so long to be with her, and now he wanted her near and warm against his chest. He hoped she would agree to go to Scone with him. As he made his way through the scrub, he asked the goddess to hold fast to his people. And he prayed that Ma-khee might want to stay with him and never let him go.

28

When I hear the news that Fergus has been spotted in the distance, I have no other thought than to get to him, so I leave Illa with Iona and run to find him.

As I run, I say his name more than once. Fergus is dirty, bruised, and cut; still, I can't help but wrap my arms about him, even though it spooks the horse and Fergus has a hard time calming it. People are laughing. But it has been so long since I saw him, days and days, and a lifetime. I didn't know if I would ever be here again with my cheek against the movement of his chest, my fingers in the weave of his coat, in the warm hair at the nape of his neck. All I know is, I never want to move again.

"Margaret? Can you hear me?"

I bury my face in his coat and don't let go until he moves. His hands are eager for me, but he has a trail of people behind him. He steps aside to have words with Rhada's father, and I can see why he might have to. I don't know how he thinks we are going to feed all these extra people when most of the flour jars sank with the crannogs. I run to see if I can find anything left in the huts by the fields. Despite the chaos, I can't keep the smile from my face. I have missed this Fergus, son of Brighde.

There's no bread, of course, and the little flour that remains is being guarded. No querns, because they were the first things to sink. It will be a cold recovery, but recovered they must be. Somehow everything will have to be set back up, like time-lapse photography moving backwards.

When I get back to the fish roast, Illa is among the children waiting in line. She stands a head taller than the Scotti children her age; her red hair marks her as another breed altogether. My auburn hair marks me as something in between, so I am allowed to stand waiting with Illa among the hungry travelers. Fergus is at the shore with a band of men, brewing plans, I expect, while the women busy themselves with the more immediate task of feeding the five thousand. I keep glancing over at him.

"Margaret?"

No. I don't hear you. I want so badly to get my hands

around Fergus again, over him, on him. But I am in a race with time that I cannot win.

Marcus walks over and stands behind me, another outcast allowed some privilege at the feast.

"What are the men talking about?" I ask.

"Brighde went east to Scone. Fergus says we must follow."

"Everyone?"

Marcus shakes his head, smiling. "Not I."

Fergus must have granted him his freedom.

Scone, I know, is in Perthshire, which I reckon must be a four-hour car drive from here. If we're all going to march, it's going to take a week or more. The "scenic route" is the old route east, around Loch Awe and then across land to Loch Earn.

I eat the half fish I am given, but pick out the staring eyes and hand them to Illa. For these children, fish eyes are as close to sweets as they get. Afterwards I walk her back to what remains of Iona's hut. Some men are already setting her roof back up. The thatch will take longer. When I notice Illa limping, I let her lean in against me. She puts her arm around my waist and holds on tightly.

She looks up at me. "You won't leave, will you?"

I am her mother. How can I leave her?

"Have you seen Winnie?" I ask.

She shakes her head, looks sad.

We find Iona seated inside her walls, her look far off. I pick the old poultice off Illa's leg and look for the dried root that Iona made her ointment from the last time. Everything is mixed in with everything else now. Iona pushes me with the toe of her shoe towards a pile closer to the door.

The mortar is still here, but the pestle must have bounced off during the quake. I go outside and bring back a stone that will do. I like the feel of the powdered root in the cup of my hand mixing together with my spit. I like the sky above the walls of the hut moving fast with the wind. It feels like I know all this, like something that was just asleep in me until now.

Illa winces as I spread my spitty mess over her wound.

When Fergus calls from outside the door, I smile to hear his voice, and because there is no roof and he could just as well look in. He says my name, and I relish the sound of it, not Maggie nor Margaret, but Ma-khee.

"Margaret, can you hear me?"

"Ma-khee?"

Illa looks just as happy to hear Fergus, but I touch her shoulder for her to be still until her poultice sets a little. It is I myself who opens the door.

I lay my palms flat against his chest. Though his face is serious, I feel his whole self alive, the warmth and movement of him beneath my fingers. He takes me by the elbow and leads me away from the hut, stopping among the rubble of field and upended earth. And he starts in on a speech so fast I don't know how he expects me to understand. I pick up some of it, about Murdoch, and it must be bad news, the way his jaw tenses and the veins form ropes under his skin.

When I put my arms around him, he shakes his head, though a smile is creeping in.

He holds me out by my arms. "When we go to Scone, Iona will stay here. In the time left, you must learn from her."

I poke him, and he writhes under the tickle. "When it gets dark, will you come to me?"

He nods but then moves off, back into his serious self. I go back to Illa.

She says, "What did he say?"

I sit down beside her and lay her hand flat against mine. It's a grubby little hand, but it's hard to tell where the heat from her palm ends and mine begins. "Your uncle Murdoch was defeated. We are going to Scone. A long distance. But not yet." I touch her poor leg. "Not until you can run fast."

I am so glad that she will run fast again, that this time she goes on to live, that I wrap my arm around her and pull her in close against me. She doesn't resist, not even for a moment.

She says, "I am glad you came to be my mother."

It is not hard to exhale, but my inhale shakes and I am unable to say anything back. Illa, if you only knew what sweet torture it has been to be your mother.

I manage quite a bright fire, relatively smokeless. I

didn't see Iona down by the loch, so I don't know what she has eaten, or ever does eat, but she stretches out on the floor of the hut by the fire across from Illa and falls asleep in no time. I sit up, waiting for Fergus, only this time I hope he doesn't call out at the door.

He doesn't. He taps, a small sound only the wakeful can hear. There is nowhere to go but inside, so he follows me in, and there is nowhere to lie except next to the others, which we do, and I can only hope that sleep lies heavily on both and they cannot see what is happening in the flicker of a fire under a very cold roof, with the wraps coming off and the tunic over the head followed by hands that want to get me down to my core skin, and bones and muscle all moving to his skin and bones and muscle until the two become one thing moving among the shadows.

"Don't leave me," I say in English this time, because I don't want him to know my need. He wants me to be strong, but here I am clinging to him, so that he will stay and stay and stay. And so will I.

"Margaret."

No. I desperately don't want to drift away. Not now.

The next morning, Fergus joins the men who strip and push their bodies through the frozen water to exhume what can be found in the crannog below the water. The children are sent off to find grasses, nuts, and grains of any kind in preparation for the quern stones drying out and beginning their toil of grinding once again.

I sit by the water, trying hard to hold on. A shake to my shoulder brings Iona into focus. She sits down beside me and takes my hand.

"The moon is a woman," she says. "The moon is Gealach. Her children are the stars."

Iona turns my hands palm up. "The hands take power from the sky."

I hold my hands up and feel first the cool breeze across my palms. But then they turn hot. I rub them together, and then hold them up again. First the coolness, then the heat. I smile to show that I know what she is saying. She takes hold of my right hand and circles her finger around my palm. She starts tapping it, chanting to Gealach, mother of all. It gives me a headache, the kind of rhythmic noise that usually sends me into an episode. I fight to stay on. She smooths my palm several times, then looks into the center of my hand. The look on her face is intent as she pulls back my fingers so that the blood runs out, leaving in my palm only white skin.

Her brow furrows under her strangely pale hair. She pins me with her pale blue eyes. "You come from what has not yet been lived."

Yes. A time of no wolves or bears or beavers, of no crannogs on the lochs, and of only a few remaining stone circles. I come from the time of witches at Halloween; of the jealous God who will have nothing to do with the goddess moon.

I take a deep breath in slowly, but she is looking at

me now as though she doesn't know if she should run or stay.

Suddenly she grips my knee. "I have seen the burnings, Ma-khee."

I lay my hand over hers. "They won't come for hundreds of years."

Her eyes suddenly fix me, so pale within the darker rim. "But it will happen. I have seen it."

I nod. "Yes, it will happen."

My gaze glances off this witch, this sixteen-year-old dreadlocked blonde with the far-off look. She's the only one who knows the whole story, and perhaps it will be better for her to keep it to herself.

I clasp her hands, and then I leave, because it seems as if there should be a space now.

Fergus is by the water with some of the men, each one naked beneath a blanket. Their nakedness offends no one, not least of all me. I sit on the shore and watch them, catch Fergus's eye and make him smile. Across the loch I see others about the same task. The men take turns out of the water shivering by the fire under woolen blankets. Slowly the end of the crannog comes up on its stilts to its former level, levered up by trunks and settled again on its island of stone. The thatch drips like a great rainstorm greedily back into the loch. The mud from the wattle walls falls in globs. I help the women hoist the walkway out of the water, heavy and weeping, until the rope cuts into my telltale palm. We bind the walkway to the end of the crannog that is still attached to the shore and repair it with fibrous rope and awls made of bone.

By evening, the crannog is still not habitable, but it is rising like the moon by degrees, drying out as much as the damp air will allow. Older boys have been dragging dead game out of the forest during the day, and there is a fair pile, but without salt it is sure to rot before we can eat it all. It's clear we are going to need to move on soon.

When Fergus sneaks back into Iona's hut and stretches himself alongside me, I take his hands from my waist and kiss the knuckles, red and sore from his work in the water. "When will we leave?"

He sits up and shakes his head. I can tell the question is on his mind, too. "How long before Illa can walk well?"

"Seven days."

"There is meat for now."

"But not for long."

He starts to talk, but I am distracted by his hands in my hair, his fingers down the ridge of my neck, his surprise to find no stretch to my underwear, in fact no underwear to speak of at all.

He lays his cold palms against my cheeks. "What are you, Ma-khee?"

"A woman. That's all."

In the dim light I see his smile, a long smile that stretches up into his cheeks on either side. And then he behaves as if I am a woman and his hunger for this woman is insatiable. As mine is for him.

He leaves in the morning before I awake. By light of day he is with the other men, back to the shivering water in search for what was lost. I imagine all the fine leatherwork from the crannogs sinking into the loch, to be found in fragments in over a thousand years by archaeologists who will make their sketches and speculate about what everything was for.

When the crannog is repaired, it looks greyer from the mold that has set in. Men and women alike have sat at the shore weaving new mats to cover the sodden and moldy ones. The fire in the main area is lit for the first time, sending up cheers and radiating a damp warmth to the walls and floor. The air is heavy with the smell of steaming grass and reed. The people from Dunadd have woven their own mats to sleep on by a fire on the shore and in the fields where they feel safe next to Iona, their *ban-druidhe*, and her newly thatched hut.

I continue in my lessons, only now Iona can't look at me when she speaks. It must seem strange to teach me the tricks of her trade that are going to incriminate her sisters in the future. She tells me about the great festival of Beltane, when thanks must be given to the goddess for bringing them through the cold months. Everyone must be purified by fire at that time of sowing. Many babies will be conceived then and throughout the summer.

The leatherworker comes from the crannog up the

loch to teach us how to preserve the best of the leather from the animals that must be stripped and stored for our journey. It takes a lot of scraping with sharp stones to take off the flesh, and my fingertips are bleeding. Sometimes we can come by a knife and get the hides down faster to the soft leather that will be good for clothing. The tanner brings us a barrel of brains, he says, brains and water to soak fat into the hide and keep it soft. Whose brains, I want to know. The brains of the animal, says the tanner. It takes days and many women pulling and stretching to make the bags that will carry our food. Iona helps me stuff one with samples of the herbs we might need along the way for common ailments, and especially for sore feet.

We have been able to beg a little salt from the crannog dwellers, small but precious pay for our help. It screams in the cuts of my palm as I help to rub the strips of meat down and set them out to dry on racks under the trees. Before it gets dark, we have to move the racks into the confines of the crannog wall. Even so, a bear comes early from hibernation and paces along the shore; Fergus appoints two men each night to stand guard with a fire torch. I can see the animals are going to be a problem as long as we are carrying food.

No one seems to know, though, when we will leave. Fergus consults with Iona. She teaches me to track the stars, to throw her stones across the lines in the dirt. She puts the stones in my hand and seems to want me to decide. At first, they seem to fall into a random selection, but after a while the patterns I expect become different. Small collections of stones straighten out to make a single line. Iona nods her head.

"Now?" I say.

"Tomorrow," she says. "The moon will be coming into its fullness. The stones say the time is close. Tell your man."

I spot Fergus cross-legged on the shore by the fire with Illa next to him leaning in close. I am stuck in this moment, a bystander observing a man and a girl, their faces lit by the fire, the smoke rising off into the night sky. For a while he was mine. For a very short while, she was mine again, too.

"Margaret? Time to wake up now."

It's all a shadow of time, just reflections in water. Everything that is happening in my time is happening right now, too, just at a different level of the picture. At this moment I am lying on a hospital bed, and then now because of a change of perspective I am here waiting ahead of a journey that will eventually be historical. Dunadd fell to the Picts in 736. No one recorded the exact earthquake that tipped the bay below Dunadd out to Crinan and rendered it useless as a fort except in the ramblings of a dotty aristocrat whom everyone ignored.

This particular trail of Scots east to Scone will make it into no annals; the presence of a strange woman from time not yet discovered will be lost. Downright misconceptions will surface in time. The women of the future will be held guilty for the fall of man, and the last vestiges of their wisdom will be tied to a post and her most holy icon of flame will be used against her.

What is to become of me, once Maggie Livingstone, then Margaret Griggs, now Ma-khee? Iona might know; Sula might have guessed by now. But I cannot say. I am not a witch tried and true. Like everyone else, I am just a traveler in time.

The moon, about seven months pregnant, drifts slowly along the ridge of filigree trees. I move out of the shadows towards the fire and kneel at Fergus's back, my arms around his neck, my mouth against his ear.

"Fergus MacBrighde," I whisper so that he can't hear me over the crackling of the fire, "there will never come a time I do not remember you."

29

M argaret?"
        Dr. Shipshap lifted Maggie's hand and patted
the back of it. "Margaret, can you hear me?"

Graeme let go of his mother's other hand and stood
up from the bed. "She's been asleep for four days," he
said. "This can't be normal."

"Not usual," said the doctor, "but not without prec-
edent."

He clicked on his little probing light and lifted Maggie's eyelid. Her head was swaddled in yards of gauze
with a tube coming out like a spout. An oxygen mask
obscured her face. Monitors by the bed ran different
colored lines in and out of the covers. The sharp sting

of methylated spirits mingled with the leftover food on a tray by the door.

Jim patted Graeme's shoulder. "Look, the heart is strong. She'll be fine."

"But she didn't wake up when she was supposed to," said Graeme, turning to the doctor. "Maybe she's never going to."

Dr. Shipshap shook his head. "People just have different ways of responding to anesthetic."

Graeme's face was flushed. "But if you couldn't wake her up, how did you know which part of the brain to take out?"

The doctor stepped back from the bed. "Experience."

He was finished with questions for today and felt put upon by the woman's teenage son. He walked out to the nurses' station to ask the ward sister to lower the level of analgesic. He set the patient's chart on the desk and left. His shift was over.

Two young nurses in short sleeves and little starched hats watched the older man comfort the boy.

One nurse nudged the other. "Is that the father, then?"

The other shrugged. "I suppose so."

"It's a shame. She should have come round before now, eh?"

The two nurses watched the son pace the floor at the foot of his mother's bed. The older man went to the window.

"Dr. Shipshap is one of the best neurologists in the country," interrupted the ward sister. "Nothing has ever gone wrong before."

An hour later, the woman's husband confused the nurses by ringing to see if anything had changed. If the woman had a husband, who was this man sitting on the end of her bed?

Close to midnight, one of the nurses took the man and the woman's son cups of tea.

"You should go home and sleep," she said. "We can give you a ring if anything changes."

Graeme shook his head.

"At least let me find you a daybed where you can go and catch a few hours. You'll do yourself in like this."

"Go on," said Jim. "You'll feel better for a snooze."

Graeme began to get up, but his body was working against him and was trying to sit him back down.

Jim got up to help him. "Off you go. I'll stand sentry."

Graeme got as far as the door before he turned back. "Thanks, Jim. I don't know what we'd have done without you."

Jim smiled. "On you go, before I chase you down the corridor myself."

After Graeme had left with the nurse, Jim stood by the window looking out at the headlights of a car pulling into the hospital car park, at the black night sky gently fading around the stars. Behind him the elevator sounded its sonorous bell. A woman's laughter echoed from down the corridor. A call for a doctor crackled over the loudspeaker.

At length, he walked back to Maggie and sat on the bed by her hip. He wondered if she was dreaming. He still didn't know what to make of all of that. But whether Fergus was real or not, he was still too real.

"Look at you," he said to Maggie. "You've made a mess of it now." He fingered one of her tubes and by the warmth judged it to be the catheter.

For a moment, Maggie's eyes seemed to flutter. Jim looked towards the nurses' station, to the wall of cupboards and the bin marked TOXIC WASTE.

He said, "I know a certain son who won't survive if you don't come back, Maggie."

Again he saw a flutter. This time he was sure. And then off to the side of his vision, he caught a movement of the finger onto which her pulse monitor was attached.

Jim slipped his own finger under the one that had just moved. "It's time to come back now, Maggie Livingston. It's time to leave your crannogs and Loch Glashan. You have to say good-bye to that Fergus brute now."

A tear ran down Maggie's face, and then another. Jim half stood up to call the nurse, but he sat back down again and wiped her tears with the edge of the sheet.

"Maggie, I know you can hear me."

"No," she said, muffled inside her mask, "I can't hear you."

He smiled and sat back in his chair, drumming his

fingers on his thigh. "You're a big teaser," he said. "The worst I have ever seen."

She opened one eye. Jim lifted the oxygen mask so that she could speak. "Am I back in the land of the living?"

Her eyes closed again, and for a moment it seemed she had drifted off.

"Are you going to stay?" Jim asked.

Her eyes fluttered, then opened a little. "It looks like it."

Jim blew out his breath. She closed her eyes. A thin line of water forced them back open a crack. Another tear fell off the side of her face onto the pillow.

Jim kept talking to keep her with him. "The doctor said the operation went well enough."

She didn't respond.

After a while, he stood up and tucked her sheet under her chin. "Well, there's a boy I know who wouldn't mind at all being woken up at this time of night to hear some good news."

Maggie kept her eyes closed. "Yes," she said, "bring that boy to me, will you?"

The nurse appeared at the door, smiling. "I heard the talking. Is she awake, then?"

Jim stood back from the bed and pulled his jacket off the chair. "She's awake and as cheeky as ever. I thought the doctor was going to fix that."

Maggie smiled, tried to lift her hand to her bandaged head.

The nurse intercepted Maggie's hand. "No, we can't do anything about cheekiness. You'll have to deal with that yourself."

"I've been trying," said Jim. He slid his arms into his jacket. "She's a useless case."

He walked to the door and stood for a while watching as the nurse checked the monitors. "Bye then, Maggie."

Maggie lifted her hand a little off the covers and listened as the squeak of Jim's shoes passed the tap of Graeme's down the empty hall.

Maggie turned to the nurse peering at her monitor. "Does it tell you up there if I'll have any more seizures?"

The nurse gently tapped the screen. "It's much too soon to know about that. The thing you have to work on is feeling better. Sometimes there are no more seizures. Sometimes there are a few and then they stop. Sometimes they keep on as before. But I'm sure that won't be true in your case. All we can do is hope for the best, right?"

"Yes," Maggie said, "all we can do is hope for the very best. Here he is."

Graeme came towards her, stifling a sob before he ever made it to her bed. "You're back," he said.

He buried his face in her pillow next to her cheek.

Maggie tried to reach for him, but she was held back by the drip. "Here I am," she said, "as though I'd never left."

Maggie lay with her son beside her, breathing in the smell of his hair, clasping his hand when it searched for hers against the covers.

The nurse stepped close when she saw the look on the woman's face. "Are you in pain?"

The woman turned her face away, so the nurse gathered all the cups onto the tea tray and left efficiently.

Maggie could see the brightening eastern sky begin to creep up her window. Before long, the first of the tourists would be setting out along black ribbons of road to climb the path and set their foot in the imprint in the rock. They would stop by the information board and read about the people who once lived at Dunadd.

But they wouldn't read about Fergus or Illa or the woman who came to them from a very great distance. They would find out that the people of King Murdoch lost Dunadd to the Picts, but they would get no sense of what Maggie lost.

From the top of Dunadd, the wind would be still now; the mist lifting off the Mhoine Mhor, the clouds off the sea. The walls of the fort that had kept it strong were this morning, just as every morning, a cold rubble in the wet grass.

Fergus and Illa weren't there anymore. But one day they might come back. And if they did, one day, perhaps the woman Ma-khee might find them there.

VEIL OF TIME
CLAIRE R. McDOUGALL

INTRODUCTION

Caught in a period of transition between her divorce and an operation that could put her epileptic seizures behind her, Maggie Livingstone decides it's time to get away. She leaves Glasgow for a three-month stay at the foot of Dunadd Hill in the Scottish highlands, where she intends to finish her PhD thesis on witch burnings that for so long took a backseat to marriage and motherhood.

Dunadd is a quiet place. Maggie's only company is a friendly widower named Jim and Winnie, the black cat who quickly finds a home with her. There's plenty of time to think about the daughter she lost to a seizure, and the son for whom she needs to pull herself together. But when Maggie's seizures start transporting her into vivid dreams of eighth-century Scotland, she becomes consumed with thoughts of Fergus, brother to the king, and his daughter, Illa, who reminds her of her own lost child. As the date of her operation approaches, Maggie must decide whether she can leave her newfound loves of that world to be present for her son in this one.

QUESTIONS AND TOPICS FOR DISCUSSION

1. When Maggie goes to stay at Dunadd, she notes, "I have unearthed the old Maggie Livingstone of childhood and pasted it over the Margaret I had become" (page 4). Later in the story Fergus calls her Ma-khee. How do each of these variations of her name identify a different part of who she is? Discuss your own nicknames, if you have any, and how you relate to being called by different names.

2. The story intersperses Maggie's point of view with Fergus's. What does this bring to the story? How different do you think the book would be if we got only Maggie's perspective?

3. What do you make of the almost instant attraction between Maggie and Fergus? What do you think draws them to each other? How might their past relationships have played a role in bringing them together at this point in their lives?

4. "'But what if time isn't what we think it is, one damn thing after another? What if what we know isn't just a series of pictures, but more like a hologram? If the whole thing is contained within each piece, then traveling through time isn't so much a question of traveling anywhere so much as looking deeper into the image'" (page 203). What do you think about this interpretation of time? Do you think Maggie's dreams are more than dreams?

5. After Maggie asks Jim (on page 206) what period in time he would like to visit, she is struck by the emotion in his response, noting "Sometimes you just happen on the thing in a person that stirs the quick. It's a nice thing to see, the quick. . . ." What do you make of the phrase *stir the quick*? What stirs the quick in you?

6. Maggie sometimes worries about altering history, and whether or not she should warn Fergus about the future. Do you agree with her decision?

7. Discuss Maggie's role as a mother. How does her relationship with Illa compare to her relationship with Graeme?

8. How do Maggie's relationships with Sula and Iona influence

her thesis? Do you think Maggie herself could be considered a witch?

9. There are a lot of things Maggie fears about undergoing the lobectomy. She worries, "will normality just be deathly dull?" (page 345). Discuss the concept of being normal. What does it mean to you? Is it something you seek out, try to steer clear of, or something else in between?

10. Aside from losing Fergus and her dreams, there are a lot of risks involved with undergoing brain surgery. Would you have the surgery if you were Maggie?

11. Discuss the relationship between Maggie and Jim. Could there be more to it? Where do you imagine things going for each of them beyond the pages of the book?

12. In the final chapter of the book, the author switches narrative style to a more omniscient point of view. Why do you think she decided to use this perspective? What do you think it accomplishes?

ENHANCE YOUR BOOK CLUB

1. Dunadd is a real place in Scotland—complete with the footprint in stone and the mark of the boar. Do some research online and check out some images of the sites and setting in *Veil of Time*.

2. Maggie goes to Dunadd for a few reasons— to get away and have a fresh start, to slow down and prepare for her operation, and to finish the thesis she started long ago. Where would you most want to escape to for three months? Are there any projects from your past that you've always wanted to finish?

3. When we in America think of witch hunts, we think of the Salem witch trials. What can you find out about witch hunts in Scotland, or Europe in general? Look online or check out Anne Llewellyn Barstow's book *Witchcraze: A New History of the European Witch Hunts*.

4. Discuss what period of time you would most want to travel to

and why. Would you want to change history or just experience a different way of life?

A CONVERSATION WITH CLAIRE R. MCDOUGALL

How did you first get the idea for *Veil of Time*? How long did it take you to write it?

I write quickly, so I probably had a first draft within six months, but it traveled a circuitous route before being picked up by a publisher. I already had another book placed with my agent, though he had had no luck in selling it. I kept *Veil of Time* in my drawer, because I didn't want him to stop plugging the first novel. After a while, I heard that a film version of Diana Gabaldon's *Outlander* was in the offing (which turned out not to be true!), so I thought I had better get *Veil of Time* out. Time travel seems to be a topic of great popular interest, and my agent was able to sell it relatively quickly. Between the time I started the book until it sold was probably a couple of years.

My working title for *Veil of Time* was always *Dunadd*, because it is so central to the book and I hold the place very dear. I grew up only a few miles away, and later a childhood friend bought the farm at its base. Often when I go back, I stay in one of her holiday cottages on the property. When I'm there, I climb up the fort at least once a day, because it is so magical walking through those old ruins, and the view across the sea and islands gets under your skin and won't ever leave you. For a long time I had been mulling over the idea of writing about it. I have written other novels set in the area, but all take place in the present. I couldn't see writing about Dunadd in any time but its heyday, the eighth century, when it was one of the major ports of the Celtic world and a place of great importance for the kings of Scotland. I didn't see myself as a writer of historical fiction, though, so I resisted going that route. I thought of myself, probably too rigidly, as a writer of literary fiction, and didn't want to switch to the romance genre either. So for a while I was a bit stuck. And then Audrey Niffenegger's widely acclaimed book *The Time Traveler's Wife* came out and it was like light breaking on the problem: If time travel could be taken seriously in mainstream fiction, then that was how I was going to approach my book about Dunadd.

Did you do any research for the story? If so, how did you go about it, and where does the history end and imagination take over?
There isn't any history anywhere in which imagination doesn't take over. As Maggie says, "History is a selective bastard." It's no accident it is called his-story. (German is more honest: *Geschichte* simply means "story.") I did try to hang my novel around an "historical" framework: there was a King Murdoch around this time period at Dunadd; Christianity was making inroads into the indigenous pagan religion; and there were a series of earthquakes. While these events probably took place over a longer period, I brought them together into one historical moment for the purposes of the novel. I did do research, but only as needed. I didn't do years of research ahead of time like Dan Brown. There just isn't that much known about the period in terms of daily life. There have been a few archaeological digs at Dunadd that have unearthed jewelry and evidence of a forge, some wineglasses (which for that time in Scotland is quite remarkable), a few other artifacts, all of which I used in the story.

One thing I did do was to look at other primitive cultures. I have a great picture from *National Geographic* of a quite extensive African village with thatched round huts and meandering lanes. The thatch there would have been made of straw instead of heather, but I think the village at the base of Dunadd must have looked quite like this. The circle is sacred in primitive cultures, so I made the houses round; and from what we know, that seems to be accurate. The crannogs certainly were. And then, too, before monotheism made inroads, primitive cultures were goddess oriented; the earth and women were venerated. Joseph Campbell says there is only one mythology, and so I had no qualms about lifting part of the ceremony at Loch Glashan from, say, Native American culture, with the seven directions being acknowledged. For other parts of goddess worship I turned to the modern-day practices of Wicca.

Some of it will no doubt get me into trouble with historians, for instance whether or not the Stone of Destiny was ever at Dunadd or whether the sea ever came up to its cliffs, but there is evidence both ways. Some historians even try to deny that the culture at Dunadd was ever matrilineal, but in these cases I chose to go with my hunches and tell her-story.

How familiar are you with Dunadd and its surroundings?

I grew up just a few miles from Dunadd, which sits in a glen full of ancient sites, some going back so far no one knows who put them there or what they mean. The cup-and-ring markings in the stone that Fergus takes Maggie to see on their first night ride fall into this category. But when you grow up in any setting, you stop seeing it. Dunadd for me was just a place where kids got on the school bus. I saw it every day and my family took visitors there, but I didn't think about it too much. The religious folk thought all that ancient stuff had to do with the devil, but I had the sense that there was more to it, and I did appreciate the mystery of it all from a young age.

Loch Glashan was out of sight, and I only knew the name because there was a signpost on the main road. Near Dunadd there is a museum where I probably first saw artifacts from Loch Glashan. The water is peaty and acidic there, and the things they brought up from the silt at the bottom were relatively well preserved (like the leather in the jerkin I have Fergus buy from an artisan down the loch). A little research told me that people had lived out on crannogs at Loch Glashan for millennia, and so it came in useful when I needed a place for Maggie and Fergus to flee to. There is actually a reconstituted (for tourists) crannog on Loch Tay in Perthshire, and it is quite eerie to go in and sit under the thatched roof by the fire. But it wasn't until after I had written *Veil of Time* that I finally drove up the bumpy road through overhanging trees to Loch Glashan to stand on its abandoned shores in the rain and imagine the people I had created moving about there. It's always a surreal experience to see your art take shape and live in real places.

What other authors or books have influenced your writing? What are some of your favorites?

I suppose that way back C. S. Lewis's *The Lion, the Witch and the Wardrobe* had an effect and chimed with my own tendencies as a child to put stock in imaginative realities. As a teenager, Anthony Quinn's autobiography, *The Original Sin*, showed me a world that didn't sit well with my evangelical upbringing and yet I knew it couldn't be dismissed. Another nonfiction book, which has never gone out of print and which I still recommend heartily, is Jean Liedloff's *The Continuum Concept: In Search of Happiness Lost* for a challenge to the way we normally think of human nature. Literaturewise, I spent my late teenage years and early twenties drooling over D. H. Lawrence and his oeuvre. I read all of Herman Hesse and loved Emily Brontë, both her novel and poems. I spent way too many years in academia, but at least I read all of Nietzsche, who was and remains an important voice. The Scottish writer Lewis Grassic Gibbon presented me with a haunting yet beautiful reflection of Scottish life, and perhaps brought up for me the possibility that Scotland could be represented in literature. Iain Crichton Smith (who taught at my high school) put a devastating part of Scottish history, the Highland Clearances, into a novel.

Poets have been a great influence on me, too. Particularly Yeats and particularly Dylan Thomas. It's an intoxication that is hard to pull yourself away from and a very good place to do any writing from.

These days I am a fervent fan of John Steinbeck, because of his lucid prose and his light touch even when tackling heavy subjects. Dialogue doesn't get any better than Steinbeck's. Once I read one of his books, I have to read the rest. I tend in any case to go back and reread books, because if it is good literature, you get more out of it each time. I do this with Frank McCourt, too. As for modern-day fiction writers, I like Paul Harding, James Galvin, and Joe Henry—they give me a vivid world of words and images to loll about in.

Do you have a specific writing process? At what point did you know how the story was going to end?

My process is that I write in the mornings for about two or three hours. I find it difficult to write anywhere else but at my desk in my office. I get up in the morning, write, then walk the dogs and afterwards take a nap. I don't write at the weekends unless I am on a roll, and I don't write on holidays.

I start a story by putting together a group of characters in a certain setting and then I go forward, listening to how they bounce off one another. It's a bit like the setup for a reality TV show. Sometimes they surprise me with where they want to go, but as Pooh says about songs, you just have to let it come out the way it wants to. So, I never really know how a story is going to end until it gets there. Other writers, of course, have a different approach—James Joyce, for one, would painstakingly build his stories brick by small brick until they slowly took shape. I don't have the patience for that. I would rather write the whole thing quickly, then write the whole thing over again quickly. So, my process is quite haphazard: I have no plan, no three by five cards, no napkins with scribbles on the backs, no map—just a flashlight and a dark wood in front of me. Somehow, I make it through the trees to the other side.

Did you have a favorite character in your own book? How did you relate to Maggie?

I am enough of a romantic that I would have to say Fergus. Writing a female protagonist stirs up my own murky feelings and is not always comfortable. But Fergus is just a good egg: He fights for the right things and has a good set of values. And he is cheeky and appealing.

When I started this book, I had the idea that I should try for once to write a protagonist who wasn't the embodiment of my ideas and values. I thought that by creating someone out of dust, instead of spilling my guts onto the page, I would somehow be a better writer. So I gave her the name of a childhood friend, Margaret Livingstone, and really tried to distance myself. This lasted for about twenty pages, until I came to the realization that it is the job of the artist to pour herself into her art, and so I gave up and let the guts back on the page. Frankly, I wish I had done it sooner.

I had fun with the character of Jim Galvin, too, just because of his wry sense of humor and his fatherliness. I always have one of these characters in my books, a sort of touchstone that lets the reader into what is really going on. Jim Galvin is someone the reader can trust.

What are your thoughts on time travel? Has the subject always been of interest to you? If you could travel to another period of time, what would it be?

Let me answer the last part of this question first: I have always thought it would be fun to go around in those dresses and hats that women wore around the fin-de-siècle (but not to be sick around the same time). Honestly, I think we are living in exciting times these days. We are witnessing a slow dissolution of a kind of religious idealism that undergirded much of the worst evils mankind has come up with: domination, imperialism, missionary ventures, all the kinds of hierarchies that pit a few at the top against the multitude beneath. I think we are seeing a new emergence of women, not into the kind of male roles that the women's movement of the sixties and seventies catapulted them but into a real feminine power that is nurturing and compassionate. If this really is the dawning of the age of Aquarius (after a very long age of Pisces, thank you very much), then I can't think of any better period in history to be living. Maybe I would like to scoot forward and see how it all turns out.

The way physicists, theoretical and otherwise, have evolved in their thinking about time doesn't seem to have trickled down to mainstream thinking much. We are still plodding around with this clunky notion of time as a road with mile markers that we pass and finally fall off. It's a bit like believing the earth is flat. No one thinks it's flat anymore, no more do the physicists see time in two dimensions. Time isn't a thing at all, but a perspective. When H. G. Wells wrote *The Time Machine,* his protagonist had to actually get into his contraption and fly backwards along the clunky road, but that's not how I see Maggie and her experience through the veil of time. To me, she isn't going anywhere but simply making a shift. Some theoretical physicists think that at every moment every possible outcome is lived out somewhere in a parallel universe. So maybe all Maggie has to do is take a step to the right or left, just as you have to do to see different dimensions of a hologram.

Are you writing a sequel to *Veil of Time*? Can you see Maggie's future?

I have almost finished the sequel to *Veil of Time.* It is called *Druid Hill.* So, yes, I see Maggie's future quite clearly as far as that book goes. In the third book in what seems to be turning into a trilogy, things will turn quite strange for Maggie, more strange than I think I will know how to write about for quite some time.

What has been the most exciting part of the publishing process so far?

I came to the final act of getting published after many years of desert wandering. For the longest time I was just a *vox clamantis in deserto,* and no one was listening. It took so long to find an agent, and all the while I was writing novels, honing my craft, waiting in "silent desperation" (to steal a phrase from James Taylor). As I said, my agent couldn't sell my first novel, and then when I got the offer from Simon & Schuster for *Veil of Time,* it was like stepping into one of those parallel universes—for a while I was going through the paces without really believing it was happening. I think it was when I got the cover art that it really slammed into me that my book was in fact going to come out and be read by more than just me and a few friends. That was pretty exciting. Receiving installments of my advance in the mail hasn't been bad either.

What's up next for you? Are you working on any new novels?
Apart from the sequel to *Veil of Time,* I am working on the screen-play, because I have faith in another parallel universe where authors are allowed to turn their own stories into movies. I also have a little story about a wild mustang that I would like to get out into the world before we kill them all off. I have several other novels about Scotland waiting in the wings, some of which I will have to rework, but it is a goal to see all of those in print. Another thing that looms large on my horizon at the moment is the Scottish vote for independence in 2014—if my stories can further that cause even slightly, then I am a happy woman.